ZANE PRESENTS

P9-DDC-151

3 5674 05198711 4

STEALING
CANDY

CHASE BRANCH LIBRARY
17731 W. SEVEN MILE RD.
DETROIT, MI 48235
578-8002

NOV 2013

ALSO BY ALLISON HOBBS

The Sorceress
Pure Paradise
Disciplined
One Taste
Big Juicy Lips
The Climax
A Bona Fide Gold Digger
The Enchantress
Double Dippin'
Dangerously In Love
Insatiable
Pandora's Box

CHASE BRANCH LIBRARY
17731 W. SEVEN MILE RD.
DETROIT, MI 48235
578-8002

ZANE PRESENTS

STEALING CANDY

ALLISON HOBBS

SBI

STREBOR BOOKS

NEW YORK LONDON TORONTO SYDNEY

Strebor Books
P.O. Box 6505
Largo, MD 20792
http://www.streborbooks.com

This book is a work of fiction. Names, characters, places and incidents are products of the author's imagination or are used fictitiously. Any resemblance to actual events or locales or persons, living or dead, is entirely coincidental.

© 2010 by Allison Hobbs

All rights reserved. No part of this book may be reproduced in any form or by any means whatsoever. For information address Strebor Books, P.O. Box 6505, Largo, MD 20792.

ISBN 978-1-59309-280-1
LCCN 2010925102

First Strebor Books trade paperback edition July 2010

Cover design: www.mariondesigns.com
Cover photograph: © Keith Saunders/Marion Designs

10 9 8 7 6 5 4 3 2 1

Manufactured in the United States of America

For information regarding special discounts for bulk purchases, please contact Simon & Schuster Special Sales at 1-866-506-1949 or business@simonandschuster.com

The Simon & Schuster Speakers Bureau can bring authors to your live event. For more information or to book an event, contact the Simon & Schuster Speakers Bureau at 1-866-248-3049 or visit our website at www.simonspeakers.com.

This book is for Keenan Hobbs

ACKNOWLEDGMENTS

To all my readers, I am honored to present you with this novel...
lucky Number 13!

Keith Saunders of Marion Designs, I thank you for another
sensual, beautiful, and eye-catching cover.

Deb Schuler, I appreciate having your interior design inside
each of my novels.

Leona Romich, thanks for all the wonderful reviews. I was so
touched when I found out that you buy my books without even
reading the back cover.

Kyndal Hobbs, my precious daughter...I am so proud of you.

Denise Doward, Sister/Friend, so glad we've reconnected. You
are a class act.

Sonia Wells, thoughtful and kind. Thank you for always looking
out.

Charmaine Parker, your showing up at my *Pure Paradise* release
party last summer was a big surprise. Spending the weekend in
New York with you and Zane was so much fun.

Karen Dempsey Hammond, forty years of friendship...Do I
need to say more?

Zane, I think we got one! I am so pleased with this novel. Thank
you for sprinkling your magic on the pages!

CHAPTER 1

As quietly as she could, Gianna unlocked two rusted deadbolts and slipped out the back door.

She took in the surroundings. Empty soda cans, beer bottles, cellophane wrappers, and other miscellaneous debris cluttered the yard.

Four cinder blocks were stacked against a crumbling redbrick exterior wall. The cinder blocks were covered with a grease-tarnished oven rack—a crude, homemade barbecue grill where her meals had been prepared.

The aftertaste of her captor's secretions, intermingled with the flavor of charred chicken, lingered on her tongue. The bitter taste in her mouth, the bruised skin around her eye, and the welts on her legs were cruel reminders of what she'd endured.

As if she'd been oxygen-deprived, Gianna breathed in deeply. The air she gulped in was polluted by smells of poverty: rotting garbage, smoldering charcoal, burning bits of meat, and the stench of urine that wafted from alleyways.

Ordinarily, these rancid odors would have repelled her, but not now. She took another deep breath of sour air and smiled. Though putrid, the air she inhaled represented sweet freedom.

A stray cat shot across the litter-strewn yard, startling Gianna. That moment of fear was a reminder that there was no time to bask in her freedom. Her life was at stake.

She trotted quickly down a gravelly backstreet. The concrete was disfigured by cracks, and numerous crater-like potholes.

She looked around as she moved forward. Where was she? Still

in Jersey? No. While she was blindfolded, she'd heard that man named Jimmy asking Bullet if he had money to pay the tolls.

She could be anywhere: New York; Delaware; Pennsylvania. Only God knew. She'd only seen dilapidated neighborhoods such as this one in the movies or on TV.

There weren't any people in sight. Only boarded-up houses that were scarcely protected by rusted metal gates.

Gianna wasn't fooled by the desolate environment. Like the house where she'd been held hostage, these seemingly abandoned houses were probably occupied by unsavory characters, engaging in all manners of heinous crimes.

A shiver of fear encouraged her to increase her speed, but running in four-inch wedge sandals and a skimpy, tight skirt wasn't easy. Desperate to put distance between her and the house of torture, she hitched up the restrictive skirt.

With the tight fabric encircling her waist, her naked, brown backside and semen-slimed pubic hair were displayed.

No time for modesty. Pressing onward at full speed, she rounded a corner, sprinting past messy yards and vacant storefronts. Her frantic eyes sought law-abiding citizens. Adults who would be outraged when they found out what that grown man named Bullet had done to her.

Someone had to help her contact her parents.

Every few seconds, she looked over her shoulder.

Had he discovered she was gone? She swallowed down a hard knot of fear. Bullet had threatened to cut up her face…disfigure her for life if she tried to escape.

It seemed like she'd been running up and down narrow back-streets for at least a half-mile, and she hadn't encountered a single soul. Jerking her head backward, she anxiously looked over her shoulder once again.

Bullet wasn't pursuing her. Her ordeal was almost over. Immense relief washed over her. She was safe. Free!

But where was she? And how long had she been gone? A week? Gianna had no idea. It was the last Saturday in May when she'd been brought to the abandoned house, bound and blindfolded. What day was it now?

She slowed her pace, looking for a street sign…a landmark… something that would reveal her location. From the looks of the ramshackle houses and decaying streets, she might as well have been in a war-torn country or on another planet.

She felt like she was a million miles away from her family's well-tended beach house. Light years away from her parents' love.

The neighborhood was a desolate place. House after forsaken house declared itself unoccupied by the boards that covered the windows. Some windows were without boards, gapped open like wide mouths screaming in anguish.

She pressed forward, searching for a populated street. She yearned to hear the roar of heavy traffic…the sight of a police car.

Continuing her trek, she rounded another corner. A trio of boys were at the end of what appeared to be another deserted block. Though their backs were turned to her, she could tell they were teenagers.

Their style of clothes, the way they moved, the sound of their voices, told her that they were close to her age. *Thank you, God!*

Certain she'd found salvation, tears of gratitude formed as she dashed toward the boys. Trying to look as presentable as possible, she pulled her skirt from around her waist, tugging on it until it covered her bare behind.

"Hello!" She waved and trotted toward them. "Hello! I need help! Please!"

The boys spun around and regarded her with annoyed expressions.

The shortest member of the group reached toward the waistband of his jeans, exposing the butt of a gun.

"Yo, shawty, don't be creeping up on us like that. You tryna get yourself shot?" His voice was gruff.

"Excuse me. I really need help," she said, using a placating tone. These weren't ordinary teenagers. They were street tough and mean-looking.

She cleared her throat and spoke in a polite voice. "Would you mind telling me where I am? And um...today's date?"

Looking for a trace of kindness, she searched the boys' faces. She was met with pairs of eyes that took in her torn top and short, tight skirt. Eyes that were alit with vulgar desires.

"You don't know where you are? What you been smoking? Must have been some of that bubonic chronic," a taller boy jeered.

She was prepared to explain her circumstances—how she'd been abducted, beaten, and molested—but decided not to. Instincts told her that these hardened teens didn't care.

The third boy, who was wearing beige cargo pants, scowled at her. "You in Killadelphia, dummy!"

"Where?" she asked meekly. "Killa...where?"

"You retarded or something? You in Philly. Damn!" Cargo Pants spat, offended by her ignorance.

"Philadelphia, Pennsylvania?" Gianna began turning in a complete circle, big brown eyes panning the impoverished area as if the Liberty Bell might pop up and validate the boy's claim.

Philadelphia was only about two and a half hours from the beach house in New Jersey.

"Yo, I got something that'll bring you back down to earth," Cargo Pants said with a chortle. Studying Gianna while wearing a leering grin, he rubbed his groin.

"Take a walk with me to the crib..." He nodded over at one of

the boarded-up houses. "It'll only take a few minutes for me to bring you back down to earth."

She took a faltering step backward.

"Ah, you tellin' on yourself, man," the short boy accused with a snort. "You ain't nothing but a two-minute trick!"

"Nah, it ain't even like that. I can stroke for hours, but I ain't got time to knock that back out the way I usually do. I'm on my grind, yo. Hustle hard or starve…y'ah mean?"

"Man, you know it's dead out here. Go 'head and smash that real quick," the short boy suggested.

"'Spose D'wan come through?"

"Man, fuck D'wan. I know he's your uncle and everything, but making us work this dry-ass block is messed up."

"You right. Ain't no money out here. So…um, you gon' cover for me or what?"

"Yeah. If D'wan rolls up, I'll tell him you had to go take a leak or something. But don't try to impress shawty. Ten minutes is all you got. I'ma take my turn with shawty after you finish."

"What? Y'all just gon' leave me out?" Hazel Eyes appraised Gianna. "She all jacked-up with that swollen eye, but I still wanna chop it down," he said, scowling. "But I ain't tryna be at the end of no damn train. It's not going down like that."

"Yo, Money, you gotta get in where you fit in," the short boy asserted.

"You don't get no special treatment."

Hazel Eyes made a grunting sound of disagreement. "Why don't you let shawty decide who she wants to hit it first," he said with confidence. "Y'all know the deal. Once I stretch her out, she gon' be too loose for both of y'all lil'-dick niggas."

Gianna was appalled by the crude verbal exchanges. Like Bullet, these boys regarded her as nothing more than an inanimate object.

Glancing around, she was ready to make a run for it. Then her eyes locked on a cell phone that was sticking out of Hazel Eyes' pocket.

It was a thrilling sight. Now jubilant, she disregarded his vile intentions. "May I borrow your phone? I have to call the police."

Hazel Eyes gawked at her and then at his boys. "Shawty got jokes...tryna use my phone to call po-po."

"I was kidnapped." She took a breath. "And raped," she admitted. Shame caused her voice to crack.

"I'm not getting involved in no rape case," Hazel Eyes spewed. His two cohorts erupted in spiteful laughter.

CHAPTER 2

The approaching sound of feet slapping pavement cut off their taunting laughter. Gianna and the three youths whirled around in surprise.

Bullet! He was wearing only a loose pair of nylon shorts, and was barefoot and racing toward her. The muscles on his arms and his bare chest glistened with water beads. His curls were topped with the white lather from shampoo, while a stream of sudsy water trickled down his face.

Gianna screamed.

The short boy reflexively reached for his weapon.

"Whoa, whoa. Go easy, young bull," Bullet placated, slowing his approach.

Keeping a safe distance from the boy with the gun, Bullet held up both hands. "I ain't got no beef with y'all. But that lil' ho robbed me."

Shielding herself from Bullet, Gianna tried to hide behind the three drug boys. She clutched the back of Hazel Eyes' shirt. "He's lying," she murmured. Her breath came out in terrified, shaky gasps.

"Get off me!" Hazel Eyes yanked away from her clingy grasp.

"Put your piece away before you end up with a body," Bullet said to the short boy. "I know you don't wanna do no long time over that skank ho."

He fixed a surly gaze on Gianna. His face was slick with sudsy water and sweat.

Following Bullet's suggestion, the short boy returned the gun to his waistband, but kept his hand resting on the butt.

It was a small victory; Bullet cracked a smile. He ran a hand through soapy curls, a gesture Gianna recognized as a precursor to a big lie. "Do y'all really think I'd jump out the shower and chase down this hooker for the fun of it? If y'all don't believe me, search her," Bullet recommended. "She got at least five hunnit-dollar bills rolled up and stashed inside her pussy."

Snarling, the boys turned on Gianna like she was raw meat.

Hazel Eyes grabbed Gianna by the waist with one hand. Quick as a snake, he thrust his other hand up her skirt, his fingers scratching and poking at the tender lips of her vagina.

Wanting the money for themselves, Cargo Pants and the short boy double-teamed Hazel Eyes, delivering vicious jabs and brutal blows to his face.

The squealing tires of a gold Escalade brought the action to a halt. Hazel Eyes loosened his grip on Gianna as the tinted window of the driver's side slid down. The driver glared at the young thugs.

"Whassup, D'wan?" the short boy mumbled sheepishly as he fixed his clothes.

"What y'all doing? I know y'all dumb asses ain't out here bull-shitting. I saw y'all scuffling with each other…not even making an effort to get money."

"We was on it, but this block is dead," Cargo Pants explained, his palm sliding across his face, checking for bruises and lumps from the sudden fracas with his partners.

"Why y'all out here swinging on each other, instead of being about my business?"

Bullet stepped forward. "Yo, Dawg, I can explain…"

The driver frowned up at Bullet like he stank. "Who the fuck is you?"

His manhood challenged, Bullet flinched. Holding his temper in check, he wisely clammed up.

"I swear...y'all worthless-ass Negroes about to be flippin' burgers again. Get the fuck in the truck," he ordered the trio.

The boys mumbled apologies and began moving toward the Escalade. Gianna scurried to the back of the SUV. Getting her bearings, trying to figure out which way to run, she gripped the bumper.

She could tell that Bullet had respect for the hustler named D'wan. He wouldn't tussle with her while she held on to the man's shiny Escalade.

"I'ma fuck you up, bitch," Bullet roared, stomping toward the back of the SUV.

The Escalade moved forward and Gianna lost her grip. The truck made a wide U-turn, leaving Gianna exposed and vulnerable.

He stalked toward her, frowning. "I see that I'ma have to teach you a lesson, ho." His threat was spoken through lips tightly twisted to contain an explosion of rage.

"I got something for yo' ass when we get back home."

Home? I don't live in that nasty dump!

She couldn't endure any more of his lessons. Arms flailing, she ran aimlessly, the soles of her sandals pounding loudly against bumpy concrete.

Within seconds, the Escalade roared past her. Hoping the driver might rescue her from Bullet, she waved her arms in the air, trying to flag the driver down. The Escalade didn't slow down.

One narrow backstreet led to another. Weren't there any streets populated with something other than stray cats and buzzing insects?

Finally, she caught sight of two men who were sitting outside a vacant garage, sharing a bottle of beer.

The fading red script on a hanging sign read: *Lou's Auto Body Shop*. Skeletal remains of ancient cars were scattered about. The scene evoked sorrow and loss. The metal frames of the old cars seemed to plead for a proper burial.

"There's a man chasing me. He's gonna kill me," Gianna breathlessly told the men.

Both men, thin as rails and obviously intoxicated, looked at her through dull, bloodshot eyes. They looked too frail to protect her from Bullet.

Frantic thoughts raced through her mind. She needed to get to a phone. "Do you have a phone? I have an important call to make."

"You say you want a lil' taste?" Befuddled, one of the men extended his arm, offering Gianna the beer bottle.

This was a waste of time. These men were too drunk to understand the gravity of her situation.

Gianna resumed running. Every few seconds, she risked a glance over her shoulder. Thankfully, Bullet was nowhere in sight. Pumping her legs, she fled down another bleak block.

Then, like a mirage appearing in the desert, she happened upon a busy street.

"Help!" she screamed, running as fast as she could toward people—tax-paying citizens and law-abiding adults who would feel it their civic duty to help her.

Passersby stared at Gianna with curiosity and then quickly moved on. In a hurry, shoppers rushed past her. Mothers pulled their children close, and old folks grimaced and muttered, "Disgraceful," under their breath.

Gianna's ripped blouse and blackened eye spelled trouble. No one wanted to get involved.

"I need a phone. I need the police. Somebody help me!" she begged.

Feeling confused and helpless, she craned her neck, checking on Bullet's location. She expelled a loud gasp. Her worst fear was realized. Bullet was galloping toward her.

The sound of his bare feet smacking the pavement grew louder, announcing that he was gaining on her—narrowing the distance between them.

A city bus came to stop. Commuters began filing in. Gianna squeezed into the throng and wriggled her way to the front of the line, and onto the bus.

"Close the doors," she pleaded with the driver when she was safely inside the bus. "There's a man out there; he's trying to kill me."

The bus driver exhaled loudly. He rubbed his forehead in exasperation. "You gotta pay the fare."

"I don't have any money!" Gianna screamed, looking through the large windshield, scanning the crowd for Bullet.

"Well, get off the damn bus!" yelled an annoyed woman. Impatient, the female passenger reached over Gianna, and paid her fare with the swift swipes of a Trans Pass card. Muttering under her breath, the woman pushed past Gianna, her eyes panning the crowded bus in search of an empty seat.

Through the side window, Gianna could see the top of Bullet's head. He was at the end of the long line, trying to shove passengers out of his way. The commuters, mainly women, resisted. They jabbed Bullet with elbows and pulled at the waistband of his soggy shorts, trying to prevent him from getting in front of them.

Frustrated, Bullet forced his way forward from the back of the crowd. Objecting commuters grumbled and stiffened their bodies, refusing to allow Bullet to move ahead of them.

Righteously indignant, Bullet worked his way to the front of the line. He hopped on the bus. "You gotta wait your turn," an indignant woman protested.

"My lil' sister is trying to run away so she can get with some old dude. Fuck all of y'all. I gotta get my sister off this damn bus."

Face-to-face with her tormentor, cold terror swept over Gianna. He was so close, she could smell him…his scent a mixture of sweat and shampoo. She wanted to run, but was trapped between passengers who were trying to board the bus and those who stood behind her. She began to sob.

"Don't try to act all innocent now. Look at you…dressed like a hooker. Get yo' ass off this bus. Mom is all sick and laid up in the hospital and you tryna run the streets like a straight tramp!"

Wanting to be on their way, passengers glared at Gianna. All eyes held sheer disdain for the wayward young girl.

"She needs Jesus!" a woman near the front of the bus exclaimed.

"Man, get your sister so my passengers can get on this bus," the driver said disgustedly.

Gianna clamped her hand around the driver's wrist. "I'm not his sister. He kidnapped me! My name is Gianna Strand. I live in—"

Bullet shut her up with a punch in her back.

"That's enough, man," the driver intervened. "Handle your business at home. You and your sister gotta get off my bus."

"No! He's gonna hurt me!" Gianna pleaded.

"Damn right, I'm gon' hurt your lil' skank ass. Somebody gotta keep you in line," Bullet exploded as he yanked her away from the driver and pulled her off the bus.

Gianna fought like a wildcat, but couldn't break free. Bullet held her firmly with one hand while smacking her face with the other.

Concerned only with finding a seat, grumbling passengers pushed past the tussling duo.

Bullet hit Gianna repeatedly, slapping and pummeling her until she crumpled to the ground. She balled into a defensive knot as he furiously kicked her with his bare foot. A hard kick to her behind forced her body to involuntarily uncurl.

She pleaded for help again. Her eyes connected with a woman who was watching from a passenger window of the bus. She searched the woman's face for compassion, but was met with a cold, disapproving gaze.

The bus eased away from the curb and merged into traffic, leaving Gianna at Bullet's mercy.

Spewing profanity, Bullet held Gianna's arm with one hand and punched her with the other, pummeling Gianna all the way back to the dilapidated house where she'd been confined.

CHAPTER 3

S aleema Sparks ripped open the monthly bill from Philadelphia Gas Works. She looked at the total and frowned.
Here it was the first week of June and she hadn't put much
of a dent in the past due balance from the cold winter months.
Keeping a large home warm was terribly expensive.

Checking the time, she put the gas bill on top of a steep pile of
unpaid debt. Soon, her home where she also operated Head Up,
a center for troubled girls, would be flooded with young girls.

Due to Saleema's lack of professional credentials, Head Up
had to be listed as a social club. But in reality, it was much more
than that. It was a safe haven—a sanctuary for girls who were
plagued by a multitude of tribulations, including drug-addicted
and abusive parents, poor school attendance, and sexual promis-
cuity, just to name a few of their personal issues.

Saleema's own childhood and teen years had not been a bed of
roses. She knew all too well what a dysfunctional home life could
to do a girl's self-esteem and her ability to follow the rules of normal society. A former teen prostitute and adult madam, Saleema
had turned her life around and had been using a sudden financial
windfall to give back and help young girls at risk.

Seeking escape from their troubled home lives, the girls flocked
to Head Up, utilizing the center's computers, participating in work-
shops, and self-esteem building activities. Saleema had provided
her girls with a refuge where they could simply intermingle and

socialize in an environment where they weren't ridiculed…an environment where designer labels and fly weaves didn't define a girl's worth.

At precisely 10:30, twelve chattering teenagers started streaming in. "Hi, Miss Saleema," each girl greeted.

The teens lingered in the entrance hall, their noise level boisterous and inappropriate for indoors. Dreading the thought of breaking the unpleasant news to her girls, Saleema allowed them some extra time to settle down.

Amirah drifted over to the bulletin board and scanned the activity schedule. She was a gangly girl who still stood with her shoulders slouched despite Saleema's repeated encouragement for her to stand tall and proud. She wished she had more time to work on Amirah's confidence issues.

"How come the talent show rehearsal is cancelled?" Amirah asked, her voice filled with disappointment.

In the few months that Amirah had been a part of Head Up, she'd progressed from painfully shy to being able to recite a monologue with emotion and great passion. Saleema had hoped that showcasing Amirah's talent in front of an audience would help boost her confidence outside the walls of Head Up.

Amirah and all the other girls had experienced a lifetime of hurt and disappointment. Saleema had expected to be someone they could always count on. Guilt-ridden and ashamed, Saleema wanted to drop her gaze, but she forced herself to look Amirah straight in the eye. "I'll explain."

A crowd of girls rushed to the bulletin board to check out the schedule. Baffled faces turned from the schedule to Saleema.

Portia, a hot-tempered eighth-grader who had weight issues along with a dozen other emotional problems, had been expelled from three separate middle schools for fighting. Portia rolled her

eyes in undisguised indignation. "Everything's cancelled," she griped. "What's going on, Miss Saleema?"

"I have to make an announcement," Saleema said, sounding more depressed than she'd intended. But it was pointless to try to sugarcoat the situation.

Her girls deserved the truth. She took a deep breath and ran shaky fingers through her locs. "Let's go to the lavender room."

The atmosphere changed instantly. Their expressions grave, the girls trailed behind Saleema in somber silence.

The rooms inside Saleema's home that were designated Head Up areas were all painted in soft hues. The lavender room had two comfortable couches, four bean bag chairs, two recliners, a zebra-print chaise lounge, a hot pink butterfly chair, and a bright purple mitt-shaped swivel chair.

There were no assigned seats and the mitt chair was a favorite. The girls usually raced to get to that chair. But today, they flopped lethargically into any random seat.

Chyna and Stacey squatted down to the leather shag throw rug and sat with their legs crossed Indian-style.

Portia and another tough girl named Greta refused to sit. They stood, arms folded, posted up against opposite sides of the doorway. Their body language was obstinate. Defiant. Sending an unspoken message that they were mad at the world.

Saleema stood in front of the twelve girls. She cleared her throat. "It saddens me to have to inform you that, after today, Head Up will no longer be operating as a social center."

Greta sucked her teeth. "What's that mean?"

"It means I'm going to have to shut down Head Up."

Groans and sighs peppered with outbursts of profanity filled the lavender room.

"Ladies! Watch your language. I plan to reopen when school

starts. But I really can't afford to keep it going over the summer."

"You broke, Miss Saleema?" Tasha asked.

"Just about," Saleema admitted. "I'm going to look for some financial backers—"

"Why don't you file for bankruptcy?" Amirah offered.

"What good is that gon' do?" Portia snarled from the doorway.

Wearing a pleasant expression, Amirah twisted around and faced Portia. "After my auntie filed for bankruptcy, she came up. She got a new car and a wallet full of credit cards," she explained.

"Your auntie was probably getting paid on some credit card scam," Portia implied and all the other girls laughed.

"That's enough, Portia. Amirah was trying to be helpful," Saleema interjected.

"I wasn't lying, Miss Saleema. My auntie said filing bankruptcy is a good move."

"I didn't accuse you of lying. Filing bankruptcy may have improved your aunt's situation, but I have to look at other options."

Portia blew Amirah off with a hand flip. "Don't nobody care what your auntie did. Anyway, ain't your auntie in jail?"

The girls exploded in laughter.

"No, she's not in jail! Always running your mouth. You get on my nerves, Portia."

"Seriously, that's enough from you, Portia," Saleema warned.

"I'm sorry, Miss Saleema, but Amirah be getting on my nerves, talkin' that dumb shit all the time."

"Bitch, who you calling dumb?" Amirah shouted.

"Amirah!" Saleema was stunned that timid Amirah had challenged a known bully.

"Yo, I'm about two seconds from yanking that bitch for calling me out of my name." In a matter of moments, Portia crossed the room, her balled fists held high.

Swiftly, Saleema blocked Amirah, trying to protect the girl who towered over her with her own petite body. "Control yourself, Portia. You know the rules."

"You already said you closing Head Up, so fuck the rules."

The girls gasped at Portia's blatant lack of respect.

Though she hated seeing this angry, explosive side of Portia, Saleema had to admit that Portia had a point. Saleema could no longer offer her girls an incentive for good behavior.

Still, she stood firmly planted in front of Amirah. "Portia, if you don't pull yourself together, you're going to wind up in a juvenile facility."

Portia scowled. "Do you think I give a fuck?" She lunged for Amirah.

Amirah, no longer feeling her earlier sense of boldness, ducked and cowered behind Saleema. Portia easily maneuvered around Saleema, landing a resounding punch on the side of Amirah's head.

Until that moment, everyone, including Portia, had adhered to the "no fighting" rule at Head Up. Saleema felt completely to blame. Her lack of money management skills had brought the program to a halt.

But before she got the chance to accept an invitation to a pity party, she felt the sting of a slap that was intended for Amirah.

"Ooo! You know you wrong for putting your hands on Miss Saleema," Tasha shouted, indignant.

"Bitch, whatchu gon' do about it?" Greta piped in, defending Portia.

And then all hell broke loose. Tasha picked up the butterfly chair. Before Saleema could intervene, Tasha threw the chair at Greta. Greta ducked.

"I know yo' ass is crazy, flinging that damn chair at me." Greta

picked up the chair. Gripping its thin mangled metal legs, she zoomed across the room, swinging the heavy butterfly fabric, kicking tables out of her way. Girls shrieked and scurried out of Greta's path as she pursued Tasha.

Meanwhile, with Saleema running toward Greta, Amirah was exposed. Portia wound her hand around Amirah's braids, bringing the gangly girl down to her knees.

This is out of hand. How did my good intentions result in this melee? Saleema backtracked and tried to wrench Amirah from Portia's grip.

Another chair whizzed through the air. Saleema watched in horror as the mitt chair smashed a window. The sounds of shattering glass and high-pitched screams were ear-splitting.

Greta picked up a bean bag chair, and threw it toward a random group of girls. The girls scattered. Unfortunately, Saleema caught the full impact of the bean bag. She went down; her petite body smacked against the hardwood floor, face down.

"Oh, my God!" Amirah shouted.

"Call the cops!" another voice added.

From the floor, Saleema lifted her head. Gasping, she witnessed Portia's and Greta's legs racing toward the door. Saleema heard a medley of beeps and buzzes from several cell phones.

The girls were calling the police. She didn't want them to, but with the wind knocked out of her, she couldn't speak. All she could do was shake her head.

She heard Amirah giving out the address and the names of perpetrators, but couldn't stop.

"Don't worry, Miss Saleema," Amirah said. "The 9-1-1 operator said the cops gon' be here in a few minutes."

Having Portia sent to a youth detention center was not at all what Saleema had intended. She would have preferred to handle the situation herself, but it was now out of her hands.

CHAPTER 4

"**Y**ou trying to punk me?" Bullet spewed. His face was so close to hers that she could see the particles of chicken that were trapped between his teeth.

"I'm not trying to punk you."

A sharp jab to her face dazed Gianna for a few seconds.

"Number one rule...don't disagree with me."

"Okay." She yearned to rub her throbbing face, but she feared that Bullet would consider the gesture as "trying to punk him," so she kept her hands folded in her lap.

"You like fucking with my money?"

She didn't know whether to say yes or no. Taking a chance, she shook her head.

"I'm feeding you and keeping a roof over your head. I been taking my time and tryna train yo' young ass cuz you can't work the track if I don't school you."

"I'm sorry, Bullet."

"Whatchu sorry for? Sorry that you got caught?" There was fire in his eyes.

"I'm sorry for running away from you."

He raised his hand threateningly. She flinched. He laughed, mockingly.

"Look around you," Bullet demanded.

Relieved that he didn't strike her, she quickly obeyed, looking around the shabby quarters. Chicken bones and bits of charred chicken skin filled a chipped dinner plate.

Bullet pointed a finger at Gianna. "How you gon' run out on your man like that?"

"I was scared."

"Scared of what? Those lil' bit of ass whippings you got wasn't 'bout nothing. But after that shit you pulled today, I'ma make sure yo' ass is too scared to run. Real talk, bitch." Bullet huffed and sighed for a few moments, and then he grabbed Gianna by the neck, pressing his thumb into her windpipe. "You didn't even clean up behind yourself after I had the decency to feed yo' hungry ass." He shoved her.

Gasping, Gianna reached for the chipped plate that sat atop a crate. Bullet's knife was next to the plate.

"Do you think I like living in this shit hole? Jail was better than this dump." He picked up a knife. Threateningly, he ran his finger along the blade. "You ain't gon' never do right, is you?"

"Yes, I am."

"Nah. You gon' keep trying to run away." He shook his head. "I ain't wasting no more time tryna train you. It's time to cut my losses." He paused and gave her a long, sneering look. "I might as well get rid of you." Then he looked up in thought. "Yeah, I need to get myself a better bitch. A bitch that knows how to listen."

"I can listen. I'll do right. Really. I promise, Bullet."

"Your promises ain't worth shit. You a slimy, ruthless chick. How you gon' shout out your government name on a crowded bus?" He blew out a disgusted breath. "If I keep fucking with you, I'ma wind up back behind bars."

Whenever Bullet talked about going back to jail, the creases in his forehead deepened. Expecting a swift kick, a slap to the face, or a body blow, Gianna tensed, and then let out a breath of relief. Surprisingly Bullet didn't get physical; he just glowered at her.

"I can't trust a bitch that would deliberately try to get her man

locked up," he said, continuing his verbal tirade. "Do you know how much time I could get over snatching yo' young ass?"

His brows arched, meeting the creases in his forehead, a warning for her to start talking fast. "I made a mistake. I don't want anything to happen to you. I love you and I need you. Please, Bullet, can I have another chance?" In all uncountable days that she'd been his captive, she'd never once told him that she loved him.

Bullet relaxed his facial muscles. His eyes brightened. He liked hearing that she loved him.

"I really love you," she repeated. Her survival depended on him believing her.

Then his eyes suddenly went cold. "If you love me so much, why you run off without even considering the amount of time I could get on some bogus kidnapping charges."

"I wasn't trying to get you in trouble. I was scared, Bullet. You kept hitting me. I was afraid for my life. "

"All bitches gotta get they ass whooped sometimes. Damn, I wasn't trying to kill you. You ain't no good to me if yo' ass is dead."

"I was scared of getting another beating."

Bullet threw his head back in disgust. "I gotta beat yo' ass. That's how the game goes."

"I'm not used to that, Bullet. My parents don't believe in corporal punishment."

"They don't believe in what?" Bullet's vocabulary was limited.

"Hitting children," she clarified.

Bullet nodded reflectively. "Oh. So that's yo' problem? You a lil' rich girl, used to having everything handed to you on a silver platter." His expression changed from thoughtful to mean and dangerous.

Gianna was sorry that she'd spoken.

"I see that I got a lot a work ahead of me. I'ma break yo' spoiled, stuck-up ass. I'ma stay whippin' that ass so good, you gon' forget you ever had any parents."

Images of her mother and father sped through her mind. The last time she'd seen them together had not been a happy time. Her parents' pending divorce was bitter, inciting them to shouting matches and name-calling, each threatening to file for full custody of Gianna.

"What's your daddy's name?" Bullet demanded.

"Andrew Str…"

BAM! Bullet's knuckles collided with the side of her head. "What I tell you about disagreeing with me. Yo' daddy's name ain't no Andrew. What's yo' daddy's name?"

"Bullet. My daddy's name is Bullet," she uttered, fighting back the tears that would incite him to do more violence.

He brought the knife close to her face. "I own you, bitch. What I gotta do to make you understand that? Do I have to carve my name in your muthafuckin' face?"

Gianna cringed at the sight of the blade. "I won't run away anymore."

"I need some money, bitch, and that shit you pulled done put me in another setback."

"I'm sorry," she murmured.

"Fuck being sorry. We need some money to move. We gotta get out of this 'hood. All I need is for one of those mufuckers on that bus to decide they wanna be a hero." His eyes went dull and deadly. "I can't believe you gave out your government name." Bullet poked the tip of the knife into Gianna's cheek.

She shook with fear. "I won't do it again." She thought telling him that she loved him would lessen his anger, but he was now raging mad.

He brought the knife up higher and pricked the skin beneath her blackened eye. "You think you could still make me some money with only one eye?"

"Um, um, um…" Terror made her shudder. Gianna was at a loss for words. She had no idea what Bullet wanted her to say.

"I don't know how much a one-eyed hooker can make. But I bet tricks will be willing to spend a grip to fuck you in that empty eye socket." He laughed. "A horny trick will fuck anything. Trust me." Bullet glared at the shivering girl. "After all the work I put in, your head game still ain't right."

"I'll do better." The words came out in high-pitched anguish.

"Shut the fuck up." He stuck the tip of the knife in a little deeper, hushing her. "That empty eye socket probably would make a good fuck hole."

Gianna's teeth began to chatter. Bullet had proven himself to be brutal enough to remove her eyeball without remorse. Her mind went on overdrive, trying to figure out a way to break free before the lunatic poked his knife into the swelling skin beneath her eyeball.

"You gon' run away again?"

"No!"

"Try it and we gon' find out how much money a one-eyed ho can bring in."

"I won't run away again. I promise, Bullet," she said, her voice shaky.

Bullet withdrew the knife. "Peep this, ho. If I tell you the sky is dog-shit brown, whatchu 'spose to say?"

"The sky is dog-shit brown," she agreed.

"Who is Gianna Strand?"

"I don't know her. I've never heard of anyone by that name." She shook her head, adamant.

"Uh-huh," he said doubtfully. "So, what's your muthafuckin' name, then?"

"My name is Lollipop."

"Why you go by that name?"

Bullet was quizzing her. She took a deep breath and launched into the recitation that he'd taught her. "My head game is tight; trick with me and I'll suck you off like your dick is a sweet-ass lollipop." Her tongue darted out to lick her lips provocatively, the way Bullet had taught her to. Her lips were sore from all the training she'd been put through. She winced when her tongue flicked against her chaffed skin.

Bullet gave a derisive snort. "How the fuck you 'spect somebody to believe you give good brain if you gon' be flinching and shit every time you lick your lips?"

"I'm sorry. I won't flinch."

Bullet sucked his teeth. "If you really had your head game right, I'd be stacking some loot by now." He loosened the string in the front of his nylon shorts. "I'ma give you one more chance to get back in my good graces." He lowered the elastic waistband. "Show your man some love."

Dutifully, Gianna dropped to her knees and took his thick erection inside her palm. It pained her to stretch her mouth open, but she stretched it wide to accommodate Bullet's large size.

He scowled down at her and then smacked the top of her head. "Watch your grille. Don't be scraping up and mangling my shit up with those sharp-ass teeth you got."

She nodded and commenced to pleasing him. Performing oral sex on this man she hated was disgusting, but giving head was preferable to getting punched around or having an eye poked out.

Besides, she wouldn't be held hostage much longer. Everyone on the bus knew her name. Surely one of those passengers would have the common decency to call the police.

As she pulled Bullet's thick erection in and out of her mouth, she ignored her pained lips. It was only a matter of time before she was rescued. She imagined bloodhounds sniffing out the area and tracking her scent. She sucked passionately as she envisioned a SWAT team, equipped with specialized weapons, breaking down the front door and pointing assault rifles and machine guns at Bullet's head.

"It's smelly in here."

"It's cool, man. Stop trippin'."

"I don't wanna be in no abandoned house. Why couldn't you bring the ho out to my car?"

"She's young and wild. I'm still training her."

"Oh, yeah?" the male voice said, his interest piqued.

"Am I her first, uh, customer?"

"Yup, you 'bout to pop a sweet, young-ass cherry."

"She's a virgin?"

"Yeah, man. You ain't gon' get a better price than I'm giving you."

Gianna moaned in distress as she listened to Bullet's lies. The man named Jimmy had stolen her virginity and Bullet's fuck and suck lessons had ensured that her vagina was no longer tight.

The SWAT team hadn't arrived. From the bathroom, where she lay in the tub naked with her wrists tied to the faucet, she heard the sex transaction taking place. After her escape attempt, Bullet said it would be a snowy day in hell before he'd allow her the privilege of walking freely about.

She hoped that she wouldn't be expected to demonstrate her oral skills. Her lips ached and felt bruised from working extra hard on her head game.

The bathroom door opened. Bullet entered with a short man who was pale, an obvious albino who reeked of liquor. Bullet gestured toward Gianna. "That's Lollipop, man." He glared at Gianna. "Show some manners. Say hi to my man, Whitey."

"Hi, Whitey," Gianna murmured.

"My name ain't Whitey," the albino muttered, offended.

"My bad, man. Look here, Lollipop is something special," he said, beaming proudly, attempting to get the albino in a better mood. "She's worth a lot more than forty dollars, man. But due to our surroundings and everything, I'm letting you have her cheap."

The albino took in an eyeful of Gianna's youthful nudity. "Why you got her all tied up like that?"

"That young ho got devious ways. She can't be trusted. She be tryna get frisky all the time and I ain't with that, so I keep that ass on lock. Y'ah mean?"

"I...I...don't know. I think I changed my mind—"

"Fuck that. I'm not giving you no money back." Bullet's body language was confrontational, as though he was prepared to physically fight the albino over the forty dollars.

"I mean...I don't know if I want to have regular sex with this girl."

"You want something extra...you gotta come outta pocket," Bullet said firmly.

Visibly excited and apparently willing to forgive being called "Whitey," the man said excitedly, "Can I speak to you in private?"

Bullet and the drunken albino exited the bathroom.

Gianna couldn't begin to imagine what the pasty-faced man wanted to do to her. The bathroom door burst open. The albino reentered the bathroom alone. Bound and helpless, all she could do was close her eyes.

Bullet hadn't accompanied the albino man. Struck with an idea,

Gianna's eyes popped open. Perhaps she could talk him into help-ing her escape. She would explain that she'd lied about her age when she first met Bullet, pretending to be sixteen. If the albino knew her true age, maybe he'd have a heart and call her mother.

"I'm only fifteen," she confessed. "And he lied to you. You're not my first. He let a man named Jimmy have sex with me." Expecting the albino to be outraged at Bullet's deceit, Gianna waited for him to conspire against Bullet and help her escape.

"You're still young and tender. I don't mind being your second john."

She tried another tactic. "Can you please untie me?" she whis-pered meekly, yanking on the two tightly tied bandanas that bound her to the rusty faucet.

"Lookin' at you all tied up and everything is making me horny," he said, turning a deaf ear to her plea.

Appalled, she watched him squeeze his crotch. "Mister, please. You have to help me. I'm just a kid."

The albino's tongue darted out, moistening his lips. "Well… you got plump titties." His eyes wandered downward. "A hairy pussy. You look woman enough for me."

"Listen, there's a reward for anyone who rescues me and takes me home. My dad works on Wall Street. He's loaded." She didn't know if her parents had offered a reward or not, but she assumed they were doing everything in their power to bring her back safe and sound.

"Hush up," the albino said, raising his voice. "Getting my money's worth off of you is all the reward I need."

Panic rising, Gianna pulled at the restraints.

Lustfully, the albino gazed at her. "Mmm," he grunted. "All that squirming you doing is sexy, lil' mama. But you gotta hold still. I paid extra money for you to stay tied to that faucet."

Quick as a flash, he opened his fly and held his opaque dick in his hand.

The head of his dick was as disturbingly alabaster white as his face.

"Yo' pimp said you give good head," he slurred.

"He's not my pimp. My name is Gianna Strand. He kidnapped me from—"

With his legs pressed against the side of the tub, the pale man leaned in. He cut off Gianna's protest, forcing his revolting white penis inside her mouth.

CHAPTER 5

It had started drizzling outside. The night air and raindrops felt good against her bruised skin. That small pleasure didn't last long. Bullet shoved her into the backseat of the albino's car.

"I'm not comfortable with this arrangement," the albino said, starting the motor. "I gotta think twice before I get involved in this here smuggling ring you got going on."

"This ain't no smuggling ring. Lollipop is the only ho I got. She ran off from her peoples. They was abusing her. You know how that go."

"Why you keep her tied up?"

"She frisky, man. After all the time and work I put in, I'd be crazy to give her too much freedom. I don't want her running off with the first pimp who comes along and sweet-talks her panties off." Bullet turned around and gave Gianna a cold look.

She dropped her eyes. Her panties were in Atlantic City in the hands of a hack named Jimmy.

The car swerved. Bullet gripped the dashboard and spat curse words. "You want me to drive, man?"

"No, I'm good." Cautiously, the drunken albino slowed down.

"Aiight, so here's what we gon' do…You gon' take Lollipop and me to a motel that's close to a bar. After you get the room for us, I'll make sure Lollipop gives you a free piece of ass."

"I ain't got that kind of time." The albino picked up speed,

slipping and sliding through the damp streets. "Another blow job is all I need."

Another blow job! Gianna jerked her head toward the locked door. She gazed through the window, wishing she had the heart to punch out the glass and jump out.

"You can get with her at the motel tomorrow night," Bullet pacified. "She'll hook you up with something special. Tell him, Lollipop." Once again, Bullet turned around and presented a threatening grimace.

"I'll give you something special," she repeated, deliberately using as few words as possible. It pained her to move her jawbone. Adding to her misery, there was an awful taste in her mouth. After the albino had finished with her, Bullet had held a sample-sized bottle of Scope to her lips, telling her that she needed to freshen up.

It would take much more than mouthwash to rinse away the acrid film that coated her tongue. Soap and water would not make her feel clean again. Gianna was already in counseling. Over the divorce. She was mature enough to realize that she was going to need years and years of therapy to heal from this ordeal.

Soon the drizzle of rain turned into a downpour. The drunk behind the wheel couldn't control the car. The ride became jerky and perilous.

"Get yourself together, Whitey!"

"I told you not to call me that."

"Yo, whatever your name is…I wanna get to the motel in one piece, y'ah mean?" Bullet grumbled.

Gianna didn't flinch or make a sound. Engrossed in thoughts, her eyes were fixated on street signs. She was keeping track of the route they were taking, making sure she could give detailed information about her location when she got her hands on a cell phone.

As though he'd read her mind, Bullet turned around. "Why you so quiet?"

She shifted her gaze away from the window and gave him a guilty smile.

"What was you looking at?"

"Nothing. I was just daydreaming."

"It's nighttime," Bullet said sneeringly. The albino laughed and briefly lost control of the car again.

"It's just an expression," Gianna explained.

"Whatchu looking out the window for? Why you so nosey?"

She squirmed. "Curiosity, I guess."

"Mind ya business. You know what they say about curiosity?" She nodded.

"What they say?"

"Curiosity killed the cat," she muttered.

"Right. That's enough sightseeing." Bullet lifted up slightly and fished a hand inside his pocket. He pulled out the same bandana that he'd used to bind her hands.

Bullet didn't have to give instructions. Gianna realized what he intended to do. Making it easy for him, she scooted forward, stretching out her neck, and allowing Bullet to blindfold her.

Inside the motel room, Bullet removed the blindfold. Gianna's eyes had barely adjusted to the light before Bullet said, "Go 'head, man, get yourself a freebie." He waved a hand toward Gianna.

Bullet clicked on the TV, and then stretched out on top of the bed. The albino signaled Gianna to follow him into the small bathroom. Desperate, she looked over her shoulder.

Bullet frowned. "Go on, bitch. Whatchu staring at me for?"

But she wasn't looking at him; her eyes were scanning the dreary room, searching for a telephone, plotting on sending out a signal of distress. There was no phone inside the cheap motel room. The TV was the only amenity.

In a hurry, the albino didn't take long. Less than five minutes later, clamping her head tightly between his pasty white hands, he groaned as he shot his load. Trying not to gag, she rushed over to the toilet, and spit out the milky fluid. If it were Bullet's cum inside her mouth, she would have been forced to swallow. Bullet didn't allow her to waste his seed. Grimacing, she flushed the toilet.

Bullet heard the flush. His voice boomed over the blaring TV. "Damn, y'all finished already?" There was irritation in his tone, as though the speedy sex transaction annoyed him.

Zipping his pants, the albino left the bathroom. Gianna remained behind, standing at the sink, rinsing her mouth out with tap water.

Bullet appeared in the doorway.

"Yes?" she asked in a meek voice.

"I gotta go out and drum up some business." His tone implied that somehow it was her fault that he couldn't finish watching *The Jamie Foxx Show*. The TV voices grew louder. He craned his neck and smiled at the antics of actors, and then turned back to Gianna, the smile gone from his face.

"Freshen up," he said gruffly and tossed her the same miniature bottle of mouthwash. That mouthwash, along with a few other items, were Bullet's only possessions, part of his paltry worldly goods. A meager part of the things he'd brought home from the penitentiary.

Home for Bullet was wherever he could rest his head: abandoned houses, cars, men's shelters...anywhere. This cheap motel room was the most comfortable quarters yet. He glanced at the TV screen again, appearing reluctant to leave.

"Come on now. You gon' have to hurry up if you plan to catch a ride with me." The albino had sobered up. He was standing at the door, impatiently pulling back the chain lock.

Bullet sneered at Gianna. "Whitey's in a rush," he said in a low tone. "I ain't got time to tie up your hands, so I'm gon' have to use another method to keep yo' frisky self in check."

He stared at her, eyes roving, mind hard at work. "Strip outta yo' clothes."

She was growing accustomed to her captor's sexual demands. Thinking Bullet wanted a quickie before he left, Gianna resignedly took off the ripped top and wriggled out of the tight skirt. She no longer possessed one article of underwear. Her bra had been left behind when she'd dressed hurriedly, escaping the boarded-up house while Bullet was taking a shower. The bra was inside the abandoned house, lost beneath the rubble.

"Hand 'em here." Bullet stuck out his hand.

Confused, she gave him her rumpled clothing.

"Shoes, too."

She stepped out of the wedge sandals.

"Pick 'em up, bitch!"

She snatched up the sandals and gave them to Bullet.

"Ain't nothing but swampland around here. Yo' nekkid ass can try to run off if you want to. But when I catch you—" He shook his head as if the consequences for trying to escape were too gruesome for him to even verbalize.

Bullet pulled out his homemade knife, grabbed her around the neck and brought the shank close to her face. "It might be a good idea to turn you into a one-eyed hooker."

"I won't run."

"Bet not. In case they got your face on fliers and shit…won't nobody recognize you after I get finished doing surgery on yo' face. Y'ah mean?"

"I'm going to be right here, waiting for you."

In her mind, she was envisioning herself running through swamp-

land and finding her way to a highway. She knew a highway was nearby. She'd heard the familiar sound of expressway traffic a few minutes before Bullet had pushed her inside the motel room.

An hour passed. Gianna had gone to the door, unlocked the chain and peeked out so many times, a sheen of sweat covered her nude body.

Bullet was nowhere in sight. Nor was anyone else. The few cars in the gravel parking lot indicated that there were people somewhere, renting out rooms. There had to be a desk clerk. But how far was the office from her room.

There was no neon sign boasting the name of the hotel. Only darkness. In silent conflict, she wondered if she should take the chance and run out into the dark night, and then trek through the swampland Bullet had mentioned. No, she couldn't deal with a swamp in the dark.

She'd stand a better chance of escaping if she pounded on some motel doors. A butt-naked, young girl screaming for help would bring the police. Her parents had to be beyond frantic. Surely an Amber Alert was in progress. A rescue team would respond quickly.

She was ready to dart out, but stopped. She stood with the door cracked, nervously licking her chaffed lips, and trying to keep her breathing steady, she pondered the pros and cons of disobeying Bullet.

It occurred to her that Bullet was most likely hiding in the shadows, testing her loyalty. Wanting her to make a run for it so he could use his knife to disfigure her face.

Too scared to run, Gianna closed the door. She started to replace the chain lock, but left it dangling. What was the point? Bullet would get in one way or another. Why give him a reason to poke out her eye?

An hour or so later, she heard footsteps outside the motel room. Panic swept through her. She pictured Bullet waving his knife around, blaming her because he hadn't been successful in wrangling up more business.

The door opened. With an arrogant swagger, Bullet stepped inside. Three white men came up behind him. They froze in the doorway. Squeezed together, they gawked at Gianna like she was something from another planet.

Bullet waved a hand. "Come on in."

Looking over their shoulders, the three men inched forward but kept the door cracked open as if they might need to make a hasty escape.

"Close the door. This ain't for prying eyes. This here shit is on the low, y'ah mean?"

With her eyes, Gianna begged the men to help her.

"She's just a kid," one of the men uttered.

Eyes alit with curiosity, the three white men spilled into the motel room. Bullet stalked over; closed the door behind them.

After carefully putting the lock in place, Bullet swiveled his head toward Gianna. "Yeah, she's young and tender. Just got her cherry popped," he bragged. "That lil' pussy of hers is still tight. Which one of y'all wants to try it out first?"

Gianna cringed. Her stomach lurched. She wanted to run to the bathroom and vomit, but that reaction would cost her several pokes from Bullet's knife. She swallowed down the bile.

The men exchanged uneasy glances. Their discomfort with the situation gave Gianna a ray of hope.

The three men didn't look like perverts. They appeared to be ordinary people...reasonable adults...parents, educators, business-

men. She could tell by their troubled expressions that they were appalled by Bullet's suggestion. They were probably pillars of their communities with kids her age at home.

She released a breath of hope. Any moment now, the three men would band together, overpower Bullet, and conduct a citizen's arrest.

"Yo, Lollipop, meet my friends." Bullet faced the trio. "What's y'all's names again?"

"Uh…call me Manny," one of the men said with a tense chuckle.

"Moe," the second man piped in.

"Jack." By the time the third man rattled off his fake name, Gianna's eyes began to well. She blinked back tears as she began to realize that these men had no intention of rescuing her.

 CHAPTER 6

"You have any condoms?" Manny asked Bullet.

Bullet scowled. "Nah, y'all shoulda brought your own."

Moe shifted his feet. "We weren't expecting…you know…to get involved with a hooker."

"Man, fuck a rubber. That bitch is clean." Bullet's head swiveled toward Gianna; his eyes commanded her to back him up.

"I'm clean," she muttered, her head nodding robotically under Bullet's irritated gaze.

"How many johns she been with?" Jack wanted to know.

"None! I'm the only nigga she fucked with. She fresh, man. Like new," Bullet said, as if he was trying to hawk a used car.

The men stared at each other.

Bullet continued his sales pitch. "That's why I ain't got no more condoms. I used 'em all up while I was breaking her in."

Manny's, Moe's, and Jack's faces perked up, obviously satisfied with Bullet's lies.

"I'm going first," Jack said, sidling up to the bed.

Manny pushed forward. "Based on what?"

"Based on the fact that I called it," Jack replied, checking out Gianna's nude body. He let out a whistle.

"Listen up! Whichever one of y'all is willing to pay a hunnit-fifty is the muthafucka who gets to go first."

Manny frowned. "I thought you were charging us sixty apiece."

"That's when I thought y'all had some protection. Right now,

her twat is fresh and clean, but one y'all might give her something."

Manny, Moe, and Jack all frowned, indignant.

"Look, I need some extra medical coverage for that bitch. Just in case."

As the obscene transaction took place, Gianna tensed, ready to spring back out of the bed that she had just lay down in. She met Bullet's menacing gaze and closed her eyes in defeat.

Someone crawled into bed with her. He pulled the motel's threadbare bedspread over their heads, using it as a makeshift privacy wall. Groping hands and heavy breathing came from Jack or Manny. Or was it Moe? She had no idea.

Her anonymous bed partner climbed on top of her and spread her legs. She wanted to shriek in agony when he forcibly entered her. Instead, she clamped her mouth shut and lay motionless. Afraid of losing an eye…of losing her very life, Gianna endured the pain without emitting so much as a whimper.

It had all started with a pair of curtains.

Gianna and her mother had arrived at the family beach house the first weekend after school had let out for summer break. The drive to Ocean City was weird. Their first summer vacation without her father.

Her parents were legally separated, and her father had spent the Memorial Day weekend at the beach house. With his mistress.

Gianna and her mother noticed the flag-emblazoned curtains the moment they pulled into the driveway.

"The audacity of that bitch!" her mother shouted, parking the Trailblazer haphazardly. "Who gave her permission to remove my

Roman shades and put up that crap?" She ran inside the house and immediately ripped down the offensive curtains that the mistress had hung.

She'd also had the kitchen repainted...bright blue. In fact, everything inside the kitchen was different. New kitchen set. Pictures on the wall. Everything. Even the salt and pepper shakers.

"This is my goddamn house. How dare that bitch come in here, changing my fucking décor?" Gianna's mother, once dignified and soft spoken, went on a wild rampage. She broke powder blue dishes, and then hurled a microwave and ceramic canisters against the kitchen walls.

After her mother finished demolishing the kitchen, she tore through the living room.

Frantic, Gianna ran behind her, pleading for her mother to try to calm down. Thankfully, the living room was unsullied by any of the mistress's decorative touches, but her mother wasn't satisfied.

She sped to the master bedroom and began tearing the linen off the bed. Shrieking, spewing profanity so vile Gianna couldn't believe her ears.

"Stop it, Mommy. Please stop. We came here to relax and have a good time."

"How can I have a good time, Gigi? Your father has allowed that home wrecker to mark her territory...he's allowed her to piss all over the place."

Gianna grimaced. "Ew. That's nasty. He wouldn't let her do anything like that."

"That's an expression, Gigi. Listen, honey... Your father is no saint. It's time you got that through your head. Together, he and his whore have fucked up over sixteen years of a good and stable marriage. It's so goddamned humiliating."

Gianna cringed. It was out of character for her mother to curse.

"I'm not sleeping in this bed. I can smell her in here."

Gianna looked at her mother curiously, and then sniffed the air. "I don't smell anything." Maybe her father was right. Maybe her mother was becoming mentally imbalanced.

"He slept in our bed with that motherfucking whore—"

Gianna gasped. She wished her mother would stop using gutter language. Hearing her mother speak so harshly was traumatizing.

"I swear to God, I can smell her. Her stench is in the mattress… it's in the walls." Her mother shook her head furiously. "I can't do it. I can't sleep in here."

Sobbing a mournful sound, her mother collapsed to the floor. Gianna joined her, soothing her as best she could. "You can sleep in my room. Okay, Mommy?" Providing comfort to an adult… her mother nonetheless…felt foreign and very awkward.

"Where's my purse? Did I leave it in the truck?"

"It's in the kitchen."

Happy to do something helpful, Gianna trotted to the war-torn kitchen and retrieved her mother's purse from beneath the wreckage. Inside the purse was an assortment of medication, prescribed when she'd first found out about her husband's illicit affair. The dosages had been increased after he'd demanded a divorce.

With her mother sleeping peacefully in Gianna's bedroom, Gianna changed from her jeans and T-shirt to a super short and very tight skirt that she'd purchased from Forever 21. A brand-new pair of four-inch wedge sandals completed her hot, naughty look. Her best friend, Taylor, had bought a matching outfit.

Her mother would be conked out for the rest of the afternoon and throughout the night. There was nothing to do in this quiet

beach town, but she'd heard there was lots of fun in Atlantic City.

After a forty-minute bus ride, Gianna arrived in Atlantic City, New Jersey. Her girlfriend, Taylor, was staying at Bally's with her parents and was supposed to slip out and meet Gianna on the boardwalk after her parents started their gambling marathon.

Phone calls to Taylor's cell went straight to voice mail. Taylor was a no-show, which should have made Gianna check the bus schedule and get on the first thing smoking.

Fascinated by the bright lights of Atlantic City and dreading having to hear more of her mother's ravings, she moseyed along the boardwalk, lingering in front of attractions, browsing inside arcades and cheesy souvenir shops.

Young. Alone. Dressed in skimpy clothing. Gianna was a target.

Inside an arcade, he eased up behind her and watched her shoot down zombies and other monsters. She caught him watching her. Flattered by his attention, she smiled.

He looked to be around nineteen or twenty. Much too old for her. But her parents weren't around to monitor her. And he was awfully cute with his curly hair that hung past his ears.

"Whassup, yo? You by yourself?" he inquired. His street jargon and improper English sent a wave of excitement through her.

"Yeah. For the moment. I'm waiting for my best friend to meet me, but she hasn't returned my calls."

"She left you hangin', ma?"

"I don't' think she's deliberately avoiding me. Her parents may have caught her while she was getting dressed." Gianna looked down at her outfit and wrinkled her nose. "We're not allowed to dress like this."

"Looks good to me."

She beamed up at the cute boy. He had on gray nylon shorts. A wife beater. A beat-up pair of Nike slide sandals. His clothing

looked a tad shabby, but he was probably just bumming around on the boardwalk. On chill mode, she told herself. Besides, he was so fine, his clothing didn't matter.

He smiled at Gianna. "Ya girl did the right thing by staying home."

"Why do you say that?"

"Hot as you is…" He frowned as though he could feel her heat. "Two hot honeys would have these wooden planks on the board-walk going up in flames."

Gianna blushed and laughed appreciatively.

"Anyway, two of y'all would be too much eye candy for this lame boardwalk."

"I don't think it's lame." She looked around at the glowing, brightly colored signs. "I think it's exciting!"

"Man, this ain't about nothin'. By the way, my name is Bullet."

"How'd you get a name like that?"

A shadow fell over his face. "Rough life. Grew up having to dodge a lot of bullets."

"Oh." She didn't know what else to say. She felt instant sympathy for Bullet.

Her life had been so easy…so privileged. At least it had been, up until now. Her parents were at war with each other. Her father constantly accused her mother of being crazy and an unfit parent. Her mother claimed her father and his mistress were deliberately trying to drive her insane.

Gianna didn't know who or what to believe. Her home life was out of order and chaotic. Despite her family's comfortable finan-cial status—her father with a powerful Wall Street position, and her mother, a university professor—Gianna no longer felt like a privileged child.

"My name is Gianna."

"Pretty name for a pretty girl."

"Thank you." She felt all tingly inside and out.

"If you want to really party, I can take you to a club that's poppin'. I heard that Omarion is coming through around eleven o'clock. Paid appearance. You know how that goes."

"Omarion! Oh, my God. For real?" Gianna jumped up and down. She took out her cell again. "I have to tell Taylor."

"Nah, I got VIP passes waiting for me. Only two. Your girl-friend left you hangin', so why you worrying about her?"

He arched a brow and then gave Gianna the kind of smile she'd only seen on the lips of hot celebrities. His smile radiated sex appeal…the kind she'd only viewed from her TV screen. None of the corny boys from her private school had ever smiled at her like that.

"But I don't think I'll be allowed inside the club," she said apprehensively. "I'm only…uh…sixteen," she lied, adding a year to her actual age.

He winked at her. "I gotchu, ma. I got VIP status. Ain't nobody gon' bother you about no ID."

He walked her down wooden steps, leaving the glitz and glitter of the boardwalk behind. On foot, they traveled well-lit streets and then meandered to darker, less inhabited streets.

"Where's the club? I'm surprised Omarion would make an appearance in this kind of neighborhood."

"The casinos, the boardwalk, and all that other shit is for crackers and tourists. The real shit be poppin' off behind the scenes. Omarion be doing a lot of PR shit for the cameras. But behind the scenes…he be gettin' down like a real nigga should."

"Oh," she said, though warning bells had begun ringing softly inside her head. By the time the bell had escalated to a blaring alarm, it would be too late.

"Anyway, I gotta change my clothes. I know you don't think I'm going to the club dressed like this?" Bullet said with a chuckle.

It made sense that he'd want to change out of those shorts. She hoped the club was closer to the well-lit streets they'd bypassed. This neighborhood was depressing. There was a queasy feeling in her stomach. Something wasn't quite right.

 CHAPTER 7

Bullet knocked on the door of a sad-looking house on a dark street.

"Who lives here?"

"Friend of mine. I been staying with him off and on since I got out."

"Out of where?"

"Uh…college," he said with a chuckle. "Summer break, y'ah mean? I gotta change of clothes here at my man's crib. It won't take me long to change." Smiling, he traced his finger across her cheek. "Is that okay with you, sweet thing?" he asked, melting her apprehension with his smile.

Sounds of coughing were heard and then a much older man opened the door, and ushered them in.

"Hey, how you doin', Bullet?" the man said between coughs.

"'Sup, Celly?"

The house stank of cigarettes and male body odor. She held her breath for a few seconds, and then had no choice but to inhale another whiff of funkiness. She hoped Bullet changed clothes quickly.

The older man yielded a soft smile toward Gianna, his eyes appraising her. "You got good taste, Bullet."

Bullet nodded and then nudged Gianna. "Say hello to my old celly."

She controlled a grimace and fixed her lips into a smile. "Hello, Mr. Celly," Gianna replied as politely as possible.

The older man laughed, cutting an eye at Bullet. "Mr. Celly! Now that's one for the books."

Both men gave deep belly laughs. Gianna didn't know what she'd said that was so funny. She really wanted to get out of there. She didn't even care anymore about seeing Omarion at the club. The urge to get out this stinking house was overwhelming.

"Where you from? You don't talk like you from the 'hood," the older man said, his voice dry and coarse from some infirmity that had him hacking and coughing every few minutes.

"I'm from northern New Jersey—Cloverhill. Our summer home is here in southern Jersey."

"Is that right? Cloverhill is nice. Big, fancy houses. Your peoples must have a lot of money?"

"Um…I guess so," she said squirming.

The old man eyed Bullet, his gaze reproachful.

Bullet's jaw tightened. "I ain't know."

"You know better than to pick up somebody with people likely to put a reward out on her head. You was supposed to be scoping out runaways. Doped-up kids who people won't be scouring the earth, looking for 'em."

Apprehension gripped Gianna. "What's he talking about, Bullet?"

Bullet ignored her; directed his words to the older man. "Man, I got what I could get. Why you worrying about it? She ain't yo' problem."

"You made her my problem when you brought her here."

Warning bells soared to a siren's alarm. Bullet wasn't as nice as he'd seemed. There was no club tucked away in this godforsaken neighborhood. She wouldn't be smiling and posing with Omarion.

This was an abduction.

Gianna bolted toward the door.

Quick as lightning, Bullet blocked her.

She tried to push him out of her way, but he was as unmovable as a mountain.

"Please. Let me leave. My mom's going to be worried about me."

"You ain't going nowhere. Sit yo' ass down while I get my thoughts together."

"My mother's going to call the police."

"Listen, ho, sit down before I smack yo' ass down. Choice is yours." He pointed to a worn couch.

She obeyed, noticing the coffee table cluttered with an arsenal of prescription meds, a half-pint of cheap whiskey, and an ashtray that was overflowing with cigarette butts. Disgusting.

The older man shook his head, his expression grave. "You done went out and picked up the wrong one."

"I ain't know," Bullet snapped.

"You gon' have to get her outta Atlantic City before her peoples find out she been snatched."

Snatched! The word had an ominous sound. Like she was going to be kept against her will for a long time. Maybe forever.

"Can I please call my mo—"

"Can you please shut the fuck up!" Bullet bellowed.

Gianna shut her mouth.

Turning his attention back to the old man, he asked, "How am I s'posed to get out of AC? You know I ain't got no wheels."

"You done really messed up. After everything I taught you back when we were locked up together…" He squeezed his eyes closed tight and shook his head grimly, like he was trying to rid himself of the image of Bullet's grim future.

"I know you ain't trying to tell me to let this hooker go?"

"This is the kind of problem I don't need. All I'm saying is, you take that trouble away from around my front door." He nodded toward Gianna.

"You gotta finish schooling me," Bullet said.

"You don't listen."

"It's one thing hearing shit when you behind bars, but now that I got me a ho, I need you to run it all down for me again. Come on, Big Pimpin', you got a lifetime worth of experience with training hoes. I need to be hanging around here so you can help me school her...teach her how to work the track. I'll give you part of the proceeds."

"Man, you crazy. Can't no two niggas pimp a ho."

"I don't expect you to raise yo' pimp hand or nothing. I can handle all that."

"I'm sick," the older man complained. "Terminal!" He coughed as if to prove it. "My pimpin' days are long gone. That type of thing don't bring me no kind of excitement or enjoyment. I'm too sick to be beating bitches."

"I'll do all the beating. Just help school her for me. Come on, man...she green."

Bullet was planning to force her into the sex trade. Gianna had heard about human trafficking; it was something that happened to poor girls from broken homes. Not to girls like her.

Suddenly her mind was flooded with images: the moving van that had hauled away her father's personal possessions, depositing him and his belongings into his mistress's home—a stone estate in the same neighborhood where he'd lived for sixteen years with his wife and daughter. She saw her mother, wild and borderline crazy, as she trashed the kitchen of the beach home.

Seemingly overnight, Gianna had become a girl from a broken home. The perfect victim to land in Bullet's hands.

"Come up with a plan, Bullet. You can't keep yo' ho in Atlantic City."

"When we was locked up, you told me the ho stroll in AC was poppin'."

"It ain't poppin' for no young bitch with her mug posted up on milk cartons and billboards and whatnot. Nah, you gon' have to work her underground."

"This is fucked up." Bullet glared at Gianna as though she had caused the situation.

Thinking hard, the older man ran his hand down his sagging face. "Go in the kitchen, Bullet," he said, coming up with an idea. "Jimmy's number is posted on the wall over the telephone."

"Jimmy who?"

"He's the hack I use to take me to my doctor's appointment. Call him and see if he can carry you and this ho to the bus station. It ain't safe to keep her here in Atlantic City. Her peoples live too close."

"What I'ma pay the hack man with? My good looks?"

"You a pimp or ain't you?"

"Yeah, I'ma pimp."

"Well then, let yo' ho work off the fare. Jimmy ain't gon' turn down a piece of ass. Make sure you charge him enough for that bus ticket and for miscellaneous expenses."

"Where me and my lil' shawty gon' stay after the bus drops us off?"

"Figure it out!" the older man yelled, working himself into a fit of coughing.

"Don't move, shawty." Bullet stormed past the couch where Gianna sat rubbing her trembling hands together.

"Stop calling her shawty," the pimp complained. "That sounds too sweet and endearing. All your hoes should go by one of two names: bitch or ho."

"Oh, aiight. I gotchu."

Gianna shuddered as the old pimp stared her down, keeping his evil eyes on her while Bullet was out of the room. The scowl on his wrinkled face was as intimidating and mean as the devil. Mean

or not, he was in poor health. The man was dying. She would be crazy not to take advantage of the situation.

Using a technique that her track coach had taught her, she envisioned herself hurtling over the coffee table and zipping past the infirmed old pimp, using elbow jabs and a hard kneecap to the groin if he tried to subdue her.

It all happened in a blur. One minute, she was sitting on the edge of the creaking couch, trying to get the courage to make her move. The next moment, she was in motion, imagining the feeling of the smooth knob as she pulled open the front door.

Showing surprising cunning and agility, the sickly pimp quickly stuck out a thin leg, tripping her. Gianna landed on her side.

"Get out here and get some control over yo' bitch!" the old pimp yelled.

She gulped down a knot of fear as she heard Bullet slam the phone into its base.

"Bitch, has you done lost yo' damn mind?" He stood over her, glowering.

"Catching a young ho is easy…like stealing candy," the old man said, sounding winded. "Keepin' a crazy ho in line is an entirely different story."

"Trust. I'ma keep my ho in line."

Bullet snatched Gianna up by the arm, lifted her, and then tossed her across the room as if she were a lifeless rag doll. She didn't feel a thing when her body hit the wall; the impact causing her world to fade to black.

She had no idea how long she'd been out, but obviously she'd been unconscious long enough for Bullet to blindfold her and bind

her hands together. And he'd had ample time to transact business with Jimmy.

"Take her upstairs, Jimmy." The ex pimp made a gesture toward the stairs.

Jimmy didn't hesitate. "Let's go!" He clenched Gianna's shoulder, trying to guide her toward the flight of stairs.

She couldn't move. Every muscle in her body locked, defensively.

"Come on, lil' mama," Jimmy persuaded, gently pulling the frightened young girl.

"Bullet, tell that bitch to pick her feet up. She wasting time," the old pimp complained.

"Get yo' ass up them steps and handle that business before I use both my feet to loosen up yo' tight ass."

Though light-headed, disoriented, and terrified, she realized that she'd better do as she was told or suffer unfathomable consequences. Blindfolded and bound, she was slightly off-balance, lifting her feet hesitantly as she anticipated each step.

Bullet seemed barely human. He was the worst person that she'd ever encountered. She was furious with herself for being so naïve and placing her life in the hands of a brutal ex-con turned pimp.

On second thought, Bullet wasn't even a real pimp. He was taking cues from the man who was his former cellmate. From what she could discern, Bullet was a sort of pimp in training...an apprentice who was being taught the ropes by a coughing and terminally ill ex-pimp.

Numb, Gianna allowed herself to be led to a bedroom. The room reeked of stale cigarette smoke. Jimmy untied her hands. "I want to feel your fingernails clawing up my back when I get between your legs."

Before she could utter a sound of distress, he pushed her on the bed. Jimmy didn't waste any time climbing on top of her, grunting

like an animal as he dry humped her and squeezed her small breasts.

Jimmy slid his tongue inside her mouth. Deprived of sight, her remaining four senses were sharp. She could taste chili peppers and ground beef. *Tacos?* Oh, God. She wanted to puke.

He yanked up the tight skirt; snatched her panties off. The dick he stuck between her legs forced her to switch her focus from his nasty, taco-flavored tongue to the fiery pain of penetration.

She cried out. Motivated by pain, she struggled out of the wrist restraints. She tried to shove him off of her; her palms pushing against a stubble-covered shaved head.

"Don't fight the feeling. Come on, now. Work with me, mama," Jimmy crooned.

She gritted her teeth as Jimmy plunged inside her, and then gyrated lewdly as he violated her.

"I ain't nevah been with a tight-pussy ho. Uh-huh, yeah, baby. You like the way I'm making you feel?"

"No, stop. Please," she whimpered.

He yanked the blindfold off. Gianna grimaced at the scruffy man grinning down at her. "Maybe if you could see whatchu doing, we could make some beautiful love. I opened you up. Ain't no reason for you not to enjoy all these long strokes I'm giving you."

"Hurry up, muthafucka!" Bullet yelled from downstairs.

"Gimme a few more minutes!" Jimmy hollered.

He started working on Gianna again, penetrating so deeply, her insides felt on fire.

"You ready to cum with me, sweet thing?"

He kept on humping. Talking dirty. Gyrating. Thrusting. Panting and moaning.

Downstairs, an exasperated Bullet hurled curses at both Gianna and Jimmy.

Gianna squeezed her eyes tight, shutting out the repulsive sight of the sweaty man on top of her. An eternity seemed to pass by.

Finally, Jimmy bucked and grunted, "Ahh. Oh, hell yeah!" He shuddered and groaned loudly.

The dirty deed was finally over. Jimmy retied her hand. "I think I'll keep these bloody drawers. As a trophy," he explained, nodding his head and smiling with pride. He stepped inside his pants and stuffed her blood-smeared panties inside his back pocket.

"Put the rest of your clothes on. Here…" He handed her the blindfold. "Tie that back on before your pimp tries to start some shit." Then he winked at her, as though they were in cahoots together.

She tied the bandana round her head, loosely. She tried to stand but her legs gave out. Jimmy carried her downstairs. "I wore that ass out. She can't even walk right," he boasted to Bullet and the old pimp.

"Yeah, whatever," Bullet said scornfully. "Put her down. That bitch ain't crippled." He gripped her by the shoulder and guided her toward the back door. "Walk, bitch!" Taking wobbly steps, Gianna complied.

The night air hit her face. Bullet pushed her into the back seat of a car. "Let's get this ho out of Atlantic City."

She heard a screech of tires. She struggled to sit up.

"Bitch, is you crazy?" Bullet snarled. "Lay the fuck down before somebody discovers yo' dumb ass."

She dropped down. Lying uncomfortably in the back seat of the car, Gianna was transported across the state line.

CHAPTER 8

Inside the visitor's room of the youth detention center, Saleema sat across from Portia. With her face scrubbed clean… no lip gloss or eyeliner, Portia hardly resembled the hot-headed, tough teen who routinely fought and intimidated her peers. She looked ten or eleven years old.

"I like your new look. Cute."

Portia *tsked* in disagreement. "These lame asses…" Portia caught herself. "I mean these dang renta-cops who work here. Those jokers made me take my weave out." Frowning, she tugged on her short ponytail.

Despite her continual bad behavior, Portia was one of Saleema's favorites. Portia reminded Saleema of herself at that age. Saleema understood her anger at the world, her short fuse. Like the old Saleema, Portia was always looking for a reason to lash out. Hurting people before they got a chance to hurt her.

Saleema reached across the table, rested her hands on top of Portia's balled fists, massaging until the young teen's fists unfurled. "Getting to see you wasn't easy. I had to meet with the detention supervisor and practically beg him to authorize this visit. Only family members are allowed visitation, but I was able to persuade him to bend the rules a little."

"Thanks for taking the time to come see me, Miss Saleema. I don't know what got into me. I wasn't trying to hurt you," Portia said in a pained voice. "When I seen you go down, I thought you was hurt real bad. Or dead. I got scared. That's why I ran."

"As you can see, I'm fine. Had the wind knocked out me when I hit the floor, but I'm okay. But, you…" Saleema squeezed both Portia's hands. "I've warned you about that temper of yours."

"I know. I'm sorry." Portia frowned. "Man, I ain't even seen the judge yet."

"Why not? You've been here for two days."

"My mom was supposed to come down here for my detention hearing, but ain't nobody seen her."

"Have you spoken to your aunt or any other relatives?" Saleema asked, but she knew that girls like Portia didn't have much family support.

"Yeah, I talked to my aunt LaRue. I told her what time my hearing was, but I already know she ain't gon' show up.

"You brought this on yourself, Portia. You have to accept accountability. You're not a first-time offender. You knew there would be consequences."

"I know!" Portia snapped, tears forming in her eyes. "I'm wrong, but I ain't ever gon' get out of the system if my mom don't speak to the judge. I could wind up on lockdown 'til I'm eighteen years old."

Portia's mother was an addict who spent days, sometimes weeks, away from the home. "What about your aunt? Can't she stand in as your guardian?"

"My guardian!" Portia made a disdainful sound. "She ain't gon' do nothing that involves signing her name on a piece of paper."

Saleema arched a brow, waiting for Portia to elaborate.

"Aunt LaRue is too fat to work a job, so she gets a disability check. She don't leave the house, except late at night to prowl the supermarket aisles at the all-night Pathmark. Oh, yeah, and she be making her sneaky food runs to take-out spots after dark. My aunt LaRue is as bad as my mom, but her addiction is food."

"Maybe I could convince her."

Portia rolled her eyes. "She just gon' tell you she can't get involved cuz it'll mess up her disability check."

"How would making a court appearance—"

"That's her excuse for everything." Portia made a snorting sound. "In order for her to come down here and stand in as my guardian, she'd have to go file some emergency custody papers and she ain't about to get involved with all that."

Saleema tried to process the information. Portia knew a lot about the system. Probably most of the kids in here knew all the ins and outs of what was necessary to obtain their freedom. If they'd spent half as much of their brain power on their studies and making better decisions, they wouldn't have gotten incarcerated in the first place.

"So you need a custodial parent present at your hearing," Saleema said, thinking out loud.

"Right. I need my mother to act like she know and get her butt down here," Portia said angrily.

"You can't blame your mother for this particular incident, Portia." Saleema had met Portia's mother when she'd registered Portia at Head Up. The woman she'd met had seemed to be a concerned parent. *"My mom got game; she know how to represent when she need to,"* Portia had claimed when Saleema had expressed shock to learn that Portia's mother was battling a ten-year addiction and was apt to go missing whenever she got good and ready, leaving Portia at the mercy of a food addict who'd sooner allow Portia to starve before sharing one crumb from her copious food stash.

According to Portia, her aunt kept padlocks on her bedroom door, several cabinets in the kitchen were secured, and even a bathroom closet was padlocked…all this to keep Portia and her negligent mother from having access to the food she bought and

her personal belongings. No, the aunt wasn't likely to get involved in Portia's dilemma. So where did that leave Portia?

Saleema sighed in frustration. "You were already on probation; you realized another infraction would result in spending some time in a detention facility."

"Yeah, I knew I could wind up doing two to three months. But if my mom don't make it to my next hearing, these people gonna get Children and Youth involved. If don't nobody come see about me…" She paused and then spoke shakily, "I could wind up getting sent upstate until I'm eighteen."

"I doubt that," Saleema said, summoning up as much optimism as possible under the circumstances.

"If my mom is too busy getting her high to worry about me now, what makes you think she gon' travel all the way to the boonies to see about me? I ain't did nothing that bad that I deserve to get lost in this system for the next three years." Portia's bottom lip poked out into a pout.

Portia was right. She didn't deserve to be incarcerated for the next three years. Spending that kind of time in an institution would turn her into a hardened criminal before she reached adulthood.

Saleema patted Portia's hand. "I agree. You shouldn't be institutionalized. You need counseling to work on your issues. And some anger control classes would be a great benefit. You can't go through the rest of your life swinging on everybody who says or does something that you don't agree with."

"I know, but Amirah be getting on my nerves. I ain't mean to go that hard on her, though."

"You didn't go hard on Amirah. You took your anger out on me."

"Aw, why you reminding me of that? You know I wouldn't never deliberately hurt you, Miss Saleema."

"I know. But do you see the severe consequences of not having control over your emotions?"

Contrite, Portia nodded. "You gon' try to help me, Miss Saleema? They all got attitudes in here. The people who work here act like they on some kind of power trip."

Bully or not, Portia was still a child and she didn't deserve to be mistreated. She needed counseling and therapy sessions. Saleema thought about her own adolescence…how it mirrored Portia's. Other than her best friend, Terelle, no one had ever been there for Saleema either. With all her past anger issues and bad behavior, it was a miracle that Saleema had escaped the juvenile justice system and the adult penile system, as well.

"Of course, I'm going to try and help you. After I leave, I'll stop by your house and see if your mother is back. If I get a hold of her, I'll personally bring her to your next hearing. Okay?"

"Suppose you can't find her…you know, in time for my hearing?"

"We'll cross that bridge later." Saleema shifted her gaze away from Portia's desperate eyes. The girl was relying on Saleema to make her mother materialize and assume parental responsibilities. It was quite a feat to accomplish.

"If my mom don't come and get me out here, I'm gon' bust out of this place. I'm dead up, Miss Saleema. I'm not staying in here." Portia cut an eye at Saleema, gauging the effect of her threat.

Saleema shook her head, refusing to even indulge the empty threat. "I brought you some magazines and books and some toiletries," Saleema said, changing the subject. "I had to leave them at the front desk so they could label the items."

"Thank you." In an instant, Portia had simmered down. "I'm real sorry about Head Up. I been doing a lot of thinking and I know why I acted up like that."

Saleema gazed at Portia curiously.

"I was mad about you closing Head Up. I loved being there."

Saleema swallowed down a big knot of guilt. "I'm a fighter, Portia. I haven't given up on Head Up. And I'm not giving up on you."

Saleema kissed Portia on the cheek. Shockingly, bad-ass Portia wailed and wrapped her arms around Saleema, refusing to let go.

With gleaming eyes, an overzealous guard rushed over and roughly unclenched Portia's grip. It pained Saleema to watch the young girl being hauled out of the visitor's room and screaming her name.

After that heart-wrenching scene, Saleema felt like she had no choice but to comb every inch of the city until she found Portia's deadbeat mom.

Before exiting the detention center, Saleema stopped to jot down the time next to her name on the visitor's sheet. She looked up at the round-faced clock mounted on the wall. One hand was pointing to number twelve and the other had fallen off, resting at the bottom of the ancient institutional clock. If a hand fell off a clock right in the lobby, what sorts of disrepair and misdeeds were taking place behind the scenes?

Overloaded with stress from her financial straights and feeling powerless to help Portia with her predicament, she barely had the strength to search her overloaded shoulder bag for her always elusive cell phone. Sighing, she groped around, searching for her cell phone to determine the time.

"It's twelve twenty-six," a male voice offered.

She pivoted around to see who the voice belonged to. The man behind her was a brown-skinned brother who had closely cropped hair. He was tall with a lean frame. He wore glasses and that gave him a studious appearance.

Who asked you? she thought, but muttered, "Thanks," and then turned back to the visitor's sheet. She wrote the digits and placed the chained pen on the clipboard.

"Obama's in Philly today," he said, starting up a conversation. "Center City traffic is going to be at a standstill."

She faced the talkative guy, giving him a quick once-over. Wearing a crisp pair of khakis and a neatly tucked button-down shirt, his look was entirely preppy without even a hint of an urban twist. A social worker, she surmised.

"I'm going in the opposite direction," she replied coldly, intending to discourage further comments. She zipped her shoulder bag and took a few steps toward the door.

The preppy dude scrawled the time on the visitor's sheet and caught up with Saleema as she headed toward the exit sign.

"I would say, lucky you, but I heard traffic is snarled throughout the city."

He was too Joe-familiar for her taste. And he seemed to be a bit of a know-it-all, the annoying type who, during his school days, had probably waved his hand enthusiastically, trying to blurt out the answer to every question the teacher asked. Saleema used to pick fights with kids who were too smart for their own good.

She fixed an irritated gaze on him. "The president is speaking at Independence Hall. Why would traffic be jammed up all over Philly?"

Seemingly oblivious to her dirty look, he continued, "He's speaking to forty governors and other lawmakers. Those top officials are in town with motorcades…criss-crossing the city, causing major chaos. For security purposes, many streets have been completely shut down."

Saleema groaned. It was ninety-eight degrees outside. She loved Obama and in her mind, the president could do no wrong. But she sure wished he'd chosen a cooler day to shut down the city. Feeling cranky, she gave the preppy the evil eye for being the harbinger of bad news. "Thanks for the newsflash."

He held up an iPhone. On the screen was a view of clogged

traffic. "Don't shoot the messenger," he said and aimed a smile at her. Then he removed his glasses and rubbed the side of his nose. A gesture from habit? Or was he showing off what he was really working with because without his glasses, he looked like a different man. He had wonderful features. Strong jawline, sparkly, alert eyes, luscious lips…really handsome.

Seeing him in a totally different light, and feeling a little thrill of excitement, Saleema's fingers smoothed back a stray loc. Murmuring a sound of approval, she smiled back, and unconsciously lowered her eyes.

Saleema hadn't been flirtatious in a very long time. In the past, the only time she'd bothered to entice was when money was on her mind. It was a minor jolt to her system to find herself attracted to a man for his looks instead of his financial status.

"My name is Khalil," he said, replacing the glasses and extending his hand.

With his glasses on, he went back to looking like a bookworm, which was a relief. She grasped his hand and shook it courteously.

"Saleema," she told him. She gave him only a fraction of a smile, but her lips were twitching to extend into a mega grin.

# CHAPTER 9

"**A**re you driving?" Khalil wanted to know as they stood outside the detention center, meandering instead of saying their good-byes.

"Yes, do you need a ride?" she blurted, surprising herself with her eager willingness to spend time with Khalil, even if it meant being ensnarled in a traffic jam that could last for hours.

He could be a serial killer, her inner voice warned. But she chose to ignore her good common sense.

"I'm parked right there." She pointed to her five-year-old Camry across the street, parked under a shade tree. There was a time when Saleema wouldn't have been caught dead inside anything less than a luxury car, but those days were long gone.

Though her wardrobe—remnants of her past—broadcasted a fashionista, Saleema hadn't shopped for clothing in over a year. She no longer required up-to-date trappings of glitz and glamour.

"No, I drove. My car is parked in a lot at the end of the block, but it doesn't make much sense to move it with traffic at a standstill. Are you hungry?"

"A little." A coy smile flickered on her lips. She felt lighthearted. Tipsy. With great effort, she kept her mouth from spreading into an ear-to-ear grin. It was odd to engage in repartee with a man without the thought of a dollar sign in mind.

Prior to opening Head Up, Saleema had been on a paper chase. She'd been preoccupied with emptying out men's wallets and bank

accounts ever since she'd taken a job at a massage parlor called Pandora's Box during her teenage years.

Later, motivated by her lust for money and having grown tired of the sex trade, she'd almost taken a disastrous trip down the aisle with a wealthy man who was a former trick.

But a horrible tragedy had changed her, made her reevaluate what was important in life. She'd opened up Head Up with the plan to dedicate her life to prevent young girls from straying down that wrong path she'd taken. She'd wanted her girls to know that their sense of self-worth was their most precious and valuable possession.

Khalil didn't have to coerce Saleema into agreeing to have lunch with him. On impulse, she accepted the impromptu lunch date with this intriguing stranger.

The pair trekked on foot for several blocks until they reached the place Khalil described as one of his favorite restaurants in the area.

When they entered a very small and cozy Caribbean restaurant, the hostess wore a smile that was aimed at Khalil only.

"Hello, stranger," the woman said in a tone that was a mixture of joy, accusation, and longing.

"Stranger?" Khalil protested. "I was here last Wednesday."

"How convenient that you came on my day off," she replied in a voice filled with complaint.

"My bad," Khalil said, slipping into jargon, his hands spread wide in apology.

Saleema felt an uncomfortable stab of envy. Were Khalil and the hostess sexually involved? *Don't even go there*, she sternly reprimanded herself and surveyed the restaurant while the petulant hostess sashayed away.

What was that all about? she wanted to ask, but didn't dare show

that kind of vulnerability. She gave her undivided attention to an expansive menu that was printed on numerous chalkboards posted on a wall.

"Anything look interesting?" Khalil's voice was silk and Saleema was officially smitten.

Perhaps it was the daggers being shot at her by the hostess on the other side of the counter, or maybe she just felt feminine and flirtatious, which prompted her next move. Whatever the case, Saleema felt compelled to let Khalil know that she found him appealing.

Gently, she placed her hand on top of his folded hands. "Nothing on the menu seems half as interesting as you. I'll have whatever you're having." *Bold!* And not bad for a woman who had indulged her earth mother inclinations for so long, she'd totally neglected her sensual side.

Unprepared for Saleema's personality that had suddenly shifted from demure to aggressive, Khalil removed his glasses and did that finger-rubbing thing against his nose. He was nervous and that fact was absolutely adorable.

A male server approached. "Something to drink?"

"Strawberry lemonade," Khalil said.

"Two?"

"Yes, two."

Two. It had a nice ring to it.

As Saleema sipped the sweet and tart beverage, Khalil gave the waiter their lunch order: stewed chicken in mango sauce, rice and beans, with a side order of cabbage and fried plantains.

"For two?" the waiter wanted to know.

Khalil and Saleema both nodded.

Wanting to know more about Khalil, she leaned forward. "How many kids at the detention center are on your caseload…and what

exactly do you do for them?" She was hoping he could give her some advice regarding Portia's situation.

"I'm not a social worker. I run an alternative school for young men. Boys who haven't been successful in the traditional classroom." He rose up a little, pulled his wallet from his pocket and withdrew a card and handed it to Saleema.

Changing Lives Academy was printed in large bold letters. She perused the address, but her eyes nearly bugged out when they landed at the bottom of the card: *Khalil Gardner, Ph.D. Founder and Director.*

Saleema's piqued interest now went beyond Khalil's good looks and gregarious nature. Like her, this man was trying to make a difference in the lives of troubled teens. He was a kindred spirit.

Then her heart sank. *Kindred spirits? Maybe not.* While Khalil possessed a Ph.D., Saleema was a high school dropout. They certainly were not evenly yoked. In an instant, she felt small and inconsequential.

Back when she'd been guardian of her goddaughter, Markeeta, she'd made sure that Markeeta was educated in the best private school in the area. While running Head Up, she always stressed the importance of education to her girls, yet she hadn't even put forth the effort to get a GED. What did that say about her? Saleema wondered.

"One of my students…a misguided but good kid nevertheless, is being detained at the detention center." He shook his head ruefully. "He'd been making so much progress…but like I said, keeping young men off the streets is often more difficult than keeping an addict clean."

"I'm still recovering from the fact that you're the founder of an alternative school. That's major. I'm so impressed," she said in quiet admiration.

"Well...don't be. Not yet. The school just opened last year with fifty-three ninth-graders. By the end of the term, we were down to forty-one. Hopefully, enrollment will increase and the boys will all be attending the academy's first graduation ceremony in three years." He gave a sigh. "Wish us luck."

"I'm sure you'll get there." Typically, Saleema exuded confidence. She was an intelligent woman who read everything she could get her hands on but, at the moment, she was mentally focused on her own educational shortcomings and could offer only a few measly words of encouragement.

"Trying to educate my boys is a constant battle. Keeping them interested in books and away from the allure of the streets is very challenging," he said with sardonic laughter.

"I bet," she said simply, intent on keeping her comments to a minimum and hoping he didn't ask where she'd gone to school.

Never had Saleema felt so out of her depth. She'd known plenty of educated men. Wealthy, educated men. But she'd always felt superior because she had what they wanted...sex! Sex that she doled out according to their ability to pay.

Unaware of Saleema's waging internal battle, Khalil went on. "I was at the detention center visiting one of my students—a fourteen-year-old who got caught with four Klonopin pills in his pocket."

Saleema frowned. "Seems like a minor offense."

"He has a long history of minor offenses."

"Yeah, one of my girls is at the detention center..."

Khalil looked shocked. "You have a teenaged daughter?"

"No. I run...well...I used to run a social club for troubled girls. I was at the detention center visiting a young lady who has anger management issues and a lengthy history of fighting. She swings on teachers, students, neighbors...anyone who has the misfortune

of being in her path when her anger erupts. I was her latest victim."

"What happened?"

"During a heated verbal exchange with another girl, she threw a bean bag chair and accidentally clunked me in the head. I hit the floor with the wind knocked out of me. One of the other girls called 9-1-1 before I could catch my breath."

"I'm glad you're okay. But I meant…what happened to your social club?"

Saleema looked glum. "Long story."

The arrival of their food drew their attention away from Saleema's troubles. Her eyes sparkled at the sight of the large heaping of exotic cuisine. "My goodness, this looks and smells scrumptious. And such a large portion. I don't think I'll be able to eat all this—"

"We'll request a take-out container. You'll be happy that it's in your fridge when you get hungry tonight."

"You're right," she readily agreed. "I'm not much of a cook. I survive on microwaveable packaged meals; having delicious left-over Caribbean food will be heavenly."

Like a perfect gentleman, Khalil carried Saleema's leftover food during the walk back to her car. Though they'd chatted about everything from voting for the first African-American president to Michael Jackson's untimely demise, the chasm between them widened as they both avoided the taboo topic of Saleema's social club.

"Thanks for lunch," Saleema said, sitting in her car with the takeout container placed on the floor of the passenger side.

Standing outside her car, Khalil held his iPhone, checking on traffic reports. "Which direction are you…?" He paused and gave

her a long look. "What's with the mystery woman routine? We've been talking nonstop for two hours and I hardly know anything about you."

"I apologize for being vague, but I didn't expect to have to go into detail about my life. I'm a very private person these days."

"These days?"

"Yeah," she answered without delving deeper.

"I'd like to get to know you better. Can I get that number?" he asked, chuckling as he once again slipped into street vernacular.

Saleema swallowed. She wanted to get to know him better, too. But not now. Not while her life was in shambles. She needed to do some serious self-improvement. She had to up her education game if she expected to roll with a scholar.

"I enjoyed myself, but I'm going to give it to you straight." She took a deep breath. "I'm a high school dropout. I never bothered to get a GED." She paused, letting that sink in for a couple of seconds. Khalil looked unfazed, so she plowed on. "You and I are worlds apart and I'm not comfortable with this feeling of inferiority."

"I'm sorry you feel that way."

"So am I. I thought I'd shed that old skin back in middle school, but it's back and the new layer is thicker than ever."

"Interesting," Khalil said with a hint of a smile.

"Seriously…the moment I saw the credentials next to your name, I felt…well…out of my league. I have to work on me before I can get into any type of relationship. Okay?"

"Are you serious?" There was a glimmer of amusement in his dark eyes.

"Yes."

"I wish I could change your mind, but if that's how you want it—"

"That's how I want it," she said firmly.

Khalil nodded.

Saleema exhaled. Though a weight had been lifted, she realized that her work was cut out for her. There were no coincidences. Khalil's presence today was a reminder that while she'd been so busy trying to help others, she'd totally forgotten the adage, "physician, heal thyself."

Khalil whipped off his glasses, and swiped the bridge of his nose as he seemed to be gathering his thoughts. God, he was so good-looking, Saleema had to avert her gaze. She couldn't bring her-self to stare at the gorgeous man that she was allowing to get away.

"Saleema, I want to be completely honest and aboveboard with you."

She ventured a quick glance at him. His glasses were in his hand. His face was so cute, it was completely unfair.

"I admit it…I'm physically attracted to you," he said in a serious tone. "But if you're going to sever our new-found association, I'll suppress my feelings." He laughed. "I promise…I'll stay in my lane."

Saleema couldn't find any humor in his promise. She wanted him in her lane—bumper-to-bumper—but not until she was feeling more secure.

"I'll settle for a platonic friendship. Will that work for you?"

Saleema pondered the suggestion and shrugged. "Sure, why not."

Khalil put his glasses back. "As I was saying…can I get that number?"

She recited her number, unable to hold back the smile that spread across her face.

CHAPTER 10

S aleema stubbornly pressed the doorbell for the third time, and then strained to hear it chime. Competing with the loud hum of a gigantic air conditioner jutting out of a first floor window and the volume of a TV that was turned up sky high was challenging.

Someone was home. Through a crack in the vertical blinds, she could see a pair of flip-flops on the floor and fat feet hovering above them. From Portia's description, the fat feet probably belonged to her aunt LaRue.

After pressing the button for several long moments, she realized that either the bell didn't work or Portia's aunt couldn't hear it over the sound of the blaring TV. Considering the urgent nature of her visit, she felt justified in pounding on the door.

"Who is it?" shouted an irritated female voice.

"Saleema Sparks...from Head Up!" she yelled loud enough for her voice to penetrate the closed door.

"From where?" LaRue barked out.

Formerly from Head Up, Saleema thought to herself with a sad sigh. "I'd like to speak to Glennis Burnett."

"She's not here." Agitation coated the woman's voice.

"Do you know where I can find her? It's about Portia!" Saleema hollered from the porch. The shouting match was absolutely ridiculous. Why didn't the lazy heifer get up and open the door?

The door magically swung open and Saleema was face-to-face

with a woman who wore a pissed-off expression on her face. LaRue was huge and seemed to fill the entire width of the doorway. It seemed as though the sound of pounding footsteps should have announced a woman her size, but somehow she had silently hefted herself off the couch and with stealth and agility she didn't appear to possess, she'd crept to the door. For a woman who weighed over four-hundred pounds, LaRue was very sprightly and light on her feet.

"What about Portia?" LaRue inquired, breathing hard from the effort it took to move stealthily across the living room.

"She's in the youth detention center—"

"Tell me something I don't know."

It was too hot and humid for Saleema to be putting up with this woman's funky attitude. It took all her self-control not to curse her out. She should have been ashamed of her lack of concern for her niece's welfare. "Portia needs her mom to show up for court."

"Portia needs her mom to do a lot of stuff, but that don't mean her mom is gonna do it." LaRue didn't have much of a neck, but the couple of thick rolls that were visible beneath her chin were rotating in a confrontational manner.

Fuming inside, Saleema wanted to give this no-neck heifer an ass-kicking or at least a long-winded, profanity-laced scolding. But resorting to violence was no longer an option for Saleema.

"LaRue," she said softly, pushing back the barrage of cuss words that were lined up on her tongue.

"That's my name…don't wear it out!"

Saleema gawked at her.

"Why you staring at me like I'm some damn mirror?" LaRue was wild-eyed; she looked ready to fight.

God! The woman was impossible and uncivilized. Saleema took the insult and asked politely, "Do you have any idea where I can find Portia's mom?"

LaRue erupted in laughter. The sound was loud, long, and derisive. "Do I look like I know where crack addicts hang out?"

Saleema's eyes traveled LaRue's large frame. *No, but I bet you could point me to the nearest Popeyes.* A dozen similar zingers came to mind, but releasing them would not be beneficial to the cause. She reminded herself that she was here to try to get help for Portia, and not to exchange barbs.

"Portia is in a desperate situation. If you have any idea where her mother might be, I'd appreciate it."

Saleema braced herself for another verbal attack, but the aunt looked at her with a hint of pity in her eyes.

"Searching for Glennis is a waste of time. My sister ain't thinking about Portia or nobody else. Look, I'm not trying to blow you off, but I was in the middle of watching one of my favorite shows."

"I apologize for disturbing you, ma'am," Saleema said courteously.

LaRue grimaced and looked on either side of her wide frame. "Ma'am? You and me look to be around the same age. I ain't but twenty-six years old, so don't be talking no 'ma'am' shit to me."

Saleema couldn't win for losing. She could see why Portia was such a hothead, growing up around this volatile woman.

"Lemme make you understand something," LaRue said, her big boobs heaving up and down, a meaty hand waving around, and neck rolls undulating. "I intend to enjoy this peace and quiet while it lasts. Glennis can stay gone for as long as she wants to. And Portia...Hmph!" She rolled her eyes in disgust. "Can't nobody tell her grown-ass nothing."

"I understand...I know Portia has a short fuse—"

"Short fuse or not...Portia needs to learn a lesson. As far as I'm concerned, she can stay in that detention center 'til she's old enough to take care of herself."

LaRue stepped back. She made a big show of stretching out an

arm and grabbing the edge of the door, opening it wider before giving it a powerful slam. Right in Saleema's face.

Saleema stared at the closed door in disbelief. The TV volume shot up to a deafening pitch. She had no idea what to do next. For a few humiliated moments, she stood on the porch, trying to get her bearings.

Having marinated in its juices for a day, the chicken in mango sauce was even more delicious than when she'd had it for lunch. The encounter with Portia's evil aunt, and then driving around rough neighborhoods asking drug boys if they'd seen Glennis, had worn Saleema out and given her a huge appetite.

Sitting up in bed with a tray in front of her, she licked sauce off her finger and then picked up the remote. The ten o'clock news on Fox filled the TV screen. The weather segment was on. Tomorrow would be even hotter than today. *Damn.*

The day-old Caribbean food was banging. A glass of that delicious strawberry lemonade would really top it off.

She thought about Khalil. Pictured him ordering their food. Reminisced about their walk to the restaurant. Saw him standing outside her car. Umph, umph, umph. When her mind began conjuring up X-rated images of her new friend, she forced thoughts of Khalil aside. *We're platonic,* she told her mind.

Determinedly, she forked a chunk of chicken dripping with savory sauce. Eyes back on the TV screen, but she wasn't watching. She couldn't stop thinking about Khalil. Good looks aside, it was his candidness, his self-assuredness, his commitment to troubled kids that touched her at a deep level.

Still, she had no choice but to accept the platonic friendship he'd

extended. She was a woman with a past. A practically broke and uneducated woman with a past. Even worse, she held a horrible, nightmarish secret.

Thinking about the ghastly night in the swamp caused dreamy thoughts of Khalil to instantly fly right out of her mind. Shaken, she also lost her appetite as well. She closed the lid of the container and put the wooden tray on the table next to the bed.

Scooting out of bed, ready to return the exotic food to the fridge, her cell rang. She checked the display. Unavailable. Frowning, she answered. "Hello?"

"Hey, Miss Saleema. This is Amirah. My cell got cut off so I'm using a friend's phone. Guess what?" Amirah asked excitedly.

"What?" Saleema humored Amirah.

"I was over Greta's house, kicking it with her sister, Brandi. You not gon' believe this, Miss Saleema. You know Greta didn't have any priors or anything and she was supposed to get out of the detention center today, but she can't because they're all on lockdown."

"Why?"

"You ready for this?"

"Amirah…what happened at the detention center?"

"According to Brandi, Greta was allowed to make a phone call and she said that Portia and some Puerto Rican girl broke out. They tied together sheets and got out through a window…like in the movies."

"Oh, my God!"

"I know, right? Portia is a hot mess. Always finding ways to stay in trouble. But she's messing with the wrong people now. This isn't like getting in trouble in school. Brandi said that if they catch up with her, she's gon' have to do some hard time. We might not see her 'til she's eighteen." Amirah sounded overjoyed about that prospect.

Saleema's entire body tensed. Her mouth hung open. *Why would Portia do something so stupid?*

And why did the city have them housed in that temporary location in the East Falls? The place had been plagued with escapes in the past few months.

"I have to go, Amirah." Saleema disconnected and immediately scrolled through the list of numbers and called the detention center.

Amazingly, she got a live person on the phone, but when she asked if Portia was okay...if she was present and accounted for, the woman told Saleema that she couldn't give out any information.

Saleema hung up.

She dressed quickly. Sliding her feet into a pair of sandals, she grabbed her handbag and the keys to her dependable Camry.

Twenty minutes later, she pulled up to the curb in front of Portia's house. This time, she didn't bother to ring the bell. With a balled fist, she banged on the door. She heard grumpy mumbling and then the door flung open.

"Can I get a break? Damn! First the cops, now you. What do you want now?"

"The cops were here?"

"Duh...don't you watch the news? My niece and some other female convict escaped; they on the loose."

Saleema felt her heart tug for Portia. The girl was not nearly as street savvy as she thought. She knew nothing about surviving out on the streets. That poor child was headed for unimaginable trouble.

"I know one thing, Portia better not even think about bringing her fugitive ass nowhere near this house. She ain't dragging me in this mess. I'm on disability. This kind of nonsense could mess up my check."

"Mess up your check? How?" Saleema wondered aloud. Portia

had warned her that her aunt suspected anything and everything other than her out-of-control eating could mysteriously interfere with the continuation of her disability income.

LaRue glared at Saleema. "Don't worry about it, cuz it ain't gon' happen. Portia knows that I'm not the one. There's not a chance in hell that I'd be stupid enough to mess up my check by harboring a fugitive. Now can you please get off my steps so I can lock up my house properly."

"Aren't you worried about your niece?"

"Hell no. She thinks she grown, so let her worry about her own damn self. The police said I should get a security system installed—just in case Portia tries to slip in to get some of her things. Hmph. I'd like to know who's gonna pay for some dang security system. I'm on a fixed income."

"Did you give the police any information on Portia's mom… you know…her whereabouts?"

"I don't know her whereabouts." Agitated, LaRue rolled her eyes. "You sure ask a lot of questions. Who you s'pose to be, the FBI or somebody?"

"I'm concerned about Portia. I told you earlier that she used to be a member of my social club, Head Up. She has so much potential—"

"Uh-huh, she has the potential…to be a pain in the butt," LaRue interjected.

"Aren't you concerned about Portia?"

"No! I'm concerned about changing these locks." She squinted at the top lock on the door. "I'm washing my hands of both Portia and her mother. My grandmother left this house to both me and Glennis, but I'm the one who pays the taxes. With a drug addict coming and going and stealing anything that isn't nailed down, and now with her wild child running from the law, I think I'm

within my legal rights to change these here locks. Enough is enough."

"I understand your frustration. But Portia…" Saleema held out her hands, a plea for Portia. "She's only a child. It's so dangerous for a young girl to be without adult supervision and a secure roof over her head."

LaRue smiled coldly. "Maybe you'll get lucky, and little Miss Potential will turn up on your doorstep. Have a good night," she said and closed the door.

The discussion was over. The sound of the lock clicking into place was Saleema's cue to be on her way.

Defeated, she returned to her car.

 CHAPTER 11

Driving his recently purchased Cadillac, Bullet pulled into a side street behind the Rite Aid Pharmacy…far from the entrance and out of range of the security camera. It was a ten-year-old car, needing a new repair every other week, but Bullet kept it shiny and looking good.

He sweet-talked and caressed his Caddy all the time, treating the car much better than he treated Gianna.

It was the second day of torrential rain. Gianna didn't have an umbrella or any type of rainwear.

Bullet began rolling a blunt; he cut an evil eye at Gianna who remained in her seat. "Whatchu waiting for? Go get me some Sudafed. You know this weather's got my sinuses bothering me." He rubbed his nose and shot her an angry glare.

"I need some money," she said in a meek, apologetic tone.

"Damn! You a pain in the ass. You know that?"

Gianna nodded quickly, knowing that if she didn't acknowledge his statement, she'd be backhanded or worse.

Bullet set the blunt and the weed on the console. Irritated that the blunt rolling procedure had been interrupted, he slung a twenty-dollar bill at Gianna.

She cracked the door open and tried to estimate how fast she had to run before she'd get drenched. She wished Bullet had parked closer to the entrance, but he felt it was his duty to make her life hard.

"Hurry up, ho!"

Motivated by his harsh tone, she darted out into the pouring rain. Her clothes were drenched by the time she entered the pharmacy.

The security guard standing at his post near the door took one look at her and said, "They got umbrellas on sale today."

"Thanks," Gianna muttered and kept moving. Bullet would give her a terrible beat down if she used any of his money to buy an umbrella. He'd also smack her around if she spent too much time inside the pharmacy, so she picked up her pace and grabbed a box of Sudafed.

She perused the cashiers and selected the one who had the shortest line. In front of her was a young woman holding a baby. A cute little girl. Gianna smiled at the baby. The baby gurgled loud and happily, causing the mother to turn around.

"She's cute," Gianna said.

"Thanks." The mother smiled at Gianna and then beamed at her baby. The mother, who looked to be in her late teens, was wearing low-cut jeans and a short top that showed a butterfly tattoo below her navel. She was light-skinned with reddish-colored hair and light brown eyes. Her brown-skinned baby didn't favor her at all.

"How old is she?" Gianna asked, sticking out a finger and allowing the baby to curl her hand around it.

"Five months," the mother replied.

Gianna didn't normally initiate conversations. She was conditioned not to talk to anyone other than Bullet and the tricks he lined up for her. But the baby was so cute.

It was refreshing to interact with an innocent baby. But was it worth the risk of Bullet plowing through the front to door to see what was taking so long?

Seized with terror, she extracted her finger from the gurgling baby's hand and focused her gaze on her water-sodden sneakers.

"Do you sell gas cans?" the teenage mother asked when she reached the front of the line.

"No," the cashier replied, "but you can get one from the Sunoco station at Twenty-second and Fairmount."

"I don't know this area. How far is that?" There was a distinct tremble in the young mother's voice.

"Just a couple blocks south." Through with giving out directions, the cashier said, "Next," and beckoned Gianna to move forward.

While Gianna paid for Bullet's medication, she could see from her peripheral vision that the mother was standing near the exit, cooing to her baby. The mother had an umbrella but appeared hesitant to run out into the rain.

Holding a crinkly bag, Gianna headed for the door. She gave the teenager a tight smile and pushed open the door.

"Excuse me. Are you driving? I don't think I have enough gas to make it to the Sunoco station."

"No, I don't drive. I'm…with…uh, my boyfriend."

"Do you think he'd mind giving us a ride?" Her eyes pleaded with Gianna. "My name is Brielle. I drove all the way from Wilkes-Barre, Pennsylvania and I wasn't paying attention to the gas gauge."

Bullet would not like it if Gianna brought this woman and her baby to his car. Her mouth was fixed to say, *Sorry, I can't help you.* But when she looked at the baby, her heart melted.

"Okay, I'll ask him to give you a ride." Gianna swallowed a lump of fear. Her fate was sealed. Bullet was going to punch her dead in the mouth for this. She'd be tricking tonight with busted lips.

When they reached the car, Bullet was kicked back, seat reclined, puffing on a blunt. Gianna opened the passenger door and poked her head in. "She ran out of gas," she explained, inclining her head

toward Brielle and her baby. "Can you give her a ride to that station on Twenty-second Street?"

Jolted from his blissful high, Bullet scowled at Gianna. His look promised punishment. "Yeah, aiight," he mumbled, adjusting his seat and turning the ignition before Brielle and the baby were situated in the back seat.

Wheeling out of the lot, Bullet instantly started chatting with Brielle. "What's a nice-looking chick like you doing stranded in the rain? Where's your man?"

Brielle laughed. "That's the question I've been asking myself. And that's why I drove to Philly. He hasn't called me in a week. That bum hasn't even called to check on our daughter."

"Is that right?" Bullet said in his slimy way. "Shame."

"If I were a no-good mother, I'd drop Samantha off at his house and keep rolling. I swear, I'd love to give him a taste of what's it's like to be a single parent."

"You doing the right thing, by forcing him to accept his responsibility."

"You think so?" Brielle's tone was uncertain.

"Yeah, let that nucca take care of a screaming baby for a minute. That'll make him get his act together." Bullet laughed heartily.

"That's exactly what I intended to do, but I don't know…I'm too attached to my daughter. It would kill me to be separated from her…for even a day."

"Sometimes you gotta go hard to get whatchu want," Bullet counseled.

Gianna was perplexed. Why was Bullet acting so friendly? Doing good deeds and engaging in light chatter wasn't his style. Maybe he had a soft spot for the baby.

Bells chimed when they pulled into the service station lot.

"I'll be right back," Brielle said cheerily. "Can you hold Samantha for me? I don't want her to catch a cold out in this weather."

Gianna's eyes darted to Bullet's, silently asking for permission. He gave a curt nod and she twisted around and took the baby in her arms.

Giving her daughter a proud smile, Brielle got out and trotted inside the convenience store.

"Hey, Samantha," Gianna said, smiling. The baby smelled good.

"Listen up," Bullet said gruffly. "Fuck all that coo-coo, baby talk bullshit. We gotta put some plans together. Quick."

Through the picture glass window, Gianna could see Brielle standing in line, holding a red gas container. "What kind of plans?"

Bullet glowered at Gianna. "You a slow learner or something? I'm 'bout to snatch that bitch. You think I wanna be wheeling this 2001? A nigga deserve a come-up. That light-skinned honey can make me a mint."

Gianna pulled the baby closer, nuzzled her hair, inhaling her baby fresh scent. "What about the baby?"

"Lemme worry about that crumb snatcher. All you need to do is play your part. Put on your game face, bitch. I'm 'bout to catch me another ho."

Brielle came out of the store and walked toward the gas pump. She waved at her daughter, who was in Gianna's arms.

Wearing her game face, Gianna smiled back. She took the baby's hand and let her wave back.

Gianna wanted to scream…RUN! But she knew Brielle wouldn't run without her daughter. And Bullet would beat her to a pulp if he realized that she was thinking about giving Brielle any kind of warning.

Maybe she could make an excuse to get the baby out of the car… hand her to her mother and then whisper that she needed to run for her life.

As if reading her mind, Bullet cautioned, "Don't fuck this up. Just follow my lead. Play your part."

"Okay." Gianna held the baby tight.

Brielle slid into the back seat. The baby turned and reached for her.

"Mommy has gas on her hands, Samantha. Your wipes are in the car. I'll pick you up after I clean my hands."

Whimpering, the baby kept reaching. Gianna turned in her seat so Brielle and her baby could communicate. Brielle made funny faces at her daughter. Samantha's crying was replaced with laughter.

Gianna's eyes latched on to Brielle's as she tried to silently connect with her. She tried to communicate with her eyes that she was in danger. Her eyes screamed for Brielle to take her innocent baby and run for her life. But Brielle's trusting smile forced Gianna to give up, and shift her gaze away.

"Whatchu driving?" Bullet asked as he approached the Rite Aid where Brielle's car was parked.

"That's my car over there." She pointed to a dark-colored Honda.

He parked on the same sidestreet as before. "Gimme your keys. I'll get the diaper bag while I fill your tank."

"You're such a gentleman. Thanks."

Gianna felt guilty. And sad.

Bullet took the car key ring that dangled a plastic framed picture of the baby. "Hand me my cap," he told Gianna. She took a cap out of the glove box. Bullet pulled the brim down low to conceal his face from the security camera. Then, braving the rain, he dashed to the parking lot, carrying the red gas can and dangling Brielle's keys.

A few minutes later, he returned to the Cadillac. He got back in the driver's seat and tossed Gianna the diaper bag, and then shifted his car into gear.

"That was fast. Uh, can I get my keys back?" There was a nervous shiver in Brielle's voice.

It had finally dawned on Brielle that something was amiss.

Shame and fear bowed Gianna's head.

"Nah, I'ma hold on to 'em." Looking over his shoulder, Bullet pressed down on the gas pedal, moving down the small street in fast reverse.

"Why are you keeping my car keys?" Brielle shouted. "What's going on? I thought you were going to put gas in my tank."

"I am. Eventually, but not right now."

"Why not?" she shouted. She poked Gianna in the shoulder. "What's wrong with your boyfriend?"

Gianna didn't open her mouth. She tightened her grip around the baby.

Brielle rose up and tried to yank her child from Gianna's arms.

Gianna shook Brielle's hands away. "Get off me, bitch," Gianna snarled, playing her part.

"Girl, are you crazy?" Hysteria rose in her voice. "You better give me my baby!"

Driving fast down another small street, Bullet suddenly hit the brakes. The car screeched and lurched to a stop. Bullet lifted his T-shirt, revealing the butt of his newly purchased gun. "Settle yourself down, sexy." He pulled the gun out of his waistband and aimed it toward Gianna and the baby.

Gianna flinched. Bullet had just bought the gun a few days ago and already he'd pointed it at her more times than she could count. Having a gun aimed in your face was scarier than being poked with his knife.

"All this tussling and struggling might make me lose control of the car. Who knows, I might skid out of control or hit a bump or something. All I'm tryna say is…I don't want to make a mistake and put a hole in lil' Samantha's head. You don't wanna make me do that, do you?

"No," Brielle whispered.

"Aiight, then. Sit back and relax."

Brielle went silent. Probably from shock.

Bullet pressed the gas pedal. He put the gun under his seat. "Damn, I hate that I had to fuck around in the rain. Now my sinuses are acting up." He rubbed his nose, made a loud sniffling sound. "All this trouble over a piece of ass."

From the back seat, Brielle began to cry softly. It was a pitiful sound.

Grimacing, Bullet's hands gripped the steering wheel. He spoke through clenched teeth. "Didn't I say my sinuses are acting up?"

"Yes, I bought the Sudafed," Gianna answered promptly.

"Well? Give it to me, bitch."

Gianna knew Bullet was apt to pop her upside her head if she didn't react quickly enough. With his eyes concentrating on the road, he might accidentally punch the baby while swinging at her and that would be tragic.

With her arms protectively encircling little Samantha, Gianna ripped open the package of Sudafed, and quickly shook out two tablets and handed them to Bullet.

CHAPTER 12

Four weeks had passed since the night Gianna had been abducted. During the first two, she'd broken free a couple times—slipping out of the abandoned house, slithering out of a motel window, persuading a trick to allow her to stow away in the back seat of his car. But every attempt to escape failed. Bullet always caught up with her, thwarting her getaway, and then dragging her back to some remote, shabby quarter.

But despite the harsh punishments that Bullet dispensed, Gianna kept trying to break free.

Then he bought a gun.

With his finger on the trigger, Bullet shoved the barrel inside her mouth, demanding that she suck it, imploring her to stick her tongue inside the muzzle. And threatening to blow her head off the next time she tried to flee.

He also made her write down both of her parents' separate addresses as well as the location of their summer home. He said that he knew people who would kill for him. Former inmates whom he'd served time with. The kind of people who would knock off her parents—put them six feet under without batting an eye. A swift death would be too good for Gianna's parents. Bullet promised they'd suffer slow, torturous deaths if Gianna ran away again.

So Gianna stopped running.

She also forced herself to stop thinking about her parents. There was no hope of ever being rescued… of ever being reunited with her family.

She belonged to Bullet, and was growing accustomed to trading sex for pay.

The hardest part of her day was keeping Bullet satisfied. Trying to not give him a reason to hit her or do the other cruel things he did for fun.

But her compliance to his wishes didn't matter. Bullet still tormented her, instilling fear by tying her to trees in secluded areas and shooting rounds over her head, using her for target practice. Scaring her out of her wits—keeping her in line.

Now Gianna leaned against the metal door, her rain-slicked hair plastered to her face.

Bullet held a large black umbrella over his head. His full attention was on Brielle, but Gianna wasn't even tempted to run. With the diaper bag slung over her shoulder, she waited to be let inside.

She held Samantha close, providing warmth and protection from the rain. Gianna loved babies and used to pretend that she was the mommy of the toddlers she used to babysit during the summer vacations in Ocean City.

Brielle stood stubbornly near the car, unfazed by the steady drizzle of rain. "I don't know what this is about, but that girl shouldn't be holding my daughter."

Bullet's eyes sparked with anger. "Fuck your daughter."

"Oh, God," Brielle said, her voice a long screech of disbelief. "Please. Don't do this. Give me my baby." She stretched out her arms, wiggling her fingers anxiously.

The baby was sleeping peacefully, but Gianna rocked her anyway. Gently…comfortingly, hoping to ease some of Brielle's anxiety. It was the least she could do.

Bullet sneered. "Bitch, please. Get yo' ass back in the damn car. Lollipop gon' take care of the baby while me and you take care of some business."

"I'm not going anywhere with you!" Brielle started striding quickly toward her child. Bullet caught her by the scruff of her collar. Using the butt of the gun, he bashed her on the side of her face.

Brielle dropped like a rag doll, her body splayed on the wet concrete.

Gianna's heart sped. "Is she dead?"

Bullet flashed her a look of annoyance. "Can a dead bitch sell ass for me?"

"No." Gianna nibbled on her fingernail, eyes shifting downward.

"Aiight, then. Stop asking dumb-ass questions." Shaking his head at the ridiculousness of Gianna's inquiry, Bullet took out a key ring and opened the door.

Without instruction, Gianna went inside. Being held captive inside different storage spaces in the Philadelphia area had become routine.

Pulling Brielle by her wrists, Bullet dragged her across concrete. Gianna gawked at Brielle's bloody face, and then quickly looked away with a shudder.

Carefully, she placed the baby's blanket on top of the lumpy, stained mattress that was on the floor—the mattress where she had been turning tricks for the past few days.

She scrounged inside the baby's diaper bag until she found a bottle of milk. She wanted the milk close at hand. Who knew what Bullet would do if Samantha awakened, screaming from hunger?

Bullet tossed Brielle onto the mattress. He frowned at her sprawled body and then grunted in disgust when he observed the gash in her face.

"Damn! How dis bitch gon' make me some money with her mug all dented up? Damn!"

Gianna dug a hand into the diaper bag and retrieved a wipe.
"Did I tell you to make a move?" Bullet snarled.

Her hand was poised to clean the blood from Brielle's face, but
Bullet's growl stilled her.

"She's bleeding."

"So!"

"I was going to clean the wound."

He raised his eyebrows. "Oh, you a doctor all of a sudden?"

"No."

"A paramedic?"

"No, I'm not a paramedic," she responded in a shaky whisper.

"I know you ain't no paramedic. You a ho. The only thing you
need to be concerned with is getting my money."

"You're right." She forced a "what was I thinking" smile, convincing Bullet that she was grateful for the reality check.

With a look of self-satisfaction, Bullet sauntered over to a plastic
lawn chair. The scruffy mattress and the green plastic chair were
the only items in the storage space. Gianna's wardrobe, a scant
collection of hooker wear, was kept in the trunk of Bullet's car.

He tinkered with his cell phone, checking messages, frowning,
and then scrolling through his address list.

After a series of beeps, he said, "Yo, Flashy. I need a favor, man."

A twinge of apprehension worked its way down Gianna's spine.
Flashy was one of Bullet's prison buddies. She'd never met him,
but she knew he usually assisted whenever Bullet called him. And
Bullet didn't call for ordinary favors.

"Straight up. Don't I always take care of you?" Bullet growled
into his cell phone.

Gianna held her breath. Maybe Flashy would show some
humanity, stand up to Bullet, and refuse to assist in his corrupt
and immoral deeds.

"Money ain't no thing," Bullet roared, indignant. "Look, I gotta dump a car. And I got another serious issue. I'll get at you in a minute so we can put our heads together."

Her hopes dashed, Gianna picked up Samantha. She clutched the sweet-smelling baby to her chest. Her lips brushed the top of the baby's head, affectionately. She had no idea what favor Bullet needed from his jail friend, but she had a hunch he had a devious plan that involved the baby. She didn't wish any further harm to Brielle, but she felt much more protective toward the innocent baby.

"Hand me the baby," Bullet said, his tone a low drone, as though he were asking Gianna to pass the salt.

"Um…" Cradling little Samantha, her hands shaking, Gianna struggled to control her anxiety. She shot a worried glance at the baby's unconscious mother.

"What you lookin' at her for? That bitch is knocked out. But even if she was wide awake, I don't need to ask her permission." Bullet made a disgusted, hissing sound at her. "I'ma muthafuckin' pimp."

Afraid for the baby's safety, her lips started to tremble. "I can take care of Samantha until Brielle is feeling better." She smiled down at the baby. "I…I took Child Life classes in school."

"I don't give a fuck!"

"I babysat for neighbors. For extra money." Her voice took on a desperate tone. "I'm really good with babies." She nodded her head, strengthening her case.

"Is you crazy? Didn't I tell you to gimme dat goddamn baby!" With savage force, Bullet ripped Samantha from Gianna's arms. He tucked the wriggling baby under an armpit, like he was holding a football.

Gianna gaped at Bullet, shocked by his careless handling of the young child.

"Whatchu staring at?" The fury in his eyes intimidated her into shifting her gaze downward.

"Nothing," she mumbled, suppressing a natural desire to protect a defenseless infant.

Samantha kicked out her little legs in protest and made tiny yelping sounds. Then she took a deep breath that signaled the coming of a full-blown wail. Her scream echoed.

"Shut the fuck up!" Bullet snapped at the baby.

Samantha screamed louder. Struggling, her small chubby fingers tore at Bullet's shirt, fighting the brute of a man whom Gianna didn't have the guts to lift a finger to.

Brielle moaned in response to her baby's wail. Her eyelids fluttered. Fighting for consciousness, her moans grew stronger. Her bleary eyes cracked open into slits. Blinking in confusion, she tried to push herself up on an elbow. With a low groan, she flopped down.

Bullet sneered at the groggy, teenage mother. He tossed Gianna a knife.

Reflexively, she caught it.

"Shank her if she tries to get out of hand," Bullet ordered, pointing at Brielle.

"Okay," she said agreeably, though she wanted to shed tears. Her life had taken another bad turn. Now her captor wanted her to resort to violence, expecting her to wield the very weapon he had used to torment her with before he'd purchased the deadly gun.

Gianna held the knife loosely.

"Don't act stupid. If she gets feisty, you know what to do. Poke a hole in that bitch."

"I will," she said with a tremor.

"Convince me."

Gianna could feel tears welling, but repressed the urge to cry.

Nervously, she bit her bottom lip. "I don't know what you want me to say."

"I'll put it to you like this…"

The baby shrieked; her arms flailed as she tried to get to her mother. Bullet gave the child a forceful shake, shocking her into a brief silence.

"When I get back; she better be ready to rock and roll. If I gotta waste time whooping that ass in order for her to make me some money, ain't gon' be no more target practice for you." He shook his head grimly "Nah, no more target practice. It's gon' get real. I'ma put some hot lead in your shoulder…or maybe your arm. Or leg."

Gianna legs were ready to buckle as she imagined getting shot in one of them.

"I know a coupla people who real good at digging out bullets and patching the hole up with cotton balls and shit."

She clenched her teeth together to keep them from chattering.

"Tell that ho that I expect her to make me ten stacks. That's how much I expect it's gon' cost me to feed her and pay somebody to take care of this youngin'. After she's paid up in full, she can have her brat back."

The baby cried and fought mightily as Bullet strode toward the door.

With renewed strength, Brielle shot upright. She looked around, uncomprehending as she scanned the barren storage unit. Her eyes landed on the pink diaper bag.

"My baby!" she gasped.

Too late.

CHAPTER 13

Bullet was already outside, clanging the lock into place. The baby's cries became distant. Muted.

Brielle shot across the concrete floor, racing toward the door. Wildly, she kicked the sturdy door, making anguished sounds as she banged her body against it to no avail.

She whirled around. "You bitch! You let him take my baby!" Hands clawing the air, she dashed toward Gianna.

Survival instinct kicked in. Gianna steadied her hand and held up the knife. She had no choice. She had to subdue Brielle or feel the heat of Bullet's scorn.

"You better back the fuck up," Gianna spat, the venom in her voice halting Brielle.

Brielle's sandals skidded on the concrete as she came to an abrupt halt. She looked stricken, but Gianna didn't feel an ounce of pity for the young mother. Brielle was her enemy.

Seeming to sense that Gianna would not hesitate to use the knife, Brielle looked around helplessly, and then spoke in a controlled whisper. "Where did he take Samantha?"

"That ain't none of your business." Gianna stepped forward, her stance confrontational, her tone belligerent. Mimicking Bullet, she was deliberately irrational; using bad grammar, wielding a weapon…absurdly angry. Bullet would be proud.

Confused, Brielle blinked rapidly. "My baby is my business."

"Not anymore. That baby belongs to Bullet now."

"No! Samantha is my child!" Breathing in rapid pants, she patted her chest several times.

"If you want her back, you gotta work for Bullet." Gianna now spoke in a droning tone. She was speaking on Bullet's behalf. Her own personal emotions, thoughts, and beliefs were removed from the conversation.

"Okay." Lines of desperation creased Brielle's forehead. She wiped blood from her face, but didn't seem concerned about her condition. "He forgot Samantha's diaper bag. She's probably wet and hungry."

"Fuck dat." Gianna pointed the knife near the open wound on her face.

Brielle recoiled. "Oh, God!"

"That lil' cut on your face ain't about nothing. Bullet only gave you a love tap with his gun. But if you fuck with me, I'm gon' poke you up and let you bleed like a stuck pig." She was channeling Bullet. Her new persona was starting to feel natural.

Brielle was afraid of her and Gianna was afraid of getting shot.

Tears filled Brielle's eyes. "I just want my baby back. Her clothes, food, and extra diapers are in the trunk of my car."

"He'll pop the trunk when he moves your car."

"He's moving my car?"

"Uh-huh. Bullet said you can't get your car or your baby back 'til after you pay your tab."

"My tab!"

Gianna nodded. "Bullet's a pimp. He caught you," Gianna said in a matter-of-fact tone. "He gon' keep you until you pay the cost of feeding you and taking care of your baby."

"How much is that?"

"Ten stacks."

"He wants me to pay him ten thousand dollars?"

"That's what he said. So you better cooperate. If you make Bullet mad, he'll kick your ass and jack the price up."

"He expects me to be a prostitute?" Brielle asked, her expression both shocked and pained.

"Yup," Gianna replied, ignoring the horrified look in Brielle's eyes.

"I can't—"

"It won't take long to get the money," Gianna said encouragingly. Feeling empathy, and allowing a fragment of her personality to come through.

"Do you know where he took my baby?"

"No, and that's enough talking. When Bullet comes back, you gotta prove that you can suck some dick. Don't make him pull out his gun. Just act like you're happy to see him and show him how well you can work your head game."

Brielle's mouth was open, speechless.

Gianna took the pack of wipes out of the diaper bag. "You look gross. Get yourself cleaned up before Bullet comes back."

When Bullet reentered the unit, he was sniffling from his allergies, wiping his nose with the back of his hand and looking fiercely angry, like he was eager to hurt somebody.

"Is Samantha okay?" Brielle said in a pitifully squeaky voice.

"What the fuck is up with this bitch?" Bullet exploded.

Gianna elbowed Brielle. "Do what I said!"

"Hi. You want me to make you feel good?" Brielle said, without emotion, and walked woodenly over to Bullet. She knelt in front of him and tugged on the waistband of his shorts.

"Stand up." Bullet grabbed a handful of Brielle's hair.

She rose.

"Turn around. I ain't really get a chance to see whatchu workin' with."

She turned slowly, allowing Bullet to critique her.

"Damn, you got a flat ass. You built like a white girl. I can't have a bitch representing me with a flat ass."

He smacked her rear end. "This here is presenting a problem. And I'ma have to fix it."

Blinking in confusion, Brielle darted a glance at Gianna.

Gianna gave a tiny shrug. She had no idea what Bullet was talking about.

Bullet pulled down his shorts and sank into the green chair. He stroked his dick.

"Get over here, Lollipop, and get me ready. It's a good thing I don't mind a lil' peanut butter, cuz I'ma be spending a lot of time plumping up that bitch's pancake ass."

Gianna moistened her lips and squatted between Bullet's legs.

Twenty minutes later, Brielle was on her knees, her torso and face pressed against the lumpy mattress. Behind her, Bullet tried to insert himself inside her tight anus.

"Stop clenching up on me, bitch. I told you to relax. Lemme do this." He maneuvered her body, pulling her buttocks closer.

"I can't. It hurts. Stop. Please stop." Brielle stiffened her body, moaning as Bullet struggled to get inside.

"You want that lil' brat back, don't you?"

"Yes," she said in a painful moan.

"Then act like it. I'm starting to think you don't give a shit about your youngin'."

"That's not true. I love my daughter."

"Show me. If you wanna get that money up quick, you gon' have to get used to dealing with this back door action."

Gianna sat in the green chair, relieved that she wasn't involved in the disaster on the other side of the room. Her stomach growled, a reminder that she hadn't eaten since yesterday. She was starving. Her thoughts turned to McDonald's fries. Bullet had promised to take her to McDonald's when he finished with Brielle.

Bullet picked up a small container of lubricant and squeezed a generous amount onto four fingers. He swiped the gooey substance inside the crease of Brielle's buttocks. Angrily, he resumed thrusting.

Moaning, Brielle clutched the stained mattress.

Bullet stopped moving. Frustrated, he released his grip on Brielle's hips. He smacked her backside harder than before.

He yanked his sweaty face in Gianna's direction. "How long I been trying to get up in this ass?"

"A long time," Gianna replied flatly, shaking her head. Gianna sighed inwardly. Nothing was being accomplished, and she found herself resenting Brielle.

"This ain't working," Bullet complained as he mopped sweat from his face.

"I tried," Brielle sobbed.

"How you trying with your flat-ass cheeks all clenched up?"

He flopped down on the bed, lay flat on his back, panting. "Lollipop," he bellowed.

"Whatchu want me to do, Daddy?" Gianna asked eagerly.

He shot a look of contempt at Brielle. "She ain't loosening up for me, so bring me my shank. After I catch my breath, I'ma have to cut my way up in that ass."

Brielle scrambled to an upright position. Her eyes were wild with disbelief as she watched Gianna stride over with the knife in her hand.

Brielle gasped. "No! Please don't cut me! I'll loosen up!"

Gianna handed the knife to Bullet. He placed it on the mattress.

"Aiight then, we gon' try this shit again. You ready?"

Brielle flinched. "Yes," she said in a choked whisper.

He mounted the girl. "You gon' loosen up for me?"

"Yes," she promised and then closed her eyes tight and gritted her teeth.

But instead of penetrating with his dick, he rammed the handle of the knife inside Brielle.

Her scream was long and anguished.

"Bet I'll get up in there now!" Bullet boasted.

Gianna covered her mouth in shock when Bullet withdrew the bloody end of the knife.

The night was hot. The asphalt was dry, without even a drop of moisture left from the downpour earlier that day.

Bullet was at the wheel. In the passenger seat, Gianna, changed from her wet clothing, was dressed for work in a short pleated skirt and a white blouse knotted in the front.

Incapacitated, Brielle was left locked inside the storage unit.

Using her daughter's life as leverage, Bullet told her to rest up and not to make a sound.

They cruised through the drive-through. Bullet placed the order.

He reached a hand out of the window and accepted the large-size bag filled with twenty-two dollars' worth of burgers and fries. "You my bottom bitch now," Bullet informed Gianna.

"Wow!"

"That's all you got to say?" He took a large container of fries from the bag and handed it to Gianna.

"Thank you, Daddy." Calling Bullet "Daddy" used to conjure up images of her father and it was hard to say, but the word rolled off her tongue with ease now.

"I like the way you handled that bitch for me. You came a long way. I'm putting my trust in you," he said, his eyes filled with sincerity.

"I got your back." She unwrapped a cheeseburger and sank her teeth into it.

"Yeah, baby. Me and you gon' conquer the world. And you gon' help me snatch up some more young hoes. I can see it now…me pimpin' a whole stable fulla hoes. All of 'em young and dumb with lil' pussies, sweet as candy."

She swallowed. "You said you were gonna let Brielle go after she pays you the money she owes."

As if the very thought was hilarious, Bullet guffawed, coughing and choking on French fries. "Hell, no. Her narrow ass gon' make me a fortune. That shit I kicked back in that storage unit wasn't nothing but game. That hooker ain't goin' nowhere."

"What about her baby?"

"Fuck that baby." Bullet glared at Gianna. "You turning on me?"

"No, I just thought—"

"Let me do the thinking, bitch." He pointed a finger at Gianna. "You know what tomorrow is?"

"Yes." She bit into a cheeseburger, but it suddenly lost its flavor.

"Tell me." There was a cruel glint in his eyes.

"It's target practice."

Bullet smiled. "That's right. Who should I practice on—you or Brielle?"

"Brielle," Gianna blurted without hesitation. "That ho ain't nothing but trouble," Gianna reminded him, speaking the street language he preferred.

"Yeah. I gotta practice on Brielle. Let her know what's really good. Feel me?"

"Yeah." Gianna smiled broadly. The next bite of the cheeseburger tasted much better.

"I don't like the name, Brielle. I gotta call her something else."

"Passion?" Gianna suggested.

"Nah. Y'all young girls are like candy. She needs a name that's sweet, and that suits the kind of work she specializes in."

"Oh, yeah," Gianna said absently as she began gobbling up fries.

"Help me come up with a name. I might take her to Ridley Park tonight. Use her new talent for some extra dough. Them crackers you been sucking off would probably love to switch it up and dip they dicks into some peanut butter."

Now deep in thought, Gianna was struggling to help Bullet come up with a name for Brielle. The fries tasted so heavenly, her mind went blank.

"Peanut Butter might work," Bullet mused. "But that name ain't sexy enough."

"How about Reese's Cup?" Gianna suggested.

"Nah, that don't have a good ring to it, either." He shook his head.

"You're right." Hungrily, she resumed munching on the fries.

"You killin' them fries," he said, laughing at the way Gianna was shoveling them in.

Gianna laughed as she was expected to do. "I know. Dey so good," she said in dialect.

Hoping to stay on Bullet's good side, she refrained from using the standard English that tended to rile him. He claimed her proper way of talking drew undesired attention. People knew the missing girl from New Jersey went to private schools and talked like a white girl.

Bullet smacked the dashboard. "I got it! I got a good name for that ho."

"What?"

"Tootsie Roll! That's a good name for a hooker who specializes in Greek."

"That's perfect," Gianna agreed, careful to not add anything that might piss Bullet off. Being in his company when he was relaxed and in a cheerful mood made her existence easier to bear.

"After she stops worrying about her youngin', Tootsie Roll gon' thank me for bringing her into the life. She gon' be happy she got a good man like me to look out for her and whatnot."

"You right. She gon' be so happy once she gets the hang of it."

Poor Brielle. Gianna gave a regretful sigh. Like her, Brielle was trapped in "the life" forever. She wondered who was taking care of Samantha. She hoped the person loved babies as much as she did.

 CHAPTER 14

Where would a pair of fifteen-year-old runaways hide out? The location of the detention center was not familiar territory to either girl, so it wasn't likely that they'd stick around that area for very long.

They had probably flagged down a ride minutes after they escaped. It was easy for teenage girls to hitch a ride. Men pulled over for young girls, and most often the offer of a ride was not an act of chivalry.

Saleema hated the thought of some perverted creep picking up Portia and her partner-in-crime and then taking them to God knows where.

Where would Portia go? Home? She'd want to slip in and get some of her things, but common sense would tell Portia that it was too risky to go anywhere near her home.

Fortieth Street? Possibly. The vicinity of the University of Pennsylvania campus was a shopping and entertainment hub. Teens flocked to the arcades, movie theaters, and the fast-food joints.

She made a quick left on Market Street and accelerated toward Penn's campus. Maybe she'd spot Portia if she cruised around that vicinity. Driving slowly, she circled the area twice, squinting at the swarm of young people, hoping to spot Portia. No luck.

South Street, with its touristy atmosphere, was another teen magnet; an area where Portia could easily blend in. Tall and chunky, with overly large breasts, Portia looked older than her age. She

could easily pass for eighteen or nineteen. No one would think it odd for her to be hanging out past curfew.

At Forty-sixth and Market, Saleema pulled into the parking lot of a supermarket and brought the car to a stop. With the engine idling, she tried to get her bearings and gather her thoughts.

She was trying to play detective but was clearly in over her head. Driving all over the city looking for Portia would be a huge waste of time. The most sensible thing to do would be to go home and wait. Maybe Portia would reach out.

But what kind of help could she offer? She could be the voice of reason and persuade Portia to turn herself in. Portia was safer in the detention center than wandering the streets.

Glancing at the clock on the dashboard, she realized Portia had been on the run for several hours—more than enough time to hitch a ride or even take a bus to Saleema's house.

Now convinced that Portia would turn up at her doorstep, Saleema tore out of the lot and sped home.

Her cell hummed from her purse that was set on the floor of the passenger side. Leaning awkwardly, she kept one hand on the steering wheel, while she lifted her bag from the floor with the other. She plopped the durable black leather on the passenger seat. Eyes on the road, she dug inside and pulled out the cell. A quick glance at the screen revealed a number she didn't recognize. *Portia?*

"Hello!" she said anxiously.

"Hi, how are you? This is Khalil," he said cheerfully.

Her heart did a little tumble.

"I hope I didn't catch you at a bad time."

"No. Well, actually—"

"Oh. Should I call you tomorrow?" Disappointment took his voice down an octave.

"No, I can talk. I *need* to talk. I'm a wreck."

"What's going on?"

She told him about Portia's escape and ended with, "I've been driving around the city, hoping to spot her. I haven't been successful. The police will be keeping an eye on her house, so I figured she might try to contact me. I'm on my way home."

"Where's home? I'll meet you there. Keep you company, if you'd like."

"I'd like that. Thanks." Despite her anxiety over Portia, she couldn't hold back a blushing smile as she gave him her address.

She parked at the curb. Her oversized, single home on the corner had no driveway in the front. She'd have to drive around the block to get to her garage, which didn't have an entrance that led inside her house. Real estate in the city always lacked in something. In her case, she had a lot of house but not much else. No land; no convenient parking.

A planned marriage of convenience had almost led her to live in the Cayman Islands, but a deadly encounter in a North Carolina swamp had yielded an unexpected windfall. Financial freedom had allowed her to turn her life around. She had cancelled the wedding. Helping young women in distress had replaced a former lifestyle of using sex for profit.

She got out of her Camry, aimed the remote, and hurried toward her house.

"Saleema."

Her name echoed, intruding the silence of the night, but she wasn't startled. She turned around, a soft smile already in place.

Wearing Dockers and a serious expression, Khalil dashed toward

her. "I parked down the street; wasn't sure if you gave me the right address. Is this you?" He inclined his head toward her three-story house with its large white exterior columns.

"Yes, this is where I reside," she said uneasily. With the threat of foreclosure breathing down her neck, she felt no pride in admitting ownership of the impressive structure.

They went inside. Adjacent to the vestibule, gapping door pockets revealed an azure blue room. He took a visual sweep of the room. A grand piano dominated the room.

"Do you play?"

"No. The girls love to play around on it. A few of them used to take lessons."

"Here?"

"Yes, my social club was once a hub of activity."

"This place is nice. Very tranquil," Khalil offered as he followed Saleema down a long corridor with walls painted a lighter shade of blue.

They reached the dining area that also served as a lounge for the girls. This room, a splash of peach.

"Would you like something to drink? Tea? Juice?"

"Juice."

Saleema motioned for him to follow her. The hue of the kitchen was citrus yellow. The room was bright and airy. Large sunflowers set in clear vases added to the pleasant setting.

"I see you're not afraid of color."

"Not at all."

"The walls in my place are all white. Really boring, now that I think about it. Maybe I'll explore some color."

"Color soothes me. The girls like the colorful environment, too."

"I can see why. It's very welcoming."

"Thanks." The mention of her girls put her on alert. She took her cell out of her purse, set it on a counter. "I need to keep this within reach, in case Portia calls."

Khalil took a seat on a stool.

Saleema took a container of Tropicana from the fridge. She poured the juice—a combination of orange, banana, and pineapple, into a tumbler and handed it to him.

He took a swallow. "Ah, refreshing."

Saleema smiled.

Khalil downed the drink

"More?"

"I'm good." Then his expression turned serious. "So what's your plan? You know, if Portia shows up?"

"I'm not sure. I guess I'll try to talk her into turning herself in. You know...I'll um, ask her to let me escort her back to the detention center."

"How much time do you think it would take to convince her?"

Saleema sighed. "I don't know."

"You really don't have a choice. If she comes here, you're going to have to inform the police of her whereabouts."

She groaned and nervously ran her fingers through her hair, separating tangled sister locs. "It seems so underhanded to lure her here, only to throw her to the wolves."

"You'd risk criminal charges if you allowed her to stay here for any length of time. What I'm saying is, coddling, cajoling... spending time with her, could be viewed as harboring an escaped criminal."

"Portia is not a criminal. You make it sound like she's a thief or a murderer. She's a misguided child...with anger management issues."

"Breaking out of the detention center doesn't look good for her.

Her rap sheet is getting longer. You don't want to get too deeply involved."

"I *am* deeply involved. I care about her." Saleema stared at Khalil. "What happened to the man who was all about looking for the redeeming qualities in troubled teens?"

"I'm still that man."

"Could have fooled me. You're starting to sound like the establishment…viewing Portia as a blemish on society, not seeing that she is a troubled young girl. You have no clue what it's like to grow up like Portia has."

"You're right. I don't know, firsthand. But I know what's going on in the streets. My students all come from—"

"Your students!" Angrily, she shook her locs from her face. "I know what Portia is experiencing, firsthand."

He made a low grunt of compassion.

Saleema patted her chest heavily with four fingers. "I used to be like Portia. Fighting everybody. Angry at the world because I didn't have parents who had my best interests at heart. From the age of seven, I was on my own. I grew up in a household filled with cousins and an absentee aunt. And a long list of 'uncles' who were no relation to me."

For the first time in her life, she was letting it out. The sympathy in Khalil's eyes made her pause, but didn't deter her from telling her story.

"I've been hurt and abused. And violently molested."

Khalil winced. Saleema continued. "Seems like each one of the steady stream of uncles all had a thing for kids. I don't know what they did to my cousins, but I know what happened to me. 'You better not tell,' some threatened. Others paid me hush money. Some change. A dollar or two for services rendered."

A look of horror covered his face. "That's awful."

"Yeah, tell me about it," she muttered sarcastically. "When I was about nine, my aunt found some money I'd been saving, stashed in the back of a drawer. She asked me where I got the money. I told her that I didn't know." Saleema gave a pained chuckle. "She whipped my ass with a broom handle, accusing me of stealing the money from her pocketbook."

"Did you tell her where you got it?"

"No."

"Why not?"

Saleema shrugged. "I don't know. I was scared. And ashamed of myself for freakin' with all those grown men."

"But it wasn't your fault."

"No, it wasn't. But that didn't stop me from despising myself. From being disgusted with myself, every time I had to get yet another treatment. Yeast infections, bacterial infections, STDs, venereal diseases   you name it, and I had it. All before the age of twelve."

"Who did your aunt point the finger at after you contracted those sexually transmitted diseases?"

"Me!"

"Why? You were a mere child."

"She called me a fast ass; accused me of messing around with teenage boys. In our house, I was called fast-ass, slut, ho, hooker, heifer…everything derogatory; hardly ever called by my given name.

Uncomfortable, Khalil looked down at the floor. "Wow. That's messed up. So did you inform her…about the…uh, uncles?"

"No."

"I can't understand why the physicians who treated you didn't file a report with Children and Youth Services?"

"It ain't go down like that." Dredging up those memories reig-

nited feelings of unworthiness. Ugliness. Pain. Unconsciously, Saleema had resorted to her old way of speaking. "You don't need a doctor's 'script in my 'hood. My aunt could buy antibiotics and anything else right off the streets."

"My God!"

"My sentiments exactly. Those were the words I cried every time I endured the trauma of a grown man forcing his manhood inside of me. Every time I itched between my legs. Every time there was a foul smell in my cotton panties."

Khalil removed his glasses; wiped unseen perspiration from around his eyes.

She'd heard that purging provided relief…a cleansing of sorts. But Saleema did not feel cleansed. Telling her story, reliving her harrowing childhood, made her feel dirty. Defiant. And furious.

And Khalil was starting to seem more like an enemy than a friend.

"Your secondhand, textbook knowledge ain't shit compared to real life experiences," she snapped.

Acknowledging the slur, he frowned. "You're right. I'm sorry you went through all that, Saleema."

"Yeah, me too. Sorry that I didn't get a chance to be a child," she spat resentfully. "I'm sorry that I got teased so badly for wearing outdated, grungy clothes, and for having uncombed, kinky hair that I rarely went to school. And when I did, I ended up getting suspended for fighting…for trying to defend myself…my honor, the only way I knew how. I'm sorry that all that early sexual activity has ruined me…messed up my insides so bad, I can never bear a child."

The words she'd spoken had never been uttered to a soul. Not even her best friend, Terelle, knew the truth about Saleema—that she was unable to conceive a child.

Her sudden admission hit her with the force of a gunshot, crumpling the features of her face, stooping her shoulders, as if the pain was too much to bear.

She trembled. Her body rocked gracelessly as she suffered her tragic childhood anew. She brought a hand up to her forehead, clasping it as if this action would prevent her from falling down.

A low moan that began deep in her throat grew louder and more insistent. It was a guttural sound, erupting from the pit of her soul, announcing itself as an anguished howl.

Khalil sprang up from the stool. Reaching for her, he caught Saleema before she fell.

CHAPTER 15

"Look at those two hoochies over there."

Gianna looked in the direction Bullet was pointing to. Two girls were loitering in the McDonald's parking lot, approaching people, apparently asking for money. Most of the customers rushed past the girls and hurried into the fast-food place. But a few stopped, dug inside their pockets, and handed the girls cash.

Instead of pulling out into traffic, Bullet made a quick left, reentering the parking lot.

Hey, papí, you got ten dollars?" a girl with a Spanish accent asked as she approached the car. Though she was grinning from ear to ear, Gianna could see the desperation in her eyes.

"What for?" Bullet inquired.

"Food," the girl replied.

"A bus ticket," the girl with the large breasts chimed in at the same time as her friend.

"Oh, y'all can't even get your stories straight. Why y'all out here tryna scam nuccas?"

"No, papí, we ain't like that. You got it all wrong. We had nothing to eat all day long." Her wide smile was replaced with a downturned mouth. She rubbed her tummy, indicating severe hunger.

"Yo, hold up. I ain't with all this begging shit," the other girl said, rolling her eyes.

She stepped closer to the car. "We don't need no food. We tryna get outta town. Can you let us hold something?"

"And what do I get in return?"

The girl scowled in disgust. "Whatchu mean?"

"Don't nothing in life come without a price tag. What do I get for my money?"

"Man, ain't nobody tryna hear all that. I only axed you for a coupla dollars. We ain't tryna trick with you or nothing."

"I ain't no trick," he said, insulted.

"So why is you frontin' like somebody axed you for a stack." She scrunched her nose like Bullet stunk.

Wearing an unpleasant expression, the Spanish girl backed away and resumed pestering the new arrivals to the McDonald's parking lot.

Not giving up easily, the bigger girl tried to shame Bullet into giving. The girl held out her hands as if perplexed. "I know you ain't blind. You see me and her—two young girls—out here struggling." She eyed the big bag of food in Gianna's lap. "You and your girl eating good, so why you acting like you can't help us out?"

Bullet's jaw tightened at the blatant disrespect, but he kept his temper in check.

Gianna knew that beneath Bullet's silence, there was controlled rage. Anger was simmering while his mind went to work, hatching up a double kidnap plan.

She felt a little sorry for what was about to happen to the Spanish girl, but had no pity for the loud-mouthed girl who had her arms resting on the open window ledge with her head stuck inside the car.

Gianna felt a mixture of emotions stirring: anger, irritation, and impatience. She disliked the brash girl and wanted Bullet to pull off and leave her behind. She didn't think she could get accustomed to hearing her loud, coarse voice every single day.

She hoped that Bullet used her for target practice after he got her in his grip. In Gianna's opinion, the loud mouth deserved to be tied to a tree more than Brielle did.

Bullet looked up, as if in thought. "Aiight. I'ma help y'all out. Where you tryna get to?"

"Well…see…Philly's kinda hot for us right now. But Maria got peeps in New York, so we tryna be out."

"I can dig it," Bullet said, drawing out his words, excitement glinting in his eyes. "Aiight, aiight. Tell you what. I'ma be a gentleman, since you calling me a cheapskate and whatnot."

The girl folded her arms and poked out her lips. "That's how you was acting."

"Tell your friend to come on. I'ma give y'all a ride to the bus depot. Shit, the way I'm holding, I can get y'all a first-class flight anywhere in the world. I can put some loot in y'all pockets, too." Bullet lifted up and pulled a wad of cash out of his pocket.

"Woo hoo!" The big-busted girl waved her friend over. "Come on, Maria. Fuck them broke-ass people. Ya boy over here got bank. We ridin' with him!"

Bullet slid Gianna his shank. "Handle shit in the back seat."

Gianna got out the car. "You can ride up front," she told the chunky girl.

"Don't be giving me attitude; I don't want your man," the girl replied back.

Bullet laughed. "She's a jealous type of female," he said, referring to Gianna. "But it's all good. Y'ah mean?"

"I'll be up in that grille if she don't watch how she talks to me."

"She'll be aiight."

Playing her part, Gianna sighed audibly.

Instead of walking over to the car, the Spanish girl was still working the parking lot, begging for money.

"Tell your friend to come on. I ain't got all night to mess around with y'all."

The big girl opened her mouth, ready to shoot off some more sass. But Bullet started peeling off the top of his knot. "How much y'all need?" he asked, using the money as bait.

The big girl actually licked her lips. "Um…we can use about um…a hundred dollars." Drooling over the knot of money, she licked her lips. "A hunnit a piece," she added, her words coming out in a breathy rush of lust.

"Aiight, ain't no thing." He held five bills. "Yo, your girlfriend is a straight nut. Walking up to niggas, asking for chump change. You wanna hang out in the parking lot with her or do you wanna hang with me and my girl? We about to hit up this after-party at a hotel near the King of Prussia Mall. I only got two VIP tickets, but I might be able to get you in."

"Oh, yeah? Whose party is it?"

"Soulja Boy."

"Oh, my God! I ain't hear nothing about him being in town."

"He's here on some hush-hush shit. Private party. Y'ah mean? You don't need no ID or nothing. So whatchu wanna do? You gon' hang out in this parking lot with your loser girlfriend, begging for change, or roll out and party with us?"

The chunky girl looked at him like he was crazy. "I'm not sticking around here! Me and that chick ain't joined at the hip. We just happened to get out of a situation together, but we ain't tight like that."

"That's what I'm talking about. Now you using your head. Drop that dead weight." Bullet smiled with approval. "That enchilada-eating mami is in your way. I got a big surprise and I really only need one of y'all. Two is a crowd in this particular situation."

As he cruised out of the lot, the Spanish girl yelled, "Portia!"

"Fuck outta here, bitch!" the loud-mouth girl yelled out the window at her and then began helping herself to a burger and some fries.

"You hard core," Bullet complimented. "You and Soulja Boy might bump heads, but then again, he might like a feisty chick like you."

"Really?"

"Yeah, see what had happened was...uh—" He scratched his head.

Gianna knew that Bullet was weaving together more lies.

"Soulja Boy's main man told me to grip up some hot girls to dance in his next video. I'm a recruiter for most of the stars that come through Philly. So if I don't get you in this video, don't even worry about it. Bow Wow supposed to be coming through next week."

"Nah, I'm not waiting on Bow Wow. I'm feeling Soulja Boy." A sudden worried look covered Portia's face. "They shooting the video here in Philly? Cuz like I said, I'm in a heated situation right now and I need to be out."

"Nah, they not shooting here. They gon' fly you out to Miami, if they pick you."

"Yes!" She smacked her hands together. "I'm *on* that private jet. You feel me? Portia is heading for Miami!"

The girl was grating Gianna's last nerve. "You're blowing everything out of proportion. No one mentioned a word about a private jet," Gianna blurted, totally annoyed.

Portia whipped around. "You need to keep your mouth shut, talkin' all corny and proper. Where you from, anyway? I know you ain't from Philly, talkin' like a damn white girl."

Bullet let out a burst of cruel laughter. In the rearview mirror, he glared at Gianna, giving her a narrow-eyed look that promised

punishment for being grammatically correct in public and for potentially blowing her cover.

Worried that she'd be used for target practice tomorrow, Gianna shrank into the leather upholstery.

Meanwhile Portia, without a care in the world, began bouncing and busting moves in the passenger seat of the car.

"Work it, shorty," Bullet cheered, turning up the volume of a Jay-Z CD. "You got serious moves, with your sexy self."

"Shit, put me on the stage with Beyoncé and I'll work it better than she can. I won every single dance contest at the girl's club I belong to," she said with pride.

"Is that right?" Bullet said. His eyes narrowed and calculating, he wheeled onto I-95 South, toward the airport.

# CHAPTER 16

"Why you got Gucci Mane on blast? You should be playing Soulja Boy's CD so I can practice to one of his songs."

"Where's the Soulja Boy CD?" Bullet barked at Gianna.

"Um…I forgot to bring it."

"Damn!" He gritted his teeth, appearing furious.

"Sorry," Gianna placated, still playing her part. In reality, Bullet didn't own a Soulja Boy CD.

"Umph," Portia grunted in disgust.

"Ain't no thing," he said to Portia. "When we get to the audition joint, you'll have time to rehearse." He frowned, scratched his chin in thought. "How much did you get paid for winning those talent shows?"

"Nothing. I got a few trophies and a certificate."

Bullet grunted. "Damn, you was on some sucker shit. Fuck a talent show. You 'bout to bust it up with the A-list stars. I might even take you under my wing and be your manager. Stop wasting your talent at some neighborhood girls club. You 'bout to get paid."

"You really think I'ma get picked for the video?"

"Yeah, after I get you hooked up with makeup and some new gear."

"The malls ain't open this time of night."

"Fuck a mall. I keep all kinds of fly gear in storage. You know, so the girls I pick can stand out when they audition. See…I get an extra bonus when one of my girls makes it to the top ten."

"Well, start counting your money cuz I know I'm gon' make the top ten," Portia boasted.

Despite the fact that Bullet was lying to Portia, Gianna still felt left out and jealous. She rolled her eyes again, detesting the obnoxious and conceited girl.

"What size you wear?" Bullet wanted to know.

"Twelve."

Bullet eyeballed Portia's bosom. "What about your bra size? I wanna put you in something that showcases those big tits you rockin'."

A smile lit her face. "Thirty-six double D!" she bragged.

"Yeah, I got a rhinestone bustier that will fit you, perfect."

"A what?"

"A sexy top that pushes your titties up so high, Soulja Boy won't be able to miss 'em."

"Oh, aiight. I'm with that."

"We gotta give you a new name, though. Portia ain't gon' get it. You star material, boo. You need a name that shines."

Portia furrowed her brows in thought. "Star! That's a good name for me."

"Nah, you gotta cute baby face. You look sweet and delicious." He scrunched his face, thinking hard. "I like Bubblicious. Bubbles for short."

Portia frowned. "I'm not feeling that name at all."

"Trust me. I know this business. That name matches your assets."

"Aiight," she reluctantly agreed.

"Just trust me. You'll get used to your new name. Let me manage your career and we'll all be moving to Miami."

Portia shrugged. "Okay. Getting out of Philly and hanging with the stars in Miami is exactly what I need to be doing. Fucking around with that damn Maria was slowing me down. I'm glad I bumped into you."

Bullet looked in the mirror and winked at Gianna. Gianna smiled back, glad for some attention, and praying that the wink was a reprieve from any punishment he had in store for her.

He turned his attention back to Portia. "You owe me an apology for calling me a cheapskate. It wasn't about no coupla dollars. I was trying to check you and your girlfriend to see which one of y'all would work best for the video, but you was coming at my neck, playing me like some kind of sucka."

"My bad."

Gianna snickered. It was the most she could do to taunt the obnoxious girl.

Portia shot her a hostile glance and then asked Bullet, "Is she gon' be trying out for the video, too?"

Bullet fell out laughing. "Nah, that's my boo, but she can't dance. If you think she talks like a white girl, you should see how bad she dance."

Portia cracked up in malicious laughter.

"Whatever!" Gianna snarled from the back seat. She'd been cued to play her part, but the growl in tone was real. She disliked Portia intensely.

"Trust. Lollipop ain't no competition for you. I have another girl named Tootsie who was gon' audition tonight, but she way out in the boonies. I ain't got time to pick her up."

"Less competition for me," Portia said.

Bullet nodded. "I like your confidence. Me and you gon' go far together."

Watching Bullet giving Portia so much extra attention and so many compliments bothered Gianna. She felt a twinge of envy. She knew Bullet wasn't being honest with the girl, but she couldn't help worrying that there was a grain of truth in his words.

Portia was competitive and would probably want to be his bottom bitch after she made peace with the situation. But Bullet had

promised that spot to Gianna. She wanted it. She'd earned it. She was his first piece of candy. That had to count for something.

"How can you stand being with an insecure female?" Portia asked.

"She can't help herself," Bullet replied, his words followed by taunting chuckles directed at Gianna.

"I don't want your man; I'm checking for Soulja Boy," Portia informed Gianna and then attacked the burger—her head, neck, and shoulders moving in time with the music that poured from the speakers.

"Work it, Bubbles. I'ma put in a special word for you. I'ma see if I can get you the number one spot in the video."

"For real?"

"Hell, yeah. I'm tired of recruiting girls. I need to play a bigger part and get the big bucks. You and me need an agreement."

"What kind of agreement?"

"I'm taking you to the video shoot and everything, getting you the kind of exposure you could never get on your own, so I wanna represent as your manager. You know, get my percentage."

"Oh! Aiight. For sure!"

"Now don't be trying to ditch me after you get all cozy with Soulja Boy. Stay loyal, aiight? We gon' split your video profits down the middle. Fiddy-fiddy, aiight?"

"Aiight. That's cool."

Bullet's cell pinged. He glanced at the display and frowned. "Soulja Boy's man done hit me four times. We gotta speed it up. You might not have time for hair and makeup, Bubbles."

Responding to her new name, she said, "It's cool. When Soulja Boy sees my moves, it's gon' be a wrap for all them other chicks."

"I like your confidence." Bullet took his eyes off the highway and gave Bubbles a quick glance of appreciation.

Bouncing to the music, Bubbles stared out the window. "Seems like we going in the opposite direction from the King of Prussia mall."

"That VIP party was on some other shit. Soulja Boy wasn't even gon' be there," Bullet explained. "We headed to the private audition. Out of the way spot…in the sticks. Everything ain't for everybody. Feel me?"

"Oh. Okay." Bubbles pulled down the visor and checked out her reflection in the mirror. "You got any lip gloss?" she asked Gianna.

"No," Gianna said with an edge to her voice.

"Can I hold a comb or brush or something?"

"No!" Gianna spat. She wasn't allowed to carry a purse. Bullet kept all her personal items. Unless she was working. When she was working, she kept a work kit…a plastic pouch filled with condoms and packets of moisturizer. Lip gloss was included but not to enhance her beauty. Lip gloss was used as a sex tool to allow customers more glide.

"Yo, Bubbles. Stop worrying about your appearance. You look sexy without makeup. They looking for fresh faces, anyway. You know…a schoolgirl look," he explained, seeming to forget it was he who had earlier brought up the topics of hair and makeup.

Bubbles tried to finger comb her hair into a different style. "I need a perm," she complained, frowning at her reflection.

His cell buzzed. "I'm on my way," Bullet grumbled. He ended the call with a click of a button.

"Why you bang on Soulja Boy's main man? S'pose they already finished with the auditions?" Bubbles shook her head in disgust.

"Ain't nothing popping off 'til we get there," he hissed. His hands tightened around the steering wheel as he regarded Bubbles contemptuously from the corner of his eye.

Gianna could tell that Bullet was doing everything in his power

not to pull over on the shoulder and beat the crap out of Bubbles for shooting off her mouth.

Jaws tight and uttering agitated sounds, Bullet went from cruising mode to speeding onto the ramp that led to Ridley Park, Pennsylvania.

Bullet rented storage areas all over the tri-state area. The space he used in Ridley Park was near a bar where a special clientele waited impatiently, watching the clock and waiting for Bullet to let them know that he and the girl named Lollipop were in town.

The Ridley Park crowd would be waiting at the usual place. Eager to have their desires satisfied as quickly as possible so they could get home to their families at a reasonable hour.

It was bowling night for that group of husbands and fathers. A few drinks with the boys before they headed home. And then a pit stop at the remote area where they leased Gianna's glossy lips.

Gianna sat back and relaxed, knowing that the Ridley Park team of creeps would be easy to please.

Bullet's training had been so rigorous, he'd often leave Gianna's lips swollen and numb. But the harsh training worked. Gianna always got each customer off in less than five minutes. Her head game was tight.

She wondered if Bullet would put the new girl to work tonight. Probably not. Bubbles seemed hard-headed and stubborn, with entirely too much mouth. She didn't impress Gianna as the type who would take orders easily. She'd probably need three or four days of Bullet's personalized training before she was ready to start making money.

With a smirk on her face, Gianna tried to imagine which sex act Bubbles would be trained to specialize in.

CHAPTER 17

As if she'd been injected with a truth serum, Saleema had poured out her heart to Khalil, revealing so much of her painful past she had lost her breath and collapsed into his open arms.

Khalil had held Saleema while she cried a river of tears.

She was all cried out, but instead of feeling purged, Saleema was horrified that she'd let down her defenses and had blurted out her sordid history during a moment of extreme weakness.

She stiffened in his arms, dreading to hear his comments.

He didn't say a word. With feelings so close to the surface, Saleema felt that Khalil's contemplative silence was proof that she'd said too much. She should never have bared her soul and admitted that she'd been a prostitute and a madam.

Thankfully, she hadn't mentioned a word about that night in the murky swamp in South Carolina. Somehow she'd managed to restrain herself from confessing that horror event. The brutal death of Kai Montgomery was a secret that Saleema would take to her grave.

On the bright side, it was best that she'd aired most of her dirty laundry before she allowed him to get too close. Now she could continue her single-minded commitment to helping troubled teen-aged girls without any distractions. The last thing that she needed was to be encumbered by an emotional attachment while she was at such an all-time low in her life.

She eased out of his embrace.

"You okay?" There was unmistakable concern in Khalil's voice, but in Saleema's state of self-protectiveness, his tone sounded very close to pity.

"I'm fine," she huffed, giving him an indignant sidelong glance.

He brushed the top of her hand. "You had it rough, I know. I'm sorry about everything you've gone through."

She pulled her hand away. "I don't need your pity. I'm good!"

"Whoa. I didn't—"

"Seriously," she said, cutting him off harshly. "I didn't ask you to come over here, bothering me and disrupting my life." Saleema knew she was speaking irrationally but she continued to release the angry flow of words.

"Disrupting your life? You're taking things way out of context. I was just checking on you."

"That's rather arrogant. Who appointed you to do that?" She laughed bitterly. "I've been taking care of myself for a long time. I don't need you or anyone else to check up on me."

"Bad choice of words."

"You're the scholar. I would expect you to choose your words more carefully." Biting sarcasm was the only defense mechanism she could access easily.

"Ease up, Saleema. I'm not the enemy; I'm trying to be your friend."

"I'm not feeling very friendly." She gazed toward the doorway, indicating his visit was over.

Taken aback, Khalil frowned. "Believe me, it's not pity that I feel for you. The other day…over lunch…it seemed we'd established a connection."

Convincing herself that it was for the best, she folded her arms, looked him in the eye and said, "We didn't establish anything. I was merely killing time. Honestly, Khalil, you're not my type."

He flinched and then glanced away.

It was a bold-faced lie. If Khalil wasn't her type, then who was?

Sickening images of the men who used to be her type raced across her mind. They were exceedingly wealthy men who wore Italian suits, had secure investments, and traveled the world. She was paid to be an amorous companion to men who were more passionate about their stock portfolios than their lackluster performance in bed.

There were so many reasons not to get involved with Khalil. He was ambitious, highly educated, and an honorable young man. Someone who was destined to succeed in life.

It was Saleema's own fault that she'd made inappropriate choices. She was quietly making amends by helping young girls stay on the right track.

She'd be damned if she'd put herself in the position to seek Khalil's approval. He was out of her league and that was that. Being around Khalil dredged up old feelings of unworthiness. Feeling unworthy fueled a desire to lash out.

"I'll walk you to the door," she said, tightening her folded arms.

"I have something to say."

Saleema sighed audibly.

Attempting to put her at ease, Khalil smiled. "Forgive me if I sound condescending, but I get the feeling that you think you need to put up a wall between us."

"I don't *think* anything. I know what I need. I need distance between us. A lot of distance," she added. "This is not a good time for me to start a relationship of any kind."

"I'll accept friendship, if that's still on the table." Khalil tried to be lighthearted but the hurt was still in his eyes.

"Why are you being so stubborn? I guess you're accustomed to getting everything you go after."

"Stubborn sort of fits my character, but nothing ever came to me easily. We have a lot more in common than you think."

"I doubt it," she huffed, discounting their dedication to helping troubled teens. She glimpsed at him. His lips were parted, as if preparing to launch into a soliloquy regarding his hard climb to academic success.

She inched closer to the kitchen's archway, expecting him to follow her lead. She wasn't interested in hearing how he'd grown up poor, had worked two or three jobs to put himself through college…how he had studied during breaks while working as a dishwasher or some other menial job.

Whatever route he'd taken to achieve his doctorate's degree and to become the founder of an alternative school would be another blow to her self-esteem. She'd always taken the quick and easy route to get what she wanted. Even the money she'd used to open Head Up had been ill-gotten gain.

There was a degree of cowardice in rebuffing Khalil. Putting up an impenetrable wall of resistance between them was based on an irrational fear of rejection. To have convinced herself that he hadn't spoken during her crying jag because he was repelled by her sordid past had been a handy excuse.

"Khalil, I find you irresistible," she said softly. "You've given me no reason to distrust you, but I'm feeling too vulnerable to start an intimate relationship right now."

He nodded in understanding, encouraging her to continue.

"To be honest, I've never had an actual boyfriend. All my involvements with men were based on what they paid me." She lowered her eyes. "I'm damaged goods."

"Don't say that."

"I'm being honest. That's how I feel."

"Listen, I'm not asking for anything you can't give freely."

"I know. You seem to be a good man, but I feel so awkward in your company. I've always taken pride in feeling self-assured and in being a strong woman...I don't like feeling off kilter."

"If it's any consolation, I felt the same way when I met you at the detention center, but I didn't allow my lack of confidence to stop me from trying to get to know you better."

Saleema chuckled. "You didn't seem insecure at all. In fact, as I recall, you were really cocky."

"I talk a lot when I'm nervous." He laughed.

Instantly comfortable, Saleema unfolded her arms and laughed, too.

Stepping forward, he entwined his hand with hers, and looked into her eyes.

"I promise to respect your parameters. But please, don't push me away. Can we let this...can we allow *us* to evolve the way that we're supposed to? Even if it's no more than a platonic friendship, I have a feeling it will be life-lasting."

Emotionally drained from reliving her past, and weighed down from fear and worry over Portia, Saleema had no energy left to speak.

Silently agreeing to give their association a chance to blossom, she gave Khalil's hand a tight squeeze.

CHAPTER 18

Preoccupied with dance moves, Bubbles paid no attention to the two cars, the pickup truck, and the SUV that were parked in the shadows.

Gianna recognized the vehicles. They belonged to some of the members of the Ridley Park bowling league.

Bullet stopped in front of the space he rented, hit the lights, and turned off the ignition. Without a word, he got out and went to collect cash for the services Gianna would soon render.

"What the fuck he doing out there?" she asked Gianna.

"Talking to Soulja Boy's peoples." The lie rolled easily off Gianna's tongue.

"Why ain't we meeting up with them at the hotel or wherever they holding the auditions?"

"He probably trying to get them to go along with letting an overweight girl audition," Gianna said maliciously. She detested everything about Bubbles: her boisterousness, her cocky demeanor, her bad manners, and her boobs. Bubbles' breasts were so big, they looked fake…totally in-your-face annoying.

"Who you calling overweight? Just cuz I ain't built like a toothpick don't make me overweight."

"That's your opinion; you're entitled to it."

"You jealous cuz I got moves and you don't."

"Whatever."

"Yeah, whatever, bitch." Lips drawn tight, Bubbles gave Gianna her middle finger.

"Ugh, you're such an ignorant low-life. I wish Bullet would have left you in the parking lot, begging for handouts."

"You better watch your mouth, hooker!" Bubbles exploded.

"Takes one to know one."

Bullet opened the trunk of the Cadillac and then slammed it. Holding Gianna's work pouch, he motioned for her to get out of the car.

Standing outside the car, Bullet gave Gianna the key to the storage unit, along with the plastic pouch that contained the essentials for working her trade.

"They brought a new dude along, so treat him extra special. We need all the repeat customers and extra business we can get," Bullet said in a low tone.

"Okay."

"Now that I gotchu some extra help, I should be getting rid of that old Caddy and pushing a new Escalade in a coupla weeks."

"Or sooner, if they work as hard as I do."

"Yeah," he said thoughtfully.

"Bubbles and Tootsie Roll gon' have to step it up real quick so you can be driving the whip you deserve." Gianna was kissing up, staying on Bullet's good side.

"You right. I ain't got time to be babying those bitches. Aiight, handle those tricks while I go handle Bubbles. Be back in forty-five minutes. No more than an hour. You know the drill."

"Okay. I love you," Gianna said.

Bullet frowned, grunted an unintelligible response, and then turned toward his car.

Bubbles scooted over to the driver's seat. Taking a liberty, she honked the horn and then shouted out the window, "What they say? They gon' let me audition or not?"

"Yeah, it's all good," Bullet said, manufacturing a smile.

"Well...hurry up. Let's get it poppin'. I can't be fucking around in Philly all night."

He regarded Bubbles with disdain. "Yo, the audition is private. Don't be putting my man's business on blast."

"My bad," she said resentfully.

Through clenched teeth, Bullet cautioned, "Lay off the horn and calm yourself down before yo' loud ass fucks up my chances to make us some real paper."

Lips poked out, Bubbles surveyed the trio of vehicles and then grudgingly slid over to the passenger seat.

Dutifully, Gianna unlocked the unit. She looked over her shoulder and watched as Bullet pulled the car door open. He said something to Bubbles that caused her shoulders to shake with laughter.

Bullet sped off into the night with Bubbles riding shotgun. Like Gianna had been, Bubbles was lured by the hopes of rubbing shoulders with a celebrity.

Gianna wondered where Bullet was taking the coarse girl. Her dislike for Bubbles was so intense, she could only hope that Bullet was en route to the nearby woods...an area that Gianna was all too familiar with.

It would be a humbling experience for Bubbles to be tied to a tree. Absolutely horrifying to be used for target practice...in the dark.

Moments later, as Gianna was smearing on lip gloss, the first bowler entered the storage unit. His eyes roamed her long brown legs and then cruised up to her chest.

"Can you undo your blouse...let me see some tits while you blow me?"

"Sure." Obligingly, she unbuttoned her blouse and then undid the knot.

There was no bed inside this unit. Just a doormat for Gianna to kneel upon.

After the ninth and final bowler had been serviced, Gianna gargled, using a container of travel-sized mouthwash. She spat the acidic liquid into a drain that was centered in the middle of the concrete floor. Then, following Bullet's instructions, she locked herself inside.

Waiting for Bullet to return, she sat on the mat, her back resting against the wall, her mind occupied with anxious thoughts. During free time, she often reminisced about fun times with the friends in her New Jersey social circle.

But not tonight. Gianna's mind was busy scheming up a plan that would keep her in Bullet's favor. She figured that since she'd experienced more fear than anyone deserved in a lifetime, she needed a break. A permanent break from the paralyzing terror.

If she played her cards right, perhaps she'd be taken out of the equation. Bubbles and Tootsie Roll…both stubborn and defiant, could alternate as human sacrifices for Bullet's target practice.

Two hours after he'd left, Bullet opened the steel door with the spare key. Bubbles wasn't with him. He was alone.

"Hi," Gianna greeted, wondering where he'd left Bubbles. Then she noticed the long, angry scratch that circled his right eye and then zigzagged down the bridge of his nose and across his cheek.

Bubbles had probably tried to fight Bullet off, refusing his training. Gianna imagined that the thug chick was lying in the gutter somewhere with a bullet hole in her head.

"What happened?"

"Mind ya damn business!"

"Here's your key," she said sweetly, somewhat relieved that Bubbles was history.

She stuck a hand inside her blouse and pulled a twenty out of the B-cup of her bra. "The new guy tipped me," she said with pride.

"That's all he gave you?"

"Yes." Her joyful mood vanished. Suddenly ashamed and guilt-ridden, her gaze shifted downward.

"That cheap mufucka only gave you a twenty-dollar tip?" With a fire blazing in his eyes, Bullet stared at Gianna.

Her breath caught in her throat. Slightly hunched, one had gripped her forehead while the other protectively covered her abdomen as she steeled herself for a head blow or a hard gut shot.

Surprisingly, he paced a few steps in the tight quarters. "Twenty dollars is a fuckin' insult!" Bullet shouted, and smacked the crinkled bill out of her hand. "What about the rest of those tricks? How much they tip you?"

Guiltily, she swallowed. "Nothing. They said they already paid you."

"Yeah, but you supposed to work your lips and make those mu-fuckas happy to empty out the rest of the dough in their pockets."

"You didn't tell me to get tips," she said gently. "I thought you handled all the money transactions."

"Why I gotta tell you everything? Ain't you got a brain?"

Did she have a brain? Gianna gnawed at the corner of her lower lip, unsure of what she should say.

He sighed. "Yeah, I get the money off the top, but you 'spose to get the rest. If you wasn't a snotty, suburban bitch, you'd know that getting tips goes without saying. Damn! You ain't got no kind of hustle in you."

"I'll get some hustle," she promised, her voice a desperate plea.

"Shut the fuck up. Let's go." Bullet yanked her by her collar and then pushed her out of the storage unit. "How the fuck I get saddled with three green-ass bitches?"

Gianna pondered the question, but remained mute, realizing that Bullet didn't expect an answer.

Inside the car, in the passenger seat that had been occupied by Bubbles, Gianna was dying to know what had become of the wannabe video star. By the looks of Bullet's face, Bubbles had not taken well to the idea of following his orders.

If Bullet's face looked like this, how did Bubbles look? she wondered. Probably a whole lot worse. It was highly likely that Bubbles was somewhere shot in the head and left for dead.

"It's bad enough that I can't put y'all young asses out on the ho stroll," Bullet continued ranting. "I'd make so much more dough if y'all wasn't on that missing kids list. Shit!"

"Brielle...I mean, Tootsie Roll is seventeen. I think she's too old for the police to have her name on an Amber Alert."

"Amber what?" He grimaced, uncomprehending.

"An Amber Alert. You know...it's a bulletin that law enforcement issues when a child has been abducted."

"Oh, yeah. I heard of that. Shit. I ain't abduct nobody. You came with me on your own free will."

That wasn't true. Gianna had been conned and held hostage, but she'd never contradict Bullet.

"Ain't nobody tell that bitch, Tootsie Roll, to hop in my ride. The same thing goes for Bubbles. Bubbles wiggled her fat hips into my whip cuz she wanted to be with me. I ain't abduct those bitches."

"I know. I was just telling you what an Amber Alert means."

"You schoolin' me now?" He furrowed his brows threateningly.

"No."

"Then keep your mouth shut unless I ask you something. I hate when you start talking like a know-it-all. You think you be sounding all intelligent and shit, but on the real, you be sounding like a stupid, stuck-up bitch."

"I'm sorry. I was just trying to be helpful."

"It's not helpful to hear you sounding like a spoiled rich girl. That crap you was just talking is starting to give me a migraine."

"You want some of your medicine?" She reached inside the pocket of the passenger door.

"Did I say my allergies was kicking up? No! I said that all that proper talking you be slipping into is giving me a fucking migraine."

Gianna dropped the Sudafed back in the door pocket.

"Why can't I get me a ho who know what the fuck she's doing? Y'all green-ass bitches ain't nothing but a liability. I'm wasting all my pimpin' skills and wisdom trying to school a bunch of underage hoes. I could do a twenty-year bid from fucking with y'all."

"You ain't gon' catch no case off me." Gianna shook her head emphatically. "I always be listening to all your pimp wisdom." She sucked in a deep breath, needing more air to plead her absurd case further. "Plus—"

"Plus what?" he snarled. "What else you do for me? Not one of y'all hoes is worth the trouble y'all causing me. I need to cut my losses, line all three of y'all up and...Pow! Pow! Pow!" His weapon was tucked in his waistband, but he used his finger as if he were pointing the gun.

Gianna flinched. "Plus, um..." She had no idea what she was going to say, but Bullet, a man who giggled at her facial contortions every time one of his bullets whizzed over her head during target practice, wanted to hear why she deserved to live. She had to come up with something.

"Well…when I'm by myself…you know, when you don't be with me, I make sure my ass be on the low," she said, using atrocious grammar, trying not to rile Bullet into accusing her of trying to be an uppity, proper-talking ho.

"I got your back, Bullet. I'ma get big tips so you can hurry up and get that brand-new Escalade."

Her promise put a faint smile on his lips. "Come here, bitch," he said softly. His voice held a tenderness Gianna had never heard.

One hand released the steering wheel. He reached for her.

Accustomed only to Bullet's savagery, never gentleness, Gianna froze with fear.

"I ain't gon' hurt you. You my bottom bitch now."

Gianna inched close enough for Bullet to drape an arm over her shoulder. Her body tensed. His one-arm embrace was oppressive. Like bondage.

Bullet steered the car. "Relax."

Uneasily, she rested her head on his shoulder.

He stroked her hair.

Her guard up, she bristled, expecting at any moment his tender touch would turn into a violent clawing. Facial pinching. Or eye gouging with a strong and determined finger.

When his gentle caresses did not switch to a vicious mauling, Gianna finally relaxed. Despite herself, she purred like a kitten, enjoying her captor's touch. Confidence restored, she possessed a sense of peace, knowing that she'd dodged another day of being used as a human target.

CHAPTER 19

They exited I-95 South on the Edgemont Avenue ramp and made a left. He drove along Morton Avenue. When they approached a familiar intersection, Gianna realized that Harrah's casino was around the corner.

She figured Bullet had rustled up some patrons from the casino. Bullet would hit the crap table while the horny men would drive Gianna to a remote street where she'd give as many blow jobs as were paid for. But this time, she'd be sure to ask for tips.

Bullet made a right, driving in the opposite direction of the casino. She was curious where they were going, but knew better than to ask questions.

"You know where we are?" he asked, after making a series of turns designed to disorient her.

"No." Gianna pretended not to know that they were in Chester, Pennsylvania, a small town outside of Philadelphia. A town Bullet visited frequently.

"Good," he said, pleased with her response.

He parked on a residential street. The street sign read *Tilghman Street*. Other than the area where the casino was located, she didn't know much about Chester. Or any other area where she worked for Bullet.

When she wasn't working, she was kept inside various storage units and motel rooms, denied permission to venture outside. He moved her around constantly...a day here...a day there, never

allowing her to become acquainted with her surroundings. Never permitting her to mingle with anyone other than paying customers.

They approached a row-house that stood out from the other lowly houses on the block. The front entry door was grand, with a glazed glass surface and deep, carved etching. Using a key, Bullet opened the door.

Gianna stepped inside a house that was small but so elaborately decorated, it could have been a celebrity's secret hideaway.

The living room was white. Every furnishing from the long sectional sofa to the coffee table, chairs, throw pillows, drapes, area rug, lamp shades, silk flowers, the candles, and vases, all were entirely white.

A glimpse into the dining room revealed more white and another super fabulous room with an elaborate bar surrounded by flashy white bar stools. At first, Gianna thought she saw a willowy woman in the kitchen, but upon closer inspection, she realized it was a man. A slender man with short, chemically straight hair, and wearing tight jeans, a red wife beater, and oddly...red maribou feather heels.

The obviously gay man sent a beaming smile toward Bullet. That smile twitched into a grimace when he noticed Gianna.

Nose turned up, he slammed the lid on the frying pan, containing the wafting aroma of fried chicken.

He pranced into the living room. Holding a spatula and batting elaborate false eyelashes, he said, "Oh, no you didn't bring another young ho up in my crib? What the hell is wrong with you, Bullet?"

He shoved Gianna aside and he switched past her, leaving behind a mixed scent of fried chicken and a musky cologne. With a dramatic gesture, he flung the front door open. "Get that young bitch outta my house, right now," he demanded, motioning with the spatula.

"Chill, Flashy. Lollipop is cool." Much stronger than his feminine friend, Bullet pushed him aside and forcibly pushed the door closed.

So this is Flashy. Gianna had heard Bullet talking to Flashy numerous times, and despite his name, she'd never suspected that he was gay.

"I've been in the kitchen working like a damn slave. I was going to play some slow jams and set the table so me you could enjoy a romantic late night dinner." Flashy rolled his eyes at Gianna. "Now here you come, bringing another young ho into my crib. Damn, Bullet, why you keep messin' with these minor children?"

"The younger the better."

"The better for what…doing a long bid? These girls have families. They got peoples who must be wondering where they at. Ain't it bad enough that you brought that little baby over here?"

"I paid you for your services."

"I thought that was gonna be the extent of my services. Now you're dragging one young hooker after another right to my front door. I don't know what you think this is, but it ain't no damn whorehouse. Damn, Bullet, this ain't no fleabag motel. This is where I lay my head!"

"Man, chill!" Bullet insisted. "Ain't nobody looking for Lollipop."

"How do you know?"

"I had her for over a month. If somebody really wanted her ass, don't you think they would have found her by now?"

Flashy sucked his teeth. "What about that other one?" He nodded toward the carpeted stairs.

"Bubbles gotta couple lessons to learn."

"Why she gotta learn 'em over here? Take her to one of those sheds you rent out," Flashy shrieked, sounding on the verge of a tantrum.

Gianna felt a stab of guilt at the mention of Brielle's baby, but was unsympathetic toward Bubbles' plight…whatever it was. She wished the worst kind of punishment on Bubbles. Other than Bullet, she'd never felt such an intense dislike for another person. Her feelings for Bullet were changing now. She still feared him, but was beginning to kind of like him. She liked his softer side. Had enjoyed the warmth and comfort of his arm around her.

She liked being treated nice by Bullet and would strive to get more of the nice treatment.

"I'm gon' move Bubbles in a coupla days. But Lollipop needs to stay here for a while."

"Why?" Flashy frowned at Gianna.

"I gotta keep my eyes on my bitches. And I can't watch 'em all at the same time. I need you to be my other set of eyes."

"I don't know."

"Two of 'em is still in training. They need a lot of attention. Ain't too many niggas I trust the way I trust you, man."

"I'm not tryna catch another case."

"I got this shit under control. Lollipop is already trained. She easy-going. If I say the sky is dog-shit brown, she say…" He nodded at Gianna.

"The sky is dog-shit brown."

"See what I'm saying?"

"I don't see shit. She just a parrot, repeating what you say."

"She's better than a parrot. Lollipop is like a faithful puppy. For real, man. I'm all she got."

"She's scared of you. Don't confuse fear with loyalty."

"Her pops done married the bitch he left her mom for. Him and the new bitch done started a family of their own. Her pops ain't thinking about Lollipop no more." Bullet nudged Gianna. "Speak your piece."

"My pops not thinking 'bout me no more."

"I'm not listening to this lil' robot bitch."

"For real, though. Her mom was a few steps from the psych ward when I caught this lil' bitch. Shit, she grateful that I brought her into the life. Ain't that right, Lollipop?"

"You right. Ain't nobody looking for me," she said emphatically, repeating words that Bullet had been drilling in her head for the past month.

"Tell Flashy what you'd do if somebody tried to grab you."

Gianna's face hardened. "I'd cut a mufucka for trying to steal me away from Bullet," she added venomously.

"See what I'm saying, Flashy? She's ride or die, man," Bullet boasted, giving Gianna a nod of approval.

Flashy sneered at Gianna. "Yeah, well…this ride-or-die hooker gon' get us both put underneath the jail if the police find out you kidnapped her from her peoples. I thought you were keeping her locked up in some hideaway place?"

"I can't be three and four places at the same time. She staying here 'til I get situated."

"What about us?"

"Ain't no us. Stop tripping; I ain't no fag."

"Uh-huh," Flashy said, rolling his eyes up to the ceiling. "First, you drop a damn baby on me. I took care of that. Then you bring in that wild-ass, thicker-than-a-Snicker chick…" He pointed the spatula toward the stairs and then he glared at Gianna. "Now this?"

"Don't worry about Lollipop. She's cool."

"You full of shit, Bullet. You ain't no real pimp and you know it."

"Why ain't I?"

"From my recollection, you did time for armed robbery, not pimpin'."

"I changed occupations. Pimpin' is easier."

"Don't seem like it." Flashy raised a brow. "That's a serious scratch on your face." Flashy placed his long, manicured fingers on Bullet's face. "You should let me put some cocoa butter on that nasty mark before it leaves a scar," he said softly.

Looking perturbed, Bullet pulled away from Flashy's reach. "Fall back, man," he growled.

"You don't have to act so touchy all of a sudden. You didn't mind my affection when we were locked up together."

"Stay focused, man. We talking about *now*."

"Whatever." Rejected, Flashy screwed up his lips.

"Anyway, this scratch ain't nothing compared to that bitch's face."

"True. And that's exactly why I want you to move that battered child out of my house. Take her off to the boonies to one those storage spaces. I don't want her in here. Seriously."

"It's cool."

"No, it's not! I'm not trying to go back to prison, Bullet!" Flashy shouted, waving the spatula through the air.

"Stop being so negative all the time."

"Ain't no hope for you." Flashy lowered his lengthy lashes and shook his head. "You better be glad I got love for your pretty ass. I wouldn't take this kind of risk for no average-looking man."

"Yo, is that food ready yet?" Bullet said, changing the subject.

"Oh, Lord. My chicken is burning," Flashy shrilled. He twirled around and daintily trotted toward the kitchen.

# CHAPTER 20

B ullet and Flashy were in the kitchen arguing. Clearly, Flashy had a crush on Bullet. Gianna could understand why. Bullet was so cute when he wasn't mad. But Gianna was certain he was as straight as an arrow. Flashy would never be more than a friend.

While Flashy ranted about his ruined meal, Gianna sank into a white leather barrel chair and focused her attention on a rerun of the MTV Awards.

On the TV, Miley Cyrus took the stage. A sudden pang of nostalgia gripped Gianna. She was a huge fan. Hannah Montana posters adorned the walls of her bedroom in New Jersey.

A severe case of homesickness stuck like a punch to the gut. Nauseous, she jumped up. "Bullet, I'm about to throw up."

"The bathroom's at the top of the stairs!" Flashy shouted. "Don't be spilling your guts in my living room!"

Gianna covered her mouth with her hand. Dry-heaving, she waited for Bullet's permission to go upstairs.

Frowning, Bullet gave a head nod.

As she took the stairs two at a time, she heard Flashy ask, "Is that lil' ho knocked up?"

"Better not be," Bullet replied.

She rushed inside a bathroom with walls painted bright pink. Blinging shower curtains were splashed with beads and rhinestones. An elaborate mirror was outlined in light bulbs overtop a vanity sink, which was covered with a scattering of makeup, hair clips,

lip gloss, a container of Tic Tacs, and an assortment of colored condoms.

Gianna knelt on a fluffy pink rug and lifted the cushioned toilet seat. Hovering over the toilet, she gagged and heaved, causing her eyes to water, but nothing came up. Her bout of nausea had passed, but a deep sorrow intensified.

Her life was hopeless. Bitter tears spilled down her cheeks. She cried softly.

Someone should have rescued her by now. Bullet was right. Her parents had stopped trying; they had moved on with their lives. It wasn't fair. She was so lonely and missed being with her friends. Her neighborhood. She wanted to be in New Jersey—back to her real life when classes resumed in the fall. She wanted to sleep in her own bedroom—not on a mattress inside a storage unit. She wanted to go home!

But it was a hopeless dream. Bullet would kill her before he let her go. Tears fell harder.

"What's taking you so long, Lollipop?" Bullet shouted from downstairs.

She flinched in terror and stood up immediately. "I'll be right down."

Gianna grabbed a tissue from a sparkly tissue box. She wiped the tears from her eyes and blew her nose. She turned on the faucets and splashed water on her face. Looking at her reflection in the mirror, her eyes were puffy from crying. She shrugged in resignation, and began to quickly pull herself together. She ran a palm over her tousled hair, and then smoothed out the rumpled pleats of her skirt.

As she exited the bathroom, she heard something that sounded like sniffling and muffled sobbing. *Bubbles?*

Downstairs, Bullet and Flashy were engaged in a heated discussion, their voices raised, oblivious to the sound of crying.

It had to be Bubbles. Curiosity sent Gianna creeping toward the bedroom at the end of the narrow hall. She opened the door and gasped.

Standing stooped, Bubbles held a blood-soaked pillowcase to her face. A trail of blood trickled down her arm.

"Oh, my God!" Gianna was astonished by the large amount of blood. "You need a doctor," Gianna whispered.

Bubbles pulled the crumpled pillowcase away from her face, revealing blood-stained gauze taped to her face. "Your boyfriend cut me," Bubbles said in a hushed voice. "That faggot who lives here bandaged me up, but the blood is seeping through. You gotta do something to help me. Call the cops."

Gianna tensed. Her eyes grew large with fear. Shaking her head, she backed away from Bubbles. Closed the bedroom door and hurried downstairs.

Pouting, Flashy was wrapping pieces of chicken in aluminum foil. "All this damn work just so you can rush out of here and take my food to some stank ho."

"I'll be back. The bitch ain't ate nothing all day. That greedy bitch upstairs ate the burgers and shit I was gon' take back to the spot I'm keeping her in."

"Buy the bitch some more burgers. You got plenty of money these days. I don't see why you gotta give a dirty ho the fried chicken that I lovingly cooked for you."

"Yo, I'm running a business. I gotta keep my workers fed. Now, fall back, man." Bullet pushed past Flashy, knocking his slim friend off balance.

"You ain't shit, Bullet! I hate you!" Flashy drew his lips into an angry knot as he steadied himself, wriggling his right foot back into the pump.

Bullet smiled indulgently, like Flashy was a spoiled child. "Keep your eye on Bubbles. I don't trust her." He glanced at Gianna. "I

want you to have my man's back if that bitch tries some slick shit."

"Okay." Gianna nodded, and then decided to take this opportunity to tell Bullet about Bubbles' condition.

"Bubbles was up there crying, so I looked in on her."

"You was supposed to be upstairs throwing up. Ain't nobody tell you to go poking around, opening up closed doors."

"I'm sorry. I heard a noise, so I opened the door to make sure she wasn't trying to climb out the window."

"She ain't going nowhere. That window is nailed shut."

"Her face…it's bleeding real bad. Blood is everywhere."

"What!" Flashy screeched. "I know she ain't bleeding all over my expensive bed linen." He kicked off his heels and ran up the stairs.

"That bitch ain't even started basic training yet, and she already giving me problems." Sighing in resignation, he flung the brown bag filled with fried chicken on the coffee table. He motioned for Gianna to follow him and then stomped up the stairs.

"What the hell is wrong with you, bitch?" Flashy shrieked at Bubbles.

"I'm trying to stop the blood," Bubbles whined.

"Well, I could have given you a raggedy towel or something if you'd asked. Why the hell would you use using my good linen to soak up blood?" He folded his arms and shook his head. "No damn home training."

"Why she bleeding like that?" Bullet inquired.

For a few seconds, Flashy's mouth hung open in disbelief. "You the one who cut her. How the hell do I know?" he finally responded.

"Yeah, but I told you to hook her up."

"I did! I slapped a triple-ply gauze pad on that cut."

"So why is all that blood gushing?" Bullet demanded.

"You need to ask yourself that question. Your crazy ass cut her so deep, she probably needs stitches." Flashy frowned at the ruined

pillowcase. "That pillowcase is part of a two-hundred-dollar set."

"Man, I gotchu. We gotta worry about closing up that gash."

"*We* ain't worrying about shit," Flashy said in a high-pitched voice. "I might be able to sew some glamorous pieces for my fashion shows, but I ain't no surgeon, so don't even hint that you want me to try to close up that nasty wound."

"Man, you was always treating niggas who got cut in the pen."

"With bandages. I wasn't trying to close up no open wounds with a needle and thread."

"How about I go out and get you a staple gun. Can you work with that?"

Appalled, Gianna gasped. Bubbles groaned, obviously horrified by the direction the conversation had taken.

"Where you gon' get a staple gun at this hour?"

"Pathmark is open."

"Pathmark is not a hardware store and I don't feel like trying to play doctor." Flashy folded his arms stubbornly across his chest.

"There's gotta be some other way you can close her face up."

Flashy sighed. "You know what? It's time for you and both these lil' jailbait bitches to roll out of my crib. I'm not with all this insanity you're bringing into my life."

Bullet glared at Flashy. "You gon' leave me hanging like this? That's how you gon' do me?"

Flashy didn't respond. He was too busy gaping in disgust at Bubbles, who was whimpering as she now used the lacy trim of the pillowcase to wipe dribbling blood from her arm.

Flashy fanned his face, as if to keep from passing out. "This is a hot, bloody mess. Look at my good pillowcase. It's completely drenched." He strutted across the room and opened a drawer of neatly folded items. He tossed a shirt at Bubbles.

"That was my ex's favorite T-shirt. Use that on your face."

Flashy shot an evil look at Bullet. "You need to drop her off at the emergency room."

Next Flashy pointed at Gianna. "And she needs to go back to that shed you keep her in. This is too much for me. I'm about to pass out from looking at all this blood…and the smell of rank fish is turning my stomach." Turning up his nose, Flashy fanned his face repeatedly.

Gianna sniffed. "I don't smell any fish."

"Females are fish!" Flashy exploded.

Bewildered by the association between females and fish, Gianna cut an eye at Bubbles. But Bubbles didn't make eye contact.

Quivering and moaning, Bubbles looked like she was having a fit. The gauze pad was hanging off her face. An outpouring of blood pumped from the vicious slash.

# CHAPTER 21

Bubbles tussled and struggled as Flashy and Bullet lowered her to the floor, trying to place her on top of a pallet made of plastic bags.

Flashy didn't want Bubbles to leak blood into the mattress and Bubbles wouldn't go down easy.

"Flashy is going to stitch your face up. Now quit all this twisting and turning, bitch."

"I don't want that muthafucka sewing on me. This some foul shit y'all doing. Y'all not right," Bubbles accused, her voice raspy and tearful.

"Shut up! Calm the fuck down before I poke a hole in your eye," Bullet snarled.

Bubbles released a grunt of surrender as she lay splayed on the green plastic.

Flashy waved a manicured finger in the air. "I'm not sewing or stapling a goddamn thing. Do you hear me, Bullet? You need to go to Pathmark and pick up about twenty packs of Band-Aids. I'll try to patch that wound together the best way I can. But this ho is going to have to keep her big mouth shut for at least a week or so until it scabs over. All that moaning and crying is the reason that cut opened up so wide in the first place."

Unable to help herself, Bubbles wriggled and moaned in obvious agony.

"Didn't I tell you to be still?" Bullet kicked her, his shoe collid-

ing with her hip. "Don't make me stomp yo' ass." He raised his foot threateningly, and Bubbles became as still as a statue.

Gianna felt real bad for Bubbles. The girl had been given a brutal punishment that Gianna would have never wished on anyone. It would be somewhat refreshing to hear Bubbles' loud mouth again. Seeing her hurt and helpless was awful.

"While you're out, go holla at my drug connect over on Pennell Street."

"Who you talking 'bout, that nigga, Smiley?" Bullet said, looking mad. "Lemme find out…"

"Please. Smiley ain't my type but he has a serious stash of pharmaceuticals. Tell him I said to hook you up with some some Xanies, Vicodin, OxyContin, and anything else he got."

"I don't like that slimy mufucka. He be tryna charge a nigga up."

"So what?" Flashy snapped. "Pay him whatever he wants. Don't even try to bargain. I need this bitch to be highed up or better yet…knocked out while I'm working on her."

A couple hours later, Bubbles was back in bed. The mattress, however, was protected with plastic. Drugged with something powerful, Bubbles was blissfully unconscious. Flashy had closed the cut on the left side of her face with what appeared to be a zillion or so criss-crossing Band-Aids.

"I'm tired as hell," Bullet complained.

On cue, Gianna rubbed his arm. From the corner of her eye, she could see Flashy shooting daggers at her.

"We outta here, Lollipop. I gotta go feed Tootsie Roll before she starves to death."

"What about this ho?" Flashy asked, fluttering his lashes angrily.

"Man, I said I need you to take care of her 'til she ready to work."

Flashy stuck his hand out. "In that case, I need some money for my troubles."

"I gotchu. What's the word from the babysitter? Any offers yet on that hooker's baby?"

"It's hard to get that kind of money you looking for in the 'hood. Niggas ain't spending a lot of dough for no goddamn baby."

"I thought the sitter had connections. That baby gotta be worth at least twenty stacks to one of those freak mufuckas."

Flashy rolled his eyes. "Please. You watch too much TV. You'll be lucky if you get a couple stacks. Nobody I talked to was even feeling your baby-selling plan. They don't want any parts of it. You gon' have to be happy with whatever you get. Your main concern should be getting that baby out of the picture. A-S-A-P!"

"I can dig it, yo. But tell that sitter to put out some more feelers for me, man. I was hoping to get enough loot to trade in my whip. A baby should be worth enough for me to be pushing a new Escalade, y'ah mean?"

"Umph. So selfish. Always have been. It's all about Bullet. What about my cut?"

"I gotchu, man. You gon' get yours."

"Uh-huh," Flashy said doubtfully.

Gianna's stomach dropped. *They plan on selling Samantha?*

She'd heard about babies being sold on the black market, but never dreamed she'd be involved in such a heinous act. She wondered about this babysitter person. She hoped the person would do the right thing and take little Samantha to the nearest hospital. Or police station.

She wanted to plead with Bullet to spare the baby, but feared she'd end up like Bubbles if she said a word. As cruel a person as Bullet was most of the time, he had finally started treating Gianna slightly better than trash and she wanted to remain in his good graces.

Bubbles' condition was a wake-up call. Gianna wanted to live.

She didn't want to be cut, kicked, or shot at anymore. She was determined to be Bullet's favorite girl.

"With three young hookers, you should be gettin' major paper. All this bloodshed, mayhem, and unnecessary trouble is getting on my last nerve. Do you hear me, Bullet?" Flashy wasn't as tall as Bullet, but with heels on, he came to Bullet's shoulder. Not exactly face-to-face, but close enough.

"Fuck you!" Bullet gave him a shove. "Your faggot ass can't tell me how to handle my business." A vein popped up in the middle of Bullet's forehead. He looked seconds away from snatching up Flashy by the neck and choking the life out of the thin, gay man.

Flashy didn't seem phased at all by the slur. There was no fear in his eyes. Despite his small frame, Flashy had a visible six-pack imprinted against his tight shirt. Maybe he was stronger than he appeared. At any rate, he seemed ready to go toe-to-toe with Bullet and continued to berate him.

"Your hustle ain't shit. You supposed to be getting money, not cutting up and maiming bitches."

"Look, I got a reason for everything I do."

"Don't seem like it."

"What? I gotta run shit by you before I make a move?"

"You should since you felt the need to drag me into the middle of this crazy bullshit. I'm just saying..."

"Just saying what? You think you can school me on the pimp game?"

"Somebody needs to school your wild ass. I ain't claiming to be no pimp, but at least I got common sense. You spazzin' out like some maniac from a slasher flick."

Bullet laughed at the comparison.

"You're losing perspective. If you used your brains, you could be iced out by now, like the big ballers."

Those words seemed to sink in. Bullet scowled in thought. "Nah, I got this. I ain't listening to you. I know how to run my business."

Flashy folded his arms. "There's other ways to control your assets. Injuring these hoochies to the point where they can't work is stupid. You're acting like a dopeman who snorts or shoots up most of his own product."

"I said I got this."

"No, you don't. You got two injured bitches that you can't make a dollar off. And I got bills to pay!" Flashy yelled. "If you don't start making it rain up in this dip, I'm gon' cut you loose! That's a promise!"

Bullet's face softened. Gianna watched the vein in his forehead disappear. "Stop threatening me. I don't like that shit."

"I gotta keep you focused. I'm innocent, but in the eyes of the law, I'll be considered as an accomplice to your deranged ass. Listen, you maniac, I'm not trying to go back to jail."

Bullet smirked. "Man, stop bringing up jail. A muthafucka will have to put my ass in a body bag before I do any more time. Get it through your head...ain't nobody looking for these bitches."

Flashy took a deep, disgusted breath. "Do I need to remind you that ya girl, Bubbles, broke out of a detention center?"

"So what? Do it seem like anybody is really trying to find her? Po-po got better shit to do with their time than search for a run-away juvenile."

Bubbles escaped from a juvenile detention center! Gianna's ears were perked, but she kept a straight face, pretending that she had no interest whatsoever in the conversation between the two former convicts.

She didn't know how the news about Bubbles would come in handy, but she had a feeling it might be useful information.

CHAPTER 22

The next day went by slowly. Portia dominated Saleema's thoughts. Worrying about Portia took precedence over her dire financial state.

Hour after hour, she abused her newly acquired friendship card, calling Khalil relentlessly, asking him to use whatever influence he had in the juvenile system to try and find out any information he could about Portia.

Through a connection inside the detention center, Khalil found out that the girl who had escaped with Portia had been apprehended outside a McDonald's in South Philadelphia. He had no other information…no encouraging news about Portia's whereabouts.

"I need to talk to that girl," Saleema said determinedly. "Can you arrange that?"

"No, I don't have that kind of pull. I believe she's being transferred to a more secure facility."

"When?"

"I'm not sure."

"Can you dig a little deeper? Ask your informant—"

"She's not an informant…not a snitch…nothing that dramatic." He chuckled. "She's a friend. A colleague, who happened to be there when the girl was brought in."

Colleague. The word evoked connotations of an elite society in which Khalil was an esteemed member. It was a harmless expres-

sion, pertaining to anyone from a coworker to an associate of the same profession. In this instance, hearing that the colleague was a *she* caused an irrational bubble of jealousy to fizz up, briefly distorting Saleema's priorities.

She reined in her emotions. There were important issues to deal with…namely, getting some pertinent information that could lead her to Portia.

"Can you ask your colleague to give you the girl's name?"

"What good will that do?"

Holding the phone cradled to her ear, Saleema shrugged. "I don't know. It's a start. Having the name of the girl who escaped with Portia is the closest thing I have to a lead."

"If my friend does know the young lady's name, she obviously wasn't comfortable committing a breach of confidentiality."

Saleema sighed in frustration. "I'm so worried about Portia."

"I know you are, but this is a case for law enforcement."

"Law enforcement doesn't care about Portia's safety like I do. Khalil, you don't know the really ugly side of human nature like I do. Believe me, Portia is in serious danger."

"You seem to think that I've lived in some cloistered environment where bad things never happened. I told you why I opened the alternative school. I'm not blind to the horrors of this world."

"Khalil, as much as you'd like to think we're alike, I know that we've had totally different experiences. I used to be so greedy, so callous, that I was part of the problem with society."

"You don't have to reopen that old wound."

Saleema ignored his advice. "I graduated from turning tricks to becoming a madam."

"You told me." Khalil sounded extremely uncomfortable.

"Who do you think I hired…bored housewives…hardened prostitutes? No, I hired young women who either had dreams of money

and wealth or were so destitute they felt they had no other choice."
She paused for a beat. "I hate that I was so selfish that I robbed
those girls of their dignity."

"Did you hire underage girls?" Khalil sounded appalled and
Saleema couldn't blame him.

"No, not intentionally. I had some scruples and required identification…proof that they were at least eighteen years old."

"At the time, you couldn't have been much older yourself," Khalil
said, trying to cushion the self-flogging Saleema was administering.

"I was in my early twenties. Really self-centered. It was all about
getting mine."

"You were young," he said, being the voice of reason.

"I never deliberately put those girls in harm's way. But one of
them, a young girl named Chanelle, was practically murdered.
Perhaps you heard about it. It was all over the news. She was held
captive in a nice house in Mount Airy. Turned into a sex slave by
a man who seemed like an average guy."

"No, I don't think I heard about that."

"Well, that's when I got out of the sex business. But instead of
bettering myself, I decided to marry one of my wealthy tricks."

"Uh, how'd that turn out?"

"It didn't. I stopped the wedding in the nick of time. But back to
Portia. She's in serious danger. Those antisocial, bottom feeders
prey on the helpless."

Khalil grunted in discomfort.

"In a case like this, I think it's your friend's duty to do whatever
she can to save Portia's life."

"I'll try and twist her arm."

After several agonizing hours of searching her mind for clues as to where Portia might have run, Khalil finally called.

"I can't talk. I have to meet with my board of directors in a few... but I have a name."

"Really?"

"Maria Gomez."

"She's Hispanic?"

"I would assume."

"That's such a common name."

"I know. Listen, I'll call you back after the meeting. We'll put our heads together and figure out a way to get you a visit with the young lady."

"Okay. Thanks, Khalil."

They disconnected and Saleema's wheels started spinning. Time wasn't on her side. Khalil had mentioned earlier that the girl was being transferred to a more secure facility. She could be upstate by now.

Surely the girl's family members had been granted a phone call. If only Saleema had a way of contacting the girl's parents, she'd plead Portia's case and ask them if Maria had provided any information that would help her find Portia.

MySpace! Most teens had a MySpace page. She searched and found Maria Gomez, fifteen years old, and living in Philadelphia. The page was private, so Saleema clicked on the page of Angelica Galarza, one of Maria's friends.

On Angelica's page, Saleema found a picture of a smiling Maria Gomez wearing a tiara and dressed in a sparkly gown. She was flanked by Angelica and another girl. The running caption boasted: *Maria's Sweet 15!*

There were tons of PictureTrail flicks of Maria's coming-of-age celebration. Apparently, Angelica and Maria were best friends.

And it was just Saleema's luck that one of the photos was taken outside. A big sign bore the name of the banquet hall.

Latino parents spent a pretty penny to commemorate their daughter's passage to womanhood. The owner of the venue would have kept records and would be able to point Saleema in the direction of the Gomez household.

Excited, Saleema searched the internet for the phone number of the venue. When she found it, instead of keying in the seven digits, she merely looked at the phone.

Like Khalil's colleague, the owner of the venue would most likely consider his clients' address as confidential.

Saleema needed the scoop, but she didn't have the rat-like cunning of a journalist or the smarmy investigative cleverness of a private detective. She'd have to rely on good, old-fashioned mother wit, which informed her that someone working at that venue could put her in touch with the Gomez family for the right price.

Her cash on hand totaled ninety dollars. She sure hoped that was the right price.

Saleema grabbed her purse. She didn't have time to wait for Khalil. He was rational, level-headed, and much too prudent to go along with this impulsive idea.

It was crazy. Journeying to the area that had the largest Hispanic population in the city had seemed like a good idea, but now deeply in the trenches, Saleema began to second-guess her decision.

The drive had begun smooth and without incident, but now she was slamming on her brakes every few seconds.

Kids darted out from behind parked cars and right into traffic at an alarming rate. Packs of teens at varying intervals would

meander across the street, defiantly dragging their feet, deliberately halting traffic as if it were their right. Honking horns did not deter them or hurry their pace. Frustrated drivers were met with glares and a cluster of raised middle fingers.

Saleema had scarcely avoided collisions with other motorists who drove by their own rules. Some made sudden turns without using their blinkers, others pulled out of parking spaces without warning or any concern for oncoming traffic.

Unable to deal with the bad drivers, she turned off the main street and took a series of narrow, residential blocks.

Big mistake.

Mischievous children who played in water from an uncapped fire hydrant made sure Saleema's Camry was splashed as she drove by.

The next block she ventured onto was a one-way street, where she narrowly avoided a head-on collision. Absurdly, a man who was either drunk or crazy, got in his car and began driving in the wrong direction—fast. The lunatic forced Saleema to swerve onto the sidewalk that was occupied by pedestrians and children at play.

Where the hell are the police when you need them?

For a few minutes, she was reluctant to move from the safety of the pavement, but for Portia's sake, Saleema had to get back in the trenches. She had to press on.

It was summer madness at its height. Her journey across town was turning out to be an epic and perilous adventure.

CHAPTER 23

It seemed to have taken forever, but she finally reached Front Street and Lehigh Avenue. She spotted the banquet hall on the busy street, but it provided no parking lot for patrons.

Over and over, Saleema circled the block. Eagle-eyed, she searched for a parking space.

A spot finally opened up in front of a meter. Looking over her shoulder, she quickly parallel parked into the space.

Outside the comfort of her air-conditioned car, she could hardly draw a breath. The air was thick with stifling heat and humidity. She searched inside her purse and scrounged up two quarters, which she hastily inserted into the meter.

Passersby, their faces scowled, were slowed by the heat. They moved sluggishly…cautiously…as if a faster pace would lead to heatstroke or some other life-threatening condition.

At the corner, the light changed to green and Saleema hurried across the busy intersection. She could feel the searing sun on her mahogany-colored skin, but thankfully, salvation was only a few feet away. The Lehigh Banquet Hall promised a cool refuge from the oppressive hot weather.

Three concrete steps led to the front door. She tugged on the sun-scorched metal handle, but it was locked tight. Unable to find a doorbell, she knocked sharply on the plate glass, and then peered inside.

From what she could tell, the lights were dim. No bustling activity. Too early for business, she supposed.

Maybe there were workers behind the scenes…prepping food in a kitchen or going over books in an office that was obscured from her view.

Hot and miserable, she rapped again. Harder. Still no one came to the door. She turned at the sound of footsteps behind her, and practically bumped smack into a tough-looking Hispanic youth who had bounded the steps.

"Whoa." Sighing in exasperation, the surly youth grudgingly gave Saleema space to pass by.

Saleema stood, staring at the teen's innumerable tattoos. Not only were his arms and legs inked, but there also tattoos above his brows, on the sides of his face, and both earlobes. Additionally, a vivid Puerto Rican flag was splashed across his neck.

His white wife beater was dampened with perspiration. A white towel, draped around his neck, accessorized his summer look.

Using the end of the towel, he mopped beads of sweat from his sullen face. "See something interesting?" Glowering with unprovoked teenage rage, he reached inside a deep pocket of his army green cargo shorts and pulled out a set of keys.

"I was wondering—" She had no idea what she was wondering. Unprepared, Saleema cleared her throat and pondered briefly, trying to formulate a question in her mind.

"You looking for Don?" he asked, helping her out, but sounding aggravated by the imposition.

She figured Don was the owner. "Yes. Is Don inside?" she asked hopefully. She'd left home looking cool and city chic in a loose cotton sundress and wedge sandals. Beaten by the sun for approximately ten minutes, she was already sweltering. She felt grubby. No longer crisp, her sundress was now rumpled and damp, and was sticking to her skin. Wanting some relief from the heat, she eyed the door, yearning to get inside and enjoy the glacial chill that an industrial air conditioner could provide.

"He don't come in on Thursday." The boy lowered his head dismissively and began studying the keys on the ring. Sweat dripped onto the towel as he clinked and clanged, sorting through the collection of keys.

"Damn." She was unable to conceal her disappointment.

"Yo, I don't have nothing to do with renting out this spot. I just clean up."

"Do you work here?" she asked, though she was pretty certain that she already knew the answer since he had possession of the keys to the front door.

He leaned back, indignant. "What's it to you?"

She was handling this all wrong. *Stop interrogating him*, Saleema told herself sternly. Changing her approach, she said, "My sister—" Then, as if she were too choked up to go on, she closed her eyes, pitifully and shook her head.

"Come on, lady. It's too hot for this shit. You think your sister is locked up inside the banquet hall or something? Get real." He grunted a sound of disgust.

Saleema pulled her hands away, taking a peek, gauging the situation. The boy turned his head toward the glass doors of the banquet hall, no doubt longing to get inside and cool off. He pulled his white T-shirt up and wiped his face. As suspected, his narrow chest looked like it was splattered with graffiti.

He pulled his shirt down. His scowling face was soon drenched by another outpouring of perspiration.

The mixture of sweat and a greasy complexion made the boy appear to be melting. Cranky and restless, he rattled the keys.

She knew she had to act quickly before he completely dismissed her. "My sister escaped from that detention center in the northeast."

"Huh?"

"My sister and a girl named Maria. Maria Gomez had her Quinceanera at this banquet hall—"

"Oh, yeah? The black girl who talked Maria into breaking out of the center—that's your sister?" His eyes twinkled with interest.

She didn't appreciate his assumption that Portia had been the mastermind. Saleema wanted to defend Portia, but held her tongue. "Do you know Maria?" she asked calmly.

"Yeah, she lives around here." He paused. "Well...she used to live around here before she got knocked."

"Do you have her address? I really, really need to speak with her parents."

His eyes shifted as he considered Saleema's request, and then he shook his head. "No, I'm no snitch."

"Portia...my sister. She's still missing."

"Sounds like you need to be talking to the cops."

"They're not cooperating. Would you help me out? I can pay you," she said sheepishly.

Saleema and the boy shared an uncomfortable silence.

"How much are you talking about?" He moved in closer.

Wearing all those tattoos, the boy gave the impression of being street savvy and highly experienced in conning people.

"Thirty bucks?" she offered, starting low.

"That'll work." He stuck out his hand, surprising her when he didn't demand more money.

"The address, please?"

"Oh, yeah, right. It's 315 Erie Avenue."

Satisfied, Saleema exhaled and peeled off three tens.

"Ain't nobody home. Maria's mother is in Pittsburgh. That's where they took Maria, you know," the boy said after pocketing the money.

"Why didn't you say that in the first place?"

"You didn't ask," he said, grinning like a Cheshire cat.

"What about her father? Is he around?"

"Nah, Maria's old man is back in Puerto Rico. Yo, that black girl…uh, your sister…Word is she got in a white Caddy with some dude who was flashing dough."

Saleema's stomach clenched painfully. *Portia got in a car with a stranger?* This was terrible news. Her greatest hope was that one of Portia's girlfriends was helping to hide her. Whenever ugly, terrifying thoughts crowded her mind, she'd managed to push them away and imagined that Portia was stowed away in a friend's basement, scared of being caught, but safe from harm.

"The dude tried to sweet talk Maria…tried to lure her into his car, but Maria's loyal to her roots. She would never mess around with a black cat."

"Who told you about the man driving the Cadillac?"

The boy started backing up, gesturing with his hands. "Yo, what's with the twenty questions? I gave you all the information I have."

"I just need…I'm wondering how you could know…um, who exactly told you about Portia…my sister?" She was so shaken, she stumbled over her words.

He shrugged. "Word gets around."

"Will another twenty buy a name?"

Saleema reached in her purse and extracted a twenty-dollar bill. "I need a name."

"Angelica," the tatted boy said. He snatched the money out of Saleema's hand. "Twenty more will get you a last name," he said, smiling and posturing like he'd just won a game of craps.

But Saleema didn't need a last name. She knew it. She rolled her eyes at the boy, whirled around.

"Twenty bucks!" the boy shouted. "I'll give you Angelica's last name and address."

Ignoring him, Saleema trotted off to her car.

"So this is the last place Portia was spotted?" Khalil asked, surveying the McDonald's parking lot.

"Yes, Portia and Maria were hanging near the entrance, bumming money from patrons as they came and went. The guy driving the Cadillac took the ramp that leads to I-95 South."

"I'm impressed by your investigative skills."

Saleema shrugged off the compliment. "That inked-up kid led me to Maria's best friend, Angelica. I hit her up on MySpace. Angelica was very eager to tell me everything that Maria had confided over the phone. Teenage girls love to gossip."

"Still, you did some pretty good detective work."

"Getting this far was easy. Now, I'm at a dead end. That predator could have taken Portia anywhere. Who knows what he's doing to her?" She shook away images of a maniac having unlimited access to Portia, torturing her at his leisure.

"I know, but what else can you do at this point? It's time to step back and let the police handle this."

"I can't step back. Portia's not at the top of anyone's list… not her family and not law enforcement. Besides, even if the police knew something, they wouldn't tell me. I'm not family."

Khalil nodded in understanding. "And her family's not particularly interested."

"Not in the least," Saleema huffed.

He gave her a comforting pat on the back as he started the ignition.

Saleema sighed in frustration. "I hate giving up."

"We're not giving up, but there's no point in hanging around here."

"I know," she conceded, studying the parking lot as Khalil wheeled

around, exiting the lot. Taking one last look over her shoulder, her eyes swept the area, as if Portia might be hiding somewhere in the shadows.

"Do you have a recent picture of Portia?"

"Yeah, I took a group photo of all the girls. Why?"

"I'm getting an idea." Eyebrows crinkled, Khalil wheeled out of the parking lot and merged into the traffic on Oregon Avenue.

"What's your idea?"

"We can crop Portia's image out of the group shot."

"Okay..."

"Portia has been abducted and we're going to get the community involved in finding her."

"Portia is considered an escaped criminal...not a kidnapped child."

"But we both know whoever was driving that white Cadillac abducted a minor."

"True." Saleema gazed at Khalil, nodding, encouraging him to continue.

"Portia's family may be apathetic, but I'm sure we can generate some interest in the community; persuade people to get involved in helping to find her."

"How are we going to do that? If Portia's own mother doesn't care that she's missing, what makes you think we can rouse the neighborhood?"

"We can start by posting fliers. I could get some of my students together. Section by section, we can blanket the city with Portia's picture."

Saleema's heart lifted. "That's a great idea." Feeling a rush of warmth toward Khalil, Saleema couldn't hold back a smile. Not only was Khalil intelligent, he was also a problem solver. A very appealing trait.

"I love it when you smile," he said sincerely.

She blushed and ducked her head shyly. Pulling herself together, she looked up and gazed at Khalil with a no-nonsense look in her eyes.

"Back to the subject..." he said, taking a hint and redirecting himself to the topic. "I'm thinking...a candlelight vigil in Portia's neighborhood might be a good way to get the ball rolling." Tapping the steering wheel with his finger, he waited for Saleema to respond.

Cynically, Saleema shook her head. "They do vigils for murder victims in Portia's neighborhood. I seriously doubt anyone will have any sympathy for a runaway."

"Hmm." He stared ahead at traffic, which had slowed.

"Honestly, you and I are probably the only people who are actively looking for Portia. The police couldn't care less. And her neighbors..." Saleema frowned. "Put it this way, Portia is an acquired taste. She's boisterous and has a bad attitude. Her neighbors are probably thinking, 'good riddance.' I can't imagine them experiencing a sense of loss."

He absorbed her words and then said, "We can make them care."

"Obviously, you're not from the 'hood."

"You don't know everything about me," he said with a sly smile.

Saleema went silent. He was right; she didn't know everything about him. She only knew that he was charming, kind, educated, ambitious, successful, and oh so handsome. She knew enough about him to realize that until she got her life together, she would feel vulnerable if she allowed Khalil any role in her life that extended beyond friendship.

But we have so much in common, she argued with what she perceived as rational thinking and sound judgment. Sighing, she stole a wistful glance at him, and then quickly averted her eyes. She'd be so

embarrassed if Khalil caught her in the midst of a longing gaze.

"If you think a candlelight vigil is over the top, then how about a community meeting? I know the director at the Haverford Recreation Center. I could talk to him."

"Khalil," she said, with strained patience. "The people in that neighborhood are concerned about surviving another day; they're not going to go pouring into a recreation center over a girl who had daily fistfights with their kids, cursed out and even got violent with teachers, and kept trouble brewing everywhere she went." Saleema shook her head. "Portia was a piece of work. But I understand her. She reminds me of myself."

"You didn't give up on yourself, did you?"

"No, of course not."

"And you haven't given up on Portia…"

"Where's this going?"

"You have faith in yourself and obviously you believe there's hope for Portia, so don't be so quick to give up on the people in the 'hood. Our ancestors had an indomitable spirit. It's still alive, lying dormant. We can bring the black community together and make them care about all the Portias of the world."

"How?" she questioned softly.

"The offer of a reward will lure them to a meeting. It can also be an incentive for someone who knows something that will lead us to Portia's whereabouts."

I don't have any money to put up for a reward. Saleema swallowed as she tussled with a bout of guilt over all the frivolous spending she'd done before opening Head Up. If she had even a portion of the money she went through on reckless shopping sprees, she'd be able to put up the reward money without a second thought.

She was flat broke. To help find Portia, she'd gladly take out a second mortgage on her home…but that wasn't even an option.

The mortgage company had done all they could to help her; it was just a matter of time before her home went into foreclosure.

"I honestly don't have any money to put toward a reward."

"Most people don't. Don't worry. We'll get donations," he said with self-assurance, as he weaved through traffic.

Her shoulders began to relax. She wasn't fighting this battle alone. Khalil was lending his support. Coming up with ideas, making plans to help find Portia.

Though Saleema kept a straight face, a smile was blossoming... this one was in her heart.

CHAPTER 24

At Thirty-third and Brandywine Streets, the heart of the section of West Philly known as "the bottom," Saleema and four girls from Head Up waited for Khalil to arrive with the fliers.

She'd called eight girls the previous night, but Portia was so disliked, she'd only been able to persuade Amirah, Stacey, Tasha, and Chyna to hit the streets with her in an effort to help find the missing girl.

"What's taking your friend so long to get here?" Tasha wanted to know, frowning as she took a swig from a bottle of water.

In sullen silence, Amirah stood with her shoulders slumped, groaning and shifting from foot to foot.

"I wish he'd hurry up. It's too hot to be standing around like this." Stacey twisted her lips into a petulant pout.

Chyna was showing off her thick, shapely legs in a pair of cut-off shorts. "I was on my way to Kelly's pool, Miss Saleema. I could be chilling with the lifeguard, but I came out here on the strength of you."

"I know and I appreciate your support. I wouldn't have asked if I didn't feel so passionate about Portia's situation." Saleema glanced at her cell phone, checking the time. "He would have been here on time, but the copy center didn't have the order ready when he went to pick it up."

There was a collective sigh, followed by impatient utterances.

Chyna slathered on some lip gloss. "I don't even like Portia like that. I'm dead up. I feel like changing my mind."

Saleema looked stunned. "How can you say that? If something bad happened to one of you, wouldn't you expect someone to care?"

"Yeah, but it's not like Portia is innocent. She escaped from that place and got in some man's car. That was her choice," Chyna responded.

Saleema looked into Chyna's brown eyes. "She made a mistake."

"Why we gotta burn up in this hot sun over Portia's mistake?" Chyna mumbled.

"Because her mistake could be deadly," Saleema said grimly. "It's our obligation to try and help find her."

"I don't see why. Like I said, I'm out here because you asked me to," Chyna insisted.

Slouched against the brick wall of a dry cleaning business, the four girls began pointing out Portia's many flaws, and openly questioning their sanity in even trying to bring her rowdy behavior back into their lives.

If they were at Head Up, and having a sharing session, Saleema would allow each girl to vent and then they'd discuss ways that they could help Portia to mirror their good behavior. But at the moment, she had too much on her mind to successfully alter their attitudes.

She stared at the moving traffic and sighed in relief when she saw Khalil's SUV barreling along Thirty-third Street.

There was a stretch of silence as the girls gazed at the Nissan Murano, their eyes filled with suspicion and hostility.

Armed with bright yellow staple guns and carrying boxes containing flyers, Khalil and four broad-shouldered, young men poured out of the SUV.

Straightening up their postures, all four girls became enlivened

and wore pleasant expressions. There was no indication of the resentment they each felt toward Portia and the task that lay ahead.

Chyna flipped her ponytail over her shoulder and quickly applied more lip gloss.

"This is Dr. Gardner, girls," Saleema said. She glanced at the students from Khalil's school. They all wore serious expressions, indicating that they were here to get the job done. She hoped their sense of civic duty would rub off on her girls.

"Dr. Gardner, would you introduce your students?"

"Sure. This is Mel, Fabrio, Rashan, and Evan." Khalil pointed at each boy as he spoke his name.

"Hi," the girls chorused together. No longer disturbed by the rising temperature, they seemed instantly soothed by the presence of the quartet of good-looking young men.

Before Saleema could introduce them, Chyna cut in. "My name is Chyna, better known as Classy C."

Not to be outdone, each of the other three girls presented herself with a catchy alias in addition to her given name.

Mel, Fabrio, Rashan, and Evan all kept their cool, nodding in acknowledgment after each introduction, and sprinkling in a few deep-toned, "What's up?"

The girls blushed and giggled, obviously enamored by the physical attractiveness of Khalil's students.

Khalil got down to business. "It's already eighty-four degrees and it's going to get hotter. I apologize for asking you to work in this heat."

"That's okay," Amirah murmured, forgetting that she'd been complaining about the weather. Amirah placed her hand on the waistline of her drawstring shorts, and stood in a feminine manner in which Saleema had never seen her stand.

Chyna's glistening lips parted, showing off even, white teeth.

"We don't mind." She flashed the boys with a big, flirtatious smile.

"I realize that this would be less daunting if we put up the flyers after the sun goes down," Khalil said. "Unfortunately, we don't have another second to waste. A young girl…one of your friends… is missing. An eyewitness states that she got in a car with an adult male. She hasn't been seen since. We believe her life is in danger and want to get her away from her kidnapper and back home safely."

There was something about Khalil's serious attitude and professional demeanor that encouraged the girls to be on their best behavior. Surprisingly, there were no more complaints about the heat or their dislike of Portia.

Working in pairs, Khalil and Saleema and the group of young adults covered the area with Portia's image on sheets of paper, headed by the word: *MISSING.*

# CHAPTER 25

"How do you like her hair?" Flashy asked Bullet. His devilish grin expressed malicious triumph.

In the makeshift beauty salon in his basement, Flashy had spitefully tinted Brielle's hair with streaks of blue, raspberry, and yellow.

Brielle hadn't been given a mirror. Her drowsy eyes shifted to Gianna's face, searching for an answer regarding the status of her hair.

Unable to meet Brielle's medicated gaze, Gianna looked away in embarrassment.

Both Bubbles and Brielle were given an assortment of drugs on a daily basis. Gianna was often given the task of administering the pills.

Bullet said Bubbles needed medication to keep her from fighting with the customers. And Brielle was drugged because he was sick of hearing her whining and crying about her baby.

With a squinted eye, Bullet took in the botched dye job. "Where'd you get your beautician's license? You got her dome looking like a pack of Skittles," he said, laughing.

"You told me to fix it so she'd be unrecognizable."

"It's all good. I like the look."

"You do?" Flashy asked, shocked and annoyed.

"Yeah, I wasn't feeling that name, Tootsie Roll. This bitch is getting a new name. I'm calling her Skittles from now on."

Flashy threw up his hands in defeat. "That name is stupid." He

plopped into a chair and sulked because Bullet was pleased with the hairstyle he'd created out of malice.

"All I need is a few more pieces of candy and my stable's gon' be tight," Bullet bragged.

"You need to make it happen with the three hoes you already got." Flashy fanned out the masculine fingers on his left hand and turned up his nose. "I thought you'd have all the fingers on at least one of my hands blinging by now. I'm supposed to be Chester's version of Kimora Lee Simmons. When is my fabulosity gonna pop off?"

"I ain't on your timeframe."

"Obviously, you ain't on no type of timeframe. You slackin', boo."

"I'm not putting these young hoes out on front street right now. They gotta keep working on the low until we can move to the West Coast, Hawaii, or somewhere."

"Another pipe dream. Now that you've discovered Chester, you ain't going anywhere. You like the feeling of being a big fish in a small pond."

"Fuck Chester. Ain't nobody trying be lingering in this lil' hick town."

There was some truth in Flashy's words. Bullet could never be a heavy hitter in Philly. Gianna recalled how Bullet had backed down to the baller dude who was driving the Escalade that day when Bullet had tracked her down, barefoot with his curls wet with shampoo lather.

Though Bullet was secretive about his sex operation, Gianna knew that in Chester he'd been getting a level of respect that he'd never gotten in Philly. She'd overheard Flashy fussing plenty of times about the way Bullet was drawing unnecessary attention by flashing his knot of money when he bought drinks for strangers and gave out big tips in the local bars.

"So take your ass back to Philly; ain't nobody holding a gun to your head, either. You and these drugged-up bitches ain't doing nothing for me but tearing up my beautiful house."

Bullet's cell pinged. Body leaning, he checked out the screen with a big, twisted grin. "Money call," he announced and then put the cell back in his pocket. He clapped his hands together. "Let's bounce. Lollipop and Skittles...you two hoes about to showcase your talents in a freaky duet."

Heading for the front door, Skittles walked unsteadily ahead of Bullet and Gianna. Bullet whispered in Lollipop's ear, "While the trick is up in that ass, you need to be rustling through his pockets. You know the drill."

"Yeah, I know it."

Bullet slipped Gianna his knife. "Poke that muthafucka if he tries to rewrite the script."

The motel room stank to high heavens, but the trick didn't seem to notice. His moans of ecstasy filled the room.

High as a kite, Skittles' mouth hung open, her tongue lolled, and her eyes were at half-mast as she endured anal penetration without a care in the world.

Revolted, Gianna looked away. Then forcing herself to focus on the task at hand, she returned her gaze to the trick.

His wrinkly eyes were squeezed shut as he plowed into Skittles. Normally, this would have been a good time for Gianna to strike. But she couldn't get near his wallet with his pants hanging around his ankles.

Shit! The old, crusty trick was making her job harder than it needed to be.

She hadn't done her share of the sex work because the gray-

haired, white man was so excited about getting between Skittles' tiny butt cheeks; he seemed to forget that he had paid Bullet for services from both girls.

Bullet would be heated if she didn't leave the motel with all dude's money and valuables. *Fuck!* She'd started using a lot of profanity lately…out loud and in her head.

While Gianna tried to come up with a plan, she heard ol' boy groan. The sound of him climaxing was loud and torturous, as if he were on the verge of a massive heart attack.

Ol' boy pulled out and Skittles collapsed on her tummy with a smile on her face. Gianna couldn't tell if Skittles was glad that the session was over or just blissfully high.

Gasping and breathing hard, the trick rolled down the feces-spattered condom and flicked it inside the waste bin.

Ew! She felt like gagging. The room smelled worse than before. She hated doing duets with nasty-ass Skittles. Working with Bubbles was easier on Gianna's weak stomach.

"I'll be ready for you in a minute," he gasped, his breathing so ragged and uneven, he sounded like he was about to croak.

Gianna's eyes scanned the room as she tried to figure out how to separate the trick and his assets without him noticing.

He reached downward and dug inside a pants pocket. "I know I brought another condom."

"What do you need another condom for?"

His eyes, clouded by glaucoma or some old folk's disease, lit up like sunshine. "You don't mind if I go bareback?"

Gianna turned up her nose. "I'm not doing anything unless you take a shower." Then it hit her! Get the nasty old geezer in the shower, and then scrounge through his pockets.

She'd take his money, credit cards, and anything else worth having, and then she'd grab Skittles, and be out.

But Skittles was naked. Best to get her dressed before she tried to carry out her scheme.

Her voice turned to honey. "Wanna know what turns me on?"

"What's that?"

"Sex in the shower."

"Really?"

"There's something about the feeling of warm water splashing against my back while I'm on my knees, taking your big dick between my lips. Mmm." She licked her lips, suggesting that he possessed the key to her own sexual bliss.

The trick gave a groan of sexual delight. He kicked off his pants, allowing them to fall on the floor. He gave her a wink as he began to unbutton his shirt. Slowly, teasingly, as if he were a male stripper preparing to reveal an oiled and well-sculpted torso. What he revealed was a skeletal frame with ripples of loose, dry skin.

His dick, now limp, was average size...not big as Gianna had claimed to pump up his ego. At this man's age...fifty or sixty, Gianna couldn't tell, she simply had him pegged as an old fool who should have known that it would be next to impossible to get his pecker back up and operating.

Gianna looked worriedly at the bedside clock.

"What's wrong?" the trick asked.

"I only have a half-hour left to spend with you." She poked out her lips, pouting as if a mere half-hour would deprive her of quality dick-sucking time.

"I can pay you more," he said eagerly, reaching inside a pants pocket and extracting a worn leather wallet.

"Okay." She didn't set a price. She held out her hand and accepted the extra fifty-dollar bill that he placed inside her palm. Her eyes, however, were set on the bulk of the wallet as he folded it and returned it to his pocket.

"Ready for the shower?" the trick wanted to know.

"Um…we should get her dressed. When my boyfriend calls, I have to be ready to go."

"Does he beat you?" he asked, his voice a mixture of excitement and repugnance.

"All the time."

"How old are you?"

"I'll get in trouble if I give out my age."

"Okay, I don't want to cause you any problems."

"Help me get her dressed." Gianna nodded her head toward Skittles, who was sprawled out and snoring.

"I guess I gave her a real workout?" he said, taking credit for Skittles' state of exhaustion.

"Yup, you sure did." Gianna put Skittles' bra and panties in her bag. No point in wasting time trying to get her into her underwear.

Holding Skittles by her shoulders, the trick held her upright while Gianna worked her tank top over her head. But getting Skittles into her skintight jeans proved to be a difficult task.

"Why don't we finish getting her dressed after you take care of me?" the man suggested, his tone changing from patient to agitated as he pushed strands of gray hair from his sweaty face.

"No, I have to get her dressed and ready to roll. I can't be late. My boyfriend…well, he's more like my manager, but he'll get mad if I'm not on time for my next appointment. "

"Oh, yeah? This manager of yours…Does he slap you around when you're late?" The trick's eyes widened with interest.

"I wish."

"Really? You wish he'd slap you around?"

"No. What I meant was, I wish that was the worst of what he does to me."

"Wanna talk about it? You can be honest with me. This manager guy sets up your appointments. Do you get to keep any of the profits?"

"No."

"So he's actually your pimp?"

If there wasn't so much freaky excitement in his eyes, she might have thought she could trust the man with the big secret—that she was not turning tricks on her own free will. But it was apparent that her status of unwitting flesh peddler would simply be another turn-on for this pervert.

"Yeah, he's my pimp."

He shook his head at the shame of it all. "Does this pimp of yours beat you with a wire hanger?"

She zippered Skittles' jeans. "I don't want to talk about it."

"Okay. That's understandable." Fondling his dick, the trick sprang up from the bed, wielding a full-blown hard-on.

Viagra, Gianna told herself.

"That pimp of yours told me you were a very experienced young woman. I guess you inner city girls start giving blow jobs from the crib," he said, and then chuckled at his wit.

His comment had Gianna steaming on the inside, but she smiled at him as if she had taken the slur as a big compliment.

"Get the water ready while I get undressed," she said, using her best interpretation of a sexy voice. "Make it nice and warm for me."

He didn't have to be told twice. The trick took off his watch and raced to the bathroom, leaving Gianna alone with his pants and his bulging wallet.

The first thing she did was inspect the watch. It was a worthless Timex. *Fuck!* She clipped his wallet and stuck it in her bag. She should have grabbed up Skittles next and quickly yanked her out of the motel room. But Gianna was too mad to let the trick's

comment go unpunished. She strolled into the bathroom with Bullet's shank in her hand.

Like the famous scene from the old movie, *Psycho*, Gianna yanked back the shower curtain.

Startled, the trick wiped water from his eyes. "Why didn't you take your clothes off?"

Gianna didn't answer. She swiftly attacked him with the knife, poking his left hip, and then his thigh.

"Ahh!" he yelled. "What the hell is wrong with you?" he screamed when she stepped inside the shower and punctured both his arms with amazingly rapid speed.

"I should disembowel you, you pervert bastard," she spat, leaving him hanging onto the shower curtains, cut in several places, but not seriously injured.

Slipping around inside the shower stall, the trick tried to assess the damage.

Meanwhile, Gianna, angry at the world, smacked the shit out of Skittles. "Get up, girl. We gotta bounce."

 CHAPTER 26

T ired of living out of storage spaces, and sick of listening to Flashy bitch about the invasion of his privacy, Bullet moved the three kidnapped girls into a rented house in a remote section of Chester.

The ramshackle single house was a two-story residence that needed exterior and interior repairs. Not wanting to draw any unnecessary attention to his trio of young captives, Bullet did not request that the landlord make any of the badly needed repairs.

No one in the town of Chester seemed interested in how Bullet earned his livelihood. No one had inquired about the young girls who were seen riding around in his car. The residents who lived nearby, ravished by drugs and poverty, were either too high or too preoccupied with their own daily survival to be concerned about Bullet's association with the girls.

He had felt vulnerable and paranoid in Philadelphia, a city with an assortment of missing kids' posters stapled to telephone polls. All eyes cast in his direction seemed filled with suspicion. Fingers appeared positioned to point at him with accusation.

It was hard to transport the girls back and forth in a city where there was a strong law enforcement presence. Avoiding the cops in Philly was impossible. Too many cops. Squad cars cruising on damn near every city block.

Inside Chester, Bullet felt cocooned in apathy. The people appeared to move about with blinders on their eyes…unseeing and uncaring of what was taking place around them. The small

police department, challenged by the steadily escalating drug war and plagued by a high murder rate, was too busy to notice Bullet and his captives.

Chester became a safe haven from the law. It was the perfect place for the girls to hustle.

Right now, he was excited to be in close proximity to the casino where he'd uncovered a large amount of out-of-town clientele. Men just passing through, who didn't want trouble and who wouldn't seek justice when their wallets or other goods turned up missing after a tryst with Lollipop and the other two girls. Lollipop, trained to stick and move, was becoming an experienced bandit while Bubbles and Skittles were sexual decoys. Human props.

Gianna was asleep in Bullet's bedroom. The oversized, decrepit air conditioner set in the window was turned on high, sending out blasts of frigid air and creating a loud squeal. She snuggled deeper beneath the blue comforter.

Skittles and Bubbles were in the second bedroom, handcuffed to the metal headboard of the bed they shared.

"Yo, Lollipop," Bullet called from the living room where he was smoking a blunt and watching a rerun of *MTV Cribs*. Overpowered by the blaring TV and the loud air conditioner, his voice wasn't heard. He called her again.

He stomped to the bedroom, yanked her arm. He leaned down and bellowed in her ear. "Get the fuck up!"

"I'm sorry," she said, bolting upright, unaware of what she was apologizing for.

"Get up! Wake them bitches up and take 'em to the bathroom before one of 'em pisses the fuckin' bed!"

Gianna scrambled out of bed. "You want me to give 'em some more pills before I put 'em back on lockdown?"

Face scrunched, Bullet searched the ceiling for an answer, and

then shook his head. "Nah. I'm sick of seeing them dragging around all doped up. I could be making a helluva lot more dough if you didn't have to babysit their asses."

"I know," she agreed, hoping that if she went along with his tirade, she could speed things along and get back in bed. She was trying her best to stay focused, but she was sleepy as hell.

"If I had three bitches working in three different locations, I'd have my new truck by now," he complained.

Naked and cold, Gianna hugged herself. She'd worked until six in the morning, and according to the bedside clock, it wasn't even noon yet. *What the hell is he doing up so early in the morning? Snorting that stuff.*

Her feelings for Bullet fluctuated all the time. There were times when she thought she loved him. Believed that he was her man… her daddy who looked out for her best interests.

Then there were times like now, when he was high as a damn kite. During moments like this, she despised his ass. She imagined herself holding his gun and making him kneel while she fired the weapon at close range, killing the muthafucka, execution-style.

Though she was extremely sleepy, she knew better than to yawn or even lower her eyes to rest them. Bullet expected her undivided attention. Without protest, she waited for him to come to a conclusion.

His eyes continued to dart upward in thought. "Umph," he grunted, and then shook his head in disgust.

"You want me to hurry up and get Bubbles and Skittles to the bathroom before they piss all over the place?"

"Nah, fuck those hoes. I want you to get on this dick." He smiled. "Some good head might take my mind off my problems."

Bullet dropped his boxers and sat on the edge of the bed. "Start on my balls. Lick 'em nice and slow…the way I taught you."

"Lay down, Daddy. Relax; I gotchu. I know how you like it." Cringing inside, she displayed a big fake smile.

Bullet kicked off his boxers and settled into a comfortable position on the bed, his head resting upon the palms of his hands.

She dove under the covers, anxious to warm her cold, quivering body.

"Suck it like you Superhead," he grunted, thrusting his dick between her lips so violently, the knob collided with the roof of her mouth.

Slowing him down and trying to control his forceful movements, she gripped the base of his rock-hard dick and then licked the drops of moisture that oozed out of the crown.

"Mmm, you taste good," she murmured. She made smacking sounds with her mouth, intending to further arouse him.

His dick pulsated in her hand. Her lips engulfed his length, sliding gently over the smooth top and the thickened veins, doing him the way she'd been taught. With her head bobbing up and down, she sucked hard and fast, trying her best to get him off.

Suddenly Bullet's dick went soft.

Oh no! She wanted to scream. Times like this were terrible. Gianna would rather suck a strange trick's dick than give Bullet head after he'd snorted cocaine. When he was high like this, his dick refused to stay hard, but that didn't diminish his desire or dissuade him from trying to bust a nut.

Determinately, she seized his limp soldier and tightened her hold, struggling to stimulate the flaccid dick into a firm erection. She wanted to get out from under the blue comforter and catch a breath of fresh air, but she remained under the stifling covers, hand-stroking as though her life depended on it.

Making no progress, she switched up her approach. She teased his meat with a feathery touch. She applied gentle caresses, lightly rolling her thumb over the head of his dick, and up and down the

shaft. But despite these attempts, Bullet's manhood hung limp.

"Stop playing. I didn't ask you for a hand job. It'll come back to life if it's pumping up in something hot and juicy."

She rubbed her jawbone, trying to quickly massage away the weariness and the pain.

"Hurry up!" He threw the covers off of her. "No wonder I can't keep it up; I need to see my pipe sliding in and out of your mouth."

With puckered lips, she drew his droopy dick inside her warm mouth.

"You want Daddy to cum on your face?"

"Uh-huh," she mumbled, which was a lie.

She sucked and sucked, but her extensive oral training could not get his burned-out soldier to stand up straight.

"Damn! You sucking too hard. Making my jawn sore." Grimacing, he pulled out of the suction-hold she had on his dick.

Thank God! This coked-up fool is finally giving up. Sweet, merciful sleep was just a few minutes away.

"You slippin' on your head game." Bullet arched a brow accusingly.

"I'm sorry, Daddy," she said, batting her lashes at a rapid rate. Fighting sleep, she was having a difficult time keeping her drowsy eyes open.

"Sorry don't satisfy my needs." Pouting, he fondled his sagging dick.

Bullet was feeling sorry for himself. Not good. His self-pity usually led to aggression. She braced herself knowing that, at any moment, a smack upside the head was coming. Next, he'd curse her out and call her vile names. His last act of violence would be to shake her until her brains rattled. Then he'd stomp back to the living room where he'd snort some more lines of cocaine.

When his freakish desires reawakened, he'd return to the bedroom holding his rigid dick in his hands.

Gianna hoped she could catch at least a half-hour or so worth of sleep before he launched the next sexual assault.

Bullet was so insensitive. Why didn't he understand that breaking up her sleep like this made her jumpy at night, preventing her from being able to concentrate when she needed to pull a sleight of hand to clip a trick?

Every time she made peace with her existence, whenever she convinced herself that she could endure living under Bullet's control, he did something callous that reminded her how hopelessly fucked-up her life truly was.

She wished Bullet would take his coked-up, crazy ass back to the living room so she could snuggle up under the covers and catch at least a couple of z's.

But Bullet didn't make a move. He lay on his back, silent. His eyes bounced around crazily. His demented mind was busy at work.

Gianna tensed, knowing that Bullet was cooking up some lewd act for her to perform.

She gave a shuddering breath, recalling how the last time he couldn't get it up, he'd made her lick cocaine off his flimsy dick. *Lord, please don't let this grimy nigga turn me into a drug addict.*

Hit with a sudden bright idea, Bullet sat up straight. "Go unhook Skittles. Bring her in here." Changing his mind, he frowned. "Nah, I ain't fucking with her nasty ass. Get Bubbles."

CHAPTER 27

Bullet had flipped the script. He wanted to fuck with doped-up Bubbles. She found the request surprising since Bullet hardly ever had sex with Bubbles or Skittles. It was about time. She wished he'd give her a break and use their services more often.

But there was a problem. Where was she going to sleep if Bubbles slept with Bullet? The living room was practically empty. The only furnishings were a sixty-inch television, a coffee table, and a lumpy chair that should have been on top of the trash heap.

She sure wished Bullet would stop spending so much money on coke and buy some decent furniture for the house. There was nowhere for her to rest comfortably except Bullet's bedroom. Bullet had a nice queen-sized bed with a brand-new mattress and box spring. New bed linen as well.

Naked with the key ring in her hand, she made her way to Bubbles and Skittles' bedroom. The instant she crossed the threshold, she stopped shivering. The small room was as hot as a sauna. A funky sauna. The urine-stained mattress gave off the odor of a foul-smelling public restroom.

Though the bedroom windows were opened a crack, metal bars ensured that the girls could not break free. There was an oscillating tower fan near the bed that circulated only hot, fetid air.

Gianna stared down at Bubbles and Skittles. Both girls lay on top of a bare, pee-stained mattress. Skittles had on a yellow top

with a dirty collar. It was time for Bullet to buy the girl some clothes or take the ones she had to the Laundromat. Nude at the bottom, the jeans Skittles wore daily were tossed on the floor beside the bed. Gianna shook her head. Skittles was looking real bad. Sickly. Getting skinnier by the day.

Bubbles was naked and plump as ever. Being drugged most of the time didn't interfere with her appetite. Slobber trickled out the side of her mouth. The slobber, along with the unsightly scar on her face, was not a good look. Gianna shook her head, feeling a mixture of pity and disgust. It was hard to believe that this poor slob was the same loud-mouth, obnoxious girl she'd met in the McDonald's parking lot.

Gianna poked Bubbles in the shoulder. Bubbles mumbled incoherently.

"Get up, Bubbles. Bullet wants to get with you."

Bubbles muttered more nonsense and tried to shift into a more comfortable position, but couldn't. Seemingly in an OxyContin coma, Skittles was stock still. She didn't so much as twitch or utter a sound.

"Bubbles! Get up, girl." She unlocked the single handcuff that secured Bubbles to the rickety metal headboard. Eyes closed, Bubbles rubbed the wrist that had been shackled and then turned onto her stomach.

"Come on, Bubbles." Frustrated, Gianna tugged on Bubbles' arm. Bubbles yanked her arm away and tucked it beneath her tummy, her big butt tooted up in the air.

Catching sight of a bottle of air freshener on top of the dresser on the other side of the room, Gianna came up with an idea.

Sorry, Bubbles, but you should have cooperated with me. She sprayed Bubbles' bare ass cheeks.

With a grunt, Bubbles flopped over and lay on her back. Gianna discharged another burst of tropical-scented air freshener. This

time she aimed at Bubbles' face. Bubbles sputtered in agitation and wiped the moisture from her eyes.

Using all her strength, Gianna heaved Bubbles out the bed and onto her feet.

Bubbles staggered and stumbled. Gianna entwined their arms and dragged the sluggish girl down the hall. Tired and irritated, she shoved Bubbles forward when they finally reached Bullet's bedroom.

"Here she go," Gianna announced, giving Bubbles a hard shove. Bubbles lurched forward, her big titties bouncing as she plopped onto the bed.

"Cock her legs open for me," Bullet instructed.

Aggravated, Gianna gripped Bubbles' ankles and pushed her legs up until her knees bent, and then she spread the girl's thick thighs, creating space for Bullet. He smacked Bubbles' crotch with his limp appendage and laughed. He kept smacking the mound of her pussy until his dick rose and came back to life.

Her work complete, Gianna scooted over to the far side of the bed. She tried to make herself as small as possible, just in case Bullet needed more room to get his fuck on with Bubbles.

"Where you want me to fuck you? Your pussy or your mouth?" Bullet asked Bubbles.

"Uh-huh," Bubbles answered nonsensically.

"Oh, yeah? You like giving your daddy head? That's how you get down?"

The headboard slammed against the wall as Bullet plowed into Bubbles.

"You like licking pussy juice off my dick?" Bullet said, sounding perverted.

"It's all good," Bubbles said, in a droning tone similar to someone being hypnotized.

Gianna wished Bullet would hurry up with Bubbles. She couldn't

sleep. Her head jerked to the rhythm of the mattress bouncing up and down.

"I'ma give you some oral action in a minute." The words came out gruff; sounded like a threat.

"Do you like feeling a big dick slippin' and slidin' up and down your tongue?"

Gianna turned up her nose. Bullet sounded perverted...like a slimy trick. She imagined Bullet forcing his dick down Bubbles' throat and flooding her mouth with a huge eruption of cum.

"Damn, you a good ho. Got Daddy's dick hard as a brick. I'ma flip you over and get some from the back. You like it doggy-style?"

"Sometimes, I do," Bubbles murmured.

That's a shame. Bubbles is so out of it, her voice is slurred. She don't even know what she's saying. Gianna wanted to cover her head with a pillow to block out Bullet's raspy sex talk.

Gianna woke up to the sound of crying. Shielding her eyes from the bright sunlight that filtered through wooden shutters, she sat up and looked around. Bullet and Bubbles were snuggled together like lovers. They were both knocked out cold from a night of drugging and fucking.

The crying started again, along with the annoying rattle of metal scraping metal. It was Skittles, trying to break free from the handcuff that kept her confined in bed.

I'm not getting up to walk her to the bathroom. She pulled the covers over her head, but Skittles' sounds of misery grew louder.

Damn! She flung off the comforter and stalked across the room, grabbed the key ring off the dresser, and noticed Bullet's phone. She reached a shaky hand toward the cell phone.

Bullet coughed, startling her.

She dropped her arm and rushed out of the bedroom.

Holding Skittles by the scruff of her collar, Gianna lugged her to the bathroom. Skittles moaned and cried for her daughter. Most times, Skittles' motherly lament softened Gianna's heart. But not today. She rolled her eyes at the whining girl and focused her thoughts on Bullet's cell phone.

"Hurry up, Skittles," she snapped, anxious to get back to Bullet's bedroom so she could get her hands on his cell phone. He usually kept his phone next to him in bed. This was a one-time slip-up and a perfect opportunity for her to sneak a call to her mother. Gianna smiled, picturing the police kicking in the door and coming to her rescue.

Thoughts of freedom filled her mind as she led Skittles back to confinement.

Back in the bedroom, she quietly crept past the bed where Bullet and Bubbles were cuddled together. She glared at both of them, wishing she had Bullet's gun within reach so she could give him a shot to the head.

Bubbles could get a pass. She was not the enemy.

Motivated by righteous anger, Gianna picked up the cell phone. She pushed the first digit. The beep was so loud, it made her flinch. She looked over her shoulder at Bullet. His head was beneath the comforter. Both he and Bubbles snored in concert.

After releasing a deep breath, she hit the second number of her mother's area code. This time the sound seemed louder than before, jarring her. She stole a nervous peek at Bullet, and then sighed in relief. He was still sleeping peacefully.

She took another fortifying breath and readied herself to press the third digit.

Bullet cleared his throat.

Shook by a chilling fear, Gianna dropped the phone. Her eyes expanded in alarm, she jerked around, and was prepared to meet Bullet's piercing gaze. Her mind raced frantically to come up with a convoluted explanation for touching his phone.

But he was still buried beneath the covers. *Thank God!* She bent down and quickly scooped up the phone, assessing it, praying it hadn't been damaged.

The light emanating told her the cellular was still operating. But a closer look showed an ugly crack running down the center. *Oh shit! Bullet's gonna kill me when he sees this.*

Using brute force, Bullet had intimidated Gianna into accepting that there was no possibility of ever being free. He brainwashed her into believing that she should gladly embrace the oppressive lifestyle he'd introduced her to. He demanded that she denounce her parents and scorn the square's life that they offered.

The thought of trying to escape hadn't crossed her mind for such a long time, she thought she'd lost the urge. But she was wrong. An overwhelming desire to be free had returned.

Grabbing the phone and pushing buttons was risky. That reckless act could have caused her some serious punishment.

 CHAPTER 28

In a way she was relieved that Bullet was sniffing white lines so regularly. The drug took his mind off target practice. But it would be real fucked-up if he decided to start engaging in his depraved leisure activity again.

If he caught her trying to make a call, and wanted to teach her a lesson by tying her to a tree, she would be in deep shit. That coked-up nigga had no business shooting off rounds. His aim definitely had to be off.

She grimaced as she envisioned Flashy playing doctor and digging a slug out of her shoulder. He'd dope her up on OxyContin to ease the pain.

Gianna did not like the mental picture that came into focus. She visualized herself shuffling lethargically toward a paying customer. Even worse, she saw herself drooling while she gave a slow-paced blowjob.

She refused to allow herself to get turned out like Bubbles and Skittles. She had to be more cautious. Think smarter.

Moving swiftly down the hallway, clutching the phone like it was a sacred object, Gianna intended to make the call in private.

Locking the bathroom door behind her, she closed the lid to the toilet seat and sat down. Before pressing the series of numbers that would end this vicious nightmare, she wondered if she should stay inside and wait to be rescued or leave the premises…maybe walk a few blocks away from the house.

Fuck! The keys were on the dresser. She needed the key ring to unlock the front door. Funny that when she picked up the key ring to unlock Skittles from the headboard, she hadn't felt any fear and no guilt at all. But now that she needed the keys to slip out of the house, she was terrified that clanking keys might awaken Bullet.

While she pondered her strategy, the most awful thing happened. The phone rang! The blare was like a screaming alarm. *Holy shit! What the fuck!* She'd frantically pressed the ignore button, shutting off the tattletale cellular.

A surge of panic had her breathing hard. She stared at the cell phone in shock. Then it dawned on her…when she dropped it, she'd accidentally switched the ring tone from vibrate mode to ring. With her heart hammering inside her chest and a bad case of the jitters, there was no way she could carry out her plan.

Maybe tomorrow.

Gianna pressed END and then scowled at the cracked screen. There would be hell to pay when Bullet saw the condition of his phone. Self-preservation was her top priority, so she had no choice but to play her position as Bullet's snitch and point the finger at the person known for destructive behavior…Bubbles.

"Don't you remember the way she was wilding out when I brought her to you?" Bullet would have no choice but to believe her. At that point, he'd direct his wrath toward Bubbles.

Satisfied that she had concocted a believable story, Gianna unlocked the bathroom door.

She bumped smack into Bullet.

"Move out my way, bitch. I gotta take a leak." He was holding his dick as he squeezed past her. Then he froze. His gaze shot down to his phone, which Gianna clutched in her hand.

"Whatchu doing with my phone?"

Briefly speechless, she could only shrug.

He snatched the cell phone from her hand, nearly breaking her wrist in the process.

"Ow." She rubbed her pained wrist.

"If you don't start talking, you gon' be screaming in pain."

"Bub...Bubbles dr...she dropped your phone and broke it." Gianna felt tongue-tied and scared out of her wits.

"How Bubbles break my phone? She 'sleep."

"I know. I know. But she was messing with your phone when I brought her in the bedroom last night." Gianna didn't like the way her voice was quaking. She sounded nervous. Her story didn't sound credible.

She cleared her throat and spoke in a measured tone. "Bubbles was acting the fool last night."

He frowned at the damaged screen. "How Bubbles get her hands on my phone?"

"She was spazzin' out. Swinging on me and throwing shit around. Don't you remember, Daddy?" Her account started sounding plausible to her own ears.

Bullet slid his fingers through his mass of curly hair. He shook his head. "Nah, I don't remember none of that." Sleepily, he scratched his balls as he treaded inside the bathroom.

"I'ma give you some privacy." Gianna turned to leave, relieved that she had literally dodged a bullet.

"Hold up. I ain't through talkin'."

Oh, shit. She gulped. "Okay," she said pleasantly.

He gripped his penis with one hand and aimed inside the toilet bowl. The other hand held his cellular.

While urinating, he studied the cracked screen, his thumb moving swiftly as he scrolled through the list of calls. He squinted at the screen, cocking his head from one side and then the other,

as though he had encountered a mysterious cryptogram that had left him completely confounded.

"Bubbles don't have good sense," Gianna said with a nervous chuckle. "It's just a minor setback, Daddy. You know how we do. You gon' have a new phone by tomorrow. I'ma make sure of that." She was trying to distract him, trying desperately to take his mind off his broken cell phone.

"What's this?" He shook droplets of urine from his dick into the toilet, replaced his privates and started walking toward her.

"What's what?" Gianna's breath caught in her throat.

Bullet froze. "609?" He said to himself, squinting at the cracked screen. "609 is a Jersey area code. Who did I call in Jersey?" He stared at Gianna, waiting for her to enlighten him.

She shook her head and shrugged. "Maybe Bubbles pushed those buttons by mistake."

Disbelief was written all over Bullet's face.

A smoldering rage replaced the confusion in his eyes. "Who the fuck was you tryna call in muthafuckin' New Jersey? Huh, bitch? Who did you call?"

"Nobody. I ain't make no calls on your phone. I swear."

He smirked at her. His eyes alit with suspicion. "I told you if you kept it one hunnit with me, I wouldn't hurt you no more."

"I do. I always keep it one hundred," she said, enunciating by mistake. "I mean, uh, one hunnit," she corrected.

Bullet gave her a sneering look.

"I really do."

"Is that right?" he asked, clenching his jaw and eyeing her with suspicion.

She nodded nervously.

"So what's this about?" Taking quick steps, he stood in front of her and shoved the phone directly in her face. "That's an outgoing call. Who made it?"

Gianna peered at the cracked screen. Frowning, she shook her head as if she had no idea how the numbers had materialized on his phone.

"You done lost your mind." Seething, Bullet snatched her by the neck, knocking her against the bathroom door. "The last thing I need to be dealing with is a treacherous bitch!"

She tried to deny any wrongdoing, but could only gurgle. Her tear-glistened eyes pleaded for mercy as he dug his thumb into her windpipe, cutting off her air.

She gagged and struggled. He released the grip on her neck, and waved the cellular in her face.

"I thought I could trust you!" Furiously, he smashed the cellular into her forehead.

The battery popped out the back; the screen shattered.

Dazed, Gianna could swear she saw stars. Fearing that she was only seconds away from being beaten to death, she got her bearings and raced to the front door.

Gianna froze when she reached the double-locked front door, and it dawned on her that there was no way out. The key ring was on the dresser in the bedroom. *Can I dart past Bullet and grab the keys?* She looked over her shoulder to check Bullet's position. She gasped.

Bullet's trampling movements announced his fury. He charged toward her with a homicidal look in his eyes. Then he bumped into the coffee table, looked down, and stopped cold. Something had caught his attention.

Instead of attacking Gianna, Bullet moved around the table and took a seat in the lumpy chair. He picked up a broken mirror and a rolled-up dollar bill and began sniffing lines of coke that was left over from the night before.

He closed his eyes briefly, and then threw his head back and gazed at the ceiling with a faint smile on his lips.

Gianna stood with her back pressed against the locked front door, her teeth chattering, her knees knocking. Severely frightened, her booming heartbeat threatened to explode and throw her off her feet.

She slipped her hand behind her back and grabbed the doorknob, steadying herself. With her hand curled around the knob, escape seemed a sudden possibility.

Bullet had snorted a lot of coke last night. There was a chance that he'd been too preoccupied to remember to secure the two locks on the door. She gave a frantic twist to the knob, but it refused to turn.

Bullet watched her desperate attempt to flee with amusement sparkling in his eyes. "I done choked the shit outta you and clocked you upside the head, and you still ain't learned no lesson," he said scornfully.

She released the doorknob. "Yes, I did! I learned my lesson," she said, her eyes watering with tears.

"No, you didn't. If you learnt something, you wouldn't still be trying to run away from me."

"I wasn't going nowhere."

"I know you ain't. That's why I spent extra money getting all those locks installed."

He twisted his lips in disgust. "After all I did for you. I trusted you. I made you my bottom bitch." He shook his head. "If my bottom bitch is capable of being this treacherous, I might as well line all y'all bitches up and pop you...one at a time...get me some new hoes who know how to show some respect for the game."

He rose, and sauntered slowly toward her. Taking his time, taunting her as he cracked the knuckles of both hands.

Sweat began beading up on Gianna's injured forehead, causing her increased pain.

Bullet punched his palm with a balled fist, his mouth spreading into a sinister smile.

"It's 'bout to get ugly." Bullet's voice rang with malicious pleasure. He practically sang out the vicious threat. He flexed up. Ripples of dangerous muscles popped up on his arms.

"Please, Daddy. Don't hurt me." I'm sorry," she cried.

"Yo' sorry ass should have thought long and hard before you betrayed my trust."

"I won't mess with your phone anymore. I swear I won't." Her brown eyes were wide with panic.

"I know you won't." Roughly, he grabbed her by the shoulder and yanked her away from the door.

She stumbled. After she steadied herself, Bullet raised his fist, and pulled it back, adding power to his punch.

# CHAPTER 29

Flashy sat next to Gianna. She was lying in bed with her head propped up by a pillow.

Bullet's punch to her face had knocked her out. She had no memory of how'd she'd ended up in Bullet's bed. Nor did she recall Flashy coming over for a visit.

"All this playing doctor is getting old," Flashy complained as he applied an ice pack to Gianna's cheek. "I really didn't want you to leave, Bullet, but I needed you to get a crib for your hookers. If I'd let you keep fucking them up in my spot, I would've wound up right back in the pen."

Bullet screwed up his face. "I thought that Lollipop had my back, but I caught her trying to call her peoples on me," Bullet spat.

He kicked the railing at the bottom of the bed. The vibration sent another jolt of pain to Gianna's swollen jaw.

Now awake and in tremendous pain, she wished that she were still unconscious. Or dead.

Life with Bullet had been a living hell that she had tried her best to accept. But now that she'd lost his trust, her living hell would intensify.

What else can he do to me? she wondered. He could keep her drugged like Skittles and Bubbles. Those two hardly knew what was happening to them, while Gianna was keenly aware that her life had been stolen. Maybe living like a zombie wasn't so bad.

So terrified of additional violent consequences, she had hardly

flinched or made a sound that indicated the severe pain she was in.

But after coming to the realization that Skittles and Bubbles, in their medicated state, were better off than she was, Gianna ended her silence. She moaned, squealed, and grunted with fervor. Her vocalized pain sounded very much like a wounded animal.

She hoped her wailing would result in merciful relief of the throbbing in her jaw and the end of the torment of living in captivity. She prayed that her groans would encourage Flashy to suggest that she be given the same drug cocktail that Skittles and Bubbles were given.

"Oh, my God!" Flashy responded, dropping the ice pack. "Why the hell is she going off like this? Maybe you broke her jaw."

Enthusiastically agreeing with Flashy, Gianna bobbed her head up and down with the hope that she would be given some pills and quickly taken out of her misery.

Bullet sneered at her. "I ain't break nothing. I would have heard the bone pop, if I had cracked her jaw."

Gianna amped up her routine, whimpering and whining pitifully.

"Shut the fuck up!" Bullet demanded. "Put that shit back on her face so the swelling can go down."

Defiant, Gianna continued moaning and violently thrashing. Though she couldn't open her mouth wide enough to raise the volume of her cries, her lament increased in intensity.

Cringing as if afraid to touch her, Flashy gingerly reapplied the ice pack to her face. "Maybe you fractured it. If so, I don't know a damn thing about fixing no shit like that, so don't even try to go there."

"Do I look like a fuckin' idiot? I ain't fracture her jaw. Why would I break up the face of a good, dick-suckin' bitch? Huh? What kind of sense does that make?"

Flashy curled his lips in disapproval. "I can't figure out why you

keep fucking these girls up the way you do. Ain't no hope for a hustlin' backward nigga like you," he taunted.

The verbal jab caused Bullet to blink several times. "Ain't nobody hustlin' backward. You better watch your mouth before I put my fist in it."

"I ain't worried about you, Bullet. A little pain might be a turn-on. You wanna hit me, Daddy?" Flashy teased.

"Stop playing, man. I don't even get down like that no more."

"I know. You got Skittles playing my part, and it has been duly noted," Flashy commented snippily.

"Man, we ain't locked up no more. We bulls now. We friends."

"Whatever. I don't see where I'm getting anything out of our so-called friendship."

"Don't I always hook you up?"

"With dribs and drabs. I'm still waiting for the big payday you promised." Flashy planted his hand on his hip. "By the way, you owe the babysitter ninety dollars for Pampers, baby food, and shit."

"Damn! Every time I turn around, you hittin' me up for more money for that fuckin' baby."

"That little crumb snatcher costs money to keep in good health."

Gianna's ears perked up at the mention of the baby. Despite her own physical pain, she felt a degree of relief in knowing the baby was still safe and sound.

"When you sell that damn baby, we can both start living better."

"If you would stop being so stubborn and bring the price down, I can make it happen. Until then..." Flashy's voice trailed off.

"See, that's your problem. You not thinking big enough. You listening to them small-time niggas who think on a small scale. You need to put out feelers. Why don't you put the baby up on Craigslist or something? Ain't that where the freaks wheel and deal?"

Flashy's face twisted into a grimace. "Fuck that! I'm not putting myself in a position to have the FBI tracking me down with their sophisticated computer technology."

"Yo, I'm gon' handle selling that baby as soon as I get some extra time. Just take care of Lollipop's jaw…make the swelling go down, so she can work tonight."

"Umph," Flashy grunted in dissatisfaction.

"I'll break you off and pay the babysitter when my hoes bring me some dough tonight."

Flashy sighed. "Why are you so hard-headed? How is Lollipop going to work her magic if she can't hardly open up her mouth?"

"Trust, she gon' open her mouth. She gon' open up wide and suck as many dicks as I tell her to. Ain't that right, Lollipop?"

Opening her mouth was not possible, so Gianna nodded her head in agreement.

Bullet was working himself into a rage of fury. Gianna had no choice but to agree with his outrageous claim—or deal with his wrath.

Flashy shook his head. "Open your eyes, fool! Her mouth is out of commission. Lollipop is gonna have to work on her back tonight."

"No, the hell she's not!"

"What's the problem? You don't like sharing Lollipop's little pussy hole?" Flashy said with undisguised jealousy.

"It ain't even like that."

"Then why can't she switch up her routine and fuck instead of sucking. Damn!"

"She got regulars who ain't got time for fucking. They got wives and kids to get home to. They on a tight timeframe."

"Since when do tricks care about their families?"

"These ain't regular tricks. They got family values."

"Family values and tricks don't even belong in the same sentence," Flashy pointed out.

"Lollipop has an appointment with a bowling team. Feel me? About fifteen muthafuckas be lined up to get their jawns sucked. They gotta be out at a certain time."

"Send one of them other hoes to do the job."

"Nah, they feelin' the way Lollipop gives brain; they don't want nobody else."

"Let Bubbles handle those family men. The way she slobbers all the time, she should be able to keep those dicks lubricated."

"Bubbles gives a good titty fuck, but those bowlers ain't with that." Worriedly, Bullet ran his fingers through his hair.

Flashy pulled the ice pack away from Gianna's face. With pursed lips and squinted eyes, he examined her face. Ever so lightly, he pressed his fingers against her swollen cheek.

Gianna yelped like a hurt puppy and pulled away from Flashy's light touch.

Flashy smacked the ice pack on the nightstand. "I don't know what to tell you, Bullet. She's in bad shape."

Bullet looked at Gianna with disgust. Incensed, Bullet began pacing again. Agitated, he wiped his palm against his own jawbone, breathing heavy, his temper flaring.

In a sudden flash of rage, he rushed toward the bed. Bending down, he positioned himself between Flashy and Gianna.

With his face only inches from Gianna's, he said, "That's good money, yo. I'm not letting yo' dumb ass mess up a steady stream of income."

She winced under his hateful gaze.

"Y'ah mean?" he shouted.

Gianna nodded quickly.

"Calm down, Bullet. You're breathing all hard—like a damn

dragon. Making me nervous." Flashy maneuvered around Bullet. He stood up and fanned his face dramatically.

"This bitch must think I'm soft," Bullet announced, looking off as though he were speaking to an invisible audience.

He yanked his head toward Gianna. "You think I'm soft?"

"No!" Though it hurt like hell, she forced herself to part her lips and defend herself with coherent speech.

"You see that shit?" Bullet asked, looking at Flashy and then turning to the unseen spectators. "She opened her mouth," he said, with an expression of astonishment.

He flopped down on the bed beside her. His eyes looked demonic. "Why you trying my patience?"

She shook her head. "I'm not," she said, her phrasing soft and almost inaudible.

"Oh, you forgot how to talk, huh?"

Again, she shook her head. Then, confusedly, she nodded. She was so scared, she didn't know how to respond.

"This lil' ho is tryna play me," Bullet said to Flashy.

Looking bewildered, Flashy stood with his chin cradled in his hand.

Bullet shot an evil eye at Gianna. "You got a lot of game for a young ho from the suburbs."

"No, no. I don't." She was able to say those words without moving her jaw.

Bullet sprang up from the bed. "I'm gon' have to teach you a lesson. You got to face some consequences." Bullet's body jerked with rage, his shoulders bobbing as if to the sound of pulse-thumping music.

"Calm down!" Flashy said in a high-pitched voice. "This is way too much drama for my nerves. Now, let's just figure out who you're going to send to do her work for tonight. She'll be back in business and ready to handle those bowlers next week."

"Fuck them bowling alley muthafuckers. They don't run shit. They can get with Lollipop when I say so. You feel me, Flashy?" There was spittle in the corners of Bullet's mouth.

"I guess so," Flashy whispered. "But seriously. Do you realize you're actually foaming at the mouth? Not sexy. You look a hot, scary mess." Flashy turned up his nose.

"I'ma show you what scary looks like," Bullet retorted. He stalked toward the dresser, and yanked open a drawer. In his hand, he held the handle of a knife that was encased in a leather holder.

# CHAPTER 30

Gianna's eyes bulged. She had never set eyes on the knife handle that Bullet was holding, and she refused to allow her mind to conjure up visuals of what Bullet planned to do with it.

Flashy gasped in shock. "I'm leaving. I'm not about to be an accomplice to murder."

"Murder? I'm not gon' kill that bitch. You think I'm crazy or something?"

Immense relief washed over Gianna. Though she'd had thoughts about dying, her natural survival instincts kicked in. She was too young to die. Too young to give up hope that there was a chance to once again experience a normal life…to enjoy her God-given right to freedom.

Flashy also looked visibly relieved that Bullet wasn't contemplating murder. "I'm just saying…You acting like you got a couple of loose screws."

"I gotta handle some unfinished business. That's all." Bullet shrugged like his unfinished business was no big deal.

But Gianna knew Bullet's many moods. She detected a simmering rage that made the hairs on the back of her neck stand up.

Slowly, he unsheathed the knife and smiled at it. It was a vicious-looking weapon that looked sharp and smooth at the top, while the center was curved with cruel, jagged edges.

She considered wriggling off the bed and making a mad dash

to the front door. Maybe when Bullet let Flashy in, he'd left the front door unlocked. Unfortunately, her legs were paralyzed with fear.

"Put that ugly thing away, Bullet!" Daintily, Flashy covered his eyes as though the sight the serrated blade might cause him to faint.

"I thought you had my back."

"Why should I?" Flashy screeched incredulously.

"Because."

"Because what?"

"You know…" Bullet's lips spread into a cheesy smile. "You know, man."

"I don't know a damn thing," Flashy snapped.

"Yo, stop being difficult."

"Hmph. I'm not making any assumptions. You gotta tell me what's what." Flashy waved his manicured hand around with great flourish.

Bullet's facial expression softened. "It's like this…if you help me out with this, we can get it back like it used to be."

A flicker of a smile crossed Flashy's face. "Seriously? Are you for real?" He giggled and then self-consciously smoothed down his short, permed hair.

"I'm dead up." Bullet wrinkled his brow and nodded, attempting to convey a large degree of sincerity.

With a hand on his narrow hip, and bending at the waist, Flashy covered his mouth to contain the girlish giggles that had him twitching and shaking with glee. Pulling himself together, he stood straight. "Oh, my God! You're not going to believe this. I went to a psychic. That woman was on point! She told me it was just a matter of time before you realized that you and I are destined to be together."

With his forehead knotted in a frown, Bullet looked confused, like he didn't really know how to respond.

Batting his fake lashes, Flashy gazed at Bullet with unmistakable love.

Gianna prayed that Bullet intended to slice up Bubbles. Or Skittles. It didn't matter which girl, as long as that wicked-looking knife wasn't used on her. She had already been sufficiently punished. Her bloated jaw was a testament to that.

She hated herself for being so gutless, but she'd endured more than her fair share of physical abuse from Bullet. She hadn't developed a friendship with either girl, and owed them no loyalty. She had to save her own skin.

If she had the courage, which she didn't, she'd appeal to Bullet's common sense. If her throat wasn't so dry from fear, she'd clearly point out to him that from a business perspective, a few lacerations on those drugged-up hoes would keep them in line.

Giving them flesh wounds with his knife would be a great replacement for the coma-inducing medication they'd been taking. Bubbles and Skittles could make a lot more money for him if they were alert and could put more enthusiasm in the tricks they turned.

"What do you want me to do?" Flashy asked, using an overly feminine voice.

"That bitch like playing with my phone, so I got something for her. She gon' think twice before she try to make another muthafuckin' phone call."

Flashy nodded in solemn understanding.

Then, as if following a choreographed routine, Bullet and Flashy moved in concert.

Worriedly, Gianna's eyes followed the two men.

Flashy yanked a pillow from behind Gianna's head. "Sorry," Flashy said, flinching at the sound of her head thumping against the headboard.

"Hurry up, man," Bullet barked.

Gianna heard a clatter as Bullet knocked contents on the nightstand crashing to the floor. She began to shake uncontrollably.

Following orders, Flashy ripped the pillow from inside the case and tossed it on the other side of the bed.

Gianna didn't know what Flashy intended to do with the pillowcase, but her instinct propelled her into action. She bolted up straight and tried to swing her legs off the side of the bed, but her limbs felt heavy and stiff as though paralyzed.

Flashy pushed her backward and held her down. She put up a feeble struggle, but Flashy was much stronger than he appeared. Forcibly, he stuffed as much of the pillowcase as he could inside Gianna's mouth.

An explosion of agony erupted throughout the swollen side of her face.

At the same time, Bullet grabbed her wrist. Forcibly, he stretched out the length of her arm, and then smacked her palm down on the wooden nightstand. He held the menacing blade over her index finger.

"You like playing with phones?" he asked in a grating voice.

Energized by fright, she bucked, trying to throw Flashy off her. He placed his bony elbow into her chest, keeping her torso in place.

"Let's see how many calls you make with a chunk of finger missing."

Frantically, she whipped her head from one side to the other. She pummeled the mattress with the heels of her feet, and then brought her knees up and then pushed them back down—changing to leg motions that resembled doggy-paddling in water.

The bed linen became intertwined and wrapped around her legs, prohibiting further movement of her legs.

Using the tip of the knife, Bullet stroked the length of Gianna's index finger. Up and down, he dragged the sharp point. Then tauntingly, he broke the surface of her skin.

Tears spilled from her eyes, but her sobs were muffled by the blue fabric that invaded her mouth.

He pressed the saw-toothed blade in a horizontal position across the center of her nail, which was polished in a sky blue shade.

Gianna's heart shuddered in her chest. She swung wildly at Flashy with her free hand. Flashy ducked and dodged, and finally pinned her arm down.

"Yo, Flashy...How much should I cut off? You think losing half an inch will stop this ho from tryin' to fuck with my phone?"

"Hell if I know!" Flashy shouted in a high soprano. He grappled with Gianna, who was fighting for her life. "Hurry up! Don't you see me sweating like a field slave? I didn't come here to struggle and tussle with this lil' bitch," Flashy gasped, wiping sweat from his forehead.

Flashy was practically sitting on Gianna. Unable to move, her frightened eyes were drawn to her imperiled hand.

Bullet was staring at her finger with his face scrunched up like he was stumped on the answer to a troubling question. She watched in terror as he studied her finger, trying to decide where he should cut.

It was too much to bear. She squeezed her eyes closed and turned her head away.

The chipping sound of the serrated blade cutting through her fingernail was amplified in her ears. She tried to snatch her hand away as the cruel little teeth of the knife began to chink into her flesh. But Bullet held her wrist in an unyielding grasp.

Blazing, red hot pain sent her body into tremors as steel chopped through flesh.

In an uncontrolled reaction, her head jerked in the direction of the nightstand. She gaped at the unbelievably grotesque spectacle.

The top of her finger was split open. It had the appearance of a macabre, flip-top lid. *My finger! Oh, God. My finger.*

"Ew!" Flashy squealed as blood spurted. "Oh, this is disgusting. Just nasty. I can't believe I let you get me involved in this brutal bullshit."

Blood spatters decorated Bullet's white T-shirt. Red sprinkles dotted his jeans. He looked down at his stained clothing and then at Gianna's twitching, mangled finger and gave a belly laugh as if he were watching a comedy show.

"Damn! I paid a grip for this shank. Why the hell is the top of her finger still hanging on?"

"Stop playing, Bullet. I can't take any more of this bullshit. Get this mess over with, dammit!" Flashy yelled, putting some unexpected bass into his voice.

Determined to subdue her, Flashy flexed the manly muscles of his lean arms, and firmly held Gianna down.

With the smooth part of the knife, Bullet made a clean slice through the final layer of skin. The severed tip of Gianna's finger popped off and skidded across the nightstand.

Savagely butchered, her finger looked decapitated. A trail of thick red blood oozed down her hand.

As if electrocuted, Gianna's body jerked and danced. Her teeth began to chatter as she slumped over, passed out from shock.

CHAPTER 31

I nside the multi-purpose room of the Haverford Recreation Center, Saleema, Amirah, Stacey, Tasha, and Chyna were seated in the front row. Saleema and the girls wore T-shirts bearing Portia's image.

Although Khalil and his students had gone door-to-door notifying residents of the importance of the community meeting, only a sparse few had bothered to show up.

"Dag, ain't hardly nobody even here," Tasha complained, looking around at the vast number of empty metal folding chairs.

Grumpily, Chyna slouched in her seat. "How come Dr. Gardner's students didn't come?"

"They had something to do at school," Saleema said absently, noticing that the few people who had come out were frowning and looking down at their watches.

Chyna fidgeted in her seat. "Summer school is over at two. How come they're not here?"

"I'm not sure what they're doing, Chyna. I'm focused on Portia right now." Everyone knew that Chyna was boy crazy, but times like now, her obsession with the opposite sex was particularly inappropriate and annoying.

Saleema looked in the back of the room. A few people lingered near the doorway, to ensure a speedy getaway in case the meeting turned out to be the snooze fest that it appeared likely to be.

At exactly five-thirty, Khalil and the director of the center stood

in the doorway. Upon seeing the poor attendance, they spoke a few words and then turned around and disappeared down the corridor.

"Hey, what time is this meeting supposed to start?" barked a forty-something man who was posted against a wall at the back of the room. He was dressed in paint-splattered clothing. His face, arms, and even the thick hair on his head were also speckled with flecks of white paint.

"The meeting will be starting soon," Saleema said. "We're just waiting for a few more people to arrive. We don't plan to keep you very long, I promise," she said with a warm smile.

Frowning, the painter sighed and folded his arms. He inched closer to the doorway.

Finally, a stream of senior citizens were escorted into the room by the recreation staff members. Khalil and the director followed.

A scant few walked in on their own accord. Some came hobbling in using canes, some pushed walkers, while others rolled wheelchairs. Those on oxygen therapy arrived with the dual-pronged nasal cannula attached to their nostrils.

After a few minutes of helping get the seniors situated in their seats, the director introduced Khalil, listing his credentials.

Standing in front of the podium, Khalil said, "Good evening. I want to thank you all for coming out to this important community meeting."

"I didn't want to come to no meeting," grumbled a seemingly sturdy senior, who had walked into the meeting without any assistance. "What's so important that I had to be snatched away from a game of checkers?"

"What's your name, sir?" Khalil asked.

The man stood up. "William Daniels," he said in a strong, clear voice.

"Mr. Daniels, I apologize for interrupting the senior social hour. I assure you that we're not going to keep you long. We want to share some important community information, and after that, you'll be escorted back to the activity room."

"My name is Ruth Ann Wakefield," a woman in a wheelchair introduced herself without prompting. "I left my daggone teeth home. Do you know if we're getting applesauce with our snack? I'm not going to be able to eat anything else."

"Hush up, Ruthie!" yelled a woman with a scratchy voice. "You said the same thing when they handed out snacks a half-hour ago." She shook her head. "Ruthie's forgetful," the woman explained to Khalil.

"This meeting concerns Portia Hathaway...a missing teenager. Portia was born and raised right here in this neighborhood, but nobody is trying to find her—"

"Oh, you're talking about that bad-behind girl from around on Wallace Street." The painter reared back in disgust. "I keep seeing her picture plastered all over the place, but I didn't know that's what this meeting was about. That girl's not missing; she ran off from the detention center."

"Oh, shoot. I might as well turn myself around," said a gray-haired woman gripping a walker. Struggling with it, she tried to get the stubborn wheels to turn.

"Wait a few minutes, Miss Hattie," the director encouraged the woman with the walker.

Unsuccessful, Miss Hattie scowled over her glasses at Khalil. "When they hauled us out of the recreation room, we were told this was some kind of community meeting...something about making changes and improving the neighborhood."

"We certainly want to bring about some changes in this neighborhood," Khalil began. "But—"

"But nothing!" William Daniels cut Khalil off. "Most of us who got yanked out of our social hour have been living in this neighborhood since long before you were even born, son. So let's talk about the issues that concern us." He paused and gave Khalil a stern look.

"Go right ahead, Mr. Daniels. You have the floor."

"I bought my house with the GI bill back in nineteen fifty-nine. Being a homeowner was something to take pride in. I thought I had got myself a little piece of the American pie."

There was a murmuring of agreement among the seniors.

"Back then, we helped one another. Looked after each other's kids. We took pride in the appearance of our neighborhood," Miss Hattie joined in.

"Men had good jobs back then. And women stayed home and tended to kids," said the woman with the scratchy voice.

The meeting was going off topic and there wasn't much time. Saleema gave Khalil a look of concern, but Khalil gave the senior attendees his undivided attention, allowing them a voice that was seldom heard.

"We all collaborated," Miss Hattie continued. "Christmastime, the houses on every block had matching lights."

William Daniels exhaled loudly. "But that was a long time ago. Those were the good old days. Decades have passed since then. Times have changed for the worse."

"Sure have," someone called out.

"The sixties brought gang violence. Kids getting hold of guns and shooting each other for walking around in the wrong neighborhood," William Daniels said grimly. "After the Vietnam War ended in the seventies, we had young boys coming home all messed up on heroin. That caused a wave of petty robberies around here. Dope fiends were figuring out crafty ways to get inside working

people's houses during the day, snatching television sets and anything else of value." He shook his head.

"That's around the time we had to set up the town watch program," Hattie reminded him.

"Yeah, hard-working men folk had to donate their time, patrolling the streets, trying to do our part to keep our streets safe."

Wanting to have his say, a chunky, elderly man tapped the end of his cane on the tiled floor. "That town watch didn't do much good when that crack epidemic started up in the eighties."

"Whoo-wee!" Hattie whooped. "That crack was the beginning of the end. Young mothers would go missing for days and weeks at a time. They didn't even remember that their young children were left at home to fend for themselves."

"The nineties wasn't much better...probably worse with drug wars sending bullets flying around in broad daylight. Shooting up parks and playgrounds. Terrible times," recalled William Daniels.

Hattie sighed. "Don't forget how the teenagers was risking their lives anytime they left their houses wearing gold jewelry, designer clothing, or even a new pair of sneakers."

"Is that true, Miss Saleema?" Stacey whispered, finding it hard to believe.

"Yeah, I got stuck-up at gunpoint over a pair of gold earrings," Saleema said in a whisper. "I was lucky that the dude holding the gun didn't use it. But I've known kids who were murdered over designer items such as a Tommy Hilfiger shirt, a Nautica belt, Pelle jackets, and Alpina sunglasses."

Chyna turned up the corner of her lip. "Kids in Philly got killed over their clothes? That's crazy."

"I know, right. Those designers Miss Saleema named sound too wack to be losing your life over," Amirah commented in a loud tone.

Saleema held a finger to her lips. "Shh! No designer's gear is worth dying for."

Too weary to continue standing, William Daniels sat down and spoke from his seat. "We're ten years into the new millennium. You'd think we'd see some kind of progress by now." He shook his head grimly. "Most of the houses in this neighborhood are nothing but boarded-up shells with rats, bums, and whatnot taking up residence. I'm eighty-three years old and I don't expect that I have much more time. So tell me, young fella, how do you plan to improve this deteriorated neighborhood?"

Standing in the rear, the paint-speckled man folded his arms tighter and furrowed his brows as he waited to hear Khalil's response.

"The summary of this neighborhood's decline was very infor-mative. I found it particularly interesting when Mr. Daniels described the glory days of the nineteen-fifties when people looked after each other. It seems that the expression, 'it takes a village to raise a child,' was taken seriously during those times."

There was a chorus of agreement.

"That's right."

"You ain't never lied."

"Yes, indeedy. We sure did look after each other's kids. If the mother wasn't around when a child was acting up, any neighbor had the right to take a strap and whip the daylights out of that child."

"Uh-huh," a woman with a hair net joined in. "And when the mother got home, that child had another whipping coming."

The girls gave each other looks. "Ain't you glad we wasn't back in those days?" Stacey whispered to her three friends. Each girl nodded.

"I want to remind each of you," Khalil continued, "time has passed, but Portia Hathaway is a part of that same village."

"No. See...I can't agree with that," said Miss Hattie. "Children today are hard-headed and wild. They got too much sass in their mouths. Won't listen to their own mammas."

With great effort, William Daniels worked himself up to his feet again. "How are we supposed to help raise a pack of heathens? If you try to discipline one of these children today, you better have a lawyer handy. Spanking kids is against the law."

Not to be outdone, Miss Hattie cleared her throat. "That's why we have a neighborhood full of little hooligans, all walking around with their chests stuck out."

"She telling the truth, right there. Spare the rod, spoil the child," Mr. Daniels said, quoting scripture, his voice strong with religious indignation.

"We're not dealing with ordinary children anymore." Frowning, Mr. Daniels shook his head. "If you try to discipline a child today, you better be wearing a bulletproof vest because they might whip out a gun and shoot you."

At an age where everything seemed comical, Amirah, Tasha, Chyna, and Stacey found the seniors' comments to be hilarious. They erupted into girlish giggles that seemed to echo inside the sparsely filled room.

"Girls!" Saleema's voice was sharp with disapproval.

The girls apologized, but couldn't contain their shoulder-shaking laughter.

"You should be more respectful to these seniors." Saleema's voice sharpened in disapproval, shaming the girls into quelling the eruption of giggles.

"I don't want to take up too much of your time," Khalil, said, bringing the meeting to an end. "The students will be passing you fliers on your way out. We'll be gathering here again tomorrow and I'm hoping those of you who came today will tell your family members and your neighbors to come out and join us."

Suddenly agile, the seniors, as well as the small sprinkling of younger members of the community, all raced for the door, many refusing to accept the fliers that the girls were passing out.

"Another thing..." Khalil said, his voice amplified by the microphone. "Beginning tomorrow, we'll be raffling off a prize at the conclusion of every meeting."

Miss Hattie turned around. "Oh, yeah? What kind of prizes?"

"You'll find out tomorrow," Khalil said, smiling.

# CHAPTER 32

Touching the small of her back, Khalil helped Saleema into her Camry. "How'd you think the meeting went?"

She wanted to say something encouraging and show gratitude for Khalil's help, but prodded by her urgent need to find Portia, she said bluntly, "I'm having second thoughts about this whole community involvement campaign."

"The turnout was disappointing, but I didn't expect a big crowd. Not right away. Don't worry; more people will come out tomorrow. Give them some time. They'll get involved."

"I can't sit through another community meeting. Those people are so bitter. As far as they're concerned, Portia is nothing more than another blemish to the neighborhood. They have the same attitude as law enforcement—that Portia's a criminal...not an abducted teen."

"Give them time. Sure, they're a little bitter from all the years of watching helplessly as their neighborhood declined, but they'll come around. We can accomplish more and put a spotlight on Portia's situation if we speak as a united voice."

"But time is running out! Who knows what horrors are happening to Portia while we're waiting for the community to open their hearts and come on board. Seriously, Khalil, they're senior citizens who were railroaded into the meeting in the first place. Then you had to bribe them with a raffle to try to spark enough interest for them to coerce their families into attending the next meeting."

"Yeah, that was a little cheesy, but it piqued their interest. Initially, people will come out of curiosity or to see what kind of prizes are being raffled off, but after a while, they will get involved."

Saleema let out a sigh. "I can't wait to hear the newcomers tomorrow start fondly reminiscing about the good ol' days of whooping their neighbors' kids' behinds," she said sarcastically. "That kind of thinking is so outdated, it was embarrassing to hear about it."

"There are a lot of customs from the past that we don't agree with, but during their era, that was the norm. The important thing here is that they get to have their voices heard. They are at an age when no one listens or thinks that they have anything of value to share. It's great to provide them with a forum to share their feelings."

"I thought this was about Portia. I didn't know you intended to conduct group therapy sessions for the elderly at Portia's expense."

"That's cold," Khalil said with a faint smile.

"I'm sorry. I have to speak my mind. Don't you think it's odd that no one has responded to the posters? There hasn't been one phone call with even a hint of a lead. If Portia's own family isn't concerned about her whereabouts, what makes you think her neighbors are going to care?"

"Give them time."

"Time is running out. I can't sit on my hands and wait for these people to get it through their heads that a fifteen-year-old is at the mercy of some sicko."

"I'm not depending entirely on the members of the community. Rashan is a computer whiz. He and a couple of my students are setting up a Help Find Portia website that will provide links for citizens to give anonymous tips. There will be information on Portia's last known whereabouts, her picture, a description of the car she was seen getting in, and also a description of the driver."

Saleema broke into a big smile. "That's the best news I've heard all day!"

"There's more. The site is going to have a forum for teens to discuss their experiences with real or potential abductions. Who knows, maybe someone has had an encounter with Portia's kidnapper. And we're asking for small donations to assist with the expenses of the search."

"Oh, Khalil, this is so incredible. I'm about to cry."

"It gets better. Once the site is up and operating, the boys are going to link it to their own MySpace and Facebook pages. They're going to encourage their cyber friends to do the same. Portia's face will get a lot of national exposure."

Saleema started fanning her face with both hands. "I'm getting so excited, I'm overheating." Saleema frowned at her poor choice of words, "Uh, I mean…"

Khalil removed his glasses and wiped at imaginary sweat. Smile lines crinkled around his eyes. "Freudian slip," he teased, having no idea how right he was.

Khalil had become the featured star of Saleema's nightly naughty dreams, but she'd never let on that she was hot as hell for him. It was her little dirty secret.

"This website idea is brilliant," she said, giving no hint of the thoughts that were crossing her mind. "Please thank Rashan."

"You can thank him in the morning. We're still going to be hitting the streets with fliers. If the site is up, we'll put the URL on the fliers."

Saleema beamed. "Now I feel like we're finally getting somewhere."

"You shouldn't underestimate me. I always have several irons in the fire."

"I won't doubt your judgment ever again. I promise."

"So you'll be at the community meeting tomorrow night?" He had a devilish glint in his eyes.

She turned up her nose. "Yes, I will be there…sticking by my man—" Saleema gasped. "That didn't come out right."

"Another Freudian slip?" he teased.

"I meant to say, I'll be supporting whatever you do."

Growing serious, he said, "By the way, we'll be listing the community support meetings on the site as well as any upcoming fundraising events."

"Fundraising?"

"I plan to discuss fundraising tomorrow night."

"You're incredible, Khalil," she said sincerely.

"I wouldn't go that far. But everything is going to be all right. We're going to find Portia."

"I know," she said weakly, rubbing her forehead, clearly stressed.

"Hey, I want you to try to relax," he said and stuck a hand inside the car. He rubbed Saleema's back. "You're a bundle of nerves." His touch gave her a tingling shock.

"I will," she said, her voice faltering from the sudden jolt.

Khalil rubbed her back for a few more seconds and then removed his hand, and stood up straight.

From Saleema's vantage point, she had a spectacular view of Khalil's sturdy thighs. Though he appeared slim, he was surprisingly muscular. Her gaze wandered to his crotch. Experiencing a rush of excitement, that rendered her momentarily spellbound. Embarrassed, she quickly turned her lustful eyes away.

Khalil's sensuality had a way of sneaking up on Saleema when she least expected it. She let out a slow, soft sigh of sexual distress. She started up the Camry and quickly turned the air on full blast.

"I'll see you in the morning, Khalil," Saleema said, giving him a cool smile. Meanwhile, her heart thudded heavily inside her chest.

"Drive carefully." He bent. Stuck his head inside the car window and gave her a gentle kiss on the cheek.

Impulsively, she turned her head, giving him her lips to kiss.

She felt the warmth of his hand touch the side of her face, then his fingers, long and searching, caressed her chin and traveled around her neck, reaching upward and fervently clutching a handful of her hair.

Saleema shuddered. Her eyes closed dreamily.

When Khalil's tongue found hers, an intense sensation pulsed through her, making her lightheaded, making her body weak.

Though she craved his passion, Saleema forced herself to break the dangerous kiss.

They looked into each other's eyes questioningly. Neither spoke for a few seconds.

"I didn't mean for that to happen," Saleema said, organizing the locs that Khalil had rearranged with his passionate grasp.

"We'll pretend it didn't," Khalil said, appeasing her like a perfect gentleman.

But they were both keenly aware that quite unpredictably, they'd crossed the friendship threshold.

CHAPTER 33

A gravelly backstreet beneath an overpass led to a one-story, red-brick residence. Under the cover of darkness, the three captive teenage girls were herded into the secluded house.

Seven black men, rounded up from a nearby bar, were waiting. Most were casually attired in jeans and T-shirts, but one man stood out from the others—an older man with a professional look, who was wearing a suit and tie.

Gianna's mocha skin was contrasted with a white satin sheer gown. A white tiara adorned her head, replete with bridal veiling that trailed down her back. On her feet was a pair of white beaded heels. Keeping with the color scheme, white gauze covered the tip of her mutilated finger.

She admired the carefully layered bandages. *Pretty!* she thought, her mind muddled by drugs.

"I'm first and I want that one," said a man with an olive complexion. His hair was straight and black. He had a Hispanic look about him, but he spoke without a trace of an accent. He was the only man in the room who was wearing a suit. He pointed at Gianna and began moving toward her with two twenty-dollar bills clutched inside his hand.

Feeling no pain, Gianna smiled at the man with the slicked-back hair.

"It's not going down like that," Flashy announced, shaking his

head and flinging a long, clip-on ponytail. "This is an auction and there are rules. The bidding will start in a few minutes." True to his name, Flashy was wearing heavy makeup, super long eyelashes, a skintight sequined dress, stilettos, and he was carrying a sequined purse.

"Hold up! You ain't running shit," Bullet spat. "Your job is to dress the girls and make sure they look presentable."

"Keep your voice down. I'm your partner now," Flashy said in a whispered hiss. "I dressed Lollipop in bridal white so I could pass her off as a virgin."

"She ain't no virgin," Bullet said, mimicking Flashy's whispered tone. "Her cherry got popped the first night I snatched her."

"Well, she's *like* a virgin. Practically new. Didn't you tell me that you used her lips more than you knocked her back out?"

"Yeah, back when I was training her. But I smash it on the regular now."

"We don't have to broadcast it. We can get a lot more than forty dollars off these tricks if you step back and let me handle this."

Grumbling, Bullet reluctantly deferred to Flashy.

Finished bickering with Bullet, Flashy cleared his throat and turned to the waiting men with a smile. He pointed to Gianna and began speaking as if he were an auctioneer.

"Lollipop is young and eager to please. She's already been broken in, so the hard part has been done for you. But don't get it twisted, she's only been with one other man and her young twat is practically brand-new. I'm starting the bidding at fifty dollars. Do I hear fifty-five?"

"Fifty-five dollars," the man clasping the money yelled and waved his money in the air.

Tired from standing, Bubbles shifted her position, her shoulders slouched slightly. Bullet sauntered over to her. "You ready for some more target practice?" he hissed.

Looking grim, Bubbles straightened up immediately. Skittles did the same.

"Yo, Bubbles. Put a smile on your mug," Bullet growled. Bubbles instantly obeyed, pasting a strained smile on her face. Imitating Bubbles, Skittles smiled also.

Annoyed at being interrupted, Flashy rolled his eyes at Bullet and then continued, "Lollipop's little nookie can put a tight grip around a man packing any size. Big dick or little dick…it doesn't matter."

Smiling sheepishly, another man stood up. "Don't get it twisted. I don't have a little dick, by I'm willing to pay sixty bucks." Leering at Gianna, he rubbed his crotch.

"I know we can do better than sixty dollars," Flashy said. "If any of y'all want to get your grub on—" He paused and took a few dainty steps backward and patted Gianna's pubic area. "This thing right here is as sweet as candy. There's some good eating between Lollipop's young thighs."

"Sixty-five," another man proposed, smiling lecherously, his tongue flicking out and licking his lips.

"Seventy!" shouted another.

"One hundred and fifty dollars," barked the man who had placed the first bid.

"He's trying to shut y'all down," Flashy taunted the men. "Can I get two hundred?" he asked, cutting a look of triumph at Bullet.

"Work it," Bullet encouraged, giving Flashy a smile of approval.

There was a low rumbling among the men, but no one was willing to pay two hundred dollars.

"Fifteen minutes," Bullet reminded harshly as he collected the money from the winning bidder.

With his chest poked out, the high bidder grabbed Gianna's hand possessively, and led her along a corridor.

Moving wobbly down the hallway, Gianna could hear Flashy

reopening the bidding. In her medicated state, the cruel world in which she existed seemed like a wonderful place. From Gianna's drugged perspective, Flashy's voice held the quality of a melody as he began to describe the sexual attributes of Bubbles and Skittles.

"Is it true what that gay fella said about you?" the suit-wearing man asked as they neared the bedroom.

"Uh-huh," she replied with an affable smile, not recalling what Flashy had said.

"You look like the bridal doll I bought my granddaughter for Christmas," he said as they crossed the threshold into the bedroom.

He closed the door, assuring them of privacy. He gazed at his watch and shook his head. "Only fifteen minutes. I'd like to have a lot more time with you."

"Alright," Gianna said obligingly.

"It's not up to you, sweetness. But I'm going to make some kind of deal with those morons who are controlling this racket. They don't deserve a pretty little chocolate doll baby like you." He smiled at Gianna adoringly.

She smiled back.

"Come here, baby." He held out his arms. Aiming to please, Gianna moved into his embrace. He lifted her up and rested her gently on the bed.

"You're so young and precious. I can't believe you're a whore," he said, shaking his head, incredulous.

"I'm a whore," she replied dreamily.

His face tensed. "No! Don't say that. You're not a whore. You're a bridal doll."

"Okay."

"What happened to your finger?"

"Cut."

"Umph. Too pretty to be scarred. Lie still so I can check you out. I want to see if anybody's been tampering with the rest of you."

Gingerly, he removed her sexy-bride costume, kissing her feet in near worship as he pulled off the beaded shoes.

She lay naked before him.

"Perfection," he uttered, rubbing his face anxiously. "How old are you?"

"Fifteen."

A worried look crossed his face. "I thought you were around twelve. Thirteen at the most. Tell me you're twelve," he demanded.

"I'm twelve," she answered, giggling again.

"My goodness. You're only twelve years old with luscious, womanly breasts," he murmured his fantasy as if entranced. With hands that shook with excitement, he squeezed her plump and firm breasts.

His trembling fingers tickled her flesh. Gianna giggled softly.

Gently, he pushed up her legs and slowly pulled her knees wide apart until her glistening femininity was exposed to him.

Fully clothed, he crouched down at the bottom of the bed and buried his face in the thick dark hair of her pubis, his tongue stretching into the delicate opening.

Drinking from her youthful fountain, the man slurped greedily as though dying from thirst.

The bedroom door opened and slammed closed. Startled, the man jerked his head from between Gianna's legs.

Bullet folded his arms, his legs spread apart. Looking at the man with disdain, he said, "Your fifteen minutes is up."

"I need more time," the man pleaded.

"Fuck that. You trying to eat her box out. Man, you gotta save a lil' something for them other niggas. They tryna bust a grub,

too." Bullet laughed at the ludicrous notion of men paying to indulge in oral sex.

The man scooted off the bed and stuffed his hand in his pocket, extracting a wad of cash. "I'll pay more."

Bullet looked at him sneeringly. "We 'bout to have another bidding war." Bullet glared at Gianna. "Put that wedding shit back on and take your ass out there in the living room."

Mechanically, Gianna picked up the sheer lingerie.

"Don't talk to her like that," the man said reproachfully.

"Fuck outta here. That's my bitch. I talk to her anyway I want to." He shot a look at Gianna. "Ain't that right, ho?"

"You right," Gianna agreed.

Using the palm of his hand, the man wiped the sheen from around his mouth. "I can't let those slimy bastards maul her like she's a piece of meat. Take the money."

With a look of desperation in his eyes, he extended the hand that held the folded currency.

"That's two hundred dollars. Let her stay here with me. Why bother to go through the motions when you know none of those cheapskates is willing to bid more than that?"

Bullet looked up in thought and then fixed his gaze on the greenbacks in the man's hand. "Hold up; lemme go run this by my partner."

Moments later, Bullet and Flashy entered the bedroom together.

"What's the problem?" Flashy sashayed toward the bed and began picking up the pieces of Gianna's bridal outfit.

"I'm offering two hundred to keep her with me."

Flashy positioned the tiara on Gianna's head. "There's people out there waiting to bid on her. You're not the only one who wants to sample the goods." Flashy sucked his teeth.

"What's the point in parading her back out there? I'm willing

to pay whatever you want." The man smoothed his shiny black hair out of his face.

Flashy gave him a snide look. "Listen up, Senor El Creepo—"

"Yo, don't be insulting the customers," Bullet interjected.

"Well, I have a system in place. This Spanish-looking nigga needs to stick to the program. Lollipop will be back up for auction again as soon as I can get her in her costume," Flashy said snippily, picking up the pair of white beaded heels. "She goes with the highest bidder!"

"I want to purchase her for the remainder of the night," the persistent man said. "I'll pay one thousand dollars if I can have her all to myself."

"Sold!" Bullet shouted without hesitation.

Flashy frowned. "Not so fast, Bullet. We can make way more than that—"

Bullet snatched Flashy by the arm. "Who's running this shit?"

"Don't be so rough."

"You stepping out of line, man. Don't make me have to break your shit." He gave Flashy a hard shove, causing him to stumble.

Flashy straightened himself up. "You don't have to manhandle me to get your point across."

"It's a deal. Give me that stack, yo." Bullet stretched out his palm.

"I can have her?" The man fidgeted with his tie, his eyes glimmering with lust.

"You got her for the next coupla hours, then you gotta bounce."

 CHAPTER 34

The sun peeked through the dark night and began to faintly lighten the sky.

Through the back window of Bullet's car, Gianna watched with interest as Bullet and the man in the suit stood outside the house having a discussion.

Skittles and Bubbles, also in the back seat of the car, sat slumped against each other, both snoring.

The medication had begun to wear off about an hour ago. Taking a huge and desperate risk, she'd told the man who called her his bridal doll the facts…how she'd been kidnapped and forced into prostitution. In a frantic whisper, she'd provided him with her parents' names and phone numbers.

He seemed genuinely horrified that Gianna was an unwilling captive. "Though I have a fetish, I'm not a criminal," he assured her. "I'll get you away from the slimy pimp, even if I have pay twenty thousand dollars. You're worth it to me. After I satisfy my fetish, I promise to return you to your family."

She crossed the fingers of her good hand, watching Bullet and the man with the fetish, hoping for a successful outcome.

With both pockets bulging with money, Bullet took giant strides toward the Cadillac.

Looking dejected, the man in the suit walked over to a long, dark car that was parked discreetly beneath a large tree.

"Big pimpin'!" Bullet yelled happily as he climbed into the driver's seat. "That auction was off the chain!"

Gianna looked out the back window one last time, her heart sinking as she watched the long black car drive away. The man who liked dolls wasn't going to save her.

Flashy sat up front in the passenger's seat, his lips poked out in irritation.

When sunlight broke through the twilight and flooded through the car windows, Bullet threw up his arm, blocking the sun's glare.

"Find my shades," he said to Flashy, using a bossy tone.

"Do I look like I'm your goddamn servant? Find your own fuckin' shades." Rolling his eyes in righteous indignation, Flashy reached inside his purse and took out a pair of rhinestone-studded sunglasses. With great flourish, he affixed the gaudy sunglasses to his face.

"Here you go with your bullshit." Bullet fished around inside the side pocket of the car door. He located his dark shades and put them on.

"You got some nerve, leaving me out here in this stuffy car while you discuss business with El Perverto."

"Man, there's a time and a place for everything. A lot of mufuckas don't want to talk business with a homo."

"Hmph. Nobody seemed to mind the fly-ass way I ran that auction." Flashy punctuated the statement with three finger snaps.

Bullet laughed. "Yeah, you was on point with the auction."

"So what did that pervert want to discuss?"

"You ain't gon' believe what that mufucka asked me."

Gianna's body tensed as she waited to hear her fate. Maybe there was hope.

Flashy folded his arms huffily. "I'm all ears and I'm braced to hear what kind of stupid arrangements you made without my consent."

"I don't need your consent."

"We're partners, aren't we?"

"Yeah, but I don't have to run every decision by you."

Flashy frowned. "So what did you discuss?"

Bullet laughed. "That sucka wanted to buy Lollipop."

"For how much?"

"It don't matter. She ain't for sale. Lollipop is gon' be bringing in lots of dough for years to come. I told him he could keep on paying for her services, but I'm not selling my cash cow."

"How much did he offer? You know I need a big payday to get my surgery."

"He wanted to pay ten stacks. I wanted to laugh in his Spanish-looking face. But I did tell him that I had a baby for sale—"

Flashy gasped at the mention of Skittles' baby. He jerked around to make sure she was sound asleep. Relieved that Skittles was snoring, Flashy asked, "Does he have enough to buy the baby?"

"He wasn't interested. He's feenin' for Lollipop, so you know I'm gonna milk him for every dollar he's got. But in the meantime, he's gon' put me on with some dudes who are into that type of thing. You know…mufuckas with serious dough. Dudes who get their kicks off of having sex with babies."

Sex with babies! Gianna covered her mouth to stifle a scream.

"He said he's gon' put the word out. I told him that baby is worth at least fifty grand. If he can find me a buyer, he won't have to bid on Lollipop no more. I'll sell him her services at a fixed rate."

Bullet turned the key in the ignition. Pushing the pedal to the floor, he skidded out of the parking spot and then roared down Bethel Road.

"Why don't you wake up the whole neighborhood?" Flashy said, his voice dripping with sarcasm.

"What's your problem, man? Why you always gotta be acting like a lil' bitch? What? You mad cuz you wasn't included in the transaction?"

"Newsflash! There wasn't any transaction. And let me tell you

something else… We are not in the city of Chester or the city of Philadelphia. This little borough is called Chester Township, and the cops in this neck of the woods don't have shit to do except hand out speeding tickets to fools like you."

"Fuck these hillbilly cops. I'ma drive the way I want to."

"You sound so stupid." Flashy shook his head.

"Fuck you."

"You need to slow the fuck down, Bullet!" Flashy yelled as Bullet increased his speed.

"Don't tell me how to drive my whip."

"If you don't drive like you have some sense, the next dollar you earn is gonna come from selling loose cigarettes in the state pen. These township cops have all the time in the world to listen to you try to come up with an explanation for why you have three minor girls in the back seat of your car."

Quickly coming to his senses, Bullet slammed on the brakes, causing Gianna to lurch forward, jostling her about. Her bandaged finger hit the back of Bullet's seat and began to pulse.

Tires screeched loudly as Bullet slowed down the car.

Bubbles and Skittles woke with a start. Groggily, they rubbed their sleepy eyes, but didn't utter a sound.

Exhausted and demoralized, they sat helplessly mute, knowing better than to question anything that Bullet said or did.

It had been a grueling night of unending sexual abuse. No longer chemically restrained, Bubbles and Skittles were kept docile and compliant by the threatening appearance of Bullet's serrated knife.

Additionally, each girl had experienced the terror of being shot at while her body was roped to a tree.

And Gianna's partially amputated finger was a powerful deterrent to any acts of rebelliousness that might have entered their heads.

# CHAPTER 35

"Pain." Gianna whispered the complaint.

Skittles patted Gianna's thigh comfortingly.

Bubbles looked at the bandaged finger and grimaced as if she were experiencing Gianna's pain.

Neither Bullet nor Flashy heard Gianna's soft cry.

"You're feeling yourself, nigga," Flashy continued to rant. "All that money we pulled in tonight done went to your head."

Bullet made a snorting sound. "These coupla stacks ain't about nothing."

"Couple of stacks, my ass. That auction pulled in exactly three thousand and seven hundred dollars." Flashy rolled his eyes again. "Do not try to play with my money because I counts every dollar. Yes, indeed." Feeling self-satisfied, Flashy clapped his manly hands. Next, he began to bounce his shoulders like he was in church getting hit by the Holy Ghost, over and over.

"Whatever, man. I gotchu. Ain't nobody tryin' to steal nothing from you."

"Uh-huh," Flashy said doubtfully.

"Stop frontin'," Bullet said with insincere laughter. "You gon' get your fair share when we get back to the crib."

"I know mufuckin' well, I'm gon' get mine." Flashy twisted his neck, his Adam's apple bobbing excessively as he continued his verbal tirade.

"Don't get it twisted, nigga. I'm the one who set up that damn

auction. You were hustling all stupid before I stepped up the game. I'm gonna let you slide and consider that statement about a couple of stacks as a slip of the tongue. But lemme find out you trying to beat me outta my cut—" Flashy did a theatrical shivering motion and another finger pop to announce his final statement. "I will shut shit down in a heartbeat. Believe that!"

"Chill out, man." The scowl on Bullet's face indicated he was losing his patience.

"Then stop playing with me. Even though I already put plans in motion, I swear to God, I will cancel the next auction if you try to get all Big Willy on me and shit. Think I won't?"

Bullet shot Flashy a big grin. "You set up another auction?"

"Yeah, nigga. But this time, it's at a different location. I'm about my business and staying several steps in front of the law. I keeps it moving."

"When? And where's it gon' be at?"

"You got slimy ways, Bullet. If you was on the up and up, you wouldn't have had any discussions about money while I'm cooped up in the car with these stank hoes."

"Man, get over that. I told you…dude wasn't feeling you like that. He's a homophobic."

"If that's the case, then he shouldn't have been feeling you either."

"Yo, watch your mouth. Don't be calling me a faggot."

"Yeah, whatever."

"What's up with the next auction?"

"I'll let you know on a need-to-know basis."

"Oh, it's like that? I thought you was my shawty."

"Don't be trying to butter me up, now."

"Man, fuck you. These hoes is all mine. You can't hold no auction nowhere if I don't provide the candy. Feel me?" Angry, Bullet made a sudden sharp turn.

Gianna's body whipped from side to side, crashing into Bubbles and then into Skittles' hard, bony elbow.

"Ow," she hollered.

"Give her another pill," Bullet said, glaring at Flashy.

"Ain't no more. We ran out."

Bullet's jaw clenched visibly. "How you let that happen?"

"It was way past Lollipop's bedtime, but you kept giving that weirdo more time."

"Ahhh," Gianna moaned from the back of the car.

"Check your pocketbook."

Flashy jerked his neck toward Bullet. His mouth was stretched open as he enunciated each word. "The pill supply has been exhausted. We ain't got no more!"

"What about at the crib?"

"I don't keep that shit at my house."

"Oh, God!" Gianna hollered. "It hurts!" Squirming, she clasped the bandaged finger at the knuckle, her face twisted in a pained grimace.

Moaning, Gianna rocked back and forth. Her head bumping against the leather upholstery, her bridal tiara knocked askew.

Bullet turned around and glared at Skittles and Bubbles. "Damn, can one of y'all shut her up?"

"Be quiet, Lollipop," Skittles said with a sternness in her voice that she hoped Gianna would take seriously.

"My finger," Gianna wept, tears now streaming.

"We gon' get you some medicine in a minute," Bubbles said in a harsh whisper. "Now shut up!"

"I need it, now!" Gianna screamed, ripping the tiara from her hair. With pain escalating out of control, her brain censors were disabled, and she no longer was concerned about facing Bullet's wrath.

"Oh, Lord. I don't need this shit," Flashy said, fanning his face.

"We gotta get her some drugs!" Bullet shouted.

"We're close to the Fairground Projects. We're gonna have to swing through there. I know somebody who might have something."

"This time of the morning?"

"Your greedy ass should have been thinking about the time when you were allowing El Creepo to keep padding your pockets."

"That was good money, yo. I wasn't gon' turn it down."

Squinting out the window, Flashy said, "What street is this? I get confused up in these Fairgrounds."

"Man, I don't know nothing about no fucking Chester Township."

"Oh, this is Engle Street," Flashy said, after locating a street sign. "Keep going. Make a left at the corner." Staring out the window, Flashy said, "Okay, now we're on Peterson Street. I know where I am. Keep going all the way down until you get to Stewart Street, and then make another left."

At cruising speed, Bullet followed Flashy's directions.

"Right here. That's his car," Flashy said, pointing to an old-model Ford Explorer in the driveway of a white brick house that was at the end of a set of four identical, connected houses.

"Gimme some money." Flashy stuck out his hand. Despite the glittery feminine jewelry, the bright polish and intricate designs on every fingernail, Flashy's heavily veined hand exposed the masculinity he tried hard to conceal.

Bullet peeled off fifty dollars and handed it to Flashy.

"You got me showing up at the dopeman's house all unannounced and desperate. You gon' have to buy in bulk. Gimme at least two-fifty."

"The drug game done changed something serious anytime a dope boy can charge a nigga up for some pain pills and shit." Bullet gave Flashy the money.

Flashy rapped on the door and then disappeared inside. A few minutes later, he came out carrying a six-ounce bottle of water.

"Damn, these niggas provide water and shit to go with the pills!" Bullet was astonished.

Flashy gave Gianna two pills. He twisted the cap off the water. "Here, Lollipop."

Gianna gulped down the pills. A few minutes later, she was enveloped in a drugged state of ecstasy.

"Hey, Skittles," Gianna said in a whispery voice.

"Hmm," Skittles responded.

"Some men wanna have sex with your baby. Don't you think that might kill her?"

"What! Where's my baby?" Hysterical, Skittles swung on Bullet, her small fists swinging at the back of his head. "You're a fucking liar! You said my baby would be safe as long as I cooperated. Where's my fucking daughter? If anything has happened to my child, I'm going to kill you!"

"What the fuck set that bitch off?" Bullet shouted, dodging her blows. His hands gripped the grain steering wheel as he tried to keep control of the car.

"I don't know what's wrong with her," Flashy said, looking back at Skittles with disbelief in his eyes.

"Ain't nobody hurt your baby," Flashy said in a reassuring tone. "She's safe and sound."

"Liar!" Skittles slapped the ponytail off Flashy's head. "You fuckin' freaks better give me my daughter. I want my baby!"

"Yo, that bitch is skittzin'. Fuck her up for me, man!" Bullet ordered, angrily gnawing on the corner of his lip.

Flashy dove into the back seat and wedged himself between Bubbles and Skittles.

Instead of attacking Skittles with vicious slaps and scratches, or wind-milling like a girl, Flashy went into masculine mode. With

his fists balled, he held them up, positioned like a trained fighter.

Cautiously, Bubbles weaved out of the way.

Screaming, Skittles tried to fight back, but her efforts were futile. Flashy delivered a flurry of rapid-fire punches to her head and face, cutting off her shrieks, and slumping the frail girl in a matter of seconds.

Flashy turned to Bubbles. "You can get some, too, Bubblicious."

Threateningly, he drew back a fist. Dulled by Skittles' blood, the jewelry on his fingers no longer shimmered.

Bubbles shook her head. Holding up her palms in surrender, she said, "No, I don't want none of that. I'm good."

CHAPTER 36

Enticed by the promise of a raffle prize, the attendance at the recreation center had drastically improved at the second meeting. The seniors, who would ordinarily be socializing together in one of the smaller rooms, were the first to arrive and take seats.

Through word of mouth and out of curiosity, other members of the community had also shown up.

Not wanting to keep the audience waiting, Khalil went to the podium and got straight to the point.

"Thank you all for coming out. We've invited you to this meeting to make you aware that Portia Hathaway, a fifteen-year-old girl, was lured into a car by an adult man driving a white Cadillac."

"That fast-behind girl probably forced herself in that man's car while she was making her escape!" shouted a short, rotund man with an owlish face and round eyeglasses.

"If that were true, the driver should have alerted the authorities by now. Let's not be so quick to add our brushstrokes to the portrait of Portia that the system has already painted. Portia is considered a runaway and there has been no effort to search for her."

"The city's already operating over budget. So it's understandable that they wouldn't waste a lot of money trying to track down a girl who doesn't want to be found," said a woman wearing a business suit.

Khalil adjusted his glasses. "An adult male was spotted coercing

Portia into his vehicle. With the amount of time that has passed, this man probably figures he can do anything he wants to Portia and no one will ever bother to look for her."

Saleema cleared her throat.

Picking up the hint, Khalil added, "Luckily, there's someone who is very concerned about Portia. Her name is Saleema Sparks, and I'm going to turn the microphone over to her now." Khalil stepped to the side.

Darn! She could have punched Khalil for putting her on the spot. She wasn't a public speaker. She'd only cleared her throat to remind Khalil that there were people who cared enough about Portia to start this campaign to find her.

Amirah, Tasha, Stacey, and Chyna applauded. "Go, Miss Saleema! Go, Miss Saleema," the girls chanted.

She treaded to the podium with confidence in her footsteps that she didn't feel inside. Having no idea what she was going to say, Saleema tried to come up with a speech in the few seconds it took to adjust the microphone to her height. Nothing came to mind, so she decided to simply wing it.

"Good evening, my name is Saleema Sparks. I grew up in Southwest Philly, near Fifty-fourth and Chester Avenue. Like this neighborhood, mine was pretty rough. I was raised by relatives, passed around from one aunt to the other. No real foundation. No rules. I don't know what family love feels like."

There were murmurs of sympathy.

"Like Portia, I was a tough girl. I got in fights at school. I fought after school; I fought in the neighborhood; I fought all the cousins that I lived with at various times. Looking back, it seems like I spent my entire childhood engaged in battle. No one understood me and I didn't understand myself. The bottom line is, I knew no one cared about me and that knowledge made me act out in anger."

"That's a shame," one of the seniors muttered.

"You are right. It is a shame when an entire neighborhood knew that I was sent to school without being dressed properly, with my hair uncombed. It's a shame when they were aware that I came to school unprepared and without supplies. But everyone turned a blind eye."

"Umph! That's just terrible," someone in the back uttered.

Revisiting memory lane was so unpleasant, Saleema paused and rubbed her forehead, overcome with emotion.

"Take your time," William Daniels encouraged as though Saleema were a Baptist preacher, pausing in the middle of a sermon.

She exhaled slowly. "I'm not a psychologist...I don't have a college degree, but I do know how it feels to be on the brink of womanhood without a caring role model in your life. It's confusing. Your body is changing; and not only boys...but even grown men are suddenly giving you special looks. That attention can be very flattering when you've never experienced love. When you've always been perceived as not good enough."

Saleema caught glimpses of her girls. They were all looking at her with furrowed brows, their eyes filled with compassion. She'd never shared her unhappy childhood.

"I ran a social club called Head Up from my home. With Head Up, I tried to provide a warm atmosphere for girls from troubled homes. I kept them involved in numerous positive activities. Portia was a member of Head Up. During our private conversations, she divulged how embarrassed and furious she was to have a mother who was addicted to crack."

"That drug is the ruination of the black community," said Miss Hattie.

Looking for a laugh, the owlish-looking man added his two cents. "That dang drug produced a swarm of crack babies. They big now

and bad as all get out. Running around, wreaking more havoc than they drug-addicted mammas. We got double trouble: crack mammas and ornery teenage crack babies."

Saleema ignored the man's negative comments. She smiled. "Getting back to Portia…Though it didn't surface often, Portia had a smile that could light up a room. Despite her quick temper and loud mouth, she had a good side. Most people do."

"That's the truth," William Daniels said.

"I want to find Portia. She's been missing for over a month. I'm hoping that you all will assist us by taking some of the fliers we have on hand to your places of employment, to the hair and nail salons, barbershops…any businesses that you patronize."

Somber, the girls stood up. Holding stacks of fliers, they began moving to the rear.

"If we plaster this city with Portia's image, people will be forced out of their comfort zones, forced to take notice and maybe… eventually, someone will care enough to give us the information that will lead to her safe return.

"Portia Hathaway is being chalked off as a runaway…one of thousands of disposable kids. I want you to understand that a daughter of this village is an abducted teen. If we combine our energy, our efforts, and our love, I believe we can find Portia. I know that together we can save her life. Thank you."

The room was briefly silent as the community absorbed Saleema's words.

Saleema gave a faint smile and then returned to her seat.

Khalil stepped forward. "Thank you, Ms. Sparks, for your personal testimony and for reminding all of us that Portia is not just a statistic. She's a young girl. One of our own. It is our duty and responsibility to find her."

There was an eruption of applause and outbursts:

"That's right. We not gon' take this lying down."

"The police don't wanna waste their time looking for black children."

"You ain't nevah lied. Bet if she was a white girl, her picture would be flashing over the news, morning, noon, and night."

Motioning with his hand, Khalil quieted the crowd. "We're going to meet here again tomorrow at five to brainstorm ways to come up with funding that would go toward increasing the reward."

"How much is the reward?" someone shouted.

"At present, we have only five hundred dollars that I personally contributed. But we're hoping to collect donations. One of our plans is to erect billboards across the tri-state area with Portia's image, her description, and the tip line number."

"My women's group sells dinners every Saturday. We use the money to help with expenses for the rare few from this neighborhood who attend college," the woman with the business suit offered.

"We've launched a website: HelpfindPortia.com. I'd appreciate it if you'd visit the site and post any upcoming funding events. You'll also find a link where you can make donations."

"I'm too old for all that computer jazz," Hattie said, "but I intend to make a contribution."

"We appreciate it, Miss Hattie. The girls have a form you can fill out, and you'll get a receipt for your donation."

"There's a Beef and Beer Social at a little bar on the corner of Twenty-fifth and Wharton in South Philly. I'll see if we can donate a portion of the proceeds to help find that girl," the round, owlish man said in a contrite, rasping voice.

"Thank you, everyone. I hope you'll all visit the website and pass on the information to your friends, family, and coworkers."

This time, there was no mad dash to the exit sign. People mingled and discussed the numerous ways they could help.

As Saleema observed Khalil chatting and shaking hands, the woman wearing the business suit approached her. "You're such a dignified young woman. It's hard to believe that you were a delinquent during your youth."

Saleema laughed. "Yes, I think most people who knew me would call me far worse." Saleema didn't dare tell the woman about her colorful past as a prostitute and a madam. That would be too much information. "But I've changed my ways," Saleema said with a smile. "And so can Portia and all the other girls I've been trying to help."

"You're right. We shouldn't be so quick to give up on our youth. You gave us all something to think about. I'm going to pray for Portia. And I'm going to discuss this issue with my pastor…see if we can get our church involved in helping to find her."

"Thank you. Thank you so much," Saleema said sincerely.

Suddenly, Amirah's giggly voice came over the amplifier. "Hold up, everybody. There's one more thing—we have a prize to raffle off." She looked toward the back, where Chyna was holding a basket filled with ticket stubs.

Preening for the audience, Chyna graced them with her beautiful smile. She held out the basket as if she were on *The Price Is Right*, showing off a prize.

"Pick a number, Miss Show-Off," Amirah said.

"Oh!" Chyna reached inside the basket and pulled out a stub. "Number fifty-four."

"Hot damn!" William Daniels shouted, looking at his ticket stub.

Amirah held up the portable DVD player donated by Saleema.

"I don't know how to work none of those computer contraptions." Mr. Daniels was visibly disappointed.

"This is a portable DVD player. You can watch your movies anywhere you want," Amirah explained.

"Hot damn!" Mr. Daniels repeated, now thrilled at the prospect of owning a state-of-the-art gadget.

# CHAPTER 37

Filled with resentment, Gianna watched Bullet and Bubbles sharing a blunt. Bubbles sat up front, where Gianna used to sit.

"Yo, the other day when I rolled up on you and dude, you was riding him like you was trying to bust a nut. Lemme find out."

"I was acting. Just tryin' to get him off quick. You know I don't cum for nobody but you, Daddy."

Gianna's ears burned. From what she could recall, Bullet couldn't stand Bubbles and vice versa. At some point, during the weeks that she was kept high on painkillers, Bullet and Bubbles had become a cozy couple.

At the red light, Bullet turned toward Bubbles with the lit end of the cigar inside his mouth; his teeth were clenched tightly on the unburning end. On cue, Bubbles opened her mouth; her lips touched his as she accepted the blast of thick smoke that Bullet blew into her mouth.

Observing such an intimate act made Gianna shift uncomfortably in the back seat. Skittles sat next to Gianna, staring out the window. Unaffected by the lovey-dovey behavior up front, she mumbled to herself like a crazy person—lost in her own world.

Jealousy burned Gianna's face like fire. Bullet had never treated her with that degree of affection.

Yearning for some attention, Gianna said, "Hey, Daddy, one of my customers asked me if I would get with him on the side. I told him, hell no! My daddy will whoop my ass if he caught me stealing money from his business—"

"Bitch, shut the fuck up. You 'bout to get stomped for even thinking some shit like that."

"I wasn't thinking that. I was just telling you what that trick wanted me to do."

"That didn't even need to be spoken on." He gritted on Gianna through the rearview mirror. "Scoot over, baby," he said softly to Bubbles.

Bubbles moved as close to Bullet as the center gear shift console would allow. "Calm me down," he said in a grumpy tone of voice.

"You want some head?" Bubbles asked in the sweetest tone of voice Gianna had ever heard her use.

Gianna looked at Bubbles with unbounded scorn.

"Yeah." Bullet lifted up slightly, giving Bubbles access to his zipper, which she swiftly pulled down. "That bitch done got on my nerves. Got me amped up and my man done got hard." He pulled on the blunt, his features contorted and mean.

Giving Bullet a warm smile, Bubbles said, "I gotchu, Daddy. Concentrate on traffic while I calm your nerves down." Bubbles buried her head in his lap and Bullet put the burning blunt in the ashtray.

The windows of the Cadillac were recently tinted. No one could see Bullet's hand pushing down on Bubbles' head.

Every three or four minutes, Bullet yelled. "Hold up! You gon' get us killed! Stop! I'm about to cum!"

Responding to his fervent protests, Bubbles would lift her head and rest it against Bullet's stomach, waiting patiently for him to give her permission to resume sucking his dick.

When? How had Bubbles started getting so much attention. Sure, trying to call her mother was stupid, but Bullet had taught her a lesson. It wouldn't happen anymore. She'd suffered the consequences and wished they could move forward.

Bubbles didn't make nearly as much money for Bullet as Gianna

did. Bubbles hadn't even had the intense oral training that Gianna had gotten. It hurt Gianna to the core to be demoted to sitting in the back seat with crazy-ass Skittles.

"That's enough." Bullet patted Bubbles' head impatiently.

Coming up for air, she asked, "You want me to stop?"

"Hell, yeah. It's six-thirty. Shouldn't she be outside taking a smoke?" Bullet made a sharp right into a road that led into a strip mall in Eddystone, a small borough near Chester. A Shoprite Supermarket was on the left and Wal-Mart was on the right.

"Yeah, that's the time she said she goes on break."

Gianna had no idea what they were talking about. She hated being out of the loop, but dared not ask Bullet what he and Bubbles were talking about.

"There she is." Bullet pointed. "That's her!" he said excitedly.

Leaning toward Bullet, Bubbles stared out the driver's side window. "Yup, that's her."

Who? Gianna craned her neck to see who Bullet was referring to. Following their gaze, Gianna spotted a white girl who looked about sixteen. The teen had blonde hair that hung to her shoulders. She was talking with some teenage boys, all wearing Shoprite store uniforms while they smoked cigarettes. From what Gianna could see, they were typical kids…laughing, joking around…having fun.

"Aiight. Make yourself look presentable. Fix your hair and put on some lip gloss."

Bullet drove in the opposite direction of the Shoprite store. Keeping the Caddy out of sight, he parked in Wal-Mart's lot, squeezing between a van and a commercial truck that advertised the name of a plumbing company.

"Now this is how it's gon' go down," he said to Bubbles. "Tell ya girl…what's her name?"

"Amber."

"Yeah, tell Amber you got a hook-up for her when she gets off

work tonight. Take her to the side. Don't let them lil' young crackers she kicking it with hear your conversation. Be discreet."

"I will."

"Tell her if she take a ride with you tonight, you can introduce her to your Oxy connect and get her enough pills for her and her friends to get high with for a week. Yo, and tell that ho not to be bullshitting. If she want the connect, she gotta be ready at ten o'clock tonight. Make sure she understands that this is a one-time only deal. "

"Okay, I gotchu." Bubbles looked at her image in the mirror.

"Put a mint in your mouth," he barked, suddenly agitated with Bubbles. "I don't want you scaring her off with your breath smelling like you been sucking on a pair of sweaty balls."

Bubbles scrounged around inside her small purse and popped a Tic Tac in her mouth and then opened the car door.

"Don't fuck this up." He narrowed his eyes in warning.

"I won't. I'ma catch that bitch for you." With a fake smile plastered on her face, Bubbles got out. Squinting at the blazing sun, she walked across the lot toward the supermarket.

Bullet looked back, watching Bubbles with silent concentration. When Bubbles approached the group of kids, he turned around and relit the blunt.

"Aw, yeah. I need another piece of candy. And a white girl. Whew! This is a come-up! Fuck Amber. I'ma name that ho Vanilla Flava," Bullet said, speaking to himself. "She might be white on the outside, but after I school her, that ho gon' be moving them skinny hips with rhythm and working that pussy like she came out of the womb fucking big, black dick."

He released a cloud of smoke, smiling as if imagining himself lying on top of the white girl, teaching her the intricacies of fucking black men.

Gianna didn't know how or when Bubbles had met the blonde named Amber, but based on Bullet's utterances, it was clear that he was up to his old tricks. He was planning on kidnapping another girl.

One thing was for sure...they didn't need another bitch in the house. Three girls were more than enough. And judging by the way Bullet was drooling over the blonde, he intended to give all his personal time and attention exclusively to her.

While Bullet and Bubbles were picking up the white girl from her job, Flashy drove Gianna and Skittles to the current auction house. The house was hidden away on a remote block that looked more like an alley of a Third World country than an American city street.

The row of dilapidated houses looked like they should have been condemned. The windows of some were boarded up, while others had stained sheets or tattered blankets serving as window treatments.

Gianna located a faded street sign that read: *Mary Street.*

Wearing stilettos, Flashy got out of his car and stepped carefully along the crumbling concrete.

He looked around. "I don't see any cars, so I guess the bidders are parking a couple blocks over. They'll probably arrive on foot. Can't blame them for not wanting their cars to be spotted on Mary Street."

Silently, Gianna and Skittles walked behind Flashy. Having fun with his role as the wardrobe mistress, Flashy dressed Gianna as a sexy princess with a sheer, flowing cape that covered a lacy bra, panties with side straps, and a frilly garter on her thigh. She also

had a gold scepter and a jeweled crown to wear during the bidding process.

"You look beautiful, Lollipop," Flashy complimented. He screwed up his lips when his eyes flickered down to her gauze-covered index finger. "I'll be glad when that finger heals. It's distracting from the look."

Skittles was garbed in roaring twenties attire. A red flapper outfit was accessorized with a headband, boa, and a flashy cigarette holder. Poor Skittles was losing so much weight, she looked frail and ridiculous in the oversized costume.

Using a key, Flashy opened the door to one of the houses where ragged blankets were hung at the windows. "The man who rented me this spot refused to clean it, so me and a friend of mine was in here all day, scrubbing and cleaning, trying to make it somewhat presentable."

Gianna turned up her nose. The strong scent of pine couldn't disguise the odor that clung to the walls of the decaying house.

"I know one thing, I'm going to run this auction in an organized manner. Nobody gets to go past his fifteen minutes. We're gonna be outta here in three hours. These tricks got ten minutes to get here. If they don't show up on time, we're rolling out. Nobody keeps Miss Flashy waiting," he said, referring to himself as a Miss and in third person.

Minutes later, there was a series of sharp raps on the door.

Gianna recognized a few of the gleaming-eyed men who poured through the door. Scanning the crowd, she looked for the shiny-haired man who called her his bridal doll... the man who'd promised to rescue her.

With Bullet adding a white girl to the household, Gianna didn't stand a chance of regaining her status. Bullet treated her with contempt and she'd be much better off if Bullet sold her. She searched the men's faces, but her rescuer wasn't among them.

# CHAPTER 38

The auction ran efficiently like Flashy had promised. The absence of Bullet's hostile personality was a plus.

When Flashy pulled up to the house on Second Street, Bullet's Cadillac was parked in the makeshift driveway in front of the house.

Flashy handed Gianna a wad of rolled-up bills. "Give this to Bullet. Tell him I took my cut off the top."

"Aren't you coming in?" Gianna asked, her expression crinkled with worry. She didn't want to be in the middle of Bullet and Flashy's business transaction.

"I'm too tired to put up with that crazy bastard's bullshit. Tell him I'll holla tomorrow. By then I should be in a better mood to listen to him accuse me of trying to rob him blind."

"Suppose he gets mad?"

"Let him! I'm not worried about that coked-up fool." Flashy grimaced. "The only thing I'm concerned with right now, chile, is taking my ass home and soaking my feet."

Flashy fluttered his lashes to punctuate the statement.

Gianna wasn't referring to Bullet getting angry with Flashy. The expression, "kill the messenger," was echoing in her ears.

"Whew, Lawdy," Flashy added in a lilting voice, having no idea or a bit of concern that Gianna was afraid that Bullet would beat her for having the audacity to handle his money.

"Standing in these high-ass heels for all those hours was pure murder. My poor corns and bunions are screaming bloody murder to get out of these shoes. I gotta go!"

"Okay," Gianna said dryly, reaching for Skittles' hand. "Come on, Skittles. We have to go in the house now." She guided Skittles out of Flashy's car and steered her toward the front door.

Since the time when Flashy went upside Skittles' head, the girl was acting like a couple screws had been knocked out of place. Skittles no longer cried for or even mentioned her daughter. She mumbled to herself all the time.

Weirdest of all, she didn't flinch when Bullet slapped the shit out of her. She didn't yell or utter a sound whenever he used his thick leather belt on her ass.

It was like Brielle, the girl Gianna had met in Rite Aid, was no longer present. What was left behind was a vacant shell known as Skittles.

Dreading having to hear sounds of passion as Bullet trained the white girl, Gianna hesitantly pecked on the metal security door. It took almost ten minutes before Bullet began unlocking the multiple locks on the inside door.

A pile of coke was centered on the coffee table. His nostrils were outlined with the white powder.

"Where's Flashy at?" He sniffed in the excess powder that was visible outside his nose.

Gianna gave Bullet the wad of cash.

"Flashy told me to give you this money. He took his cut off the top. He'll holla at you tomorrow." Gianna spoke in a casual tone, hoping to keep Bullet at an even keel. A scared-sounding voice was apt to set him off.

He started counted the money. He sniffed the air. "Is that Skittles stinking up the place?"

"Did you mess on yourself, Skittles?" Gianna asked gently.

"Whatchu asking her for? That buggin' bitch don't know up from down. Take her in the bathroom so she can wash her stank ass."

On the way to the bathroom, Gianna stopped in the smelly bedroom she now shared with Skittles.

She clicked on the bedroom light and gasped. "Girl, you scared me," she said to Bubbles, who was sitting on the side of Gianna's pee-stained bed, bent over with her face buried in her hands.

Gianna couldn't resist taking a jab at the dejected-looking girl. "How come you're back in this room? Did Bullet kick you out of his bed? What happened? Did that white girl take your place?" Gianna snickered.

Bubbles yanked her hands from her face, revealing a black eye. "Do you see a fucking white girl?"

"What did you do to get on Bullet's bad side?"

"Fuck you, bitch. At least he didn't cut off my finger."

Gianna flinched. She didn't have a comeback. Bubbles had hit a nerve. Fighting back tears, she took off her crown and leaned her scepter against the dresser. Using her now favored left hand, she quietly poked around in Skittles' drawers, looking for a clean pair of underwear and pajamas.

While Gianna explored the dresser drawer, Skittles moseyed over to her own bed and flopped down.

"Damn, she stinks," Bubbles complained. "Didn't I hear Bullet tell you to wash her funky ass?"

Without replying, Gianna held out her good hand, beckoning Skittles to come with her.

After sitting Skittles in a tub filled with warm sudsy water, Gianna gathered up her soiled panties. With her nose turned up, she double-bagged the panties inside a plastic grocery bag.

"These are going in the trash," she informed Skittles, who muttered in gibberish.

Though Skittles didn't earn as much as Gianna or Bubbles, she

did okay for a girl who didn't communicate and only spoke in her own made-up language.

"None of this is your fault. You always mess your pants after those nasty men do it to you in your butt. Bullet messed you up when he opened you up with the handle of his knife," Gianna whispered, shaking her head at the memory.

Bullet was mean. He was a monster at times, but Gianna was starting to understand his ways. She missed being his favorite bitch. The one he kicked it with. She missed being his confidant. She wouldn't stand a chance of getting back in his good graces if that white girl started making the most money.

What was the girl doing so quietly in Bullet's bedroom? Why wasn't he in there giving her some training? Maybe he didn't like her. Curious, Gianna decided to sneak a peek at the new girl.

"I'll be right back, Skittles. Wash your butt real good, okay?"

Skittles laughed to herself and playfully splashed the sudsy water, as if she were a child.

Bullet's bedroom door was wide open. *Bitch must be fast asleep. Exhausted from training.* Bullet didn't usually let a bitch rest when he first caught her. It would be odd for her to be laying back... chilling.

Most likely, Bullet needed to snort some lines in order to deal with the no-rhythm white chick.

Surprisingly, his bedroom was empty. There was no trail of clothes leading to the bed. No rumpled sheets. No blonde-haired girl sprawled out and exhausted from Bullet's intensive training.

Where is she? Gianna wondered, though she was delighted that the white girl was nowhere in sight.

She heard the low rumble of Bullet's voice. He was talking to Bubbles. Gianna rushed back to the bathroom to tend to Skittles before she got in trouble.

As she slipped back inside the bathroom, she could see Bullet standing in the doorway of the girls' bedroom. He was holding his leather belt.

Ooo, Bubbles gon' get it! She crept out into the hallway, unable to resist watching Bubbles get a whipping.

Bullet flicked the belt. "Take your clothes off. I'ma put some welts on that blubber cuz I messed your face up bad enough."

"Why you gon' beat me again?"

"You know why. You think one black eye is enough for tryin' to play me?" He chortled. "Nah, ho. You gon' get the full treatment for fuckin' with my pimpin'."

"But it ain't my fault, Daddy. I ain't know Amber was getting off at nine; that bitch told me to meet her at ten," Bubbles explained pleadingly.

"Take your shit off. That's the second time I done told you. Make me say it again and I'm pulling out my shank."

"Okay, Daddy."

Gianna felt excited as she heard the rustling sound of Bubbles coming out of her clothes.

"What should I beat?" Bullet asked in an ordinary tone of voice.

"I don't know what you mean, Daddy," Bubbles' words came out in a terrified tremble.

"I wanna beat those plump titties, but you need them for work. Guess I might as well light some fire to that fat ass," he mused, like whipping her buttocks was a monotonous task.

Stifling giggles, Gianna covered her mouth. Bubbles thought she was Bullet's new bottom bitch. Now she knew how it felt to be on his shit list.

"You a ruthless ho," Bullet said. "Did you think I was gon' let that shit ride? You deprived me of adding a skinny white girl to my stable. Do you know how much skinny white girls bring in?"

"We can go back tomorrow. Catch her ass at nine o'clock," Bubbles appealed.

Thwack! The sudden crack of leather against flesh startled Gianna, making her jump.

Bubbles let out a scream that could raise the dead.

"Shut your big mouth before somebody calls the cop on me."

"I can't help it; that hurts," Bubbles said, crying.

Curious, Gianna eased up to the bedroom door. Bullet had Bubbles lying on her tummy, her butt shaking like jelly as she shuddered in fear.

"I ain't even get started good and you screaming like you crazy."

"Please, Daddy. Don't hit me with that belt no more. I'll get you that white girl tomorrow night. I promise."

Thwack, thwack, thwack! He struck Bubbles three times across her ass. Her screams were so high-pitched, it was a wonder that windows and mirrors didn't start shattering all over the house.

"Do you think I'd give you another chance to mess up my plans again? I don't need yo' stupid ass to catch me a ho! As long as I got my looks and keep my game tight, I'ma keep pulling in young hoes. "

Bullet noticed Gianna standing in the doorway. "She's making too much noise. Get over here and help me. Stuff her mouth the same way Flashy stuffed yours."

Responding to Bullet's order, Gianna hurried over to the smelly twin bed and shook an old lumpy pillow out of the case.

"Open up your damn mouth," Gianna snarled.

Lips sealed as if glued shut, Bubbles twisted and turned, her tortured moans emanating from her nose.

"I ain't playin' with Bubblicious," Bullet said firmly. "She got two seconds before I go get my shank."

Instantly, Bubbles, who was lying on her side, stretched out her

neck and opened her mouth wide, as if begging to be fed the balled-up cloth in Gianna's left hand.

Gianna jammed in as much of the pillowcase as she could fit in Bubbles' mouth. Then she grabbed a handful of the girl's hair and pulled it hard. "Why you fuck up *my* Daddy's money?"

Bullet took his shirt off and went to work. By the time he finished, bits of Bubbles' buttocks were welted and bloody.

"Get up and go clean your ass!" Bullet ordered. "While you in the bathroom, get Skittles out of the tub."

"Go 'head in my room, Lolllpop. No! Hold up." He studied her princess costume. "I don't like that outfit. Go put on your bride shit and wait for me in my bed."

CHAPTER 39

Gianna waited for Bullet, wondering if he'd tear up her bridal costume in a fit of rage. She thought about the tone of voice he'd used when he'd told her to change. There was an unmistakable softness. Maybe he'd finally forgiven her.

"This 'here comes the bride' bullshit had them tricks losing they minds at the auction. One mufucka asked me if he could buy you. He said he wouldn't take your virginity." Bullet laughed in remembrance. "Dumb mufucka wanted to pay me a whole lot of paper to eat your box out when he got good and damn ready."

Gianna gave a nervous smile. She couldn't read Bullet's mood. Didn't know if he was still mad at her.

"I hated that man," she said, lying. "I don't ever want to leave you, Bullet."

"You don't?"

"Never."

He sat on the bed, touched her face. "We gon' put the past behind us. You came through for me in there with Bubbles. Showed me that even though your people got money and raised you like the Fresh Princess of Bel-Air, you know how to get gangsta when you need to. I believe you'll kill a bitch for me if I asked you to."

"I would," she said softly. Tears welled in her eyes. It was the truth; she'd do anything she had to do to stay on Bullet's good side.

"Why you crying?"

She wiped a tear. "Because I love you so much it hurts. I hate sleeping in there with Skittles. I want to be back in here with you."

"You miss the way I used to let you fall asleep, buried under the covers with my dick swolled up in your mouth?"

She nodded.

He unsnapped his jeans. "Let's get it poppin'."

Gianna sat up, eager to help him out of his jeans.

"Lay back down. I ain't ready. I wanna beat my meat for a minute."

Gianna complied. She lay still as a statue, staring into space. Waiting for Bullet to tell her what he wanted her to do.

Surprisingly, he sat down at the bottom of the bed. "Remember that old pimp in Atlantic City?"

"Uh-huh." She had no idea what was coming. Bullet's disposition could go from sunshine to thunderstorm in split-seconds.

"He told me that the number one rule to pimpin' was to never put your mouth on a ho's stank cum hole. Eating a ho's box out will make her think she running shit."

Gianna was silent. Her mind raced to come up with a comment. "A ho's pussy is too nasty for you to put your mouth on, Daddy. That old pimp gave you good advice." She hoped she'd spoken words that Bullet wanted to hear.

"I know y'all nasty! You ain't gotta school me," Bullet said scornfully.

"You're right. I'm sorry." She hoped he wouldn't beat her for telling him something he already knew.

"Them tricks at the auction spend big bank just to lick and suck your stank hole. They got me curious, y'ah mean?"

Though puzzled, she nodded her head, pretending to understand.

"Did you wash your box out yet?"

"Not yet; I was taking care of Skittles. I'll go do it now," she said, eager to please him. "Do you want me to take a shower or should I give myself a whore's bath?" Grateful for an opportunity to please Bullet, Gianna was talking fast and excitedly.

"Hold up. Lemme check you." Unbelievably, he did something he'd never done before. He put his face between Gianna's legs and inhaled deeply.

"Nah, you ain't gotta wash nothing," he told her and then kissed the delicate strip of cloth that covered her moistening center.

That unexpected act of intimacy made Gianna clench up with desire.

When his tongue slipped beneath the fabric and entered her pleasure center, she screamed out his name.

"Aw, yeah," he moaned. "You taste sweet." He licked and sucked greedily, while Gianna writhed out of control.

Bullet stilled his tongue. "I'll be right back. I gotta go get my shit."

He left Gianna with her legs wide open, her vagina pooled with overflowing lust.

He returned to the bedroom with a bag of coke.

He spent the next fifteen minutes alternating between snorting the drug and licking it off Gianna's clit.

Finally, he entered her. Slowly and tenderly, as if being careful not to split her in two.

But Gianna didn't know what had come over her, she shouted for him to give it to her hard…to plunge deeply.

"You don't run shit," he reminded her in a lethal whisper and continued slow-stroking.

Once she caught on to his unhurried pace and uncomplicated rhythm, their horizontal dance was flawless.

Later, lying in Bullet's arms, Gianna decided this was where she

belonged. She felt loved and protected. She felt safe and secure.

Her parents were becoming a foggy memory. *Fuck 'em*, she told herself. They could have found her if they really wanted to. Bullet was the only person who really cared about her. He had taught her a painful lesson, using tough love to make her take the game seriously.

"I was wrong to be messing with your phone like that. But I was so confused. Now I know what I want…I just want to be with you," she whispered in his ear, meaning every word.

"But I'm sayin', though…don't ever lie to me again. I went easy on you. My mind kept telling me to cut off your whole finger, but something in my heart made me settle for taking off just the lil' tip."

"Thank you, Daddy."

"Don't play with my heart, no more." He narrowed an eye. "I won't go that easy on you the next time. Believe that."

"I won't play with your heart. I love you. I worship you!"

"Now that's the kind of shit a pimp wants to hear." Bullet smiled and pulled Gianna closer. He clipped her chin between his fingers and kissed her. A soulful kiss on the lips—another first.

"Damn, I can't believe how I'm acting. First, I eat your box out and now I'm kissing you on your mouth. You got me slippin', lil' mama," he said affectionately. Then his eyes went cold. "So don't let me catch you lying or doing nothing foul."

"I won't. I learned my lesson. For real, Daddy."

"We see eye to eye?"

"Yeah, Daddy.

He kissed her again.

Gianna closed her eyes, enraptured.

"You fuckin' the game up," he complained as he licked his lips and smiled. "You tryna flip the script?" he asked, laughing.

"No, Daddy." Gianna giggled.

Playfully, Bullet hit her with a pillow. "Yeah, you tryna make a nigga get a job and bring home a paycheck."

Gianna beamed at him. Bullet was so cute when he wasn't mad.

"Yo, stop looking at me like that, with your sexy self and those pretty brown eyes."

Blushing, her heart swelling with hope, she lowered her eyes and dreamily contemplated a life where she could get this kind of sweet loving from Bullet all the time.

They could be so happy together, if they got out of the game. They could make ends meet, if they both got jobs. Well, she wouldn't be allowed to get working papers until she turned sixteen. But she'd do her part as soon as she could.

After experiencing Bullet's tender touch, it was going to be unbearable to be stroked and fondled by a paying customer.

CHAPTER 40

S mall personal donations poured in via the HelpfindPortia website. The community pitched in with numerous fundraising events. And through Khalil's professional contacts, local businesses had contributed larger sums of money.

All total, fifteen thousand dollars had been raised as a reward for Portia's safe return.

Groups of people had organized and helped post fliers throughout every section of Philadelphia.

Manning the tip line, Saleema was swamped with lots of crank calls. There were a dozen or so from concerned citizens who sincerely believed they'd seen someone they thought fit Portia's description. But nothing had panned out so far.

Using his laptop, Khalil was seated in Saleema's kitchen, updating the website.

Saleema went to the computer center that was on the second floor. "That's it, girls. You're an hour past your allotted computer time. It's time to wrap it up."

"Aw, I need ten more minutes. I'm applying for a job. CVS is hiring!" Amirah said.

"She's lying," Stacey said, laughing. "Amirah can't even get her working papers yet."

Saleema peeked over Amirah's shoulder and couldn't help laughing when she discovered that Amirah was actually playing an online cake-baking game.

Saleema shook her head. "In my day, we played with Easy Bake ovens."

"You can do it quicker online," Amirah boasted.

"Okay, seriously. It's time for you young ladies to go home."

"Is the professor keeping you company tonight?" Chyna inquired, lifting a brow. All the girls had started calling Khalil "Professor."

"He's updating the website," Saleema said firmly, refusing to even joke around about her personal affairs. "Log off, girls."

Murmuring their disappointment, each girl gathered her belongings and filed down the stairs. Before they left, they made it a point to prance to the kitchen to tell Khalil goodnight.

"Amirah is still such a little girl. I love that about her," Saleema told Khalil. "While the other girls were flirting and playing around on MySpace, Amirah was playing some kind of cake-baking game. Isn't that cute?" Saleema moved closer to Khalil's screen to see if there were any interesting tidbits or any Portia sightings in the chat room.

"They're talking about a girl from Wilkes-Barre who went missing around the same time as Portia. She's seventeen and has a five-month-old baby."

"Oh, God. Is the baby missing, too?"

"Yeah. She brought her baby to Philly, intending to leave the child with its father for a few weeks. But they never made it. Her car hasn't been found, either. It's like she fell off the earth."

Saleema shook her head, perusing the chat, hoping to find some mention of Portia.

Khalil looked over at Saleema. "You look tired."

"I am, but I want to read all the updates before I go to bed."

Khalil pushed back his chair and stood, moved behind Saleema and gripped her shoulders, his strong hand kneading her tired muscles. "Relax."

His hands felt so good, she closed her eyes and did just that.

Then she tensed. Every part of her body was acutely aware of how close he was to her.

"Relax."

"I can't."

"Why not?"

"I don't know."

He stopped massaging. Standing behind her, he softly kissed the back of her neck.

She shivered.

His arms closed around her, his hands cupping her breasts, as he traced delicate circles around her nipples with his thumb.

"Relax," he whispered again, and then nibbled on the side of her neck.

Feeling limp, her head lulled back, resting against Khalil's chest, while his mouth teased the flesh on her neck, and his thumbs worked magic, turning her nipples into hard stones.

His lips; his thumbs were making her ache. "You know I want you," he whispered, his breath tickling her skin. "But I don't want to rush you. If you want me to stop, tell me. You know I will."

His husky, sensual voice, his coaxing lips, his masculine scent, all rendered her speechless, had her melting in his arms.

Incapable of speech, she swiveled around. In a series of motions, she removed his glasses, set them on the table, and cradled his handsome face.

"I don't want you to stop," she admitted, looking into his eyes.

He grasped her buttocks, massaging the firm mounds while his warm lips pressed against hers. His sensual tongue, exploring adventurously, sending chills up her spine while a fire raged inside.

The heat from her groin burned into his. "Khalil," she moaned.

He lifted her dress and gazed at the V-shape in her thong. His

hands slid over her slim hips, palms gliding up and down her smooth mahogany flesh.

"I want you now," Saleema gasped.

"How do you want it?"

"Huh?" she said, breathless. She was dripping with desire. This was not the time to play games.

He ran a caressing finger down her cheek. "If you need me to be gentle, I can do that."

"Oh, my God," she rasped. Khalil was way too sexy. "I just..." her voice trailed off.

"You just what?" He stroked the V between her legs until the soft cotton became damp. "You want me to take away that tension?"

"Yes," she whimpered.

"How? Do you want me to slide it in gently?"

Flashes of pleasure shot through her body. His words were making her crazy.

"Um. I'm not sure."

"Turn around."

She turned around, and gripped the edge of the table as he slipped her dress over her head. Standing in her kitchen wearing only a thong and a bra, her dress was in a lump on the floor. This was the stress release her body had been longing for.

The sound of his zipper going down echoed inside the kitchen. With her back to him, her buttocks bared, Saleema lowered her head until it was pressed against the table. She shuddered in anticipation.

The next sensation was his lips kissing a tender trail down her back, making her jerk and whimper.

"Too gentle?"

"I'm not sure." She spoke through panting breaths.

He delved his long middle finger into her moistness, stroked her clit with the pad of his thumb.

Her inner walls tightened around the thickness of his finger. Her moans were deep and anguished as her body writhed against his touch.

"You like it like this? You wanna cum on my finger?"

"It's been so long, Khalil. Don't make me tell you what I want, because I don't know," she said pleadingly.

"I know what I want," he said in a low sensual voice. "Spread your legs for me."

Bent over the kitchen table and uncertain of exactly what Khalil planned to do, Saleema slowly and cautiously widened her stance.

He lowered his body, scooted under the table, grabbed the ledge for support, and licked open her folds until his tongue was saturated with her womanly flavor.

Saleema felt as if her body was vibrating against his tongue. Hunched over the table, she allowed him to weaken her with every thrust of his sturdy tongue.

Unable to bear another second, Saleema's legs buckled, and then gave out completely. In an instant, she was in a heap on the floor.

Khalil inched forward, no longer positioned beneath the table.

Saleema crawled to him. Pushing him down, she mounted him, now knowing what she needed.

Soothing her blazing hot spot, she positioned his rigid length between her legs. She eased down slowly, taking him in inch by inch. When she felt their groins touch, she lost control, and rode him like a stallion…rough and hard.

CHAPTER 41

Gianna sat up front in the passenger seat with Bullet, while Flashy was squeezed miserably between Skittles and Bubbles in the back seat of the Cadillac.

Announcing his irritation, Flashy rolled his eyes and popped gum loudly. "I would have driven my own car if I knew you were going to stick me in the back with these two heifers."

Unhealed welts on Bubbles' rear end prevented her from sitting in a normal position. To relieve the discomfort, she sat tilted, with her big bosoms smashed against Flashy's shoulder and neck.

Twisting away from her, Flashy snarled, "Move over, heifer. You're suffocating me. Bullet! I want to sit up front. I swear I'm suffocating back here. I can't breathe with this big heifer's titties flopping around in my face."

Gianna heard Bubbles, who sat directly behind her, mumble something derogatory in response to being called a heifer.

Irritably, Bullet glanced over his shoulder. "Yo, Flashy, stop bitching all the time. You getting paid to do a job, not ride my damn jock."

"I'm not tryna ride nothing; I gotta man!" Flashy retorted.

"That's whassup. Glad to hear it."

"But I'm worried about my reputation."

"What about it?"

"I worked hard all week putting together their special costumes and you got them dressed like two-dollar whores."

"You not running shit. How many times I tell you that?"

"We're partners and I should have some say-so over the wardrobe."

"I notice you take the money for them costumes out of my cut! I ain't feeling that. I don't want them wearing all that makeup and crazy costumes. You got them looking like they trannies."

"That's a lie! They look classy in the outfits I choose for them. Why do you want them looking like skanky hoes?"

"Cuz that's what they is, man. They hoes! All they gotta do is show some nekkid ass and the tricks will spend their dough. Fuck all that extra bullshit."

"So let me get this right...I don't have any say-so about these hoes?"

"Nah."

"So why am I in this car with y'all?"

"You ain't gotta be. Want me to pull over and let yo' ass out?" Bullet hit the brakes, screeching to a stop. "What's it gon' be, man? I can work the auction my damn self."

"Puh-leeze. You don't have any finesse whatsoever. But since you don't need me, why don't you start finding your own auction spots?"

"That's what I pay you to do. But the girls ain't to be tampered with. I don't want them rockin' no more faggot-ass, transvestite gear."

Flashy *tsked* and batted his glued-on butterfly lashes angrily. "Have you noticed how much paper we pull in when I'm in charge of selecting the wardrobe?"

"If I leave it up to you, you'll have them prancing around in angel wings and whatnot. That's bullshit. I want my hoes to look like hoes; not like they 'bout to recite lines from a fairytale."

Bullet glanced at Gianna. "Ain't that right, baby?"

"You right, Daddy. Flashy was wasting your money on those stupid outfits. We stay looking hot when we wear the clothes you buy us."

"Baby!" Flashy shouted in disbelief. "My ears must be deceiving me. Don't tell me you slippin', Bullet? Are you going soft, muthafucka?"

"Lollipop belongs to me. I'm the only family she got. She belongs to me…body, mind, and soul. I can call her whatever I fuckin' feel like calling her. But you don't know nothing about feelings that run that strong."

"Hmph. Not too long ago, your feelings were so strong, you jacked-up her finger."

Bubbles burst out in titters of laugher.

Bullet narrowed an eye at Bubbles as he hit the gas pedal. "You just earned another ass-whooping, Bubblicious. You gon' be leaning on the other side of your hind parts this time tomorrow."

"I ain't mean to laugh. I'm sorry, Daddy."

"You outta pocket, bitch. Your sloppy ass thinks everything is a joke. I'ma show you how serious I am about my business. You crazy if you think I'ma let you mess up the game."

"I ain't do nothing. I only laughed a little bit. I'm sorry, Daddy. I won't laugh no more."

"Too late. You already did."

Gianna smiled at Bullet, co-signing his decision to give Bubbles more lashes of leather across her ass.

"You're a fool, Bullet!" Flashy exclaimed. "Bubbles' rear-end is already torn to shreds. How you gon' work her if you keep tearing up her ass?"

"She gon' have to fuck standing up." Bullet stroked Gianna's hair as he drove.

Flashy sighed in disgust. "As soon as this auction is over, pay

me my money so I can be the fuck out. You are turning my stomach, Bullet."

"Whatever, man."

Surreptitiously, Flashy gave him the finger. Bubbles chuckled softly, carefully muffling the sound with her palm clamped over her mouth.

"Scoot over, Lollipop. Why you sitting so far away from me?"

In an instant, Gianna was straddling the gear shift console, cuddled next to Bullet, and resting her head against his muscular arm.

She felt so special. So loved. Though she was wearing stilettos, a pair of booty shorts, and a push-up bra, Gianna felt like a princess. And her daddy, Bullet, was the king of her world.

Looking utterly lost, Skittles stood in the middle of the room.

Pointing to Skittles, Bullet told the lustful men who were at the clandestine auction house, "This bitch right here likes to take it up the ass. I'm starting the bidding at twenty dollars for her."

Flashy groaned. "You don't have to be so crude, Bullet. Let me handle the bidding. Go work the rooms so you can make sure these tricks don't try to stay past their fifteen minutes."

"Back up, man. I got this shit."

Retreating, Flashy *tsked* in disgruntlement.

"Can I get twenty dollars?" Bullet asked gruffly.

No one offered twenty dollars.

"Damn. Y'all muthafuckas tryna go hard. Aiight, then. Let's take it lower. Can I get ten dollars for this ho? What's the deal? Her pussy don't get a lot of action. It's nice and tight."

"Ten dollars," a poppy-eyed man called out.

"Twenty," said another.

Bullet clapped his hands together. "Now that's what the fuck

I'm talking about. We got a bidding war going on. Can I get twenty-five for this ho with the grip-tight hold?"

"Twenty-five," a young baller said. He was clean-shaven, dressed in fresh gear, and blinging so brightly, his presence was blinding. For a man who seemed to possess a lot of material things, the baller's eyes sparkled with excitement at this new-found sport.

"This auction jawn is off the chain. Better than watching pit bulls fight," he told his overweight sidekick.

"Thirty," the poppy-eyed man said in a huffy tone.

"Thirty-five? Who wants to pay thirty-five for the grip-tight, do it right?" Bullet said, laughing, obviously enjoying the limelight.

The baller fell silent.

"Aiight, then. Sold for thirty dollars."

The poppy-eyed man hitched up his pants and clutched Skittles by the arm, claiming her. He had to guide her gingerly...patiently... like he was escorting an old woman.

Upset over her sore and red-striped backside, Bubbles wasn't smiling.

"Put your game face on," Bullet quietly hissed at her.

He turned on a megawatt smile for the crowd of men. "Aiight, now this next ho's name is Bubblicious. Now she might present a challenge. She thicker than a Snicker, and only limber and creative muthafuckers need to bid on this ho. See, she just got that ass whooped, so she can't lay flat on her back. She got some big titties, though. Work 'em any way you see fit."

Bullet glared at Bubbles. "Pull yo' top up. Show these bidders how fat your titties is."

Bubbles squirmed uncomfortably and then pulled up her top. The crowd of men cheered and uttered lewd comments.

Bubbles revealed her double D's. Bullet squeezed her left breast. "Nice and soft."

"Big set of melons," someone commented.

"You can work your dick all up inside the crevice." Bullet demonstrated by sliding his hand up and down her cleavage.

Gianna couldn't see Bubbles' face, but she could feel the girl's shame—her palpable embarrassment.

"Drop it low, Bubblicious," Bullet demanded.

Despite a sore and welted ass, Bubbles went into action—working her thick body, gyrating the way she had planned to do for the Soulja Boy video she'd thought she was going to audition for when she met Bullet.

"Can I get fiddy dollars for a titty-fuck with this big jumbo bitch?"

"Yo!" the baller responded, starting the bidding. "She can drop it low on this." He gripped his crotch.

"If you wanna get with Bubblicious, you need to dig deep. Can I get fiddy-fi?" Bullet pulled Bubbles' tight-fitting skirt up, exposing her shaven vagina. "She keeps her grass cut." Bullet fell out laughing. "Bubblicious is ready! She rocks out with her cock out!"

"Fifty-five dollars!" yelled someone from the rear. A man wearing a blue cap moved forward when the bidding didn't progress further.

"Sold for fiddy-fi dollars to the man in the blue cap." He patted Bubbles' tender ass. "Aiight, Bubblicious. Show that high-bidder some love."

The man smiled proudly. Lips poked out, Bubbles trudged off with the man wearing the blue cap.

# CHAPTER 42

Bullet rubbed his hands together. "Now I'm 'bout to present y'all with the cream of the crop, so all of y'all need to getcha money up. This ho is so sweet and innocent, I don't even allow no niggas to smash it…" Bullet laughed, "I don't allow no white crackas that opportunity, either."

Boisterous laughter erupted from the crowd of men. Flashy sighed in disgust.

"She gives some damn good head. That's her specialty." Bullet shook his head. "Yo, her oral game is on point. She suck so long and so good, I was like…damn, Lollipop! That's how she got her name."

Bullet's antics got more guffaws from the crowd.

Gianna licked her lips as she was expected to do, though her mind was on being Bullet's wife. Maybe he'd get out of the game if she got pregnant. He wouldn't possibly allow her to hustle if she had his baby. She liked her plan. Get pregnant by Bullet. Then he'd have no choice but to take her out of the life.

"I'm starting it off at seventy-five dollars," Bullet said proudly.

Flashy groaned. "You starting too high."

Bullet ignored Flashy. "I ain't even gon' hold you. Lollipop got some juicy, sweet-sucking lips."

"A hunnit!" the baller called.

"That's what I'm talkin' 'bout. Ain't none of y'all evah had your dick sucked the way Lollipop can. Who else wants to experience

the feeling of her plump, delicious lips? I'm asking for one-twenty. Can I get it?"

"A buck-fifty!" the baller said in a cocky voice.

"Oh, aiight. Mr. Playa over there is tryin' to get Lollipop on lock. Y'all gon' sit back and let him get his pole slicked and licked? Do I hear one-sixty?"

The baller folded his arms, indicating he was through bidding. No one else placed a bid.

"Aiight, then. Sold for one-fiddy. Get your condom from Flashy over there."

As Flashy was handing the baller a condom, the poppy-eyed man came out of the room he'd been in with Skittles.

"Go get Skittles ready for the next bid," Bullet snarled at Flashy with his head bowed as he counted money.

"Damn, I'm just one person. I can't do everything."

In the bedroom with the high bidder, Gianna could smell his expensive cologne. The baller was dressed fly, but he wasn't as cute as Bullet. She decided that giving him a blowjob might not be as difficult as she thought. Now that she and Bullet were officially in love, she was grateful that the first man she had to suck off wasn't funky or gross.

"Can we go without the condom? If I give you a big tip?"

"I'm not allowed to," Gianna expressed with a sad face.

"I won't tell if you don't," he coerced.

"I'll get in trouble. I can't. You have to put it on."

"Are you the bitch with the good pussy that I heard niggas pay a fortune to eat?"

"Uh-huh."

"Well, let me try some of that. You can jack me off. You allowed to let me go raw dog if you just use your hand, right?"

"I guess," she said, giving an unsure shrug.

"Take them shorts off and get on the bed." The baller unzipped his jeans and pulled out an average-sized dick.

"Play with it," he encouraged. "It can get a whole lot bigger." He stuck his pole inside her hand. She stroked for a few moments.

"Wait. Lemme taste your twat and see if it's really all that."

"Okay, but don't do it too long. I don't know if my daddy wants anybody licking on me anymore."

"He didn't say I couldn't."

He was right. Bullet hadn't said that going down on her was off limits. She spread her legs for the baller. He slid his tongue between her folds, lapping her juices until she moaned and clamped her thighs against his face, despite herself.

At that moment, Bullet opened the door.

It all happened in a blur. Bullet lunged for the baller and wrenched him away from Gianna. The baller still had his pants down, unable to defend himself when Bullet punched him in the face.

As Gianna pulled up her shorts, the beefy companion skidded awkwardly into the bedroom, looking irate and ready to defend his baller friend.

"You aiight, Mookie?"

"What the fuck your goon-ass gon' do?" Bullet drew his gun. "I'll drop yo' ass and Mookie's, too. When yo' big ass fall, muth-afuckas gon' be yelling, 'timber'!" Bullet gave a sinister laugh.

In seconds, the baller named Mookie had his attire back in place. He swiftly pulled a gun out of seemingly thin air and fired at Bullet. But his aim was off. The shot hit a dusty, floral picture that was hanging crookedly on a wall.

Screams and shrieks sounded outside the bedroom. A stampede was heard, heading for the front door.

"Let's go, Mookie," the unarmed sidekick implored. "This nigga

ain't about nothing. He on some bullshit pimpin'. He ain't worth it. Come on; we better than this. Let's be out!"

"Nah," Mookie said. "This pimp nigga got a gun pointed at me. I ain't leaving 'til he chalked up on the floor." Though Mookie was talking tough, his words had a hollow ring. Even more telling, the hand that held the gun was shaking like a leaf.

With skills honed from target practice with his girls, Bullet shot the baller's gun hand. The gun flopped out of his grip and hit the floor with a clunk.

"Shit!" Mookie grabbed his wounded hand. Drops of blood plopped on his expensive high-top sneakers.

"Get the gun, baby," Bullet told Gianna.

"Yo, it ain't even got to be like this. Let's talk about this…man to man," the portly sidekick rationalized.

Gianna slid off the bed. On shaky legs, she crossed the room. She bent over, picked up the gun, and brought it over to Bullet.

"Hold that jawn. Point it at that muthafucker." He nodded at the sidekick, who was sweating like he'd just finished jogging a couple laps.

Target practice had made her deathly afraid of guns. Gianna wanted to scream and throw the gun down. But facing Bullet's wrath was more frightening than picking up a gun.

"Man, I'm bleeding out. I gotta get to the hospital," Mookie said in a raspy, pained voice.

"Does your hand hurt, Big Ballin'?" Bullet taunted the bleeding man. "You should have thought about needing a doctor before you stuck your face in my bitch's box. Just cuz you wearing all that ice, don't mean you can have anything you want. I'm the only muthafucka 'spose to be licking between her legs."

"Aiight, man. It ain't that deep. Lemme get to a hospital."

"Nah, you crossed the line. I'ma keep my eye on you right here.

I ain't never witnessed a muthafucka bleed to death. That shit might be interesting."

"Nigga, is you crazy?" the sidekick blurted, mopping perspiration from his forehead. "Let my man get to a doctor. He bleeding, man. He needs to handle that."

Without a word, Bullet fired off a second shot. Gianna screamed from shock.

"I'm hit!" the sidekick uttered in amazement, grimacing as he covered the bullet hole in his shoulder. Blood began oozing his fingers. He stared wild-eyed at Bullet. "Whatchu do that for?"

Bullet cut his eye at Gianna. "Give me Big Ballin's gun. He leaking too bad to do anything with his piece."

After Gianna did as she was told, Bullet looked at Mookie's gun admiringly. "Nice!" He tucked it inside his waistband.

"You niggas better not move," Bullet warned. He pointed his gun from one wounded man to the other, causing them both to flinch, cringe, and cower.

As he ushered Gianna through the door, he stopped suddenly and turned around. Frowning, he gave both men threatening looks.

"Y'all big ballin' muthafuckas fucked up my auction. Start emptying out yo' pockets. Both of y'all. Hurry up!"

"Can I call for some emergency assistance after I give you my dough?" Mookie asked.

Bullet gave Mookie a hateful gaze and then aimed his piece at the man's sneakers. "Wanna bullet in ya foot?"

"Naw." Mookie started digging in his pocket with his good hand.

"You was frontin' out there during the auction, acting like you a walking bankroll..." Bullet pointed his gun at the man's right sneaker. "You better have at least a coupla stacks tucked away."

"I do! I gotchu. But I can't get to my knot. It's in my right pocket." The baller was bleeding profusely.

Using his uninjured arm, the sidekick scrounged around in his own pocket, and then threw a nice-sized wad toward Bullet. "That's a stack right there."

"Gimme both y'all cell phones."

Maimed, both men struggled to retrieve their cell phones.

"Yo, Lollipop! Collect their phones. While you at it, get those rocks outta Big Ballin's ears. Take all that bling he wearin'. Nigga been blinding my vision ever since he stepped up and started biddin'."

Gianna did as she was told. Gun on the floor, her bare foot holding it in place, she removed all the baller's diamond and gold jewelry and gave it to Bullet. The man howled torturously when she pulled the tightly fitted ring off his bloody, wounded hand.

 CHAPTER 43

Outside, there wasn't a car in sight. Luckily, they were on a deserted street. No one had called the cops.

"Where the fuck did Flashy take my hoes?" Bullet asked Gianna.

"They probably got a ride from one of the tricks," Gianna suggested. "He left his car parked in front of the house. The trick probably drove him to pick up his car."

"I'ma whip Flashy's ass for moving my bitches without permission. Plus the fact, that punk knows I gotta stay low-key. Why he showing muthafuckers where I rest my head?"

"That was real dumb of Flashy to take a trick to your crib."

"I might have to shoot Flashy in the head." Bullet gave his words more thought. "Nah, I'ma let that punk live a little while longer. He got a buyer for Skittles' baby. I'm expecting a big windfall in another week or two."

"For real?" Gianna was overtaken with joy that Samantha was still alive. She didn't care about the windfall. She wanted to see the baby...make sure she was being cared for properly. Maybe if she told Bullet how much she loved children, he'd change his mind about selling the sweet little girl.

Skittles wasn't in her right mind anymore; it was only right that they take responsibility and raise Samantha as their own.

"Do you see that shit?" Bullet blurted. As they neared Second and Parker Streets, they saw Skittles meandering aimlessly, her gait wobbly in her high heels.

"What the fuck is wrong with Flashy? How that punk gon' leave this bitch to wander the streets like she's homeless?"

"Skittles!" Gianna yelled out the window. Skittles continued staggering.

Bullet shot ahead and hit the brakes. "I'm not playing with this bitch." He jumped out the car, snatched up Skittles, and roughly threw her in the back seat of the car.

"Where's Bubblicious?" he asked. Skittles murmured some long-winded nonsense.

"Where's Bubbles?" Gianna asked firmly, helping Bullet resolve the problem, though she didn't expect a coherent response.

"Running," Skittles replied to Gianna's and Bullet's surprise.

"Which way she go?" Bullet was infuriated. "I'ma go upside Flashy's head with the butt of my gun. That faggot know better than to turn my bitches loose like they a pair of worthless stray dogs. These hoes is valuable. I don't appreciate that punk disrespecting my property like this."

Breathing fire, Bullet pulled his cell phone out and called Flashy's number. "What the fuck's wrong with your punk ass? How you gon' drive off and leave my bitches to run loose in the streets?"

Gianna could hear Flashy's high-pitched voice, but couldn't make out his words.

"Who called the cops?" Bullet sounded distressed.

Gianna shot a worried glance at Bullet. Visibly upset, he started sniffing and swiping at his nose.

"My allergies kicking up," he told her. She quickly rustled through the glove box, searching for his medicine.

"Why'd you let a trick drive y'all to my crib? Why didn't you take them back to your crib? You knew I'd be sliding through to grip 'em up. Oh, your man wouldn't like that! I bet your man don't mind spending that money you make off my hoes."

There was a burst of ear-splitting yelling coming from Flashy's side of the conversation.

"I don't owe you shit," Bullet barked. "I only made a coupla dollars off that auction. You can blame yourself for that. Ain't nobody tell you to let all them paying customers run out the door."

Flashy yelled something indecipherable.

"Fake-ass Big Ballin' ain't get nothing but a flesh wound. His right-hand man was only grazed a lil' bit 'round his shoulder area. Them niggas ain't dead. You could have doctored them up while I kept the bidding going."

In a clear, loud voice, Flashy yelled, "Fuck you!"

"Fuck you, too, punk-ass!" Bullet exploded and then disconnected the call.

He briefly stared into space and then shot Gianna a dirty look. "Did you find my medicine yet, bitch?"

Her heartbeat thumped in fear of being smacked and, once again, demoted to being treated like dirt. She couldn't bear to fall out of grace again. "It's not in the car. I think it's home...in the bathroom."

Visibly trying to calm himself, Bullet took a deep breath and released a sigh. "It's not your fault, baby. We gotta find Bubbles. Then we gotta get out of town. Chester is hot."

"Can we stop and pick up some clothes?"

"No. That punk-ass Flashy done fucked the game up."

"What did he do?"

"That sucka claims he told Bubbles and Skittles to run cuz the trick was threatening to report a double murder."

"You didn't murder anyone!" Gianna sounded pissed.

"I know. But that's just what the fuck I get for letting a fruit loop handle pimpin' business."

"Whatchu gon' do, Daddy?"

"Soon as I find Bubbles, we gon' head to Atlantic City. I'ma call that old dude...you remember my old celly?" Bullet said in a chipper tone, as if he expected Gianna to have fond memories of her time spent with the malicious, sickly ex-pimp. "I'ma call my man and find out if we can crash at his crib 'til I get back on my feet." Bullet scowled. "But I gotta find that bitch, Bubbles, first."

Gianna felt nauseous at the thought of having to stay in the cruel old pimp's tobacco-reeking house. She dreaded having to hear him fuss at Bullet for not being hard enough on his hoes. He probably would think that Bullet should have beat Bubbles with a wire hanger instead of a belt. And...he would taunt Bullet for cutting off only the tip of Gianna's finger instead of the entire thing.

Bullet was a good pimp. He was still learning. He sure didn't need that crusty old man to be putting torturous ideas in his head.

There had to be somewhere else they could go besides Atlantic City. Then she thought of Samantha and her heart leapt.

"What about the baby?" Gianna whispered. "You gon' let Flashy collect that money and keep it?" she asked, pretending to be interested in selling the baby.

"Fuck that baby. That's the last thing on my mind. The buyer is from Wisconsin or somewhere real far. He's still negotiating the deal with Flashy."

"But Flashy's got shady ways. After what he did tonight, I don't think you can trust him to be on the up and up." She wanted Bullet to go get the baby and take her with them.

"I ain't going back to jail. Ya dig? I gotta get out of Chester. I'll deal with that baby situation when I can think straight."

"Okay." Gianna rubbed his hand comfortingly, while her mind raced to come up with an idea that would keep them from having to move in with that cranky, old pimp.

"Roll me a blunt. Nah, never mind. You can't roll for shit." He stared through the windshield. "Where the hell could that fat bitch be at? After she roll me a blunt, I'ma fuck her up for making me drive around while the Chester po-po is looking for my ass."

Continuing on Second Street, Bullet stopped near some construction work at Edwards Street.

"There she is!" Gianna shouted, pointing.

Barefoot, Bubbles was fast-walking down Edwards Street, heading toward Third Street. Her tight skirt, obviously put on in a hurry, was inside out and twisted around backward.

Bullet accelerated. The roaring motor and screeching tires startled Bubbles, causing her to jump back and shriek in fear.

Bullet jumped out the Cadillac, and began forcefully beating Bubbles about the head and face. He dragged her to the idling car, shoving her inside the back seat with Skittles.

"You know what happens to runaway hoes, don'tchu?"

"I wasn't running from you. I wouldn't do that, Daddy. Flashy told me the cops was looking for all of us. He said you killed them ballers. He told me to run somewhere and hide. But I don't know my way around Chester. I ain't know where to go." Her voice was defensive.

"First of all, I ain't kilt nobody. Second, if I do end up with a murder rap, it's gon' be cuz I put a bullet in Flashy's dome. That punk need to stop spreading rumors all the time."

He tossed a bag of weed and a cigar in the back. "Roll me a blunt." He rubbed his nose. "Damn, I wish I had my medication."

"You wanna take a chance and drive by that convenience store on Ninth and Kerlin?" Gianna asked.

"Nah, we gotta bounce outta this town. I'll be aiight when Bubbles hand me that blunt."

 CHAPTER 44

Lost in her own thoughts, Gianna wasn't paying any attention to the phone conversation Bullet was having with the ex-pimp.

Preoccupied with trying to come up with ideas to prevent Samantha from being sold, she didn't notice that Bullet had hung up and was cursing in anger and frustration.

Intellectually, she knew she was too young to be a mom, but her naïve heart told her that together, she and Bullet could give Samantha a good life. Well, maybe not a traditional life…but being with them would be better than being sold to a sick pedophile who would do awful things to the infant for the rest of her life.

Skittles was crazy, but there was a chance that she might make a recovery and return to her normal frame of mind, if she could see her daughter. Holding and kissing Samantha might give her a new lease on life. Skittles could make Bullet a lot more money if she wasn't such a loony tune.

She turned to Bullet and noticed that they were approaching a sign that read *WELCOME TO DELAWARE*.

Good! She didn't question where they were going, but was relieved that it was the opposite direction of Atlantic City and the irate ex-pimp. Her parents were in New Jersey, too. But they were the last people she wanted to see. Because of their apathy, she'd lost part of her finger. If they really wanted to find her, they could have, Bullet had finally convinced her.

"Your peoples got money. They could have hired a private detec-

tive, if they really wanted to find you. They living their own lives. Glad to have you out of the way," Bullet had told her repeatedly.

The way she felt about it…her mother and father could both kiss her ass. She despised both of them. Bullet was the only family she needed.

"Why this muthafucka ridin' my ass?" Bullet muttered.

Gianna and Bubbles both looked out the back window.

A dark compact car was tailing them…too close for comfort.

"Damn, Daddy, that little-ass car behind us 'bout to ram your bumper," Bubbles complained.

"What the fuck? Reckless sonabitch driving that lil' squatter must be smokin' crack!" Bullet sped up, putting distance between his Cadillac and the dark economy car.

The dark car picked up speed and pulled up in the left-hand lane.

"They young bulls. And they throwing up signs," Bubbles informed.

"What kind of signs?"

"I don't know. I aint never seen those signs in Philly."

"Don't fuck with the Farms!" a voice hollered from the small car.

"TF!" another harsh voice rang.

"You fuck with Mookie; you fuck with Toby Farms, muthafucka!" the driver of the hooptie yelled. He looked no older than Gianna and Bubbles. Probably about fifteen or sixteen.

Then a shot rang out. Bullet ducked his head. Gianna scooted down to the floor mat, her arms covering her head.

"Oh, Lord. Somebody's tryna kill us!" Bubbles screamed.

Bullet did a quick, screeching turn. Cars skidded. Horns honked as cars slammed into each other. During the traffic pileup, Bullet drove bumpily over the island that separated north and southbound traffic and maneuvered into northbound traffic and pushed the pedal to the floor. He looked back with murderous fury in his

eyes, but then laughed when he saw the little squatter was in the pileup, too.

"That must've been Big Ballin's peoples. That clown couldn't handle the situation man to man. Nah, that punk ass had to send a car fulla strapped kids after me."

Gianna slowly rose up and eased into her seat. "What's Toby Farms, Daddy?"

"A section of Chester," Bullet explained. "Lil' young chumps tryna be gangsta."

"They shot a hole in the back door, Daddy," Bubbles informed, examining the door while sitting on a tilt. Her buttocks still too sore to sit straight.

"They fucked up my whip?" Bullet looked over his shoulder real fast and then returned his angry gaze on the road. "I'ma squash them Toby Farms niggas like they roaches," Bullet fumed.

"I can see the bullet!" Bubbles hollered in an excited voice. "It's lodged in the door. If it woulda came through, Skittles woulda got hit. I'm dead up, y'all."

"Fuck Skittles." Bullet growled. "Damn, don't I have enough problems? Now I gotta worry about getting that hole patched up and my door painted."

"You gon' have to get the interior fixed up, too. Cotton and shit is hanging out that bullethole."

"Goddamn! Always gotta be spending money on some bullshit." Bullet blew out a stream of frustration and then fired up the blunt that was resting in the ashtray. "Damn, I can't believe them niggas was on my ass like that. Bronco sure picked a bad time to try to get new."

"Who's Bronco?" Gianna asked.

"You know, Bronco! My man. You know...my old cellmate. Dude you met in AC. That ol' pimpin' muthafucka who got me into this hustle in the first place." Bullet frowned.

He got me into it, too, she thought with a mixture of sorrow and acceptance. She'd never thought of the mean, coughing from too many cigarettes man by name. Ol' Ex-pimp, was his name as far as she was concerned.

"Count that money I took off Big Ballin'." Bullet reached up and pulled wads of money out of his pocket and tossed it in Gianna's lap. She immediately started counting.

"I thought I had a come-up; now I'ma have to spend that nigga's paper on some body work. Ain't that some shit!"

"I know, Daddy. Them some foul niggas," Gianna soothed.

"How much?" Bullet yelled.

"Um, there's seven hundred in the small pile."

"Seven hunnit? That lying sidekick told me he had a stack. Count the rest," he ordered.

Gianna obeyed, flipping through bills. "There's fifteen hundred in the thick wad."

"That's all?" Bullet's incredulous voice was as high-pitched as Flashy's.

"There's a whole lot of small bills mixed in, making the knot look big."

Bullet exhaled loudly. "I should have smoked them two punks when I had 'em leaking blood in the bedroom."

"Yup, you sure should have," Gianna agreed.

"This is what we gotta do...we gon' get a motel room while my man, Bronco, gets his thoughts together. He said we can all crash at his crib but not until after he gets admitted in the hospital. He said he can't stand all the racket and commotion of having three young hoes under his roof."

"Aw, he must be really sick. When is he getting admitted?" Gianna put compassion in her voice, as if she really cared about the ex-pimp's failing health.

"I'm not sure. He said something about needing to get his insurance approved. He should know in a day or two."

Gianna nodded in understanding. But thoughts of Samantha occupied her mind. She doubted if she'd ever have peace of mind if she didn't try to save that baby from the wretched existence that was waiting for her in Wisconsin, or somewhere.

"I see a sign for a Red Roof Inn," Bubbles alerted.

"Nah, we can't stay near the airport…too close to Chester. Them crazy, young-ass muthafuckas would be grinning and laughing while they shot up everybody in this goddamn car." Bullet's mouth turned down as he continued driving…over the George C. Platt Memorial Bridge and onto I-76 West.

Bullet rolled up in front of a hole-in-the-wall bar. "Hold this money." He threw Gianna the wad of cash.

"I'ma go holla at this hooker who works in there. She's a hard-core ho. Bitch will pick-pocket a muthafucka while she giving him a lap dance." Bullet smiled, looking wistful, as if the hooker's dishonest practices were praiseworthy.

"Why you gon' to see her?" Gianna asked with undisguised jealousy.

"Last time I saw her, she was trying to choose up, but I told her that I don't deal with no seasoned whores. They hard to control… been in the streets too long."

"So why you gon' to see her now?"

"I'ma get the keys to her crib so we can stay there for a minute."

"Suppose she got herself a pimp. What we gon' do if her man is staying at her house?" Gianna asked, trying to gauge how much time she had to be settled somewhere before the man from Wisconsin came to pick up Skittles' baby.

His eyebrows rose in disapproval. "You outta pocket. Do you want me to knock your teeth out of yo' mouth?"

"No," she said, looking down.

"Then stop asking so many questions. Stay in your lane, ho."

"Alright." She smiled at him, testing his anger barometer.

"Skittles acting like she gotta go to the bathroom," Bubbles yelled.

Gianna twisted around and checked. "Yup, she do, Daddy. She squirming and mumbling like she do when she gotta pee."

"She better not piss on my seats. Tell her she gotta wait 'til we get to the crib."

"You gotta hold your pee," Gianna translated.

"Damn, I hope this bitch got some running water in that dip."

"Huh?" Gianna blurted. She thought they were past the stage of living in abandoned houses without electricity or running water.

"I'm just saying, the last time I was at the crib, she ain't have the water on. Damn shame cuz she had got a big lump sum amount of money a coupla years ago. She went through that dough real quick. Stay high all the time, forgetting to pay bills. That's why she was trying to choose up. She needs a business-minded man like me to manage her cash flow."

"How come you turned her down?" Bubbles asked from the back seat.

"Mind your business, Bubblicious. Ain't nobody talkin' to yo' ass."

"Bubbles stay tryin' to be all up in your business," Gianna said with loathing.

"I'ma be in that mouth in she don't learn how to keep it shut." Bullet glared at Bubbles.

"Anyway, that ho who was tryna choose up ain't even my type. She too far up in age."

"How old is she?" Gianna asked.

Bullet looked up in thought. "I'd say she somewhere around twenty-six...twenty-seven. Too old to train. I like working with fresh meat. Y'ah mean?"

CHAPTER 45

Bullet came back smiling and dangling a keychain.

"She's letting us stay?" Gianna was delighted.

"Damn right. Your man got good game. That ho is happy like it's Christmas morning."

He started up the car and pulled off. "Keep your ear locked to my phone. That bitch is going to call me at two o'clock when her dancing shift is over."

"Okay."

"Nah. Fuck that. I'll get there when and if I damn get there."

"Alright, Daddy."

Bullet parked two blocks from the hooker's house. With his arm wrapped around Gianna, he and the girls trekked to Delancy Street.

En route, they had to stop to let Skittles urinate. She squatted behind a fire hydrant and sighed with relief as her yellow flow streamed down the pavement.

Bullet rolled his eyes and groaned in disgust while Bubbles and Gianna shielded Skittles from any passersby who might call the cops on Skittles for indecent exposure and for openly pissing in a residential area.

The hooker's house wasn't fly, but it was presentable—better than the house where they'd stayed in Chester. An extra bonus... all the utilities were on.

Bubbles and Skittles were assigned one of the three upstairs bedrooms. "Take y'all asses to bed. We might have to get up early and bounce to AC."

Gianna and Bullet went inside the master bedroom, which was junky with wigs, lingerie and other clothing items strewn all over the place. Bullet knocked a bunch of clutter off of the bed and pulled back the sheets.

"I'm stressed, baby. Climb on top of me. I ain't got no strength to do nothing," he said.

Wearing a smile, Gianna removed Bullet's sneakers and socks. She kissed his feet.

He raised his head, grinning. "Lemme find out you some kind of foot freak."

"For you, I am." She covered his feet with kisses. Sucked his toes, the way a trick had done her. She remembered how good it felt and wanted Bullet to have that same pleasure.

Mimicking everything the trick had done to her, she slid her tongue in and out of the spaces between his toes. When Bullet moaned, Gianna joined him, his sounds of pleasure making her pussy wet and hot.

With his participation, she stripped his pants off. "I love you, Daddy," she whispered as she straddled him, kissing and biting his neck, making him squirm.

Bullet flipped her over on her back. "I can't lay dead and let you drive me crazy. Damn, how I let you get me open like this? You fuckin' up the game, Lollipop," he accused, scowling and breathing hard.

Positioning his dick between her legs, he murmured. "I been waiting to smash this ever since I caught Big Ballin's tongue embedded in yo' pussy."

Gianna moaned as Bullet pushed in deeply.

"Yeah, baby. Slang that pussy at me. We gon' make this bed rock."

By the time Bullet was close to reaching the finish line, Gianna

was screaming promises: "I'ma get you a pair of Louis V. sneakers; a big-ass chain; I'ma drape you in ice."

"What else, baby?" Bullet asked, steadily stroking.

"I'ma...ah," she moaned, overcome by the good feeling that Bullet was putting on her. "I'ma get you a new whip."

"Yeah, baby, and I'ma keep hitting this thing right."

Gianna began pulling her own hair, wrapping her legs around Bullet's waist as she swiveled her hips.

He unwound her legs, lifted them high, placing her heels up on his shoulders.

"Daddy, I'ma get you..."

"What else you gon' buy me?"

"Seven whips! A different color for every day of the week."

With a booming roar, Bullet released his load.

Gianna didn't know what was better...being filled with Bullet's passion or cuddling afterward in his arms. He stroked her hair as his breathing returned to normal. It seemed like the perfect time to talk to him about raising Skittles' baby.

But Bullet sat up suddenly, snatching his arm from around Gianna. "Where's your lil' clutch bag?"

She pointed to a chair that was piled with clothing. "Over there," she said, both puzzled and disappointed over his sudden interest in her clutch bag. "I hid it underneath all that junk. Why? What's wrong?"

"I was thinking about that shit you was talking a few minutes ago."

"Uh-huh..."

"You know...all that shit you plan on buying me."

"Oh!" She looked slightly embarrassed, recalling that she'd been talking out of her head. How could she buy him seven cars when she was barely able to keep gas in the one he was currently driving?

But it wasn't her fault. Bullet spent a lot of money on cocaine, she thought to herself.

Naked, Bullet stalked across the room and wrenched the clutch bag from beneath the junk in the chair. He snapped it open, peering inside as he returned to the bed and emptied the contents. Wads of cash tumbled out, followed by blood-encrusted jewelry.

"Man, I forgot I took Big Ballin's bling!" Bullet smiled proudly as he picked up an earring. "This is about two carats. Wonder how much I can get off the set?"

"You gon' sell it?"

"Hell yeah. I don't need no faggot-ass jewelry. I'm about gettin' paper, some blow, and long-stroking my ho. A couple cars would prolly get my dick hard," he added, laughing.

Even though she wanted to be wifey, Gianna couldn't help from blushing.

"Go clean this shit up and lemme see how nice it shines."

She trekked to the bathroom down the hall and cleaned the jewelry, shined it up with a hand towel.

When she returned, Bullet had clicked on the TV that was mounted on the wall. It was the only thing that wasn't covered with clutter in the messy room.

Bullet kept his eyes on the screen for a few moments, and then he lit a blunt. Blowing out smoke, he picked up and admired the shine of Mookie's diamond and gold jewelry. "This is good money. We gon' hit a pawn shop first thing tomorrow."

He returned the cash and jewelry into the clutch bag and handed it to Gianna. "Sleep with that tucked under you. I told you that hooker who owns this crib got light fingers."

By the time Gianna found a comfortable position, Bullet was snoring, with his back to her. Unable to find a way back into his arms, she snuggled against his back, inhaling his male scent. Running

her fingers up and down his toned back, his neck, and through his tumbles of curly hair.

Gianna awoke to hammering! Pounding! Drumming! *What the hell?*

Bullet threw the sheet off of his body. Instantly alert, he grabbed his jeans and hopped into them. He pulled his gun from beneath the mattress and tucked it in his waistband.

"Open the fucking door!" a woman's voice called from outside.

Gianna hugged her nude body. "What's going on, Daddy?"

"That ho outside tryna cause a commotion cuz I ain't go pick her up after work."

Bullet stormed out of the bedroom and ran down the stairs. Gianna heard him unlocking the door.

"Bitch, is you outta your mind? Who you think you is? Bangin' on this muthafuckin' door like you own the place? You want me to put my foot up yo' ass?" His menacing tone humbled the feisty prostitute.

"I'm sorry," she said meekly. "I had to get a cab and um…I was scared something happened to you. That's all."

Gianna felt proud of Bullet. He didn't back down to anyone. Well…he had back in the beginning, when that big baller driving the Escalade had come to pick up his soldiers off the corners. But Bullet had manned up since then. He didn't take no shit off of anyone. Gianna liked that about him. He handled shit like a real man.

One of the things he'd instilled in her was that her father didn't have any balls. "A real man would have found his only daughter

by now. Do you think I'd let a muthafucka steal you away from me?" he'd asked. "Man, I'd blast my way through concrete walls if somebody took you. Your pops should be ashamed of hisself for lettin' you be gone all this long. I told you he done forgot yo' ass. He got a new family. Ain't it obvious your peoples don't want you no more? Huh, dumb ass? What does it take for you to understand that I'm all you got in this world?"

Gianna wondered if Bullet was going to make her move into the spare bedroom. She didn't think she could bear hearing Bullet sexing up another ho. She'd put up with him and Bubbles, but that was in the past.

Bullet and a light-skinned, wig-wearing woman entered the bedroom.

The woman looked horrified at the sight. "Why you got that young bitch in my bed?"

Bullet slapped her. "Watch yo' mouth, bitch. Get yo' belongings and go rest yo' head in that spare room."

"But—"

Bullet glared at her. "You hard of hearing? Don't make me break yo' jaw. You know I will."

The woman raced around the room, gathering stuff, her route illuminated by the dim light that was cast from the TV screen.

On her way out of the bedroom, Bullet hollered, "Ain't you forgetting something?"

She stopped and rustled around in her purse, and then pulled out a clump of crumpled bills. "It was slow," she said, looking embarrassed.

Bullet counted the money. "A hunnit and twenty dollars? That's how much you think it cost to ride this dick?"

"Wasn't no money out there, tonight," she said apologetically. She averted her gaze from Gianna's face, too ashamed to look directly in the young girl's eyes.

"Man, I oughta whoop that ass for insulting me like this." He handed Gianna the crinkled bills. "Here, baby, put that in the clutch."

"You see this fine young thing right here?" Bullet asked the hooker. "She wouldn't nevah come home with less than a stack." He looked at Gianna. "Am I right, baby?"

Gianna nodded. There'd been many nights when she'd come home with less than five hundred, but she went along with Bullet's charade.

"You tryna choose up with this lil' bit of cash?"

The hooker held her head down.

"How many pretty muthafuckers you know who would give a broke-down ho like you a chance?"

"None," she murmured.

"I know that's right. That's why you ain't got no man."

"I'ma do better."

"I know good goddamn well you gon' do better than this. I wouldn't let you give me a hand job for this amount of money. You coming in here like gangbusters; like you holding something worthwhile. Man, get the fuck outta here."

"I can make it up to you."

"How? You got some more tricks lined up for tonight?"

"No, but I got some blow for you. Maybe we could party. All three of us."

"Gimme the blow."

Smiling, the hooker tossed Bullet a plastic bag. She approached the bed.

"Back up, bitch. Lemme test this shit." Using the long nail of his smallest finger, he scooped up some cocaine and snorted. After a few seconds, he nodded his head and smiled. He brushed off the odds and ends that littered the table next to the bed. Then he shook some cocaine into a pile.

Using his shank, he cut up and separated the narcotic into un-even lines.

"Aiight, now we can party. Start off by eating my baby's box out. If you make her cum, I'ma let you suck on this here pipe." Lewdly, he grabbed his dick.

"I don't want that lady licking between my legs!" Gianna yelled, repelled by the idea.

Bullet laughed and glanced at the hooker. "Lollipop's green when it comes to getting that cat licked by another female. But I'ma let you be the one to bust that cherry."

"No!" Grimacing, Gianna twisted away from the woman who was already crouched in position, her puckered lips aiming for her crotch.

"I was forced to witness yo' lil' ass all wiggling and moaning while that big ballin' nigga was snacking on yo' goods. So lemme see how much pleasure you get from another female tonguing you out."

"Please, Daddy."

With a heavy sigh, Bullet motioned for the prostitute. "Come snort a coupla lines."

She sank down on the side of the bed. "I like mine cooked."

"Nah, it ain't that type of party."

Looking pitiful, the hooker snorted a couple of the lines that Bullet had created on a jagged mirror.

"It's like this, Lollipop. I can make you do anything I want. You know that, right?"

"Yes."

"I want you to do this willingly. You know. Show me that you're really feeling yo' man."

"I am."

"Aiight. So…You turned your first trick for me. I sold your

virginity to Jimmy. My jawn was the first dick you sucked. Now I wanna be the first one to witness you bust a nut from a woman sucking on your stuff. After that...it's gon' be like we married."

Married! That was the magic word. It was as though Bullet had been reading her mind.

"That's what I want, Daddy. I want to us to be married."

"I know, baby. We gon' take that walk down the aisle one of these days...after we retire. Now be a good girl. Lay back, close your eyes, and open up your legs real wide. I'ma be right here beside you, stroking my dick, while you cum like crazy."

# CHAPTER 46

Music blared from gigantic speakers. According to the kids, the block party was poppin', but Saleema had a pounding headache and wanted to go home.

"Have some more cake," Ms. Hill, the block captain offered. "Better get you a piece before these little rugrats eat every last crumb."

"No thanks," Saleema said, shaking her head, looking at the outrageous spread that was displayed on six fold-up tables. There was every kind of meat, side dishes, and desserts imaginable. It would take an army to eat all of the food at the first block party the neighborhood had hosted in over ten years.

People were eating, drinking, chatting, and joking with each other. Teens were dancing up and down the street that was blocked off from traffic. Morale was high now that the community had banded together.

Saleema didn't feel their joy. Despite the neighborhood unity, Portia was still missing. *She could be dead while everyone is out here partying.* Saleema realized that her agitation was irrational and she was feeling frustration toward the wrong people.

Her anger was really directed at Portia's mother and aunt, who were not in attendance.

They were definitely keeping it real. Portia's family would look so fake if they came out and tried to pretend that they were remotely interested in Portia's whereabouts.

Saleema sighed. She was ready to say her goodbyes and leave. She'd stayed long enough, hadn't she?

Standing up, she was almost knocked down by a troop of little kids who were running around and chasing each other and squealing like crazy. *They must be on a sugar high*, Saleema decided.

"You leaving, already?" Ms. Hill inquired.

Already? She'd been there for three hours, smiling all those hours, despite feeling deeply depressed. She couldn't take another second of performing this charade, when in her heart, she felt like crying.

After so much effort...hanging fliers, canvassing neighborhoods, manning the tip line, monitoring the chat room, organizing meetings, raising money...

So much work and nothing to show for it. It was so depressing that no one had called the tip line with any information that could help locate Portia.

Saleema said her goodbyes, shook hands, gave out hugs and then drove home, feeling that everyone involved in finding Portia had found an inner peace. Everyone except her.

A few minutes after she got home, Khalil called.

"How was the block party?"

"Okay, I guess."

"The neighborhood's first block party in ten years was just okay?"

"Everyone had a good time."

"Except you."

"Yeah. I felt like I was in mourning while everyone else was celebrating. It seems like I'm the only person who really wants to find Portia."

"That's not true and you know it."

"You're right, Khalil. I'm in a bitchy mood and I'm depressed. I just want to know she's alright." Saleema wiped tears.

"We all do."

"But I'm taking it personal. I sincerely feel the loss. And I'm scared. Sometimes I have nightmares about her. In my dreams, she's being tortured and she's screaming for help, but I can't find her. Then she suddenly stops screaming and I wake up with the knowledge that she's dead."

"Saleema," he said gently. "You have to hope for the best."

A lump in her throat made it hard to speak. "I know," she whispered. "But I'm starting to give up hope. Portia's a fighter. She would have found a way to call me if she were still alive." Saleema swallowed.

"You still there?"

"Yeah," she murmured softly. "Portia's been gone all summer, Khalil. The odds aren't looking good. In my heart, I believe she's dead." Saleema broke down and cried.

"I'm on my way over, baby," Khalil soothed. "If you need me to hold you all night, then that's what I'll do."

"Okay." Her voice was tiny, like a child's.

A few hours later, Saleema finally found peace when she fell asleep, enfolded in Khalil's loving arms.

 CHAPTER 47

Two weeks had passed and Bullet couldn't get in touch with the old pimp. His voice lowered to a tone suitable for mourning, Bullet said that old Bronco had probably passed away from throat cancer.

That was a relief! But Gianna put on her game face and acted sad over the pimp's possible death, for Bullet's sake.

Still, she had other problems.

Bullet had gotten entirely too comfortable at the hooker's house. Most of the houses on the street were boarded up and Bullet didn't have to worry about prying eyes witnessing the coming and goings of him and his young hoes.

The hooker's name was Sizzle and she was having a terrible influence on Bullet. Along with Bubbles, they snorted cocaine night and day. When they weren't snorting, they were sleeping. Or eating.

Gianna was constantly running to the corner store, but she couldn't keep food in the house.

Sometimes Gianna used Bullet's cell to call Flashy, pretending to be calling on Bullet's behalf. "Did the buyer slide through yet?" she'd ask, her insides trembling with dread.

Flashy usually banged on her, stating that Bullet wasn't getting a penny from the baby sale. "You can tell Bullet that since he left me to have to deal with the wrath of Mookie and his crew, I'm keeping all the profits from the baby sale."

Other days, Flashy was agreeable. "No, that hook-up in Wisconsin fell through."

Gianna's relief didn't alter her jealousy over Bullet, Sizzle, and Bubbles…new partners in crime. To Gianna's shock, Bubbles didn't even protest when Bullet told her and Sizzle to get into a sixty-nine.

Money was running low. Bullet didn't have his head into his pimp game at all.

She recalled that Bullet still had possession of the two ballers' high-tech cell phones.

"Hey, Bullet, do pawn shops buy cell phones?"

"Prolly so."

"Can I take those two iPhones and try to sell 'em?"

"Go 'head and try it, but if you don't get nothing off of 'em, then you and Skittles need to get out there and do whatchu gotta do."

"I don't know where to go."

"Take yo' ass to the closest strip…the ho stroll, dumb bitch," Bullet berated her.

Gianna had no idea how to find the nearest ho stroll, nor did she know how to work one. At first, Bullet had always supplied the willing customers. Later, Flashy had handled that part of the game. Gianna didn't know how to get out there and ho on her own.

"Pick up a lighter from the store." He clicked his red lighter and frowned at the low flame.

"Are you gon' drive me?" she asked worriedly, not really knowing her way around Philly.

"Hell no. Don't you see me gettin' high? Walk, bitch."

"Okay," she complied. "Daddy, you want me to run some bath water for you before I go out?" Gianna asked, hoping that if he cleaned himself up, he'd come to his senses and act like a pimp again.

The bedroom stank to high heaven. Bullet, Bubbles, and Sizzle were funky, seeming to forget that there was soap and water in the house.

"Nah, I'm good. While you at the pawn shop, ask dude how much he'll give you for a fiddy-two-inch plasma jawn."

Sizzle frowned. "No! That TV is the last thing my cousin bought with the money she made off telling her story."

"You got a famous cousin?"

"My cousin's a hooker, too."

"Damn! You come from a long line of hoes?"

"Uh-huh. My grandma and her mom…shit…all the women in my family are hoes," Sizzle said proudly.

Bullet laughed. "Sounds like some Lifetime movie shit. Where yo' cousin at?"

"She locked up right now. She'll be getting out soon. Prolly gon' try to move back in here."

"Yo' cousin better keep it moving and find herself another crash spot."

"I know that's right, Daddy."

Bullet and Sizzle were caught up in a conversation that sounded like sheer nonsense. Frustrated and disillusioned, Gianna grabbed one of Sizzle's large shoulder bags. She needed something with some depth, in case she got enough money off the iPhones to buy some badly needed groceries.

With Bullet and Sizzle distracted, Gianna slipped another item inside the shoulder bag, telling herself that in order to keep food on the table, she had the right to steal anything that wasn't nailed down.

"Come on, Skittles," she said. "We're going for a walk."

Trying to remember the route to the pawn shop, Gianna kept her eyes on street signs. She walked to the end of Delancy Street

and turned left on Fifty-fourth. After many long blocks, tugging Skittles along, she ended up on Fifty-second Street—a busy street with lots of foot traffic, boutiques, and restaurants featuring foods from different cultures. There were so many vendors peddling their wares, she was reminded of being on vacation in Nassau in the Bahamas. Interspersed between the many establishments were numerous pawn shops, a delight to her eyes.

It was the end of August and it was hot as a bitch. Eager to get out of the burning heat, she pulled the door handle of the first pawn shop she encountered. The door wouldn't open. The salesmen shook their heads, refusing to buzz her in. She yanked on the door again. They pointed to a sign near the door: *Identification Required.*

She didn't have ID, and she was too young to pawn anything. Disappointed, she turned around. Maybe she should ask one of the vendors if they wanted to buy the two expensive iPhones.

She scanned the many vending tables that were filled with pocketbooks, T-shirts, sunglasses, socks…everything imaginable. When her eyes landed on a table that had an assortment of phone chargers, headsets, pouches, and other cell accessories, she felt like she'd hit the jackpot.

Pulling Skittles along, she weaved through the crowd, crossing a small street where an open back truck that sold fruit and vegetables impeded foot traffic. Working herself and Skittles around the big truck and heading for the vendor with the phone accessories, she suddenly stopped.

Eyes wide, mouth gaped open…as though she'd seen a ghost.

Smiling at her from a telephone pole was none other than Bubbles. The word *MISSING* was centered over her head.

Gianna crept up to the flier and read the description. *Portia Hathaway, last seen getting into a white Cadillac on June fifteenth.*

Bullet had told Flashy that nobody was looking for Bubbles. If Flashy had known about this reward, he probably would have snitched.

Feeling like a thief, Gianna looked around and then tugged the flier away from the pole.

CHAPTER 48

A fifteen thousand-dollar reward was being offered for Bubbles' safe return. *Fifteen stacks!* With that kind of money, she and Bullet could make a deal with Flashy, buy the baby back, and she could convince Bullet to move far away from the Philadelphia area.

If she got him away from that crackhead, Sizzle, she could get him cleaned up and back to his normal self. They could get married. She'd be sixteen in a few months. She wondered if it was legal to get married at sixteen in certain states.

She needed access to a computer to do that research.

She'd seen a public library near the McDonald's. Looking around, she immediately spotted it: Lucien E. Blackwell West Philadelphia Regional Library.

She trotted across the street, dragging Skittles along. Inside the library, however, she was told she needed a library card to use a computer. And she needed ID and a parent's signature to get a library card. *Fuck!*

Back out in the baking sun, she took notice that Bubbles aka Portia Hathaway was posted up on every visible telephone poll. *This is crazy. Who would do all this work to get Bubbles?*

Sooner or later, someone was bound to discover Bubbles was right in the vicinity. For all the trouble the sloppy girl had brought into her life, Gianna would be glad to be rid of her. That reward money would secure her future with Bullet.

She tore off the tip line number at the bottom and discarded the information about Portia.

If the ballers hadn't disconnected their cells, she could be calling the tip line right now.

But first things first. She had to get some cash for the cell phones, bring home some food and a lighter. Bullet would whip her ass if she didn't. Ever since he started messing with Sizzle and smoking cocaine, he was getting crankier by the minute.

"Do you want to buy two iPhones?" she asked the African vendor.

"Let me see what you have."

She showed him the two handsets.

"Very nice. I'll give you twenty dollars apiece."

"That's all?"

"I don't buy cell phones, but those are a good quality."

"They're worth way more than forty dollars."

"That's my final offer," he said politely.

After grudgingly accepting his offer, Gianna and Skittles headed straight for the McDonald's. She'd get Bullet's lighter from the corner store near Sizzle's crib.

It was blessedly cool inside the fast-food restaurant. The smell of burgers and fries made her mouth water.

Gianna winced when her total came to thirteen dollars, but then she reminded herself that she'd be filling her clutch bag with fifteen stacks in a day or two.

Before Gianna could sit down good or even arrange the food on Skittles' tray, the hungry, frail girl began shoveling fries in her mouth, using both hands.

A man seated nearby was yelling loudly in his cell. Having a dispute with his wife...or his girlfriend. She opened her clutch and looked at the tip line number.

The moment the man finished his argument, Gianna asked if she could make an emergency phone call.

"I don't need no more problems at home. Don't need no strange numbers popping up on my shawty's phone bill. Nah." He shook his head.

A woman with gray streaks in her hair offered Gianna her phone, stating, "I have unlimited minutes. Go ahead and make your emergency call."

"Thank you. This is a private call. Do you mind if I take your cell inside the restroom?"

The woman looked doubtful.

"Please. And can you watch my…uh…sister? She's retarded. She might get up and try to walk away."

"Alright, I'll look after her, but don't take too long," the nice lady said.

"I won't. I'll be back in five minutes."

Inside the public restroom, Gianna's palms were sweating as she placed the call.

"Good afternoon. HelpfindPortia Tip Line. Can I help you?" said a woman's voice.

"Hi. Um…I know where she's at."

"Is Portia alright? Is she alive?" The woman sounded like she was going to start crying. Gianna couldn't imagine why anyone would want Bubbles back that bad.

"Yes. She's alive. I can't talk long because I'm using some lady's cell phone, but I really need to get that money. How long is this going to take?"

"What's your name, honey? You sound like a kid."

"I'm sixteen," Gianna lied. She cracked open the restroom door to check on Skittles. Looking impatient, the lady motioned for Gianna to return her cell.

"I gotta go."

"Wait! Where's Portia? Can you give me an address? Can I get back in touch with you on this number?"

"No, this isn't my phone. I borrowed it. I can see if somebody will let me hold their phone."

"No. I'll come to you. Where are you right now?" the woman asked desperately.

"I'm at a McDonald's on Fifty-second and Chestnut. Do you know where that is?"

"Yes, of course. Is Portia with you?"

"No, but I know where she is. We live at the same spot."

"Are you sure it's Portia Hathaway?"

"Uh-huh. We call her Bubblicious, though."

"Bubba what?"

"Bubblicious. Bubbles for short. Anyway, I was in the white Cadillac the night Bullet spotted her and that Puerto Rican girl."

"Oh my God," the woman uttered. "Is she being held against her will?"

"Not really."

"What do mean, not really?"

"At first she was. But she digs Bullet. We both do. He manages Bubbles' career. But it's not just business with me and him. We're in a relationship, but you know how they say…it's complicated."

"I see. What's your name?"

"Gian—Um, Lollipop."

"What's your real name, sweetie? I need a real name in order to give you the money. You have to sign for it."

"But the flier said it was an anonymous tip line. I can't give out my real name. Bullet will kill me."

"You don't mean that literally, do you?"

"Well…he loves me, but he would kill Bubbles before he'd let you take her from him. Bullet has two guns and I've seen him shoot people. We have to do this on the low. You give me the money and I'll get Bubbles out of the house."

"Listen to me, Lollipop. If you want this money, do not leave that McDonald's. I'll be there soon."

"Okay. Me and Skittles will be waiting near the door. You'll recognize Skittles because her hair is blue and a couple of other colors."

"Got it. My name is Saleema. I'll see you soon."

She was going about this all wrong. Following her heart instead of her head. But Portia was in the hands of some trigger-happy pimp, and if she told Khalil, he'd want to call the police. That could be disastrous.

Saleema had only been a little girl when the police dropped a bomb on the MOVE members' home on Osage Avenue, killing men, women, and kids, and destroying an entire neighborhood. To this day, she could still see the billowing smoke and the stench that lingered for weeks in her Southwest Philly neighborhood. The city had taken forever to repair the homes, and that was the beginning of Saleema being schlepped around from house to house.

She didn't know hardly anything about Khalil's background, but she doubted if he'd seen or experienced half of the horrors that she'd survived in her life.

Saleema had no love for cops. She knew they would eagerly engage in a shootout with a trigger-happy pimp. Portia was disposable. She could end up dead, and the police would issue a half-ass apology and move on without another thought.

Saleema couldn't allow that to happen.

The two girls were standing outside the McDonald's, sipping on beverages. The one with the multi-colored hair was as thin as a rail. Anorexic? She looked to be about sixteen. The other girl

appeared to be even younger; fourteen or fifteen at the most. But Saleema could tell she was the one in charge.

Saleema parked in the rear lot and walked around to the entrance.

"Hey, Lollipop; I'm Saleema," she said in a friendly, non-threatening voice.

"You got the money?" the girl said, trying to sound a lot tougher than she looked.

"Yeah, some of it."

"Some!"

"I have four hundred, for now." Saleema cracked open her purse, letting the girl see the stack of twenties. The girl seemed hungry for money.

"Where are you staying?"

"A house on Delancy Street. Near Fifty-fourth."

From Saleema's memory, Fifty-fourth and Delancy used to be a high-crime area. Helicopters flying around constantly. Street blocked off with yellow tape, bodies outlined in chalk was a weekly occurrence. A women in a wheelchair had been killed in her own home by her husband...a crack addict who shot her for her disability check and claimed that he'd found her robbed and dead when he came home. Police had found bloody footprints leading out of the door and down the pavement. The bottoms of the husband's shoes were stained with blood.

So much death and destruction on this one block, Saleema was surprised everyone hadn't picked up and moved.

As they cruised close to the intersection, Saleema gazed down Delancy Street. As suspected, practically every house was boarded up.

"I'm going to park on Pine Street. I need you to go get Bubbles. Meet me on Pine."

"Aiight. But you have to give me something I can give to Bullet. I can get back out when I tell him I forgot to get him a new lighter."

Saleema didn't like the idea. She looked at the quiet, skinny girl who was staring into space. "What's her name, again?"

"Skittles."

"What's wrong with her?"

The girl shrugged. "I don't know. She used to be normal, but she went crazy a few months ago."

"What happened?" Saleema had seen that vacant look in the eyes of her best friend, Terelle. After experiencing an emotional break.

"I don't have time to tell you her whole history. I need that paper." The girl stuck out her hand.

Saleema peeled off ten twenties. "Half now, and the other half when you bring Portia out."

"What about the big reward?"

"You need an adult to sign for it," Saleema lied. "You're going to have to trust me, okay?"

The girl sighed. "I guess." She got out the car. "Come on, Skittles."

"No, leave her here," Saleema demanded.

"Why? My Daddy gon' wanna know where she's at."

"Make up an excuse."

"I can't. He'll get suspicious if I don't bring Skittles home."

Against her better judgment, Saleema watched nervously as Skittles climbed out of the back seat of the car. She watched the two girls through her rearview mirror and then pulled off. She prayed to God like never before that Portia would soon be safe inside her car.

CHAPTER 49

Time ticked by slowly. Five minutes…ten…fifteen minutes elapsed. The girl had lied. She wasn't coming back. Saleema was going to have to get the police involved. There was no other way she could get Portia out of that house. But the police and a coked-up, crazy pimp did not point to a happy ending.

What should she do?

Aggrieved, she lowered her head on the steering wheel.

The sounds of footsteps made her lift her head.

Saleema's eyes became misty, clouding her vision as she gazed at an unbelievable sight. *Portia!* She seemed spaced out and smaller than she'd ever been, but it was Portia—in the flesh!

Saleema jumped out of her Camry, gave Portia a quick hug, and then tried to help her into the back of the car. Portia dropped limply into the back seat and immediately closed her eyes.

"Hi, Portia. It's me…Miss Saleema. Are you okay?" Saleema gently touched Portia's face. She winced at the scar on Portia's face, but was grateful that the teen was alive.

Frowning, Portia swatted away the hand that caressed her face. Portia turned away and balled up into a comfortable position.

"She's always sleeping like that after she goes through a drug binge with Sizzle and Bullet."

"Sizzle? That name sounds familiar," Saleema commented as she returned to the driver's seat.

"She's a crack ho," Gianna informed.

Saleema pulled away, and then it dawned on her that someone was missing. "Where's the other girl?"

"She wasn't allowed to come back out. Bullet doesn't let all three of us go out together at the same time."

"Why not?"

"Can you hurry up and take me to the place where you can sign for that money?" The girl was antsy.

"Sure." Saleema headed in the direction of her home. Portia was drugged up and scarred, but at least she was alive. *God is good*, Saleema whispered to herself. She tried to concentrate on traffic, but couldn't stop staring at Portia through the rearview mirror. It was a miracle. Saleema couldn't control her smile.

Next to her, Lollipop sat in brooding silence.

"We'll go back to my place and then I'll call the agency that's handling the reward. It will be really helpful if you give me your name."

"Damn, it's Gianna. Okay!"

"What's your last name?"

"Strand." Gianna jerked her shoulder as if giving her real name was killing her.

"Here we are, Gianna." Saleema parked her car inside her garage, something she seldom did. But today it seemed like a wise choice. In case the pimp had somehow seen her vehicle, she didn't want him to be able to spot it sitting directly in front of her home.

It was a struggle getting Portia out of the car and up the stairs that led from the entryway from the garage to her basement. Portia was dead weight, so Saleema decided to let her crash on a sofa in the basement.

"Let's go upstairs and talk," Saleema said to Gianna.

"Excuse me, Miss. But I'm not tryna be smart or nothing. But it seems like you tryna scam me. I don't wanna be here. I just want the money. Could you call those reward people, please?"

"Sure. Okay," Saleema said, still stalling. She'd been counseling troubled girls for two years now. Why was it so hard to deal with this girl?

As they paced through the kitchen, Saleema offered Gianna something to eat.

"I just ate. At McDonald's, remember." She folded her arms stubbornly.

"I want to be straight with you, Gianna. You seem like an intelligent girl—"

Gianna dropped her arms at her sides in frustration. "I don't want to talk."

That's when Saleema noticed her finger. Her mouth dropped open in silent horror.

"What happened to your finger?"

Gianna folded her arms again, hiding her deformed finger. "Nothing."

"Something happened. Let me see your finger."

"No!"

"Did that pimp do that to you?"

"Yeah, but I deserved it," Gianna snapped defensively. "He had to teach me a lesson. So he cut off part of my finger."

Saleema squirmed visibly. Enraged, she realized that the pimp was also responsible for the cut on Portia's face.

Gianna did a defiant head move. "Don't worry about my finger. It's healed now. It's all good."

Oh my God! Gianna's crazy. She's been mesmerized by a deviant pimp, and she views him as some sort of hero. She'd heard of Stockholm Syndrome, but never expected to meet anyone suffering from the mental condition.

All of her instincts told Saleema that this situation was beyond her control, but she didn't want to send Portia back to the detention center without talking to her. Who knew where they'd ship

Portia. No doubt, there'd be lots of red tape to weed through in order to get a visit. That could take months, and Portia would be under the impression that she was worthless and unwanted…and that simply wasn't true.

Needing desperately to make sure the pimp hadn't amputated any of Portia's fingers, Saleema excused herself and raced to the basement.

She scrutinized Portia's face, telling herself that the scar wasn't that noticeable. Other than being about fifteen pounds lighter and in terrible need of a bath, Portia seemed physically intact. Mentally? Good question. She was addicted to crack and had spent an entire summer in the hands of a merciless pimp.

Going back upstairs, she made a decision. She couldn't leave that other defenseless girl overnight with the pimp. She had to get her out of that house.

Saleema shook her head. She couldn't call the police. But how could she live with herself if she got that innocent girl killed? There had to be another way.

She was able to distract Gianna from questioning her about the reward by taking her to the lavender room and parking her in front of the TV.

Saleema flicked through a zillion channels that she thought might interest the girl.

Finally, Gianna settled for a BET reality show. She was entranced for hours, watching marathon reruns.

Saleema felt guilty for leaving Khalil out of the loop, but she had to handle this by herself. She'd talk to him tomorrow. Right now, she wanted to converse with Portia…to let her know that she would be there for her. She'd help her get though the rest of this ordeal. She also wanted her to know that there was an entire community ready to embrace her.

Though she'd always cared about Portia, Saleema now realized

that she loved the brash girl like she were the pesky little sister she'd never had.

And Saleema couldn't wait to tell Portia that she intended to file the necessary paperwork to become her legal guardian.

"Oh, my God!" Gianna screamed from the recreation room. Saleema rushed to the room.

Mouth opened in stunned silence, Gianna pointed to the TV screen.

Breaking news. Reporting from the scene, a reporter was talking: "A dismembered body of a teenage girl was found in this open field in Lower Bucks County today. An eyewitness to this gruesome scene thought an irresponsible resident was burning what appeared to be a bale of hay. Inspecting the burning object, the eyewitness discovered a horrifying sight. A human torso, brutally dismembered, with its arms and legs tied tightly around the torso."

Next to the reporter, an older Caucasian man wiped his forehead.

"Tell us what you saw, Mr. Cambridge."

"Well, I saw a fire. Then a cloud of smoke. As I pulled over on the side of the road, I saw a car pull off and roar down the road. A white 2001 Cadillac." The man shook his head. "Right in broad daylight. Poor girl." He squeezed his eyes shut, too choked up to go on.

The reporter moved along with the story. "Discovered approximately a mile away from this area, the victim's head was apparently tossed out of a moving vehicle. The body is believed to be that of missing teen, Brielle Harper, who left Wilkes-Barre, Pennsylvania with her infant daughter back in late June. Anyone with information on the whereabouts of little Samantha Harper should contact the number on the screen."

A missing teenage girl and her baby from Wilkes-Barre. Saleema searched her mind, trying to recall why that rang a bell.

"That's Skittles," Gianna sobbed. "Bullet chopped up Skittles and burned her up!"

Saleema quickly jotted down the number on the screen. "How do you know that it's Skittles," Saleema said, her voice panicked.

"Because Bullet told me he was going to kill all of us. He said that he'd already killed Skittles, but I didn't believe him. He was mad because I didn't come right back."

"When did you talk to him?"

Saleema had no doubt that she was in over her head. It was time to call 9-1-1.

"I called him and gave him your address when you went down in the basement to check on Bubbles. I didn't think he was serious. I thought when he got over here and I gave him the fifteen stacks, he'd feel better."

"How did you know my address? We came in through the garage."

With a guilty expression, Gianna said, "I saw your water bill... on the kitchen counter while I was talking to him on the phone."

"Why would you tell a murderous pimp how to find you?"

"He always tells me to keep it one hunnit with him. That's what I was trying to do. I didn't want to get in any trouble with him after I collected the reward for finding Bubbles."

Hearing Portia referred to as Bubbles made Saleema's flesh crawl. She used to call herself Hershey. She had given herself that name when she was only seventeen, when she'd starting turning tricks at Pandora's Box.

"All this time, you knew where that girl's baby was and you haven't told anyone?" Saleema gawked at Gianna in horror. Maybe Gianna had been so traumatized that she was now deranged.

Saleema hurried out of the lavender room and raced down the hall toward the kitchen to call the police, but her footsteps were

cut off by a gunshot blast that shattered her kitchen window. Screaming, she dropped to the floor. Gianna ran out into the hall.

"Get down!" Saleema shouted. She started crawling fast toward
the basement. "We have to get Portia," she whispered. "Hurry!"

They tiptoed down the basement stairs.

Saleema dragged Portia off of the sofa in the basement and pulled
her sluggish body across the tiled floor. "Help me get her into the
garage. Did you tell that pimp that I parked my car in the garage?"

"No, I forgot."

"Thank God! We have time to escape. He'll have to drive a
couple of blocks to get to the back of my house." They heard
another blast from his weapon. This one seemed to have shot out
an upstairs window, like he was shooting at any room in the front
of the house that had a light on.

Inside the car, with Portia on the floor in the back and Gianna
crouched in the passenger seat, Saleema reversed out of her garage,
zigzagging on screeching tires as she zoomed into the dark night.

There were no blaring sirens. Help was not on the way. Until
she could put some safe distance between herself and this maniac
pimp named Bullet, Saleema was on her own.

Speeding and handling the wheel with one hand, she scrounged
around inside her purse looking for her cell.

Shit! In her mind's eye, she could see her cell on the stand next
to the TV, where she'd placed it while looking for the remote so
Gianna could take her mind off her pimp, while she channel-
surfed.

CHAPTER 50

"He's two cars behind us," Gianna said in a whisper, keeping her voice low as if fearing the pimp might hear her.

"Oh, shit. Where's a fuckin' cop when you need one? Is he from Philly?"

"I don't think so."

"Good! Then he doesn't know his way around Fairmount Park."

Saleema made a quick U-turn and zoomed past the Philadelphia Zoo. Still no cops in sight and no time to ask for the help of her fellow man. She shot down Girard Avenue, and turned on two wheels when she got to Parkside. Her gas light came on. *Shit!*

Inside the park, she headed for Belmont Plateau, a spot she used to hang out as a teen, but would now use as a refuge, being that her gas tank was dead on E.

They couldn't make it any farther without gas. She hid the Camry under a huge tree that was hidden from view.

"Why you stopping? Bullet's gon' kill all of us. We gotta keep moving."

"Out of gas. We're going to leave Portia on the floor of the car. You and me can make a run for it. Get help when we get out of this park."

Gianna's teeth started chattering. "He's gon' find us. He told me he'd always know where to find me."

"He's not psychic. He was messing with your head. Don't worry; he doesn't know about the Plateau. He'll never think to drive up

here. He's probably still riding up and down Girard Avenue, trying to figure out what happened to us. Now stop talking, and run!"

Gianna jogged alongside Saleema. "Sizzle's from Philly."

"And?"

"She was in the car with him." Gianna was already panting.

"Why didn't you tell me that before?"

Gianna shrugged.

Headlights suddenly shone in the pitch-black park, and then went dim.

"That's him! I know it's him," Gianna whispered, her body trembling like a leaf. "He said the next time I betrayed him, he's gon' chop off all my fingers."

"Shh. Get down. Stay low. He didn't see my car; he'll move on," Saleema said. She and Gianna crawled deeper into the park and then lay on their stomachs, panting.

"Oh, God. Please don't let him spot my car. If he finds Portia, I'm gonna lose my mind."

Though the headlights were turned off, the sound of tires slowly crunching over twigs put them on notice that the car being driven by a maniac was gaining on them.

"Hey, hoes. Where y'all at?" Bullet's voice echoed ominously through the quiet night. "I can't see y'all asses, but I know you're out here somewhere. Come on out, Lollipop. I'm already mad. Don't make me have to start chopping off yo' toes."

A woman giggled.

That's that Sizzle bitch! "We have to move deeper into those trees and bushes," Saleema whispered.

Gianna didn't budge. Her teeth began chattering again. Louder this time.

Saleema elbowed her, trying to get her to clam up and move along. But Gianna lay on the ground, her body going into spasms of fear.

"Move, girl!" Saleema whisper shouted. "He can't see us. He's playing mind games with you."

The sound of a car door opening and then slamming shut sent Gianna into motion. Panicked, she slithered on her belly like a fast-moving snake. Unencumbered by the shoulder bag that she lugged along, Gianna kept up with Saleema, sliding into the shelter of a group of trees with bushy foliage and thick trunks.

The shoulder bag clunked against a gnarled root at the base of a tree, the sound giving away their position.

Slowly. Tauntingly, footsteps crunched in their direction.

Gianna uttered a moan of defeat.

Saleema prayed that they would remain unseen…that Bullet would pass them by. As her life began to pass before her eyes, she realized that the hope of staying alive was merely wishful thinking.

The worst part about viewing the scenes of her life was seeing snippets of the future she might have shared with Khalil. She wished that she could have told him goodbye.

Then she thought of Portia, lying vulnerable in the back seat of her car. She wanted to cry. No doubt, he'd get to Portia, too. Saleema had wanted so badly to protect troubled girls, but instead she'd unwittingly contributed to Skittles' brutal murder. Now she, Gianna and most likely Portia, too…would soon meet certain death. She prayed their demise would be swift and painless.

"I don't want to die," Gianna whispered, her body quaking, her elbows banging against her shoulder bag.

Gianna started wriggling her hand inside the bag. Saleema figured that the girl was religious and was routing around for a Bible or some prayer beads. It really didn't matter at this point.

The moonlight filtered through the treetops, casting a glow on a long shadow. A man with a dagger-like knife in his hand was approaching.

"I didn't want to touch this, but I was desperate. I was going to

try to pawn it earlier today." Sitting upright, Gianna gripped a gun with both shaking hands.

At a complete loss for words, Saleema watched as the man's silhouette grew larger. Was there time to take the gun from the terrified girl, who obviously didn't know how to use it?

"Oh! There you go, bitch!" Bullet said, his voice ringing with sadistic pleasure.

Though it was too dark to see his features clearly, the whites of his eyes became wide and visible when Gianna held up the gun with amazingly steady hands. The weapon shimmered in the moonlight.

"Yo! Watch yourself, bitch! Whatchu think you gettin' ready to do?" The knife in his hand now looked as threatening as a poodle.

"My name ain't bitch. It's Gianna Strand. And this ain't target practice, muthafucka!" Gianna opened fire on Bullet. She didn't stop shooting until she'd emptied the clip.

CHAPTER 51

S aleema clicked off the TV in disgust. Watching a remorse-less Joseph Oaks, aka Flashy, preening for the cameras as he was led into court was revolting.

The prostitute known as Sizzle shamelessly adored the spotlight also.

Portia would be testifying next week and Saleema would be in the courtroom to support her. Until then, she didn't want to hear anything else about the horrendous crimes that had been committed against three teenage girls. Thankfully, with Gianna's cooperation, the abducted baby had been rescued.

Gianna and Portia had provided Saleema with enough graphic details of their ordeal to give her nightmares for the rest of her life.

The only good thing that could be said about Joseph Oaks was that he'd made sure that Brielle's daughter was given good care. His motives, however, weren't honorable. His intention was to traffic a plump, healthy baby to a prospective buyer.

Little Samantha was now in the care of her grieving grandparents. Witnessing their anguish was unbearable, and Saleema wondered how Brielle's parents would be able to get through Portia's and Gianna's graphic testimony, detailing the horrors their daughter had endured up until her brutal murder.

Gianna was given the reward money. Her parents, reconnected though their daughter's tragedy, added fifty-thousand dollars to the reward and used it to set up a trust fund for Brielle's daughter.

Saleema now realized that Brielle was the girl that was mentioned

in the HelpfindPortia chat room. She'd had the girl in her car and let her go back to that brutal maniac.

Having unwittingly played a part in Brielle's atrocious and untimely demise, made it very difficult for Saleema to sleep at night.

Unable to save her home from foreclosure, Saleema moved into a small efficiency apartment. The tiny space took some getting used to, but on the flip side, it was much easier to keep clean. For Saleema, the miniscule living quarters did not represent rock bottom, but symbolized a fresh start.

Having no formal education or job training, she worked for minimum wage, stocking shelves at a grocery store at night. It was humbling but good for her soul.

She also volunteered at the Haverford Recreation Center, working with the seniors. She needed to clear her head and get away from adolescent issues for a while.

During the day, she was a full-time student at the Community College of Philadelphia.

For some unknown reason, Portia's mother, who still had not demonstrated any motherly concern, would not relinquish custody of her daughter. Saleema was denied permission to become Portia's legal guardian. The injustice of an unfit parent being allowed parental rights bolstered Saleema's desire to eventually practice family law.

She had a long journey ahead of her and she welcomed every step of the way.

Portia was being detained for eighteen months. Fortunately, she was incarcerated in Philadelphia and Saleema visited her several times a week.

Ironically, part of the detention center's mission statement was to protect the community from juvenile offenders, yet the community had not protected Portia until it was almost too late.

Portia's neighborhood was evolving and coming together since

they had banded together to help find her. Now the Haverford Recreation Center offered numerous structured recreational programs for youth, as well as giving them access to a state-of-the-art computer center that was given by an anonymous donor.

Whenever the girls—Amirah, Chyna, Tasha, and Stacey—used the computer center, they gave each other knowing glances, realizing that Saleema was the anonymous donor.

Khalil.

Saleema gave a wistful sigh.

Khalil was busy running his school, going through the rigors of trying to mold thuggish ninth-graders into college-prepared students.

Her best friend, Terelle, who resided in Montreal, told Saleema that she was making a big mistake in letting a good man like Khalil slip through her fingers.

But Saleema knew better. She couldn't accept his love.

She was too broken and fragile. Still damaged and scarred from her own childhood and calamitous recent past.

Khalil had introduced Saleema to her soft side, given her an opportunity to experience the most important aspects of a relationship: friendship, respect, and intimacy that weren't attached with a dollar sign.

It was her strong feelings for him that made her relinquish their budding relationship. She wasn't ready for Khalil.

She was still running from her demons. It would be a long time before she found peace.

If she and Khalil were meant to be, they'd reconnect one day.

Until then, she'd do everything within her power to ensure that she became healed, whole, and healthy.

Saleema prayed every day for Brielle's soul. She asked God for wisdom, strength, and inner peace. And to be forgiven for all her past sins.

PUBLISHER'S NOTE

Dear Reader:

Gianna, Brielle, and Portia, also known as Lollipop, Skittles, and Bubblicious; three young ladies that I will never forget. Allison Hobbs has outdone herself with *Stealing Candy*; in my humble opinion, her best piece of literature to date. Allison has penned an unforgettable novel with even more unforgettable characters. If you have already completed this novel, then I am sure that you were riveted to each and every page. The most prevalent message contained within is that we must protect our youth. They assume that they are prepared to go out into society, that they understand the consequences of their actions, and that horrible things only happen to other people. That is not the case.

The three girls in this book were innocent in their own way, they thought that making rash and hasty decisions were okay. Gianna wanted to go to a party with a famous singer. Brielle wanted a ride to a gas station with her baby. Portia wanted to try out for a music video. All three of them ended up being used, abused, and terrified; used for everything from sexual favors to being tied against trees for target practice by a sociopath.

And what about Bullet? Even he was a young man who fell victim to circumstances, having learned to have a blatant disregard for women from his old cellmate in prison, where he himself was coerced into having sex with other men. Another product of what happens when no one cares.

What difference can one person make? Saleema made a world of difference; she would not give up on Portia. Saleema understood about being a victim of circumstance and thus, she did not judge Portia. She only loved her. By teaming up with Khalil and rallying the neighbor-

hood together, it ultimately brought the ordeal to an end. Not a positive one for Skittles but at least Portia and Gianna had a fighting chance to begin their lives anew. Damaged but breathing, and free from the oppression forced upon them by Bullet.

I must touch upon two underlying messages in this book, masterfully executed by Ms. Hobbs; lessons that every woman must learn. One is that too many people do suffer from the Stockholm Syndrome. Not to the degree of Gianna, kissing up to a man who chopped off her finger and auctioned off her body; but by staying with men who demean them, physically and verbally abuse them, and keep them trapped in relationships and marriages out of pure fear. Unless they make the decision to get out—not often an easy one—that pain and humiliation will follow them every day of their lives.

The other message—and I love how Allison dealt with it—is that until a person is in the right place for a relationship, they should not set themselves up for failure. Saleema was feeling Khalil, yearned to be with him, but she realized that it could never work—not until she was ready. Every woman needs to do a serious self-examination and determine if they are emotionally prepared to love. Self-love is the greatest love of all. Without it, any other type of love will ultimately fail. I commend Allison for examining that fact.

I was already Allison's biggest fan but now in awe of her talent. If you have not read her other books, you are not missing only great books, you are missing out on life-changing experiences.

Blessings,

Zane

Zane
Publisher
Strebor Books International
www.simonandschuster.com/streborbooks

ABOUT THE AUTHOR

Allison Hobbs is the national bestselling author of thirteen novels and novellas: *The Sorceress, Pure Paradise, Disciplined, One Taste, Big Juicy Lips, The Climax, A Bona Fide Gold Digger, The Enchantress, Double Dippin,' Dangerously In Love, Insatiable* and *Pandora's Box.* She is one of the contributing writers of Cinemax's *Zane's Sex Chronicles.* Her novel *The Climax* was nominated for the 2008 African American Literary Awards Show.

Allison received a bachelor of science degree from Temple University. She resides in Philadelphia, PA where she's working on her next novel.

Join the Stealing Candy Movement at Stealingcandy.net.

Visit the author at: www.allisonhobbs.com, www.blackplanet.com/allisonhobbs or www.myspace.com/allisonhobbs

RESOURCES

Girls Educational and Mentoring Services (GEMS)
298 West 149th Street
New York, NY 10039-2741
(212) 926-8089
www.gems-girls.org

National Human Trafficking Resource Center (NHTRC)
(888) 373-7888
www.acf.hhs.gov/trafficking

Veronica's Voice
Kansas City, KS
(816) 483-7101
www.safecenter@veronica'svoice.org

Children of the Night
Van Nuys, CA
24-hour hotline: (800) 551-1300
www.childrenofthenight.org

Coalition to Abolish Slavery and Trafficking
5042 Wilshire Blvd., #586
Los Angeles, CA 90036
24-hour hotline: (888) 539-2373
www.castla.org

Polaris Project
P.O. Box 53315
Washington, D.C. 20009
(202) 540-5239
www.polarisproject.org